Tales from the SECUREMARKET

Lucas,

Man why do I even got to do a thing.

- Colin

Tales from the SECUREMARKET

Colin Sandel

Urbane Undead Small Press
Rockville, MD

This book is a work of fiction. People, places, events, and situations are the product of the author's imagination or have been used fictitiously. Any resemblance to actual persons, living or dead, actual events, locales, or organizations, is purely coincidental.

Copyright © 2010 by Colin Sandel. All Rights Reserved.
Published by Urbane Undead Small Press.
Cover art by Danielle Church.

ISBN-13: 978-1-4499-7170-0
ISBN-10: 1-4499-7170-9

No part of this book may be used or reproduced, stored in a retrieval system, or transmitted by any means withouthout the written permission of the author or publisher.

Acknowledgements & Dedications

This novel is for everyone who witnessed the creation and development of the Age of Corporations, particularly those who read Tales as it was being written, offering their invaluable encouragement, corrections and ideas.

Special thanks go to Julia Suggs, Lauren Harrison, and Renee Griffin for going above and beyond to help refine my work. Thanks also to Robin Sevakis, without whom New Washington might not exist. Extra-special thanks go to Dani Church, who did at least as much work on the book as I did.

Arc I

Tales from the Securemarket™

Introduction

Did you know: of the violent deaths that occur in the greater New Washington area, over 30% occur to ordinary people running everyday errands?

New Washington is the greatest city on Earth. Magic and Technology are at their peak, adventuring is a career choice, and Legends walk the streets. Sadly, it seems to be normal people who suffer the cost, oftentimes gunned down by mercenaries or blown apart by a powerful mage while trying to buy a cup of milk! No one wants to be eaten by monsters while trying to pick up produce, but few of us are given a choice in the matter.

It doesn't have to be this way.

Have you ever wondered why your office requires that its employees have Martial and Magic Certification, but your local supermarket doesn't? We seek to change this standard. The Securemarket™ is simply the safest and best shopping experience in New Washington, providing a wide selection of high-quality food *and* maintaining the best standards of protection in the service-provider industry. Our employees are all trained in the use of magics and weaponry and periodically participate in training retreats designed to hone their ability to protect and serve you. In the greatest city in the world, you shouldn't expect anything less.

Welcome to the Securemarket™. We'll take care of you.®

1

It was an ordinary Wednesday in the greatest city in the world.

The air was crisp but not cold, made warmer by the mid-day sun shining down upon acres of pavement and skyscraper. Hours ago the nine-to-five crowd had begun their takeover of the city, releasing it from the hands of the late-night workers and career partiers. The streets milled with thousands upon thousands of everyday people, dressed in suits and casual clothing alike, wearing guns and swords and wands. They poured into and out of the entrances to Rail stations, office buildings, restaurants. For many, it would be the first or last day of their lives; for others, it was merely an ordinary day.

On the fourteenth floor of an apartment building on 15th Street in north New Washington, an employee of the mighty Securemarket™ woke at the crack of noon.

He was wiry-thin and tall. Like most New Washingtonians, he had a deep tan skin tone and facial features indicating the melting-pot heritage of the city. His black hair was splayed in dreadlocks around his head which slowly drew together as he sat up.

He blinked several times, then turned to his bedstand. On top of his alarm clock were a simple black handshell, a tube of chapstick, and a nametag reading 'Matt'. He reached for the handshell and picked it up, knocking the tube of chapstick to the floor.

He tapped the surface of the shell, watching its screen come to life. A few more taps from his thumb and he had opened a contact and set the shell to call it. He held the shell to his ear and cleared his throat several times. After five rings, someone picked up.

"Steve, girl," he said into the receiver of the phone.

A female voice said something, sleep-thick, into his ear.

"Yeah, you slept through your alarm."

The female voice sounded startled.

"I know. But it's aight. The boss is going to be late too. There's a Rail delay. Chill."

The voice responded with relief, then, after a pause, sarcasm.

"If I used my second sight for anything important," the dreadlocked employee said, "You'd still be asleep when Alan got to the store. You're welcome."

The employee ended the call, set down his shell and once again cleared his throat loudly.

"That reminds me," he muttered, "I need to buy a camera."

"Hey Zap, catch!"

The black-haired young man turned just in time to see a large package of toilet paper flying toward him. He jerked his arms upward, clipping his elbow against the sharp edge of the weapon at his hip.

"Ow!" he yelped as he caught the toilet paper.

"Pff. That hurt you? It's TP, not plasteel," his coworker Steve said, her tone incredulous. Her auburn curls swayed as she carried another bundle of toilet paper toward the shelf and shoved several along the ground with one foot.

Zap swiveled, trying to bring his aching elbow into view around the large package in his hands. "No, it's this damn Forcebolt," he complained. "My elbow hit it. I'm not used to wearing a weapon."

"You'll get used to it," Steve said. "If you don't look like you can defend the place, we'll get an audit." She rose to her tiptoes and shoved the package into place on the high shelf. Her own weapon, an ominous-looking custom pistol, glinted in the store's sterile light as she turned. Zap glared at it for a moment, then laughed.

"Hey Steve, got a joke," he said, smirking as he stood on his own tiptoes to place his package on the shelf. "What's the difference between a gun and a marital aid?"

Steve turned to him and raised an eyebrow.

"The average New Washingtonian can get it up without a marital aid."

His coworker's stare hardened, her eyebrows forming a flat, angry line.

"What?" Zap said. "It's just a joke."

Steve's glare bore into Zap's face. He averted his eyes.

"Look, I wasn't trying to offend you." He paused, then said, "I just sort of think the whole arms culture thing is—"

"Whatever," Steve snapped, turning back to stock the shelf.

"I'm honestly not trying to say your apprenticeship is—"

"Whatever! Zap!" Steve said, her whole body tensing. "I don't *care*. You want to do your job or what?" She snatched another package of toilet paper and jammed it into place. Zap gingerly slid his onto the shelf, then picked up the next.

"Are you sure?" he probed.

"I'm not an apprentice gunsmith because *you* think it's cool," she said, shoving the package onto the shelf. She tossed a dismissive gesture at Zap and focused a look of uncharitable appraisal on him. Zap found himself suddenly self-conscious of his skinny frame and soft features. "You're not working on your degree because wizards make me moist. Because they *don't*."

Zap shifted uncomfortably and set the package back down where he'd picked it up. "Maybe I'd better go stock the sodas."

"Maybe you'd better," she replied coldly.

At the front of the store, a man in his fifties with a muscular, lean build pushed his shopping cart up to the checkout line, his bald pate gleaming in the CoolSun full-spectrum crystal lamps of the store. He began unloading his items, placing them in the scanning area one by one. This was not a noteworthy event until the scanner refused to recognize one of the items. The man looked puzzled and moved it out of the sensors, then placed it back in. The computer remained unresponsive.

Seemingly from thin air, a young man appeared next to the customer. He was coffee-skinned, dreadlocked, and very handsome. He had a small set of shimmering holo-tats on his face, a common sign of a yuzie or street punk, but he was also wearing the simple red apron of a Securemarket™ employee and a nametag labeled 'Matt'. He raised a hand and used it to tap a few points on the scanner's console.

"Tamarind," he murmured to the bald man, keeping his voice low. "The scanner doesn't like tamarind. Never recognizes it." Then, raising his voice to more normal levels, he added, "Also, your wife's cheating on you. Check her pea-coat when you get home."

The scanner beeped as it decided to acknowledge the tamarind's presence. The dreadlocked employee turned and sauntered away, leaving the bald man standing baffled in front of the scanner.

Now alone, the bald man scoffed, smiled and shook his head. He then paused, furrowed his brow, took out his handshell, and stared at it.

Ten minutes after Zap had begun restocking the sodas, he had a visitor. The shift manager Alan, a twentysomething with light brown hair, walked by the drinks aisle holding a tabletshell, absently tapping the screen with his finger as he took inventory around the store. "Hey, little guy," he said in an offhand tone to Zap as he approached. "What's on?"

"Uh, not much," Zap said, keeping himself busy stocking the sodas.

"Cool, cool," Alan said. "Cool." He tapped his tablet a few more times. "Hey, candy aisle's been lossy. Think you guys could keep an eye on it like after school hours? I think we've got some yuzies hanging around."

"Okay," Zap intoned rotely. Alan seemed satisfied and continued his patrol, still jabbing at the tabletshell. Before he reached the end of the aisle, he stopped and turned back to Zap.

"Oh hey, uh," he said. "Steve pissed about something?"

"We had a discussion about guns," Zap said.

"Huh," Alan said. There was a pause as he failed to think of something appropriate to say. He eventually just made a helpless gesture and moved to the next aisle.

Zap spent a few seconds staring at the space where his manager had just been standing, then stood up and shoved the soda case forward with his foot. "That's it," he growled. "Smoke break."

Moments later he was outside, leaning on the side of the building and watching cars hum by. A pink-tinted roll of paper dangled from his fingers with a glowing ember on the end. Zap let it sit for a little while, checking his watch periodically to make sure he was not outlasting his break.

It was a cool day. Spring had recently begun and now the weather was nice; Zap had been taking advantage of the fair conditions by visiting his parents often. His parents lived in the Agricultural District of Home and actually had a yard, a commodity that Zap imagined they must have paid a great deal of money for. He would visit whenever he could and used the yard as a place to study when he had the time to take the Rail there. Someday, Zap promised himself, I'll have a condominium with a rooftop garden and I'll walk there every day.

The outside of the Securemarket™ was not so picturesque, but the weather was still nice, and it provided a pleasant respite from a stressful day. Zap brought the cigarette to his mouth and took a drag from it.

Zap then heard a *clack* from the door and looked over to see it open. Steve walked out casually, then saw Zap and stopped short.

Both of them looked at each other for a moment. "Taking your break early," Steve observed dryly.

"Yeah," Zap said.

After a moment, Steve apparently decided that was all right. "Okay," she said, coming out of the store all the way and letting the door close behind her. "Alan'll do floor patrol." She leaned against the wall herself and pulled a pack of cigarettes from her pocket.

Zap looked at Steve as she tapped the pack against her opposite hand, then brought it up and drew a cigarette from the pack with her mouth. He began to speak. "Hey, listen—"

Steve's left hand flew up very quickly with one finger extended. "Don't—" she said, fixing him with a steely gaze. "Don't."

Zap faltered and let his voice drop off. Steve's eyes remained steadily on him for a moment, then her expression changed, one eyebrow raising. "Is that cig *pink*?"

"It's a rose cigarette," Zap said, thinking this explained everything, but Steve seemed to expect him to continue. "Mages smoke them."

"*Femmey* mages?" Steve asked, the edges of her lips turning up in a little smile as the unlit cigarette dangled between them. "Mages who wear *dresses*?"

"No! Iyesu. Regular mages." Zap retorted, annoyed but relieved that Steve was no longer staring him down.

Steve snorted derisively and raised her hand to the edge of her cigarette. Zap sensed a faint surge of magic as his coworker summoned a small flame to her hand, lighting her cigarette.

Eager to change the subject, Zap pointed to the newly-lit cigarette. "I didn't know you knew Color Magic, Steve."

"Took it on the side during high school," she said. "Knew I needed mag-cert to get a decent job, and CCDM looked boring."
"Yeah, I guess so."
"Zap," Steve said, suddenly very serious.
"Yeah?"
"Does your wand have a glittery star on it?"

2

The lamp came on very suddenly, its full-spectrum glory flaring into brilliance before Zap had the chance to close his eyes. He cursed and flailed in place for a moment, then grabbed the top of the ladder and waited for his vision to clear. While he was still dazzled, he heard a female voice call from below.
"You okay up there?"
"Yeah," Zap replied.
"You got the dead crystals ok?"
"Yeah," Zap said, squinting as his sight slowly returned. "I'm coming down now."
One careful, slow trip down the ladder and Zap was once again on the floor. He looked to Steve, who had already turned her attention to something else. "Check this out," she murmured conspiratorially to Zap and pointed down the aisle.
On the other end of the store, an elven toddler was throwing a tantrum while its father stood nearby. The child was giving an expert performance: it rolled on the floor and shrieked its rage as tears rolled down its face. The father had an air of baffled helplessness, seeing his child in a state he could not bring himself to control or even address.
Steve had her eyes still fixed on the child, but she leaned toward Zap with a smirk hanging on her face. "Can you believe how impossible it's got to be?" she asked him. "By the time elven kids are done with their 'Terrible Twos', they're over five years old."

"Probably why most of them are so patient," Zap murmured in agreement. "Elven puberty is what, like five to eight years long? I think that'd beat patience into anybody."

The two went quiet, silenced by the unpleasant thought. The toddler's tantrum continued, and the father moved toward the shrieking beast but seemed unwilling to do anything.

"He should smack the kid," Steve said.

"I don't think that's necessary. He could just take the kid out of the store," Zap replied. "It'd teach action and consequence without having to resort to—"

"Is that how you were brought up, seriously?" Steve interrupted. "No wonder you suffer urges to wear a pointy hat and speak in tongues."

"You're an asshole," Zap said, managing to only mean it a little.

The two went back to regarding the commotion on the other end of the aisle, just in time as the child reached up to a shelf and swiped his hand across it, knocking twelve boxes of cookies to the floor.

The two employees sprang into action without their usual snarky comments. In a moment, the toddler found himself confronting one and a half imposing meters of Steve Anderson, while Zap launched a rapid-fire lecture at the father for failing to control his child. Moments later, both parent and child were being ushered out of the Securemarket™ by a pair of employees making shooing motions with their hands.

Zap and Steve walked back into the store. "Sweet jumpin' zombies," Zap commented, looking behind him at the retreating figures.

"Friggin' larvae," Steve grumped.

"I'm just glad we got there when we did," Zap said. "Kid could've unshelved a whole aisle."

"Yeah," Steve said with a smirk. "Good thing we're such good employees."

On the other side of the store, Alan sighed as he heard raucous laughter coming from the entrance. "I need to separate those two or something," he muttered.

"Pull!" Steve shouted.

Zap hurled the jar high into the air and broke into a run toward the other side of the loading dock.

Before Zap had gone four paces, Steve's hand sped to her hip and wrapped around the grip of her custom pistol. A fluid motion brought it from its holster in an unnecessary but stylish spin, coming to bear at the jar as the latter reached the top of its parabolic flight. Steve squeezed the trigger, and the pistol barked.

The sound of a bullet hitting an IHDP wall echoed through the dock. The jar fell to the ground and bounced once, unscathed.

"So apparently the third time is *not* the charm," Zap quipped, amused.

Steve waved off the disparaging remark, then jumped down from the ledge near the loading shutter. "I'm not warmed up," she offered as an explanation. "And anyway, I'm better at making guns than shooting them."

"Can I try?" Zap asked.

"Okay," Steve replied, jogging to the jar and picking it up. She stood in the position that Zap had stood, marked with a chalk "X" by the employees. "Stand on the ledge," she said to Zap, who was already climbing up.

"Ready?" Steve asked. Zap nodded. He drew his wand from a narrow pocket of his slacks. It was elegant, for a student's wand: it had a simple burnished black design with a number of white runes etched near the bottom. Zap held it with easy expertise.

"Pull!" he yelled. Steve threw the jar.

Zap drew his energies inward and prepared the arcane syllables that he would use to cast a magic missile at the jar. As he raised his wand, there was a sharp report from behind him, and the jar shattered in midair, sending pieces of plastic scattering across the garage. Both Steve and Zap cringed in frightened surprise, Steve raising her arms to ward off the falling bits of plastic. Both turned to the source of the noise, too surprised to bring their weapons to bear.

A male half-elf wearing the trademark red apron of a Securemarket™ employee stood in the loading dock's doorway, grinning. He had tousled platinum-blond hair, appeared to be in his late fifties (were he human, he'd be "pushing thirty"), and was holding a smoking Dai-Sho Katana .45-caliber pistol.

"Iyesukristo!" Zap exclaimed.

"Holy fuck!" Steve shouted. Unlike Zap, her tone of surprise was a happy one. "To'mas!" She ran to the edge of the loading ledge and vaulted atop it. "Where have you been?!"

"Earning my Dai-Sho B-Cert," the half-elf said with a smirk, waving the gun in the air as demonstration.

"I missed you, jackass!" Steve said, leaping forward and embracing To'mas, who moved the pistol out of the way and returned the hug with his free hand.

"Yeah, I know," To'mas replied. Once freed, he holstered the gun and held out his hand to Zap. "Sorry to steal your thunder, little guy. I'm To'mas Bonvent."

"It's cool," Zap said as he put the wand back in its pocket. He reached forward and shook To'mas's hand. "I guess I would have done it too. Zap Bradshaw."

"Good to meetcha," To'mas replied. "Anyway, Alan says you guys have to come back in. Loren's done waxing the floor and you need to stock some shit before we open."

"Aren't we overstaffed?" Zap asked. "We never have this many people."

"Go-Go Cola just adblitzed," Steve explained. "I think Paru's worried that a supervisor and three people aren't going to be enough."

"Oh," Zap said.

"Anyway, somebody's gonna have to sweep up that jar," To'mas said.

Zap clapped him on the shoulder. "Well," he said with a grin, "you broke it."

Steve and Zap slipped through the entrance before To'mas could reply. He looked at the broken shards of plastic on the dock's ground and sighed. "To think I kind of missed this place," he said wistfully.

3

It was 21:25, the night shift manager was nowhere to be found, and neither were any of his employees.

Alan stood at the front of the store, his tabletshell tucked under an arm and fingers pressed to his temples. Steve was sitting on top of one of the shelves and bouncing her sneakers against it while Zap paced in front of the checkout lines. To'mas, whose shift extended into the night, was the only employee not on edge; he instead ran a mop up and down the aisles and hummed an Ellis Manteaux song.

Halfway through one of his paces, Zap halted and gestured violently with his pointer finger. "They're watching the ethcast, aren't they."

"They're watching the ethcast," Alan confirmed, his voice saturated with resignation and his fingers drawing little circles against the side of his head.

"That's so scrambled I can't even say!" Zap exploded. "It's not *going* anywhere!"

"C'mon man," Steve said sarcastically. "Don't you know it's more HD to watch it live?"

"Fucking Shadowflames." Zap muttered, kicking the ground. "Fucking Ghost Blade."

"Hey, leave Ghost Blade out of this," To'mas said from the aisle, his tone defensive. "I like Ghost Blade."

"This is so stupid. I have places to be," Zap groused.

Steve smirked. "I bet you don't."

"I do!"

"I bet you don't. I bet you have homework."

"I *always* have homework," Zap retorted.

"I bet you want to watch the end of the ethcast," Steve taunted.

"I don't! I'm not even going to watch the saved version!"

"*Enough!*" Alan barked, his eyes squeezed shut, then spoke a little more quietly. "Not now. Please."

There was a moment of awkward silence before Steve spoke. "Do *you* have somewhere to be, Alan?"

"Yes," Alan said, finally taking his fingers away from his head.

"What is it?"

"A thing," Alan said. "I have a thing to get to, and I'm going to be late to the thing."

Steve snorted, and then resumed kicking the shelf with the back of her feet. After a moment's pause, To'mas's head rounded the corner of the aisle. He was smiling. "Okay, so this sucks. We know that. So: who wants to play Dry Ice Hockey?"

"Do we have enough brooms for that?" Zap asked.

There was a pause.

"There are extra in the manager's closet," Alan said, actually cracking a very small smile as he held up his key.

The employees all bolted for the back.

4

"Scuze me, miss."

Steve looked up, startled, into the face of a man in his mid-twenties. He was wearing a simple pair of cargoes and an Ellis Manteaux '24 'Elemental' world tour t-shirt. He smiled at Steve, his expression one of nervous hope. "Can you help me with something?"

"Uh, sure," Steve responded.

The customer pointed over at the flower display, a cool jungle of colorful blossoms. Steve's confidence faltered immediately. The customer continued. "I have a lady friend who I, uh, think likes me."

"Izzat right," Steve said.

"I like her too," the customer said. "She's very shy, though. I don't think I could just tell her I like her, for some reason. So I was kind of hoping to get her some flowers. Today." He paused and looked at his watch. "Like in less than an hour."

Steve led the customer to the flower display and looked them over. She chose one of the most flamboyantly colorful displays and gestured at it. "Uh," she muttered. "That one is ... good."

"It's a little..." the customer trailed off.

"Well," Steve said as her eyes roamed over the flower display, preparing to pick another bouquet at random. Before she could do so, Zap appeared behind her, placing both hands on her shoulders and giving the customer a winning smile.

"My associate," Zap interjected, "was about to mention that she needs to know a little bit about who these flowers for. Who are they for, again?" He delicately moved Steve to the side, who tucked herself behind her rescuer, grateful for the save.

"Somebody I know," the customer said. "Well okay, I guess I don't know her really that well. But we like each other. I'm pretty sure."

"So I think it's safe to say that you wouldn't call it *love*, right?"

The customer held up his hands. "W-whoa, that's a bit much this early."

"Right," Zap said. "Let's not do red roses, then." He pointed at a tasteful bouquet with a romantic theme, but that avoided roses altogether. "How does that look? Or this one, or this?"

"I like that one," the man said, pointing at the second bouquet Zap had indicated. It had a white and pink theme to it, mostly white. Zap nodded.

"Good choice, sir. Would you like me to ring you up here? How will you be paying for that?"

"Card," the customer said, holding out a chargebus. Zap produced his workshell, plugged the bus into it, punched a few buttons and handed the card back. "That's gonna be twenty-two thirty-five. Here's your bouquet."

"Thanks!" the customer said cheerfully, taking the bouquet and walking out of the store.

"Well, that was cute," Steve said, only half-sarcastic.

Zap furrowed his brow at his workshell. "Stewve…"

"Do not start making up weird nicknames for me, Zap," Steve said in a flat tone.

"No, this flower guy's name," Zap said. "It's literally the last bunch of letters in the alphabet. How the hell do you pronounce that?"

Steve looked at the shell. "Stew-vixens."

"That can't be right."

Alan interrupted the pair suddenly. "Iyesu, Steve," he said, exasperated. "Can we *please* get you to some customer service classes? You can at least pretend that you know what you're talking about, even if you choose horrible bouquets like Zap does."

"Horrible?!" Zap snapped, indignant.

"The important thing is to make the customer feel like he is making the right choice," Alan continued. "I don't care if it's a bouquet that I wouldn't be caught dead giving my girlfriend—"

"Wait, you have a girlfriend?" Steve asked, raising her eyebrows.

"The bouquet was fine! Pink is romantic!" Zap ranted.

"—what's crucial is that you empower him. You make him think, 'I am buying this horrible bouquet and I feel *good* about it.' And I mean girlfriend hypothetically. Anyway, Zap, could you please give Steve some pointers? I've gotta go finish inventory."

Alan walked off.

"Iyesu!" Zap retorted. "Orc manners!"

"I think Alan has a girlfriend," Steve said. "I always figured he was way too boring for that sort of thing."

"Well, he never talks about himself, does he?" Zap said. "For all we know, he could be a Shadowflame. Whose magic uses infant massacre as its focus."

"Don't be a jackass; he was right about the bouquet."

"No he wasn't! Anyway, you had your chance, and you pointed at the crazy person bouquet!"

"Crazy person? It's exciting!" Steve objected. "And if it's so bad, why are we selling it?"

"Ask the distributor," Zap said.

To'mas approached from behind, pushing a shopping cart full of returns. "What're you guys talking about?"

"Bouquets," said Zap.

"Alan," said Steve.

"Girlfriends."

"Infant massacre."

To'mas stared at the two for a moment before continuing to push the cart. "You guys are too much," he said, grinning and walking by.

Zap hummed a tune to himself, watching a diagnostic program run on one of the self-checkout devices. He had been sitting through the process for about a minute and a half when a familiar figure walked out of one of the aisles.

"Hey, Little Merlin," the figure called to Zap, ambling toward him.

"Hey Matt, what's up."

Matt reached the checkout device, towering over Zap. His holo-tattooed face was grinning down at Zap, his dreadlocks framing his face as he leaned down slightly. Matt was a fairly talented employee, when he bothered to work; it was fairly well assumed that he showed up to work on drugs most of the time.

"I got one for you," Matt said, a cryptic smile on his face.

"Got one what?" Zap asked.

"An answer."

"I don't think I asked a question."

"So do it now," Matt replied.

Zap laughed and shook his head, then looked up at Matt. His smile faded a bit. "Wait, you're serious?"

It was also fairly assumed that Matt had an oracular talent. Every once in a while he displayed a prescience that was unlikely to be coincidence, but seemed to manifest itself only in useless situations.

"I'm never serious," Matt replied with a laugh.

"Yeah but ... are you serious about answering a question?"

"What else am I supposed to do with this answer?"

Zap paused. "Okay, okay," he said, his mind racing. "I don't want to ask you anything too serious, because you might not be able to answer it and anyway I don't want to know important things too early and be tied to them..."

"It's very simple, Little Merlin."

"Uhm," Zap tapped his foot. "Okay. Let's keep this all secondary school, like. When will I get together with my next girlfriend?"

"Soon, man." Matt laughed. "Real soon." With that, he turned to the failed diagnostic program. "Since that was lame, I'll give you one extra: the driver on this thing is down. You want to download another one from the franchise Ether. I'll see you five minutes after you stub your toe today."

With that, Matt turned and walked away, leaving Zap standing, confused, by the crashed checkout machine.

A girl with a pretty face and long black hair who wore a black-stained pair of overalls and a t-shirt peered through the window of the Securemarket™. She stayed there for a moment, standing on her toes and moving her head about to try to look down the aisles. Her large brown eyes swept back and forth as though spying on heavily guarded territory. After a few moments of this, she sighed and walked around the corner to the entrance.

As the doors opened, she scurried through, still sneaking like a truant student. She rushed past the self-checkout machines and approached one of the aisles, looking down it cautiously.

Steve, who had seen all of this, thought it would be hilarious to sneak up on the girl and greet her from the closest possible proximity, which she did.

"Hi!" Steve chirped. The girl started violently and whirled toward Steve, her large eyes wide with surprise. Steve noted that the girl's hands were in a similar state to her clothes, stained black with an oily substance.

After a moment, the girl calmed enough to respond. "Hi," she said.

"May I help you?" Steve asked, all smiles.

"Um, that's okay," the girl said shyly. "I just wanted to see if an employee was here."

"Unless his name is To'mas, the answer is 'no'," Steve replied, looking a little annoyed at being left alone with the half-elf. "Alan and Zap had to go pick something up from regional HQ and left me and To'mas to mind the store. We don't know *where* Matt is."

"Oh," the girl said, looking a little crestfallen. She then looked up at Steve and smiled. "Okay, thanks."

"Which one were you looking for? I can tell him you came by."

"Oh, that's okay," the girl said, ducking her head. "It's really not that important. I've gotta get back now. Nice to meet you, uh, Steve," she said, glancing at Steve's nametag.

"Well shouldn't I at least tell them who came by?" Steve asked, nonplussed.

"No, that's okay, that's okay!" the girl said, already on her way toward the door. "I'll just talk to him later. Thank you! Bye!"

A few seconds later, the girl was out of sight. Steve scratched her head.

"Huh," Steve said. She let a few moments pass, then spoke to no one in particular. "Hey Alan and Zap, some girl who didn't leave her name came by with a message she didn't give for one of you, but she didn't say which one."

She shook her head, and then walked back into the aisle. "I'm gonna sit on this one."

5

15:20: Sir Lewis Birchmore of Lorenz Municipality, Inc. was released from active duty for the day. He stepped onto the rail still in his full Corporate Knight business-combat suit and headed for the 14th and Neimuth Ave. station.

15:33: Sir Drake Kunimitsu of Better Living Ltd., who had the day off, decided that it would be a good time to do his grocery shopping for the week. He threw on a t-shirt, a pair of jeans, and his kit and rose before leaving his condominium. He started walking toward the nearby Securemarket™. While he was walking, he stopped to chat with a hot dog vendor he knew.

15:43: Sir Lewis Birchmore entered the 15th and Neimuth Securemarket™. He went immediately to the beer aisle and perused the selection.

15:45: Sir Drake Kunimitsu entered the 15th and Neimuth Securemarket™. He walked to the carts, took one, and headed down one of the aisles.

15:46: Alan Morganstern, the afternoon shift manager of the 15th and Neimuth Securemarket™, received a local ping on his workshell. He tapped his earbud and heard the voice of To'mas Bonvent, a store employee, in his ear.

"We've got two Knights in the store, Alan."

Alan disconnected the call and quickly tapped a store-wide alert into his workshell, walking the length of the store with long strides. After a moment of surveying, he got two responses back:

"Got the one in the beer aisle." Steve wrote.

"Tailing the one with the cart." Zap responded.

Alan entered a message into his shell. *Roses?*

From Steve: "*Blue with gold trim.*"
From Zap: "*Yellow fading to white.*"
"Fuck," Alan said aloud. "Political attack dogs." He tapped his earbud once more. "To'mas."
"*Yeah.*"
"Would you be a dear and go man the stun turret console? I'll alter your clearance in a moment."
"*Fuckin' sweet!*"
"That's a yes, I assume."
"*Uh, sure thing, boss man. I'm on it.*"
"Thank you."

By 15:49, the Securemarket™ employees were all prowling the store like black ops troopers getting into ambush positions.

On the far left side of the store, Sir Lewis Birchmore looked to his right and spotted a short girl with curly auburn hair in an employee's apron. She was busy doing a bad job of trying to look discreet. Realizing she had been found, the girl strode up to him and gave a tight smile.

"You seem to be having some trouble deciding," she said to him.

"I am going to a party," the knight told her. "I normally drink Dragonback, but it is too expensive to bring to a party."

"So you need something cheap?" the girl asked him, adopting a vacant expression.

"No, not cheap," Lewis said, his mouth pressing into a thin line. "I do not want to seem cheap."

"So something nice, then?" the girl asked him stupidly.

"Don't worry about it," Sir Birchmore said, rolling his eyes. "I think I can probably find something,"

"No, wait!" the girl said, her voice a bit strained and far too cheerful. "I know a lot about beer!"

Sir Lewis stared at her.

Across the store, Zap's earpiece (which he had put on ready mode) came to life with Alan's voice. "*Steve's stalling the other guy. Hurry this one.*"

Zap murmured a quick affirmation and ducked into the aisle where the casually-dressed knight was pushing his cart, leaning against it. He swept to the knight's side and greeted him warmly.

"Hello, sir!"

The knight jumped, his hand flying to the hilt of his blade. Zap backed off hurriedly. The knight relaxed upon seeing Zap's apron.

"Sorry 'bout that," the knight said, nodding to Zap.

"Hazard of the job!" Zap chirped, his eyes a little too wide. "Can I help you find what you're looking for today?"

"Oh, I've got a list," the knight responded, holding up his pocketshell. There was a full shopping list on it. Zap's smile faltered a bit.

"Ahaha! A list, awesome! Looks like it'd be best to start in the produce aisle, which is two down." Zap pointed.

"I know," the knight said, smiling. "I live two blocks away, Zap. I shop here every week."

Zap stood dumbfounded for a moment, then laughed. "Of course! Sir, um..."

"Drake Kunimitsu."

"Sir Kunimitsu! Right! I didn't recognize you without your suit an' tie."

"I'm usually coming home from work," the knight replied. "But it's my day off and I figured I'd get this out of the way. How's Alan doing? Has he played any gigs lately?"

"Excuse me?" Zap looked baffled.

"Any gigs. With his band."

Zap shook his head, his face incredulous. "Alan has a band?"

From the front of the store, Alan paced a small circle. "Come on, come on, *report*..." he muttered to himself. A moment later, he heard Zap's voice in his ear.

"*Sir Kunimitsu has a big damn shopping list,*" Zap said. "*Beer is on it. I'm sending him to the produce aisle, tell Steve to get the other guy dealt with!*"

Alan tapped his earbud. "Steve, get Sir Fuckface his beer and usher him to the front. The other guy's a regular and he's doing his shopping."

The curly-haired girl's eyes looked distant for a moment, then her smile faded and she looked at Sir Birchmore with a lucid expression. Her vapid tone gone, she pointed at a 12-pack of St. Liam brand ale.

"St. Liam," she drawled, "is a good, solid ale with a relatively obscure name but reputable packaging and an excellent flavor. It's inexpensive because it's a niche brand, but heavy drinkers favor it."

The knight stared at the girl, completely nonplussed.

"It's hard to find, but I suggested that we stock it, so we do," the girl said and gestured at the beer.

"I suppose you do know a lot about beer, Miss ... Steve..." the knight said slowly.

"I'm apprenticed to an alcoholic," the girl said, and gestured to the beer again.

"I see. And to whom are you apprenticed?"

"Messianic the Gunsmith," Steve said, gesturing forcefully at the beer. "He loves St. Liam. That's the beer you want to take to your party. You want to take it now. The beer."

Sir Lewis's eyebrows rose, eyeing Steve with a growing look of appraisal. "Such a beautiful girl, an apprentice gunsmith, and so knowledgeable about fine ales?" he said in what he imagined was an alluring voice.

Steve stared at the knight for a moment before speaking. "What are you, like fifty?"

Sir Lewis bristled. "I am *thirty-nine*."

"How bout I carry this beer to the front for you sir?" Steve said in a strained voice, hauling the case of beer onto her shoulder and bustling down the aisle.

Sir Lewis stared at her ass as she went.

"Such *fire*," he murmured, then followed her.

Alan's voice sounded in Zap's ear. "*Steve's got the other knight headed toward the checkout lanes. Try to get Sir Kunimitsu to the back of the store; if he needs any meat now is the time to get it.*"

Zap shook his head and smiled to the knight beside him. "Sorry, what was that you just said?"

"I said I'm not really into any popular music," Sir Drake said. "I kind of like the old jazz standards, the ones that survived the Snowfall."

"I don't have much experience with jazz," Zap admitted. "I mostly listen to pop music. Ellis Manteaux, Rubeus, Life Rising..."

"Rubeus is a very talented man," Sir Drake said.

"So, you needed meat, didn't you?" Zap said, his smile nervous.

Sir Drake sighed. "Ground beef," he said. "For the kids. They like burgers. Someday I'll get them to appreciate a good steak. I get mine specially delivered, you know, from Amazon farms. Until then, though ... burgers."

"Burgers," Zap commiserated, nodding with very convincing regret. "Well, let's get it over with." He patted the knight on the shoulder and led him toward the butcher section of the store.

At the front of the store, Sir Birchmore approached a checkout device to see that the girl named Steve had already placed the case of St. Liam beer in the detection area. She gave him a small, rather forced smile as he approached.

"How would you like to pay for this, sir?"

"Birchmore," Sir Birchmore said, as though Steve had been waiting for his name. "Sir Lewis Birchmore."

"Aaand how would you like to pay for that, Sir Birchmore?" Steve asked, gritting her teeth.

"Company chargebus," Sir Lewis said, producing a small, sleek chargebus and holding it out to Steve. She smiled and gestured to the console and the bus port on it. Frowning, Sir Lewis plugged the chargebus in and watched as the total appeared on the screen.

"Well!" Steve said with obvious relief. "Glad to have helped you out! I know you really must be getting to your party, so I'll let you get to that!" She deftly hoisted the 12-pack and thrust it upon the knight, who took the box with both hands before he could think of doing aught else.

The small girl hurried around him and ushered him to the door with quick, shuffling steps. "Thanks so much for shopping at the Securemarket™!" she said as they went to the door. "We'll see you later! I must be going, my manager's calling! Work, you know! Ha ha!"

"Miss Steve, I—" Sir Birchmore's words fell on deaf ears. Once she had deposited Sir Lewis Birchmore at the store's exit, she scurried away and vanished into one of the store's aisles. Frowning again, the knight shifted the case of beer under one arm and exited the store.

Alan watched Sir Lewis leave and tapped his earbud. "He's gone. How you doing, Steve?"

"I need a solvent shower," she replied. "And a shot of Dragon's Breath. And a raise."

"I'll have the first two arranged," Alan replied. He looked across the store and saw Zap and Sir Drake Kunimitsu emerging from the beer aisle, Sir Drake's cart full of groceries. He smiled and sighed.

"Okay, To'mas, you can come down from the turret console."

"Aw, but..." To'mas's voice had a definite tone of disappointment.

"What if he comes back? The other guy?"

"I'm taking it out of your break time if you stay in there."

"Eff that."

Alan watched as Sir Drake scanned the last of his groceries and paid for them. He and Zap were chatting about popular culture; with the other knight gone, Zap's relief was obvious. Zap bagged Sir Drake's groceries, then lined them up so that they could be placed in an easy-sling quickly.

It was just after Zap had bid Sir Drake goodbye and the knight had prepared to sling his groceries that Sir Lewis Birchmore walked back into the store.

The knights saw each other and froze, as did Steve, who had been standing at the edge of one of the aisles, To'mas, who had returned from the office, and Zap.

There was a long silence. The CKs stared at each other, and everyone else stared at them.

"Sir Kunimitsu," Birchmore said in a flat tone.

"Sir Birchmore," Kunimitsu replied coldly.

"You and your squad are responsible," Birchmore intoned, "for the killing of fifty-three Lorenz Municipality employees, unrestituted thus far by your company."

"And you," Kunimitsu replied, "are responsible for the killing of Better Living's Sir Dreyfuss Richmond, among other trespasses against my company."

"Roberson vs. Filene!" Alan shouted. Both knights stared at him.

Alan took a deep breath, feeling the knights' stares boring into him. *This is the Securemarket™. We are secure. We offer the safest shopping experience in New Washington.* "Roberson vs. Filene. You are *not* to fight here."

In the ensuing quiet, Alan allowed himself to think for a fleeting moment that it was going to work.

Sir Lewis Birchmore sneered, "Villanueva vs. Burrows. The rivalry between Sir Kunimitsu and myself transcends the precedent set by the duel that your company has asked you to parrot. We will determine the terms of this duel and it will be *here* and *now*."

"No!" Kunimitsu snapped. "This is not a unilateral decision, churl, and by Thrace vs. Arrowroot your insult alone should allow me to dictate *all* of the terms!"

"That old argument?!" Birchmore retorted, angry. "How many examples should I use to illustrate how out-of-date that duel's terms are?"

Kunimitsu faltered for a moment.

"Here." Birchmore said triumphantly. "Now. This duel will—"

"Sir Birchmore?" A quavering voice asked. All eyes turned toward Steve, who was standing nearby and looking pale. She cleared her throat. "Uh ... Sir Lewis?"

Sir Birchmore's face twitched.

"I, uh, I forgot," Steve said nervously, extending her personal shell with a shaky hand. "I uh really wanted to give you my ether address."

There was a dead silence. Everyone in the room gaped at Steve.

"It'd be great to see you sometime," Steve blurted, her brow sweaty. "Y-you could send me a message and we could go get coffee..."

Sir Birchmore blinked, then reached into his pocket and withdrew his own shell. Both shells chirped, transferring Steve's ether address to the knight's shell. Steve looked ready to vomit.

Birchmore put away his shell and cleared his throat. He looked up at Sir Drake, who was gaping at him. "So. Later, then." With that, he turned and strode away before the other knight had time to object.

Once the knight had gone, Steve leaned her back against the wall and sank to her haunches, crossing her arms tightly across her chest.

Sir Drake exploded, stricken at Steve's sacrifice. "Miss Steve, I cannot allow you to—" he cut off at a gesture from Zap.

Alan and To'mas hurried over to Steve. Simultaneously, Alan produced a bottle of water and To'mas produced a silver flask. The staring match that followed was broken when Steve reached forward and snatched the flask from To'mas's hand. Alan watched, then sighed and nodded.

"At some point," Alan said to To'mas, "I'm going to have to lecture you about bringing that to work."

"At some point I'm sure I'll be very sorry," replied To'mas, watching Steve take a long pull from the flask.

Having somehow managed to convince Drake to leave without delivering an oath of vengeance, Zap came over and smiled at Alan. "Steve and I are going to take all of our smoke breaks now."

Alan straightened and nodded. "Ok, fine," he said. "Good job, team. You all did awesome. To'mas, fucking figure out where Matt went; I need to go to the office. I'm going to submit a complaint to HQ. If they can't get us a duel citation that a knight won't loophole in ten seconds, I am going to do some serious yelling."

As Alan strode toward the office, Zap helped Steve up and led her toward the back of the store. To'mas, left alone, walked over to a checkout machine. He leaned against it, got a distant look in his eyes, and sighed.

"Stun turret," he said in a dreamy voice.

6

Zap walked slowly down the aisle, checking to make sure that the products were in their proper places and near their appropriate price tags. It was a far easier job than inventory; all it took was simple pattern recognition and basic reading skills. Zap always volunteered for it when he was feeling too lazy to take care of anything else around the store, and today was such an occasion. As he slowly approached the end of the aisle, he could hear To'mas and Steve bantering.

"I just don't understand how you can buy into that corporate noise," Steve said.

"Good music is what it is," To'mas replied. "It's popular for a reason."

Zap paused in front of one of the shelves. Someone had completely ransacked the soft drinks, leaving them completely mislabeled and scrambled. He sighed and reached toward the first misplaced case of Go-Go Cola.

"It's popular," Steve said as though she were speaking to a child, "because that's what Mix Media puts on the ether. They put top cred into *making* it popular. People try to *convince* themselves that they're into this music, but they're really just trying to fit in."

"That doesn't make the music any worse, though!" To'mas objected. "Ellis Manteaux is a talented singer and dancer."

"Whose songs are all written by other people."

"So what? Who cares?"

Zap hauled case after case of soda from one location on the shelf to another, occasionally referencing the price tags to make sure the cases were going to the right places. He wondered what exactly someone needed with the drinks that they had to have them all on the wrong shelves.

Maybe somebody had a Supermarket ritual they needed to do.

"So it's manufactured! How can you think of it as art when it's mass-produced and shoveled into our faces?"

"Because when you get right down to the compositional level, it is *still* composed by people. By artists." To'mas insisted.

"By sellouts," Steve snarked.

"Now you're just being bitchy, is the thing."

Zap stood back and looked at the shelf, which now at least appeared to be organized. He resumed walking.

"How about Rubeus?" asked To'mas. "Is Rubeus a sell-out?"

"Absolutely," Steve replied with certainty.

"How's that?"

Zap reached the end of the aisle and turned the corner, encountering his two arguing co-workers.

"Because he's thrown himself into the popular music mill!" Steve said.

"So what, so anybody who uses effective networking and associates himself with major promoters is a sell-out?" To'mas retorted. Zap walked up to the two of them and stuck his hands in his pockets, listening.

"Yes," Steve said.
"Then what, exactly," To'mas asked, folding his arms, "is wrong with selling out?"
"...what?"
"What's wrong with selling out?" To'mas said, now spreading his hands. "Is it making money off of art? Do you have to struggle, is that the only valid kind of art?"
"That's not what I'm saying!" Steve objected.
"I think you're just bitter because rock isn't popular any more."
"Excuse me," said an unfamiliar voice.
The three employees turned to look at the person who'd spoken, a girl with short blonde hair in cargoes and a t-shirt. A basket hung from her arm. The employees looked at her for a moment, then To'mas said, "Yes?"
"Um, do you carry genmai-cha?"
"Yeah, it's in the tea aisle," To'mas responded.
"I checked the tea aisle," the girl said, "but I didn't see it."
Steve and To'mas both looked at Zap, who sighed and started walking, motioning for the customer to follow. "Come on, I'll take you to it."
Zap and the customer walked away from the other employees, who resumed their argument as soon as the others had disappeared into an aisle.
"Look," Steve said, "I'm just saying that popular music is like ... stolen goods. Anyway the lyrics are always shit."
"Rubeus's lyrics are good!"
"But Ellis Manteaux's lyrics are shit."
To'mas set his jaw, then nodded. "Okay, her lyrics are pretty bad. But the music's good."
"Says you."
"Yes, says I."
"Were either of you," Alan said, having just emerged from a nearby aisle, "planning on doing any work this hour?"
"At some point, sure," To'mas said dismissively. "Hey Alan, what kind of music do you listen to?"
"Muzak covers of baroque music," Alan replied glibly.

The other two employees stared at him. Steve murmured, "Are you serious?"

"Iyesu!" Alan said. "No! Okay, enough of this drek. To'mas, there are customers over there. Go help some. Steve, go clean the bathroom."

The employees grumbled, but moved to accomplish their assignments nonetheless. Alan stood still for a moment, then looked around him, then exclaimed into the air, "And where the *hell* is Matt?!"

Outside of the 15th and Neimuth Securemarket™, only a few meters from the front windows of the store, Matthew Del Fye stood looking up at the sky. Passersby walked by him without pause; he paid them about as much regard. He had stood for a few minutes when he broke from his reverie unprompted. He broke into stride, his long legs carrying him swiftly down the sidewalk.

As he approached the rail station and headed into it, he received some odd looks from commuters. Not only was Matt a person with a rather distinctive appearance, but he had not bothered to remove his Securemarket™ employee apron and was still wearing it as he stepped onto the Q train.

Within a few minutes, he had reached his destination. He got off the train and strode up the stairs. Once on the street, he glanced about lazily, then chose a direction and walked in it. Three minutes later, he stopped in front of a building that had a large sign reading "Dru's Garage" on it. Matt pushed open the front door, which opened into a small lobby. He bypassed the lobby without comment, getting a confused stare from the front desk attendant, walked into a hallway, went through a door on his left, and found himself in a garage, where a sleek-looking car was being serviced.

The three engineers in the garage stared at the intruder. One of them was a girl in overalls with long black hair tied in a braid. She stared at Matt, who walked up to her like an old friend. She waited a moment, then stammered, "Uh ... can I help you, sir?"

"No," Matt replied cheerfully. "I just wanted to see what all the fuss was about."

"...what?" the girl asked.

"Don't worry," Matt said, nodding. "I see you're worth it now."

"Worth what? Do you work with—"

"I gotta get back," Matt said. "I'm going to get yelled at real good if I don't get back in ten minutes."

"Oh."

"Good to meet you, Nalley," Matt said, turning away and waving as he walked away. "I'll tell him you said hi."

"Um, thanks?"

"Sure thing," Matt said and exited, closing the door behind him.

One of Nalley's co-workers stared at her. "What the hell was that about?"

The black-haired girl tapped her lips. "My boyfriend told me that he worked with a street oracle," she murmured. "I think that was him. Matt."

"That was weird," the other co-worker said.

"Was it?" Nalley asked, turning back to the car and sticking her arm down into its hood, resuming her work. "It's kind of normal, given the way my life has been so far."

The first coworker nodded. "New Washington."

"New Washington," the other agreed.

"Whatever," Nalley muttered.

7

"MIMIC!" Steve shouted.

Zap and To'mas abandoned the inventory count they had been jointly failing to do and bolted in the direction of the cereal aisle, from where they had heard Steve's voice and where they now heard the sounds of a scuffle.

When they turned the corner, they saw a middle-aged female human customer looking on in horror as Steve used one arm to wrestle with a cereal box that was latched firmly onto her other arm. It was a box of Frutee-Oze, though rather than having a cute cartoon pixie on the front it instead had a gaping maw of sharp teeth, many of which were buried in Steve's right forearm. The cereal box was snarling and wriggling, resisting Steve's efforts to remove it.

To'mas's pistol was in his hand in a moment, and he dropped to a kneeling position, sighting the cereal box. "Hold it up!" he shouted.

Steve winced, but took her hand away and put her arm into the air, making an easier target out of the box. To'mas fired. The bottom half of the cereal box exploded, splattering blood, viscera, and teeth across the aisle. The dying top half of the box twitched angrily, and Steve gripped it and tore its teeth out of her arm. She dropped the cereal-mimic on the ground and stomped on it hard, muttering curse words under her breath.

To'mas holstered his pistol with a flourish, looking extremely smug. Zap rushed forward.

"We need to get your wound cleaned up," Zap said, his voice a little strained as he ran to Steve, "so I can cure it."

"I'm going, I'm going," Steve said, trying to sound annoyed, but her voice was shaky. She held her bloody and wounded arm a short distance away from her as she and Zap moved toward the back of the store. To'mas strode over to the woman with a confident smile.

"We apologize for the inconvenience, ma'am," he said to her, leading her away from the gory mess on the floor. "I'm going to have to go clean up the aisle, but my supervisor is on his way to help you."

Alan jogged up and resumed the spiel where To'mas had left off. "Please allow us to recommend you file an incident comment on our franchise ethersite. Your input helps us to keep Securemarket™ the safest grocery experience in New Washington. In the meantime, my associate Matt will be happy to help you continue your shopping experience as soon as I can locate him. And we can fetch cereal for you, if you still want it."

The woman meekly asked, "Do ... you have any more Frutee-Oze?"

"We don't actually carry Frutee-Oze, ma'am," Alan said.

The human woman looked perturbed. "But I saw a box of them."

Alan blinked, and said slowly, "That ... may have been a *mimic*, ma'am."

"I thought I saw one," the woman said.

"Ma'am," Alan explained patiently, "Angola Foods discontinued Frutee-Oze because ColorWheels were outselling them two to one. No Securemarket™ carries Frutee-Oze any more."

The woman scowled. "Well!" she huffed. "You can expect a complaint about this!"

"Certainly, ma'am," Alan said coolly. "You can do that when you send in your incident comment. Is there anything else I can help you find?"

"Are you *sure* you don't have any Frutee-Oze?"

Alan stared at the woman.

"Like ... in the back?" she wheedled.

"Matt!" Alan shouted at the figure who had just appeared at the end of the aisles. "Come help this customer!"

"Hey!" the woman snapped.

"I'm sorry, ma'am," Alan said, directing a big smile at the customer. "As shift supervisor, I must go see to my wounded employee. Matt is an excellent sales associate and should be able to answer all the questions you ask him and probably several you don't. Don't forget to fill out that report!"

Alan turned and walked away, pausing for only a moment to set the cereal aisle's isolation shields using his workshell.

There were several moments of awkward silence between Matt and the customer.

"Help you?" asked Matt.

The woman adopted a wily look. "Do you carry Frutee-Oze?" she asked.

"You will die in a fire," Matt replied.

In the small store infirmary, Zap gingerly cleaned Steve's bite wounds with antiseptic gel and sterile pads.

"You're being pretty thorough," Steve said through clenched teeth, eyes watering from the pain.

"I don't know if you've ever seen what happens to a mimic wound that doesn't get cleaned," Zap responded, "but let's just say that you're lucky if you get to keep the limb."

"Great, thanks," Steve muttered. "That really makes me feel great."

"That's why I'm cleaning it, you little ingrate," Zap shot back, leaning forward a little bit. "I want the wound to be clean before I cast a spell that'll close it up."

"Don't you—" Steve began, looking up, and cut her phrase short as she found her eyes locked with Zap's, their faces no more than a centimeter away from each other. (Later, she would joke at herself that it was just like in the movies.) Steve could feel Zap's breath on her lips. After what seemed like a long pause, Zap averted his eyes, turned his head down, and resumed daubing at the wound.

Steve cleared her throat, her face feeling hot. "Y'think there are any more? Mimics, I mean?"

"Knowing Alan," Zap said, "he's already on the phone yelling at Paru to hire an exterminator. He's way too paranoid about safety to ignore the possibility of an egg clutch in the store."

"An egg clutch," Steve said. "That's a fun thought."

"They're a bitch to ferret out," Zap said, placing a few oiled leaves over the bite wounds. "It's amazing that something with teeth that big can come from an egg the size of a battery. Hold still."

He pressed the tip of his wand against the edge of Steve's bite wounds and murmured a few words under his breath. The leaves began to wither and the bite marks pulled together, the flesh holding itself in place and mending.

Steve looked impressed. "Not bad," she said.

"Thanks," Zap responded with a smirk.

Alan walked through the door. "Hey," he said. "How're you doing?"

Steve pointed at the red lines where the nasty gashes had just been. "All better."

"*Not* all better," Zap objected. "They're clean and closed, but they're still there. You probably shouldn't do any shooting or heavy lifting for a few days with that hand."

Alan nodded. "We can work with that," he said. "I just got off the phone with Paru. I'm concerned there might be an egg clutch in or near the store."

Steve and Zap exchanged a knowing glance.

"Anyway, she's going to come in with a Mimic Specialist tomorrow," Alan said sternly, and pointed at the two employees. "So I want you two to keep the smartassery to a minimum, yeah?"

"Why Alan," Zap said with mock innocence.

"Whatever could you mean?" Steve finished.

Alan shook his head. "Never mind," he said. "Maybe if she sees what I have to deal with daily she'll be more forgiving."

Steve laughed. "I don't think we're talking about the same store manager, then."

"Yeah," Alan conceded. "Wishful thinking. Go ahead and take a smoke break, you two. I'll see you back in the store once I finish scolding Matt for whatever it is he just said to the customer I gave him."

8

"The Eagle has landed," To'mas's voice spoke directly into Alan's ear.

Alan slapped his forehead and was about to reprimand To'mas, but someone was ahead of him: a female voice spoke over the store's ethwork.

"The Eagle," it said, *"has indeed landed. And she is listening."*

"Uh," To'mas said eloquently.

"Brilliant, To'mas," Alan said aloud, not transmitting it over the network.

"All employees not currently engaged in customer relations to the back of the store, please," the female voice intoned.

One by one, the employees gathered in the store conference room. Waiting for them was a tall woman in her mid- to late-thirties with dark skin, silky black hair, and sharp features. She wore a fashionable pantsuit and an observant, calculating expression. She also had a bulletshield on her belt and an ornate, old-looking longsword hanging at her side. The employees lined up in front of her except for Alan, who stood just behind her and to the side.

"Good to see all of you again," Paru said. "I have Alice minding the store while we meet. I hear that you've had an exciting month."

The employees didn't respond except for a few nods and a murmur or two, so Paru continued. "As store manager, it's my responsibility to ensure that the operation of the store continues apace regardless of any on-the-job threats. I understand that things have been difficult; there has nearly been a knight's duel, and now we have a potential mimic infestation."

"Regardless," she continued, "this is not a Nouri-Mart. This is the Securemarket™. Do you all recall what we provide?" A few nods. "Tell me, then."

The employees all intoned, "We provide the safest shopping experience in New Washington."

"That's right," she said. "We do. And you have; congratulations. You have all done well. But you have come *very close* to *real* disaster. What if the CKs had dueled and a customer had been injured? What if Miss Anderson had not been present to interpose herself between the mimic and the customer?"

Silence.

"I take pride in having each and every one of you as employees," Paru said. "Unique pride for each of you. In return for that pride and the faith that you can run this store under Alan's supervision, I have one single expectation for you, and that expectation is *diligence*. You are all capable of living up to this expectation, but it will not live up to itself. I require *diligence* concerning the store's needs, *diligence* concerning the fulfilling of your duties, and most importantly *diligence* concerning the safety of our customers."

Paru paused and swept her eyes across the gathered employees. "Is that clear?"

"Yes," the employees said raggedly.

"I'm sorry, is that clear?"

"Yes!" the employees barked.

"Good!" Paru shouted back, smiling for the first time. "Then I am proud to announce that due to her proactive handling of two crises within the store and her improvements in fulfillment of duty and responsibility, Stephen Anderson shall be hereby promoted to the rank of B-Class employee upon the completion of the pursuant shellwork and shall be subject to all of the privileges and responsibilities thereof."

Steve face-faulted, and the other employees broke into applause.

"Well," Paru said. "The exterminator was supposed to be here by now. I guess I'll have to help you all mind the store until he arrives."
To their credit, the employees managed not to grumble aloud.

"Congratulations on your promotion, Stephen," Paru said, reaching stride with Steve.

Steve smiled, still looking a little overwhelmed by the news. "Thank you, Paru," she responded. "I have to admit I never really expected to reach B-Rank."

"A little ambition, I think, would suit you well," Paru responded sagely. "I know we can't have you forever, but the skills you earn here will be there for you when you become a gunsmith in your own right."

"Okay," Steve replied.

"Would you mind giving me some of your opinions about the way that your shift is operating?"

"Uh, sure."

"What do you think of Alan?"

Steve thought about that for a moment. "Alan's a good manager," Steve said. "I mean, he doesn't really share much with us—the other employees, I mean—but I guess that kind of makes sense, right? He's just being professional."

"Mmm," Paru responded, bobbing her head.

"But when it comes right down to it, he's good at looking out for us, and he encourages us when we do well. Alan's all right." She paused, and then looked up at Paru curiously. "How old is he, d'you know?"

"Twenty-four or twenty-five," Paru replied.

"Ha!" Steve said triumphantly. "Zap owes me twen—uh. An apology. Twenty apologies."

Paru magnanimously let the comment go. "To'mas?"

"To'mas is cool," Steve said, smiling. "He does his work well, but he's really easygoing. I think we'll probably lose him when he gets his A-Rank Pistol-Cert though."

"I see," Paru said. "How about Zap Bradshaw? He's the newest employee here." She stopped walking, prompting Steve to do the same, and pointed at Zap, who was talking animatedly with a customer, a blonde human girl.

Steve cleared her throat. "Zap's a good employee. Sometimes he's a bit too big for his britches, but he's enthusiastic."

"How do you feel about the fact that you outrank him now?" Paru said, turning her piercing gaze on Steve.

Steve stared back. Through a sudden cold sweat, she tried not to resemble a prey animal too much, having the very vivid impression that Paru might pounce on her and devour her. "I'm not sure what you mean," she said.

"All right," Paru responded. "How about Loren Waites?"

"Incredibly boring," Steve replied, "but efficient and obedient. Sometimes I forget that he even works here."

"Matt Del Fye?"

"Uh, Matt," Steve said, scratching her head. She watched Zap point down an aisle and lead the blonde customer down it. She noticed that Matt had been watching Zap too, standing with an unused automop resting in his hand.

"Matt doesn't really do much," Steve said. "I guess what he's got going for him is that he has weirdly comprehensive knowledge of the store. And every once in a while he just knows things that are really useful."

"I see," Paru responded, giving Steve a smile. "Do you have any other comments or questions?"

"Well," Steve said. "Not really. Unless you know something about a black-haired girl who came in looking for one of the boys."

"Doesn't ring a bell," Paru said. "Ah! There's the Mimic specialist." She hurried away from Steve to meet up with the man who had just entered the store, a swarthy, scarred man with graying hair and beard, sporting overalls.

Now alone, Steve looked to her left and saw Matt still standing in place, now carefully examining the mop. She was seized suddenly with an inexplicable curiosity. She strode across the floor toward Matt, closing the distance between them in moments.

"Matt," Steve asked, "who was that black-haired girl who came and tried to find one of the boys?"

"Nalley," Matt responded.

"Nalley?" Steve asked.

"I'm supposed to mop the floor," Matt said, in the same tone one might say *one can never truly fathom the nature of man.*

"Yes," Steve responded. "You are. Can you tell me which of the boys this Nalley was looking for?"

"No," Matt agreed, and started swabbing the floor with the automop.

"I'm going to keep this in mind," Steve said. "When I want you to work, I'm going to ask you questions that you don't feel like answering."

Matt didn't respond to that. Steve whirled and walked back toward her manager, who had just finished speaking to the exterminator. As the man turned and walked into the aisles, Steve stopped a few paces from Paru.

"Paru," Steve asked, a curious edge coming into her voice, "does the name 'Nalley' ring a bell for you?"

"Nalley?" Paru said thoughtfully. "Yes, that's familiar..."

Steve gnawed on her lip.

"That's the name of Alan's, er ... car, I believe?"

Steve let out her breath. "Oh, Alan's—wait, his *car*?"

"I think so."

"Um, thanks," Steve said, discouraged. She shoved her hands in her pockets and walked back into the now-reopened cereal aisle.

"So Matt says the girl you met is named Nalley," Zap reiterated, "and Paru thinks that Nalley's the name of Alan's *car*?"

"Yeah," Steve said.

"So I guess the question is whether Matt was screwing with you or whether Paru doesn't remember her supervising days very well."

"I think Matt was screwing with me," Steve said sourly. "Paru doesn't seem like the sort of person who forgets things."

"Why don't we just ask Alan?" Zap said innocently.

"That's embarrassing!" Steve objected. "I don't want to do that."

"What is this, a sitcom?!" Zap retorted, waving his arms. "You are not doing this. I'm going to ask Alan about this Nalley person. You can come or not."

Zap started down the aisle. Steve made some noises of protest, but scurried behind Zap and kept pace with him. They approached Alan, who was checking the expiration dates on cheese.

They stopped in front of him, and Alan paused, a piece of cheese still held in his hand. He slowly turned his head, looking at the two with a suspicious expression. Zap prodded Steve.

Steve cleared her throat. "Hey, uh, Alan?" she asked.

"Yes?"

"Who is ... Nalley?"

Alan dropped the cheese. "How do you know who Nalley is?" he asked, his tone somewhat urgent.

"She ... came to the store a few days ago. She gave me her name," Steve lied.

"Why didn't you tell me she'd come?"

"She didn't say she was there for you," she said. "Um, I asked Zap first and he said he didn't know her."

Alan stared at the two of them for several seconds, and Steve found herself momentarily nervous that he would start yelling. After a moment, he cleared his throat.

"Nalley's my girlfriend," he said.

"Aha!" Steve crowed, turning and pointing at Zap. "You owe me twenty *more* creds!"

"I didn't put any money on that one either," Zap said crossly, "just like I didn't put any money on his age."

"Whatever," Steve said. She turned to Alan and smiled. "So? So?"

"So what?" Alan asked, bending down to pick up the cheese he had dropped into the lower shelf.

"So when do we get to meet her?"

"I can't remember agreeing to introduce her to you yahoos," Alan said.

"But you've got to!" Steve insisted. "To celebrate my promotion to B-Rank. We can all go to a bar. Come *on*, Alan. I just found out you're our age, now you have to hang out with us."

Alan stared at her. Steve couldn't read his expression.

"So—when're you free?" Zap said, breaking into a smile himself.

Alan rubbed his chin. "You know," he asked, "what Paru just suggested to me?"

"What?" Steve asked.

"She said that I should make an effort to connect to my employees, to establish some rapport."

"So?"

"So my band's playing a gig at the Three Gibbet Crossroads this Friday," he said.

"You've got a *band*?" Steve said, more than a little incredulous.

"I knew that," Zap said, smug.

"I have a band. And Nalley's my bassist. You come and you see our concert, and you'll meet Nalley and we can hang out," he said. "Does that sound all right?"

Steve stifled a smile, cleared her throat and affected a tone of indifference. "Yeah, sure," she said.

9

"Have you ever had to deal with any powerful mages?" Zap asked, walking at an easy pace next to Sir Drake Kunimitsu, who was back in his professional combat suit.

"A few, yes," Sir Drake replied, leaning against his cart as he pushed it down the aisle. "Knights aren't generally the best tactical choice against a good mage, though. Few of us have much magical defense at our disposal, and a powerful mage will wipe out a squad of troops quite easily."

"What will a corporation usually do?"

"If we're talking about war, most companies keep a few combat mages on hand for situations like that. The action's usually split. The mages keep each other busy while the knights and their squads handle ground conflict."

"Huh," Zap replied.

"But there are always exceptions," Sir Drake said. "Extreme situations can occur, and a knight must always be ready to defend his company and property no matter who attacks. I have killed more than one magic-user who deigned to attack me and mine."

"Well, what do you do?"

Drake rested his hand on his sword, touching it like a lover. "The Cavalier Artisans Collective crafts their blades to be perfectly balanced, both in weight and function. A knight's sword can be enchanted for unusual situations, through the pommel," he tapped the pommel of the sword, "such that the enchantment extends through the blade. The blade itself, however, is specially treated in its design to deflect spell energies. A sufficiently skilled knight can literally parry spells."

Zap's eyes widened. "Wow."

"Miss Steve!" Sir Drake said as the two walked down the aisle.

Steve stood at the end of the aisle, a tabletshell cradled in her arms. She looked up from her work and smiled at Zap and the CK. Drake continued. "Zap has just told me of your promotion. Wholly deserved, I say, and well-received. It is encouraging to see a strong young person like yourself duly rewarded."

"Thanks, Sir Kunimitsu," Steve said, bowing.

Sir Drake's expression grew a bit more serious. "I also hear that you have been pressured into a lunch date with Sir Lewis Birchmore."

Steve's jaw clenched. "Tomorrow," she said in a clipped tone.

"Surely it is not your company that is advising this," Sir Drake said, his tone low and dangerous.

"No," Steve said. "He's been legally banned from the store, actually. I just ... don't want to make an enemy of a knight. It's not a good idea."

"You're sure? If you wished to challenge him, I would champion you," Sir Drake said confidently.

"It's fine," Steve said, letting out a resigned sigh and tucking the tabletshell against her side. "You know? We'll go on a date, he'll hit on me, I'll be charmless, I'll let him know that things aren't going to work out. Not like anybody'd want to go on a second date with me."

Sir Drake and Zap stared at Steve. A moment of silence passed by.

"Are you serious?" Sir Drake asked, wide-eyed.

"I have never been on a second date, Sir Kunimitsu," Steve said, an edge creeping into her voice. "I craft weapons of death for a living and enjoy it. That's not very fetching in a girl. I've gotta go."

She hurried away, leaving her coworker and the knight standing alone in the aisle.

"Does she ... do this often?" Sir Kunimitsu asked.

"Just often enough to confuse the hell out of me," Zap replied sadly.

10

Steve leaned back and checked out her reflection in the bathroom mirror. She was dressed in standard concert fare: a black Rory and the Prairie Dogs '25 City Tour t-shirt, a pair of army green cargoes, and her bomber jacket. She was wearing her pistol low on her hip on a finely crafted false-leather belt. Her curly auburn hair was mostly loose, save for a single barrette holding a section of it back. She had actually bothered to apply a bit of makeup, covering her freckles with a subtle base, applying a bit of kohl to her eyes and gloss to her lips.

"I don't look good in makeup," she said to no one in particular.

After a few more moments of inexpert preening, Steve gave up, strode to the restroom door, shouldered it open, and walked through. Zap and To'mas were waiting for her in the break room. Zap wore an outfit not unlike Steve's: a t-shirt that said "Awesome Elemental" in a blocky font, a pair of jeans, and a black pea-coat. To'mas, however, was dressed in a black button down shirt, black slacks, and a beautiful long white duster. His normally blonde hair had been dyed white. When he saw Steve examining his outfit, he grinned and turned around. Steve saw that there was a pair of black cartoon wings on the back of the coat. She smiled and clapped her approval.

"You know we're going to a *rock and roll* show, right To'mas?" she asked, still chuckling.

"Steve, I look good anywhere," To'mas said, self-assured. "I am going to take somebody home tonight."

"You're awfully confident about that," Steve said with a grin.

To'mas turned and gave her a predatory grin, shoving his hands in his pockets and leaning forward. Steve's heart involuntarily skipped a beat. "Do you wanna put money on it, Miss B-Rank?" To'mas asked.

"Uh," Steve said, and cleared her throat. "No, that's ok."

"Can we go please?" Zap asked, rolling his eyes.

To'mas gestured magnanimously and Steve hurried ahead, letting the boys follow behind her.

Bantering the whole way, the employees made their way out into the street, to the rail station, and onto the rail.

"Hey To'mas," Zap said, smirking, "is it true that elves are developmentally challenged?"

"Only after meeting you," To'mas shot back.

"Seriously though," Zap said. "It's been proven that along with a prolonged life comes a slower development cycle. You're, what, sixty, right?"

"Fifty-six," To'mas said, nodding. "It's a little odd. I think there's definitely truth there; it takes elves longer to grasp concepts than humans, age-wise. They can pick up skills as quickly as humans do, but stuff that relies on emotional and cognitive maturity takes a lot longer. Anyway, I'm not an elf."

"Yeah, yeah," Zap said.

"No, it's relevant," To'mas said, smiling. "I think that we actually get the best of both worlds. When I was a little kid, I developed only a bit slower than my human friends, but my aging has slowed down now. It's more like my 'teens' and 'twenties' have lasted a lot longer." He grinned more. "I'm reaping the benefits, I think."

Zap laughed. "Okay."

"Our stop," Steve cut in. The three stood, preparing to exit.

A few minutes later, the employees arrived at *The Three Gibbet Crossroad.*

To'mas looked at the entrance. "Not too bad of a venue," he said, smiling. "Alan's band must actually have a bit of a name."

"It's kinda cold," Steve said. "Awesome as it is to stand and stare at the entrance, I think I'm gonna go in."

The three walked in and dealt with the bouncer. After paying the door fee, they were let in and left to explore the interior of the club. Immediately inside the building was the bar, an area with a fair bit of standing room. At the far end of the bar, a set of stairs led down into the concert area, which had a dance floor and stage. Suspended above the dance floor, just below the lighting rigs, were three cages designed to look like old rusty iron, held up by chains.

"I wonder if they ever put dancers in those," Zap mused. To'mas beelined for the bar.

"This is an okay crowd," Steve said. She was right; there were already enough people in the bar area to make getting across the floor a bit challenging. Quite a few of the patrons had colorful skin, each one representative of an element.

"Lotta mutants," Zap noted.

"So?" Steve asked.

"So nothing, just noticed."

"Hey!" To'mas shouted from the bar. He held up his hands and beckoned. "You two going to do this shot with me or what?"

Steve and Zap hurried over to To'mas. In front of him were three perfect spheres of faintly luminescent white liquid floating in the air, just above the surface of the bar.

Steve gaped. "To'mas, that's ... Aura!"

"Does appear that way, doesn't it?" To'mas said, grinning.

"You bought us *Aura* shots?!" Zap said, eyes wide. "Aren't they expensive?"

"This is what I save for, kids," To'mas replied, bowing his head magnanimously and placing a hand to his chest. "Well. This and merc training."

"You know, To'mas, I've been meaning to ask about that," Zap said. "A lot—"

"Wait wait wait hang on," To'mas interrupted. "You've got a ball of Aura with your name on it sitting right there and you think it's trivia time? No no. We drink."

"Right, of course," Zap agreed.

"May I recommend we do this the right way?" Steve asked.

To'mas held up three fingers to Steve. Steve nodded.

The employees gently cupped their hands under the floating spheres and lifted them. They carefully maneuvered, intent on not dropping the balls of Aura, and formed a triangle facing each other. Some of the other concertgoers noticed the impending tavern ritual and stopped nearby, watching.

"As all things have a beginning, middle, and end," Zap said.

"As all things are born, live, and die," Steve said.

"As all things are less, more, or the same," To'mas intoned.

"We celebrate the rule of three," the employees said, joined by several of those watching.

"One," said Zap.

"Two," said Steve.

"Three!" To'mas shouted. All three employees brought their hands up to their face and pushed the balls of Aura into their mouths. The nearby concertgoers cheered. A slight glow passed over each of the employees after they swallowed the liquor, and they all held still as the sensation of the Aura's magic passed through them. All three were silent for several seconds, their eyes closed.

"Oh wow," Zap murmured.

"It's like an orgasm wrapped in a cashmere blanket," Steve purred.

To'mas opened his eyes and looked at them. "You're welcome," he said happily and turned back to the bar to order his next drink.

Zap's eyes fluttered open and he looked over at Steve, who opened her eyes and looked back at him. The two immediately averted their eyes, daunted by the Aura-augmented intensity of each other's gazes.

"Iyesu," Zap said. "You ever done that before?"

"Only once," Steve said. "They don't serve it many places. What're you having next?"

"I think a whiskey and cola of some sort," Zap said. "I need something profane to bring me back down."

"Not me," Steve said dreamily. "I'm going to have a Sword Dancer."

"You and To'mas are going to be broke by the end of the night," Zap retorted.

"A small price to pay for flying in the clouds," Steve said, walking back to the bar. Zap followed.

"I'll have a Grabet and Go," Zap said to the bartender, who nodded and grabbed a bottle of Grabet brand whiskey.

"A Sword Dancer when you're done with that," Steve said.

To'mas leaned in from the side. "Hey kids, you should meet my new friend," he said. He grinned and pulled a pretty elven boy with long blonde hair close to him. The boy was smiling and clearly a little tipsy.

"This is T'y," To'mas said. "He saw our Rule of Three ritual and thought we did it very well."

Steve grinned. "I'm glad I didn't take that bet, To'mas," she said.

"You bet your ass you are," To'mas said proudly. "T'y's girlfriend is here, and he's going to introduce me to her as soon as she comes over."

"Hey, look," Zap said pointing. "It's the opening band."

Steve leaned around To'mas and T'y to look at the stage. T'y turned, and To'mas twisted so that he could see the stage without removing his arm from around T'y. The band was a small group of humans with torn clothing, odd hairstyles, and cheap instruments.

"They must be punk," Steve said.

"Must be what?" To'mas asked.

"I wonder if they're any good," Zap mused.

They weren't.

11

Zap stuck his pinky in his ear, making a face. "That has to have been the worst opening band ever," he said.

"It's up there," Steve agreed, slurring a bit.

"How many drinks have you had so far?"

"Two more than I *would* have had if that band hadn't been shit."

"That's how they're trying to make a name for themselves," Matt said, nodding.

"Well it—" Zap began but cut off mid-sentence. Both Steve and Zap turned their heads to stare at the tall, dreadlocked figure standing nearby. Matt had dressed in the exact same type of outfit he wore to work every day, making it actually seem a bit odd to see him without his red Securemarket™ apron. Matt was being followed by three young, attractive girls.

"Hey Matt," Steve said, looking up at her co-worker. "Fancy meeting you here."

"Way fancy," Matt replied.

"Matthew, introduce us," one of the girls said. She had forest-green hair and emerald skin, with dark green spots running across her cheeks and nose like oversized freckles. Her eyes, too, were completely green, from pupil to iris to sclera.

"Yeah, introduce us," another girl said, a human with short blue hair.

The third girl, a human brunette, simply slipped under Matt's arm.

"Oh," Matt said. "Guys, this," he indicated the human brunette, "is Sarah. This is Fleur," indicating the green-skinned mutant, "and this is Liss," pointing to the blue-haired girl. "Girls, this is Zap and this is Steve. I work with them."

The brunette, Sarah, smiled and said "Hi," to Zap and Steve, but the other two girls didn't really do much to acknowledge the pair.

Fleur moved to Matt's front and looked up at him with huge eyes. "Tell me what you said before again," she requested in a honey-sweet voice.

Matt grinned. "You are the summer breeze," he said. "Your skin is like the velvet of lamb's ear, and your eyes speak of sunny days and fields of heather."

The girl made a happy squealing noise, and Zap and Steve exchanged a dubious look. It looked as though the other girls were going to request similar compliments, but a sudden cheer from the dance floor interrupted them.

Alan was onstage, dressed like a post-apocalyptic businessman. He wore a pair of black slacks, the cuffs of which were badly scuffed. He had a white button-down shirt that was partially tucked-in; its top button was undone and the sleeves were rolled up halfway up his arms. He wore a bright orange tie and his plain dirty blonde hair had been gelled so that it looked windblown. He was holding a well-used electric guitar.

The employees couldn't quite believe that it was Alan onstage.

The rest of the band was arrayed behind him. A male human wearing an old fedora-style hat and a suit jacket over a t-shirt sat at the drum set. An inordinately tall human girl, who had on a white hat with bear ears on it, stood behind a keyboard array. A male red-skinned and -haired mutant held an electric guitar much like Alan's.

Lastly, a pretty young woman with a long, black braid stood on the far end of stage right, cradling a bass guitar. She was wearing a pair of overalls and a green long-sleeved shirt underneath it.

"There!" Steve shouted, pointing. "That's the girl, that's Nalley!"

"Hey kids," Alan said, smirking at the crowd, his voice amplified by a remote mic.

"Is that really *our* Alan?" Zap asked, bewildered.

"We are Sixth Gear!" Alan shouted. "And we are going to open with that song we always open with!"

The crowd roared its approval and the drummer began the song with a flourish. *Sixth Gear's* opening song was an up-tempo piece with a complex bassline and vocal harmony. The employees were surprised to note that all of the band members except the drummer sang, forming harmonies and counter-melodies in both male and female vocals. Alan's voice, a bold tenor, featured particularly during the verses.

> *Love had a Tea*
> *And invited you and me*
> *I showed up early*
> *But you didn't deign to show at all*
>
> *I called your shell*
> *Too bad I couldn't tell*
> *Whether you had left the thing*
> *At home or just ignored my call*
>
> *You always ruin my day*
> *You never meet me halfway*

Zap, grinning, stumbled down onto the dance floor. It took a few moments for Steve to notice that he'd gone, but she followed him down shortly thereafter, pushing through the tight crowd.

> *You never meet me halfway*
> *and I can't understand*
> *Why you won't just take the time*

> *to take my grasping hand*
>
> *I wish I could predict the things you do or say*
>
> *But you, you never meet me halfway*

The crowd had formed the closest thing to a mosh pit possible in a weapons-allowed bar, shoving each other and dancing wildly to the music. Steve and Zap joined in, throwing themselves into the crowd enthusiastically.

> *My birthday came*
> *Expecting just the same*
> *I was surprised to see*
> *That you had figured you should come*
>
> *At my protests*
> *You took away my guests*
> *To a party you had planned*
> *And left me feeling pretty dumb*
>
> *Why do you think it's okay*
> *You never meet me halfway*

Zap turned back to Steve and shouted, grinning. "They're good!" "They are!" Steve agreed at the top of her lungs.

> *You never meet me halfway*
> *and I can't comprehend*
> *Why you would leave me alone*
> *until my bitter end*
>
> *I wish you'd help me keep my woes at bay*
>
> *But you, you never meet me halfway*

The music abruptly cut to half-time and the rhythm guitar got quieter, making room for a complicated bass solo that Nalley performed, chewing on her lower lip as she concentrated on the improvisation. Zap and Steve cheered along with the crowd as Nalley's hand danced up and down the bass's frets and her other hand's fingers flickered across the plasteel strings. As Nalley's solo came to an end, the drummer dove into an energetic fill and the band went back into a fugued version of the chorus. All four of the singing members, including Alan and Nalley, formed a layered, round-style harmony.

The song ended with a dramatic out, and the audience burst into enthusiastic applause that Steve and Zap joined.

Alan grinned at the audience, his face glistening with sweat, and held up a hand until they had quieted a little.

"I heard that I've got a few of my co-workers in the audience," Alan echoed through the mic. Steve and Zap let out a whoop and heard To'mas follow suit from somewhere behind them. "Well, this song's dedicated to you guys. I like to call it 'Fuck the Day Job'."

A few songs later, Zap and Steve decided to leave the dance floor and refresh their collective buzz. They each had a glass of water at Zap's insistence, then a shot of good vodka at Steve's insistence. They were on their next drink when they actually stopped to look around.

"Good crowd," Zap said, a little zoned out from the effects of the alcohol but still coherent. "Good concert."

"Seriously," Steve said. "Y'know, I allus thought that Alan was just boring. But there are all those people down there who just think he's the shit. Those are *fans*, you know?"

"Yeah," Zap replied. "Oh hey, look." He pointed over to a corner of the bar area.

Steve followed Zap's indication and saw To'mas in the corner of the bar. He had T'y pinned against the wall and was nose-to-nose with him, murmuring something quietly. The effect of To'mas's proximity and words was obvious on T'y, as his face was flushed and eyes were half-lidded. A very alluring, svelte elf girl with multi-hued hair, presumably T'y's girlfriend, was behind To'mas and had her arms around him, gently nibbling at his neck.

"Holy shit," Steve said.

"Did you *know* To'mas was such a smooth operator?" Zap asked.

"You know," Steve slurred, "I prolly should have. Never hit on me, though."

"That's odd," Zap said.

Steve paused for a moment. "You think so?"

"Sure," Zap said.

Steve mumbled something Zap couldn't hear.

"What was that?" Zap asked, turning back toward Steve.

"Nothing," Steve said. "Where's Matt?"

"Over there," Zap said, pointing. "Looks like he's switched out one of his girls."

Sure enough, Matt still had the mutant and brunette human clinging to him, but rather than the blue-haired girl there was instead a half-elf wearing a black golf cap backward.

Zap looked toward Steve, who shrugged and held up three fingers.

"I don't think so," Zap said. "That'd just be mean. 'Oh, sorry, this girl's cute so you're going to have to go. Rule of Threes, you know.'"

Steve gazed at Zap for several seconds.

"What?" Zap asked, knitting his brow.

Steve mumbled something.

"I can't hear you," Zap said.

"Kiss me," Steve said.

Zap's eyes widened. "W-what?"

Steve lunged across the space between them, threw her arms around Zap's neck and kissed him. After a moment's hesitation, he returned the kiss. Behind them, rock and roll music blared.

Just like in the movies, Steve thought.

12

The show had ended. Numerous concertgoers were still milling about, discussing what they thought of the show. Steve was sitting in her barstool, glowing. Zap had gotten a little bit shy after the kiss and had eventually wandered off, but Steve still wore a triumphant, self-assured smile.

Steve's shell buzzed in her pocket, and she fished it out to take a look at who was contacting her. She found an e-mail from Alan waiting for her.

3 blocks east, 1 block north. The Good Old American Diner.

Steve nodded and looked up to where To'mas and his new friends were cooing at each other. She walked up to them and prodded To'mas in the arm, who seemed surprised that anybody other than the elven couple existed.

"The Good Old American Diner," Steve said. "Should I assume you're a lost cause?"

"Yes, I'm being kidnapped for the night," To'mas said, smiling broadly.

"If I'd taken the bet," Steve asked curiously, "would I have had to pay twice?"

"Yes," To'mas replied, and then turned his attention back to his couple.

Steve laughed and turned from the amorous triad. She turned and saw Matt, still with the same three girls as when she had last checked. She walked up to them. "Hey Matt, you want to bring your harem to The Good Old American Diner? We're meeting Alan there."

Matt shook his head. "No, I have to spend a little bit more time with these ladies before I vanish mysteriously from their lives, leaving them to pine and wonder whether they will ever be able to find me again."

Fleur, the green mutant, put on a mock pout. "Don't joke!" she said.

"I think he's serious," said Sarah, frowning.

Steve shrugged and turned away. Her eyes roved once more and she spotted Zap, who was sitting at the bar staring at his drink.

"Hey, Zap!" she shouted. Zap looked up at her. "We're going to The Good Old American Diner to meet the band."

"Um, okay," Zap said.

The two left the bar and started walking toward the diner. Zap was quiet almost the whole way, speaking only when directly asked a question. Steve found it a bit strange but didn't comment.

The diner was modeled in the style of pre-Snowfall American diners, with a bar where they didn't serve alcohol and lots of booths. The band was arrayed at a long table in the corner of the room, sitting on the long seat against the wall. The chairs across their tables were empty.

Alan and Nalley sat at the end of the line. The drummer sat in the center, still in his fedora and suit jacket. The fire-element mutant was next to him, and the tall, buxom keyboardist (still wearing her cute white bear-hat) sat at the far end, a huge maul leaning against the wall next to her.

Steve and Zap sat down across from the band. "Hey!" Steve said. Zap threw in a quieter "Hey," as well.

"Hey, kids," Alan said, smiling and clearly still high on the endorphins from performing. "Where's To'mas?"

"He and Matt were preoccupied with some playthings," Steve said. "They both saw the show, but stayed with their new friends."

"Aw," Alan said. "Well, okay. So, introductions. Guys, these people here are Zap and Steve, two of my employees at the afternoon shift."

Various 'heys' were exchanged.

"This is Nalley, my girlfriend," Alan said with pride, indicating the black-haired girl next to him. "She's also a superb mechanic and bassist." She gave Zap and Steve a shy smile.

"This here's Animal Jake, my drummer. I'm pretty sure this is all he does," Alan said, indicating the guy in the fedora. Animal Jake saluted to Zap and Steve.

"The gentleman in red," Alan said, pointing to the mutant (who nodded in response), "is named Roger. And the lovely amazon on the end of the line is Michelle-Bear," he said. Michelle-Bear gave a toothy smile to the two.

"Good to meet you guys," Steve said.

"Hey Zap, you all right?" Alan asked. "You look a little queasy."

"Been drinking, you know?" Zap said, his tone wan.
"Ah," Alan said.
"So how did you guys meet?" Steve asked the band.
"Well, it started with me and Rog," Alan said, nodding to the red mutant. "We were friends in secondary, and we always thought rock was an underappreciated genre."
"We were both in the choir," Roger said, running a hand through his bright red hair. "So we knew how to sing harmony. We tried to make a band but it really didn't work with just two guys. I didn't even know how to play guitar then."
"So anyway, we both went on to NWU," Alan said. "Me as a business major and Rog as a political science major."
"You kids want to eat anything?" a waitress asked, approaching the table.
"Uh," Steve said, looking down at the menu in front of her.
"We need a little more time," Alan said. The waitress nodded and left.
Zap and Steve took a few moments to peruse their menus. Once they had decided, they set the menus down and Alan continued.
"We met the rest of our *first* band in uni," Alan said.
"Animal Jake was always hanging out at a local rock club that we went to regularly," Roger said. "We didn't know what he did for a living then, and we don't know what he does now, but that doesn't really matter so much, does it AJ?"
Animal Jake smiled.
"We also met this guy who went by Face," Alan said. "We never really found out why. We took him on as a bassist, and there was our band. The *Sixteenth Street Crazies*."
"Only problem was," Roger said, "we didn't have a keyboard, we only had two singers and our bassist was shit. And anyway I was still picking up the finer points of rhythm guitar."
"We didn't get far," Alan said. "It wasn't long before we had to kick Face out of the band because he was a terrible bassist and an asshole. But now we had no bass at all and we still had the same problems as before. By the time we graduated from NWU, we were still no closer to making it big. It was looking like the band was going to fall apart. But then our rescuer found us."

"Aw," Michelle-Bear said sweetly. "You guys rescued *me*."

"You kids ready?" the waitress said, suddenly having appeared again.

"Yeah," Zap said. The waitress looked at him, and he responded, "I'll have a stack of pancakes and a glass of milk."

"I want the All-American Breakfast Platter and orange juice," Steve said with relish.

The waitress looked at Alan, who said, "The young lady and I will share a plate of cheese fries, and I'll have a coke," he said.

"And a cup of black coffee for me," Nalley added meekly.

Animal Jake held up the menu and pointed at the chicken fried steak. The waitress nodded and looked to Michelle-Bear, ignoring Roger. "Miss?"

Michelle-Bear looked confused for a moment. "Um, I'll have the half-pound burger with fries and a chocolate malt."

"Okay," the waitress said.

"I'll have the number one skillet," Roger said.

"Anything else?" the waitress asked the table.

"Number one skillet," Alan said in measured tones, "for the gentleman in red. And water all around, please."

The waitress left.

"There goes her tip," Alan said. "Racism tax."

An uncomfortable pause slunk by.

"So! You want to take over here, Michelle-Bear?" Roger asked.

"Sure!" Michelle-Bear chirped. "I was living with one of my boyfriends at the time, and I had big dreams of being a musician. I was pretty much totally self-taught. When I got my SEC, my parents made me get enough martial cert to take care of myself and turned me loose. I stopped my formal education there and lived on my own for a bit. I kept practicing singing and keyboards and writing songs, and I paid the bills by waiting at the Reynaldo's near NWU."

"The Reynaldo's," Roger interjected, "where Alan and I became regulars after we graduated."

"So, I started dating this guy named Arnold, and he was encouraging, he said he believed in me, he thought I'd go places. He was monogamous but I really thought that he and I had something special, so I let my other partners go and just dated him," she said, her smile fading. "He sort of mooched off of me. I had to work extra hours to support him because he was between jobs, and his encouragement dropped off a little, but I thought it was just the relationship getting comfortable, you know?"

Michelle-Bear suddenly looked up, a little mortified. "Oh geez, look at me going on about my personal shit..."

"No, it's okay," Steve said, and Zap nodded.

"And anyway it's relevant," Alan said. "In case you hadn't picked it up, this guy was a serious piece of work."

Michelle-Bear cleared her throat. "So it all went down one day when I was at work. We were in trouble financially so I was going to take another waitstaff's shift to make a little bit of extra cash. I had sort of forgotten that I was supposed to lend Arnie my datasoul so that he could use some of the programs that I had. He showed up at the restaurant and just started yelling."

Michelle-Bear bit her lip, clearly affected by the memory. After a moment, she went on. "He showed up and just started yelling. He was saying that he was waiting for me to succeed, and at first he thought I was gonna be somebody, but I wasn't going anywhere, I was just spinning my wheels. And he said that he was just hoping I'd go somewhere professionally, and he never loved me in the first place. That I was too big to be human, and how could anybody be attracted to someone with a body like a half-orc, and he was tired of waiting for an ugly freak to make it big."

"He probably would have gone on," Roger said, "but Alan and I had decided we'd heard enough."

"I think you've got a very nice body, Michelle-Bear," Nalley said, smiling.

"Thank you, Nalley," Michelle-Bear said, smiling broadly. "I know it was bullshit. He was just jealous that I could bench almost twice what he could."

"Anyway," Roger said, "Michelle-Bear was obviously in no psychological shape to defend herself, so Alan and I decided to intervene. I berated the guy for his unacceptably callous treatment of his girl. He responded, naturally, with racist nonsense that failed to address any of the points I had made. I smiled at him and replied with a full dressing-down based on everything he'd said, as well as a few key points regarding his appearance and how he must be in bed."

"And then he drew his pistol," Michelle-Bear said coolly. Steve and Zap gaped.

"Iyesu!" Steve said. "In a restaurant?! That'll get you killed in some precincts."

"Yeah, well, I snapped his limb," Alan said. "Idiot locked his arm. Must have forgotten all of his C-Rank training, so a few kilos of pressure was all it took. I knew I'd get away with it, too, because I'd been studying business law that semester. I'd been doing research on local businesses and their responses to armed action. Because Shithead drew first, he basically lost most of his rights right there."

"Once the police had carted Arnie off and I took my leave, the boys talked to me for a little while," Michelle-Bear said. "We hung out for a while and talked about ourselves, just to take our minds off of what had just happened. The boys were really interested in the fact that I was a singer and songwriter."

"And that pretty much did it," Roger said. "We decided to let the band sit quiet for a while and prepped. Alan and Michelle-Bear put their heads together and started writing songs and I started auditioning bassists. Nobody else was able to pull off the bass sound that we wanted, unfortunately. It was around this time that Alan started spending a lot of time with this Nalley girl."

"That's me," Nalley said, smiling. Alan smiled and kissed her on the cheek. She made a pleased 'mmm' noise.

"At one point, on a lark, I lent her the bass that Face had left behind and jokingly suggested that she should be our new bassist," Roger said with a grin. "It turned out to be the best thing I ever did for the band."

"I took to it like I took to fixing cars, kinda," Nalley said. "It just made a lot of sense. And I liked how it was heavy, and the strings were heavy."

"She became our new bassist and we renamed the band," Roger said. "We were actually able to go on tour for the first time around July of last year. Since then we've gotten this little cult following that's just growing and growing."

"And Nalley and I started dating around Christmas," Alan said.
"There you go. The story of *Sixth Gear*."
"Awesome!" Steve said.
"Seriously!" Zap added, seeming to have gotten over his malaise.
"Look, I want all of your contact info," Steve said, holding up her shell. "You people are too cool not to see again."
"Oy," Alan replied. "Worlds collide."
"There's nothing to be done about it," Steve said triumphantly as the other members of the band produced their shells and pinged their contact data to Steve.
Steve looked at her shell, then up at Nalley. "Lumia?" she said with a smile. "That's a really pretty last name."
Zap looked up, his expression a bit surprised. "Lumia?"
Nalley nodded. "Yes, that's my last name."
"Huh," Zap said.
"Honestly, you guys are really good," Steve said. "I'm so glad that we came to the concert."
"Thanks!" Michelle-Bear said, her smile radiant.
"I'm really glad you guys all got to come, including To'mas and Matt," Alan said. "Zap, it's seriously too bad that your girlfriend had to miss it."
Steve and Zap both suddenly stood very still.
"What's her name again?" Alan said. "Pazu?"
"Pazi," Zap said quietly.
"Girlfriend?" Steve said, her voice quavering a bit.
"Yeah, you didn't hear?" Alan said, smiling. "You remember that customer you foisted off on Zap while you and To'mas were arguing about music a few weeks back? The one with short blonde hair?"
"The one who was looking for genmai-cha," Steve murmured.
"Yeah! She and Zap hit it off, and started dating recently! The girl sounds great."
The waitress showed up during the awkward silence that followed with the food. "Here you go. Pancakes, All-American, Cheese Fries, Chicken-Fried Steak, Burger, fries and shake. Did somebody order a skillet?"
"The *gentleman* in red," Alan said coldly. The waitress grunted, set the platter down and walked away. Animal Jake gave her the middle

finger as she walked away, and Roger and Alan simultaneously did the cast-off gesture, holding a fist to their chest then splaying their fingers away quickly.

"Excuse me," Steve murmured. "I don't feel well." She stood and hurried to the bathroom.

"Huh," Michelle-Bear said. "She looked like she was doing pretty well with her liquor."

Zap put his face in his hands.

"You okay, Zap?" Alan asked.

"Yeah," Zap said, standing up. "I just gotta go call my girlfriend real quick. Back in a second." He walked toward the exit.

"What was that about?" Alan asked once they'd gone.

"Ohhhh," Michelle-Bear said, her eyes wide and one hand flying to her mouth. "Oh dear."

"What?" Alan said.

"I don't get it either," Roger said.

"Don't worry about it, sweetie," Nalley said to Alan, exchanging a significant look with Michelle-Bear. "They need a little space."

13

(soundtrack: "The sun was in love with the moon", a piece by Michelle-Bear Urza, almost exclusively piano and solo voice, with sparse vocal harmony by Nalley Lumia)

The sun was in love with the moon

Though he knew that she would never know what he thought
He fell for her curves and her luminous face
He tried to run with her but couldn't keep pace
He hoped she would wait for him, but she could not

And oh, how he prayed he would be with her soon
The sun was in love with the moon

"Aw, 'yesu," Roger said, looking through the window. "I think it's starting to rain."

The band followed his eyes and saw that outside, a gentle rain had begun. The late-night pedestrians pulled up their hoods and produced umbrellas, picking up their pace a little bit.

The earth was in love with the sky

Though she knew he would never be able to see
She'd look to his heavens and wish she were there
It was what it was, but it didn't seem fair
So she pined for a thing that was not meant to be

And although she was low and he was too high
The earth was in love with the sky

Stephen Anderson sat on the toilet in a cramped bathroom stall, her eye makeup streaked down her face with tears. She held her shell to her face and rocked back and forth. After a moment, the shell connected and she spoke.

"Daddy?"

Ooh, ooh, you never knew that you let me down
Ooh, ooh, you never knew that you let me ... down

But you did
Oh, you did

Zap Bradshaw stood underneath the awning of The Good Old American Diner, his shell pressed to his face, already in the middle of a conversation. Around him, the rain beat a tattoo against the pavement.

"Yes—thank you. I need to admit, though," he said, then sighed. "I kissed her back. I did kiss her back."

A pause.

"No, it didn't mean ... it didn't mean anything."

He nodded. "Thank you. I'm glad you understand."

A girl fell in love with a boy

When she was with him, she could not feel alone
But she never said what she had in her heart
And there were some times that the two spent apart
So during this time he found love of his own

He could never have known that he'd shatter her joy

But he did...
Ooh, he did...

Sometimes we're blind to the things we destroy
A girl fell in love with a boy.

Arc II

The Retreat

News Update

Sent 0:48:04, 2227/04/08, from 12365.35.8290
From: NW News Express Online
    <noreply@express.nwfp.co.nw>
Reply-to: <unsubscribe@express.nwfp.co.nw>
X-Sender: express.nwfp.co.nw:5052
Subj: Express Online! Volume 35, Issue 15

The NW News Express Online:
The City's Finest Weekly Plain-Text News Service:
No ads, no lies, no problem!

Regional News: Precinct 8

LEAD STORY: THE URBAN JUNGLE, TWO WEEKS LATER
--
OTHER NEWS:

VARGAS'S STOCKS CONTINUE TO RISE

THE 16TH STREET STALKER KILLS AGAIN

VAGRANCY ON THE DECLINE IN PRECINCT 8

ACES EIGHT TO BEGIN LAYOFFS

THE URBAN JUNGLE, TWO WEEKS LATER

Two weeks ago, the western border of Precinct 8 saw the worst terrorist attack in three years, and cleanup concerning the event still goes on. Information concerning the incident itself, previously kept confidential by Lorenz Municipality, Inc., has now been released to the public and press.

On the day of the incident Marwyn Lewis, 38, a

Life-elemental Node Caller, allowed his magic to run unchecked in front of the 11th Ave. Securemarket™. As the location is a strong Life Node, the extent of damage that the sudden plant growth caused left 13 citizens injured and will cost taxpayers well over 9,000₢ in repair.

Authorities claim that the swift reaction of nearby Securemarket™ employees saved the city from further loss. Sergeant Loomis Blaemyre, a member of the Precinct 8 Police Force, summed up the situation: "Securemarket™ employees are trained to be ready for just about anything, and these kids really exercised that this time. We're especially thankful to [Securemarket™ employee] Miss Elwynn for summoning a fire spirit to help keep things in check."

"Honestly I had no idea I'd ever need to do any serious Calling while on the job," employee Pazi Elwynn remarked. "But this guy was wrecking everything, I had to ... I had to act."

The Securemarket™ corporate headquarters claimed no official involvement in the quelling of the disaster.

VARGAS'S STOCKS CONTINUE TO RISE

The unexpected success of upstart research corporation Vargas, Inc., has been a surprise to everyone-- a pleasant surprise for its shareholders and a nasty one for its detractors.

Vargas's chief research is in personal enchantment for civilian use. Among its front line of products has been the controversial product ElemRescue, a medical device designed to counteract the effects of magical radiation on unborn children; Vargas's press release claims that the device can, if used quickly enough, rescue fetuses from in utero elemental mutation with no adverse effects. Vargas came under fire from mutant rights groups immediately, particularly when it was suggested by some key members of Lorenz Municipality that such treatment might be required by any mothers-to-be who were exposed to elemental energies.

Despite this, Vargas's stocks have continued to grow; their additional host of useful and cutting-edge technomagical products has drawn the attention of wealthy visionaries and hopeful marketing firms throughout the precinct.

THE 16TH STREET STALKER KILLS AGAIN

A 10th victim has been claimed in a string of murders by an individual now being called "The 16th Street Stalker".

The victim was Robert Grorek, 46, the half-orc proprietor of Grorek's Falafel, a restaurant located at 16th and Rose St. As with previous killings, Grorek's cause of death has not been announced. He died on the 2nd at 23:25 in his store.

According to police, Grorek's death was consistent with the previous killings in the alleged serial murders; all victims have been proprietors of businesses on 16th Street, one of the Commercial District's most profitable avenues for independent entrepreneurs. The murders are having a chilling effect on the business environment, residents say.

"My family is telling me to close up shop," said Brielle Spelt, 168, owner of neighborhood mainstay 'Brielle's Deli'. "They think I'm going to be targeted. I'm seeing shops that have been open for 10, 20 years closing because of this. Well, I'm not going to do this. I'm not going to cave in, and I want to see some action about getting this threat dealt with."

"We will see this threat quashed, whatever it may be," Precinct 8 Lieutenant Torvald Lawson remarked on Friday. "The chief is personally involved in this case."

Precinct 8 Police Chief Doyenne Salazar had no direct comment.

VAGRANCY ON THE DECLINE IN PRECINCT 8

A survey done by the community watchdog group 'Role: Perception' has noted a marked decrease in the number of vagrant persons at large in the Precinct 8 area. Consistent with this finding, the group reports that the number of arrests for nuisances, loitering, public drug use, and related crimes have dropped significantly.

Obviously, these findings indicate a positive trend for the precinct's businesses; complaints about vagrancy come chiefly from business proprietors who feel that their customers will shy away from the frequently disruptive antics of local vagrants.

"Yeah, Crazy Mikey's gone from his corner," said Rafe DeWitt, manager of the 14th and Rose St. Donut Pass-Go. "I couldn't be happier. That [expletive] drove away more customers I can count. I feel sorry for whoever has to deal with him now."

Despite the outward positive effect, many members of Role: Perception urge citizens to be vigilant. There is no correlative indication that explains the reduction in vagrancy, nor have any of the remaining street-dwellers indicated any knowledge of a migration. Some members of the watchdog group have gone so far as to accuse Precinct 8's municipal company, Lorenz Municipality, Inc., of foul play. Lorenz's press representatives have disavowed any relation to or knowledge of the sudden change.

ACES EIGHT TO BEGIN LAYOFFS

A Press Release issued on Saturday by umbrella corporation

Aces Eight has stated that several branches of the company, most notably those involved in plastics and chemicals, will be undergoing necessary layoffs in the next few months.

This marks an unusual behavior for the company, which has prospered almost unfailingly since its inception. Federal sources indicate that some resources for consumer materials are undergoing a temporary shortage, forcing the government to increase taxes on the trade and processing of such materials.

Aces Eight's CEO and Chairman John Doxen said, in an official statement to the press:

"Now, a lot of people are going to start talking about our big 'setback'. I'm here to tell you that this situation is not a setback. Not to reinforce my reputation too hard, but there are times when one has to fold a hand to win out in the long run, and this is such a time for Aces Eight. While my sympathies go out to the workers who will need to be reshuffled in this, I am confident that with a history with Aces Eight and solid references, they'll do just fine. And so will we."

Aces Eight's competitors in the plastic and chemical industries seem to be suffering under a similar situation, and none commented on the Aces Eight layoffs.

You are signed up to receive the text-only
NW News Express Online!
To unsubscribe, please reply to this e-mail.

Please send comments or story suggestions to commentbox@express.nwfp.co.nw

14

Paru Dupree, barefoot and wearing a polysilk robe, padded out into the tastefully decorated and immaculately clean common room of her condominium. It was her day off, and she had chosen to take the rare opportunity to sleep in very late. She sighed and looked through the window, surveying her city through the post-rain haze. She went to the kitchen, where a pot of coffee was waiting for, brewed without prompting when she woke. Paru poured herself a mug, went to her desk, and sat down in front of her home-shell, which had booted up and was already displaying the news.

She was about to start reading when a dialog popped up indicating that she had a call and Handel's *Water Music* played over the condo's speakers. Paru sighed and said, "House, pick up."

"Paru?" A female voice came through the common room speakers.

"Yes?" Paru replied.

"It's Steve. Listen, I'm not feeling well, and I couldn't reach Alan. I've called Loren, and he's going to replace me for today's shift."

"All right," Paru said. "Thank you for letting me know."

"Sure thing," Steve said. "Have a good one." The speakers let out a disconnect chord.

Paru sighed and turned back to her news just in time for *Water Music* to strike up again. She gritted her teeth and leaned toward the screen, seeing that it was Alan calling her.

"House, pick up. Hello?"

"Paru, it's Alan," Alan said. "I'm running kind of late today. I'm going to call Steve and ask her to mind the store until I get there."

"She's not coming in," Paru said. "She just let me know. Loren's going to replace her. You might want to ask To'mas or Zap to mind the store until you get in."

"Okay, thanks," Alan said.

Her peaceful morning completely disrupted now, Paru paused for a few moments before she managed to get her bearings and turn back to the shell. She managed to get halfway through the listing of headlines when Handel's *Water Music* once again echoed through the condo. She read the notice on her screen and saw it was Zap.

"House, pick up," she said, her voice strained. "Zap, if this is about you not coming in, I am going to have you killed."

"Huh?" Zap said, confused. "No, no, I'm on the rail now. I just had a question for you."

"Oh," Paru said, a little surprised. "Go ahead."

"I think you said something about Alan having a car. What kind of a car was it?"

"That is a very bizarre question, Mr. Bradshaw," Paru said.

"It's okay if you don't know," Zap said.

"No, I think..." Paru thought for a moment. "I think it was something by Chiaroscuro, a recent model. I can't remember which one, though."

There was a pause on the other end of the line.

"Okay, thanks!" Zap said after a moment. "That's what I needed to know. I'll see you at the retreat."

"Mmm," Paru said, smiling a bit. "That's soon, isn't it?"

"Yes," Zap said.

"All right, have a good day," Paru said.

"You too," Zap said, and disconnected.

Paru sat motionless for a few moments after the call, then swiveled in her chair back to her shell's monitor. "House?" she said. "Shut up."

There was a tune as all notifications in the condominium's memory disabled. Paru smiled, picked up her coffee, and took a sip.

15

"Okay," Alan said, tapping his tabletshell. "Nice work, Zap. I think the only thing I've got for you right now is to go help Steve with restocking the canned goods aisle."

Zap shifted his weight onto one foot. "Uh," he said, "isn't there anything else to do?"

"Nothing more pressing," Alan said. "Got To'mas on the bathroom, and in a fit of unexpected productivity Matt went and mopped the entire store. Hop to, little guy."

Zap took his time moving over to the aisle, but couldn't help but reach it after a minute or so. Steve was there, moving goods from a cart to the shelves. She froze when she saw Zap, and then looked away.

"Hey," she said.

"Hey," Zap said back. He moved to help her with stocking the items, and both of them worked in silence.

They had been at their work for several minutes when a customer came by, humming a children's song. The customer didn't tarry in the aisle at all, carrying through and exiting the aisle within fifteen seconds.

There were several more silent moments of work before Steve started humming the song.

Zap ignored her, at first, but upon the completion of the verse she actually started singing the words aloud. "*Johnny was so poor and sad, the saddest in the town; his house was made of sticks and leaves and always falling down...*"

Zap joined her without thinking. "*Johnny was the most unlucky man I'd ever know; I thought he couldn't have it worse, but it began to snow.*"

Alan appeared at the end of the aisle. "Hey!"

Zap and Steve both looked at their manager, who stared at them for a moment, then burst into song. "*Johnny, Johnny, the unluckiest man, Johnny's is a fate that I never could stand.*"

Zap and Steve resumed both stocking and singing, accompanied by Alan, who began harmonizing. "*When the magic came back we all had it rough, but it seemed like Johnny just couldn't get enough.*"

They made it through all five of the standard verses, and then threw in a few extras that each of them had heard in primary school.

"—and things sort of got a little less weird there," Steve said, then took a sip from her coffee.

"Wow," Nalley replied, leaning against the hard back of the café's chair. "I'm so sorry all that stuff happened, Steve."

"It sucks," Steve agreed. "But the way it went down, it wasn't like he was being some kind of asshole. I'm not going to lay it on Zap. He should have told me right away and he shouldn't have kissed me back, but it's not like I gave him time to think about it. Whatever."

Nalley gave a sympathetic nod, keeping her large brown eyes on Steve. "You're being pretty even-headed about it."

"It's about time I did that with *something*," Steve said. "Anyway, enough about me. I'd love to hear about how you met Alan."

Nalley smiled. "Well, I met Alan in '25," Nalley said. "We just sort of ... met. I went through some serious difficulties a year later, and Alan was really nice and let me stay with him for a little while. Pretty soon I was able to get a job as a mechanic and I started making more money, so he and I became roommates for real. And, um, I've kind of been interested in him since I met him, but he didn't think it'd be appropriate at first. Especially when he was supporting me. But around Christmas he admitted that he liked me, and we started going out," Nalley said, smiling.

"That's a cute story," Steve said. "I wish I could have a boyfriend as thoughtful as that."

"Oh, you totally could, Steve," Nalley said. "You just have to wait to find him."

"Mmm," Steve replied, taking another drink of coffee. Her tone was not a hopeful one.

"Thank you for meeting me for coffee, Steve," Nalley said, smiling. "I ... moved from a different neighborhood and lost touch with most of my friends. I don't have a lot of them around here. It's cool hanging out with the band, but it's nice to branch out, too."

"Hey, no problem," Steve said, grinning. "I haven't got a whole lot of female friends. Come to think of it, my number of actual friends is a little lower than I'd like these days. I spend too much time with my Master."

"That's right," Nalley said. "You're an apprentice gunsmith. Who's your boss?"

"Grover Messianic," Steve said, a bit proudly. "He's an amazing gunsmith. I carry a piece of his; it's named Polaris." She took the gun out of its holster and set it on the table. Polaris was a gorgeous weapon, impressive even to an untrained observer. Its design was smooth and sleek, crafted of silver plasteel and carefully balanced.

"Polaris uses nine millimeter ammunition, but honestly it's so well-balanced it kicks like a twenty-two. Using Messianic guns just ruins you for standard models," Steve said. "Though frankly, few people can afford to carry them."

"How's it that he lets *you* carry one?" Nalley asked, smirking.

Steve laughed. "Polaris was a commission by a merc who was trying to make a name for himself. Master was just working himself raw on this piece, and had me working on a lot of the lower-priority ones. So he finally finishes the damned thing, and he's ecstatic. He says that it's one of the best guns he's made in the past year, and it was a rush job, too, so there was a *lot* of money coming in for it. He sends me out to buy a gallon of Good Old Apple Scrumpy and a case of St. Liam's, saying that we are just going to get shitfaced in celebration. I head out."

Steve drank the rest of her coffee, far more animated now than she'd been earlier in the conversation. Nalley leaned against the table, rapt.

"While I'm gone, Master gets a call. It's from a mercenary who'd previously commissioned a Messianic, and knew about the Polaris. He tells poor Master Grover that the commissioner of the Polaris ended up taking a hit job on somebody who was being defended by *Johnny Fucking Holiday*. Wachow," Steve said, making a swiping motion with both hands. "Holiday took off both of his arms with those katana, and our man bled to death before he could make it to the hospital."

"Wooow," Nalley said, her eyes wide.

"It also turns out that our man owed hundreds of thousands of creds to debtors, so all of his accounts were liquidated and distributed. Way the contract went, we could keep the down payment and the pistol, but we had no way of collecting the rest of the commission. We lost over *half* of what we would have made. Master was furious. I came back to the workshop and he was cursing this guy's name up and down, ranting and raving and cursing all over the place. Said that the last time a client died, he destroyed the gun to send it to the client in the afterlife, but there was no way he was sending Polaris to this deadbeat."

Steve cleared her throat and grinned slyly.

"Well, I could see that Master was super upset, and I wanted to calm him down a little. So after he says that there was no way he was sending this guy his unpaid gun, I chime in and say well, it wouldn't work anyway. So he stops and kind of looks at me funny and asks why. I look at him real earnest and give him a little-girl look and say because Messianic guns are too good to go to hell."

Nalley laughed earnestly, a melodic noise. Steve spread her hands in a grand gesture.

"Well that totally throws him for a loop. He starts laughing there, and says that I just made his night and that he wasn't allowed to bitch until he'd had at least one tall stein of Scrumpy. So we sit down and start drinking, and soon he gets all sentimental like he always does when he gets drunk. He says that Polaris reminds him of some of his best pieces, and he wishes that some of them were still around for him to show me. And he says that he wants to have Polaris be somewhere where he can see it until he retires, but guns are meant to be worn and used, not displayed like trophies. I want another coffee."

"What?" Nalley asked, thrown by the sudden departure from the story.

"I want another coffee," Steve said. "Mind if I interrupt the story and go get one?"

"Uh, sure," Nalley said, nodding. "I could use one too."

They got another pair of coffees from the counter, then returned to their seats.

"Okay, so where was I?" Steve asked.

"Used, not displayed," replied Nalley.

"Right!" Steve said. "Used, not displayed. So all of a sudden I see him switch gears in his head, and he looks at me and leans forward a little bit. And he says to me, he says, 'Stephen, someday yer gonna have to carry a piece o' yer own craftin','" Steve rasped, affecting an exaggerated accent and squinting one eye. Nalley giggled and Steve continued.

"'But until that time, I d'want yeh carryin' around no Dai-Sho gun. Worthless man-ya-fakkered shit,' he says. So he reaches over and grabs the Polaris and slaps it down right in front of me. And he looks at me and he says, 'My star student. I 'spect you to make yourself a standard belt tomorrah an' a dress belt th' next day. An' they better be good.'"

Steve threw her hands into the air and smiled. "And there you go. I made holsters and belts for myself, and Master gave me the gun. Until I get Journeyman Cert and can legally carry my own weapons—" she leaned toward Nalley "—and let me tell you I have one design that is going to kick *ass*—but until then I get to bear the Polaris, one of Grover Messianic's self-admitted best guns."

"That's an awesome story," Nalley said, clapping her hands.

"Thanks!" Steve said. "What kind of training do you have, Nalley?"

"Oh, just C-Rank pistol and CCDM," Nalley said.

"Oh, I don't mean just martial or magic," Steve replied. "Don't you have VC? You said you were a vehicle mechanic."

"Oh yeah," Nalley replied. "I have a history with cars, so I learned a whole lot of stuff on my own. When I finally had to make a living, I managed to get rush-certified as a mechanic because I already knew just about everything about Chiaroscuro-make cars and was quickly picking up other makes. I am pretty good with cars."

"Wow," Steve said. "That's really impressive."

"Thanks," Nalley replied shyly. She looked down at her watch, then up at Steve. "Hey, weren't you supposed to be at work ten minutes ago?"

"Oh, shit!" Steve agreed, leaping to her feet. "Really nice to spend time with you! Sorry to have to leave so quickly!"

"It's okay!" Nalley said, smiling. "I look forward to doing it again."

"Bye!"

"Bye!"

16

"Maybe they're sharing embarrassing stories about you," Zap said, grinning at the shelf of apples in front of him.

"Sure, maybe," Alan said. "Nalley really likes to get people talking. She'll listen to stories all day."

Zap turned and looked back at Alan. "I hear you used to have a car," he said mildly.

Alan looked back at Zap, his expression somewhat suspicious. "Yeah," he said. "I sold it."

"Hm," Zap said, returning to his work. "Okay. That's cool, owning a car."

"Might get another one," Alan said, his expression relaxing a bit. "Nalley's going to build me something out of salvage parts. Collecting the parts now, and she'll eventually find a frame."

"I'm here!" a voice called from the front of the store. "I'm here!"

"Don't tell me; clock in!" Alan shouted back.

"So," Zap said to Steve as the two paced the aisles, "How was coffee with Nalley?"

"It was good!" Steve said, smiling. "She's really great. Alan's caught himself a seriously awesome girl."

"She does seem really friendly," Zap agreed. "She's cool. What did you guys talk about?"

"I did a lot of talking, really," Steve said. "I told her the story about how I ended up getting to carry Polaris here."

"I should hear that story sometime," Zap said.

"Yeah, you really should. Other than that we just covered basic stuff about each other, you know, what we do and stuff."

"Nalley's a vehicle mechanic, right?"

"Yeah, why?"

"What kind of cars does she specialize in, do you know?"

"Um, I think mostly Chiaroscuro cars."

"Mmm..." Zap said.

"What are you on about?" Steve said suspiciously. "You're acting really weird."

"I want to show you something," Zap said, pulling out his personal shell and tapping on its screen.

"What?"

"Just going to the Chiaroscuro manufacturer's ethsite. Did you know that Alan used to own a Chiaroscuro?"

"Oh? What model?"

"Well, I'm not *entirely* sure," Zap said, tapping the screen a few times. "But I'm pretty sure it was this model."

He showed the screen of his shell to Steve. Steve froze. Her hazel eyes flickered from the screen of the shell to Zap's eyes several times. Her face registered confusion first, then surprise, then suspicion.

"What—" she began, and shook her head. "What are you trying to say?"

"You know," Zap said, "I'm not sure. I'm not sure what I'm trying to say. But I think there's something to be said."

"Maybe it's a coincidence," Steve said.

"You know, if not for Paru's first comment, I'd write it off as a New Washington thing and leave it at that."

Steve shifted uncomfortably. "Are you going to say something?"

"I don't know," Zap said, tapping his shell and putting it back in its pocket. "I don't think so, not yet. But I figured you ought to know."

"I guess," Steve said. Her face suddenly expressed irritation. "Man, Zap, why do you have to *think* so much."

"I know; it's a bad habit."

17

He had muddy brown hair that was thinning on top and carried himself with a pronounced slouch. A simple Wakizashi 9mm was on its standard-issue holster on his belt, obscured slightly by the Precinct 11 Sharks team jacket he wore. He was leaning over one of the self-checkout units, poking at it savagely. His face registered obvious irritation.

Zap passed by as the customer continued his futile struggle with the checkout machine. He saw the customer's face and approached, asking, "May I help you?"

"This damned thing isn't showing my Data Deal," the customer growled.

"Which Data Deal would that be?" Zap asked, looking at the screen.

"On Spun Glass Soda," the customer said.

"Hmm," Zap said, knitting his brow. "I don't ... recall there *being* any Data Deals on Spun Glass Soda."

"It was on *your* ethsite," the customer growled.

"I don't keep an ethsite, sir," Zap said, keeping his voice mild. "But if you mean the store's, I can check for you."

"This is stupid, I just want the discount!" the customer said, irritated. Noticing the customer's raised tone, Steve appeared from around a neighboring aisle to watch the altercation.

Zap kept his cool. "I know, sir," he said, his tone placating as he pulled his workshell from his belt. "Let's take a look at the store's ethwork."

"You're useless," the customer muttered. "Just like all the staff at this damned store. I don't even know why I have an account with you."

"Of the current Data Deals running," Zap said, looking at his workshell. "Spun Glass doesn't seem to be one of them."

"It's on my account! I *just* downloaded it!" the customer shouted, raising his voice. Alan had appeared at one end of the store's front, his tabletshell tucked under one arm. He, too, seemed content to watch the scene unfold rather than to take action.

Zap sighed. "Please ping my shell with your contact information, sir, and I will take a look at your account downloads."

"I can't believe this," the customer said, but produced his shell and pinged his address to Zap's workshell nonetheless. "You're all totally useless. The machines and the fucking employees, all of you. I might as well be hunting and gathering in the Great Western Forest."

"Please mind your language, sir," Zap said coolly as he tapped his workshell, sifting through the customer's data.

"Fucking useless," the customer said. "All of you."

"Okay, sir," Zap said. "It looks like there *was* a Data Deal on Spun Glass Soda that ended about a month ago. You downloaded the Deal the day before it expired, according to your account."

The customer's face rapidly turned beet red. "That's wrong!" he shouted. "That's a lie!!"

"If the Deal were still on, I'd gladly reinstate it but—"

"It's wrong!" the customer roared. "I want my Data Deal! Take the money off!"

"Look, I *can't*—" Zap began, his tone a bit more strained at being interrupted.

"Take it OFF!" the customer interrupted at the top of his lungs. To'mas, who had clambered up to the top of one of the walls dividing the aisles, now crouched there and watched.

"It's *one cred eighty*—"

"Take it off, curse you!" The customer reached to his side and grabbed his pistol with both hands, jerking it halfway out of the holster.

He was stopped abruptly by the sound of multiple safeties being turned off. Steve had advanced several paces and had Polaris leveled at the customer's head. Alan, somewhat further away, also had his Waki 9 drawn and pointed straight at the customer. To'mas's Katana .45 heavy pistol, too, was trained on the customer.

The scene was very still. The customer, finally realizing his situation, had frozen in place with his gun half-drawn. Zap gently reached out and placed his hand on the customer's elbow. He pushed down, and the customer reholstered the gun and let go of it. The other employees did not lower their weapons.

Zap cleared his throat. "As I was *going* to say, that Deal is expired; however, there is currently a Data Deal on the Too-Kann frozen dinners you purchased that would total to more than the Spun Glass Deal you'd downloaded. I would have happily uploaded it to your account to make up for the difference, but..." Zap trailed off, letting his eyes trail over to Alan.

Alan holstered his pistol and approached. "But you're banned from the entirety of the Securemarket™ chain for attempting to draw a weapon with hostile intent and no provocation." He held up his smaller workshell and tapped the shutter button, capturing the man's image. "Any creds still on your account will be refunded to you."

"You can't—"

"I assure you I can," Alan said. "Get out. My employees' arms are getting tired, and I know for a fact that at least one of them has an itchy trigger finger."

The customer watched, stricken, as Zap canceled the transaction on the self-checkout unit, humming and smiling.

The customer looked back and forth between Alan's stoic face, Zap's pleased one, and the two pistol barrels still trained on him. "But—"

"You really should go now," Alan said in a weary tone. "At this point we can legally shoot you."

The customer started walking off, and the closer he got to the exit the more his shock and fear turned back to anger. Right next to the door, he turned back and shouted, "You just lost yourself a customer!"

The employees, baffled, stared at him.

"Yes," Alan finally said. "Yes we did."

"You'll regret this!" the customer shouted.

"BANG!" To'mas shouted. The customer started violently and rushed out the door, hitting his head on the frame as he pushed his way through.

Once he was gone, Steve finally relaxed and holstered her gun, and To'mas did the same. Alan looked up at To'mas. "For the fifth time, To'mas," he began.

"I know, I know," To'mas said, leaping down from the wall. "Walls are for separating, not standing on."

"They are," Alan replied.

"You know something?" Zap said, smiling and folding his arms.

The employees all looked at him. "What?" asked Steve.

"We are going to *kick ass* at the retreat."

"Yeah," Alan said, smiling. "We are. Now everybody get back to work."

18

Alan, Nalley, and Steve were sitting at The Kaiser Roll™ on Neimuth Avenue, about a block away from the 15th and Neimuth Securemarket™. The time was 21:53, and the three were having a post-shift dinner together before going their separate ways. All three were grinning widely as Alan told a story.

"—but of course, his weapon belt had already come loose," Alan said, "and when it fell, it went and took his slacks right with it."

"Oh my God!" Nalley said, her hands flying to her mouth. She giggled madly as Alan continued.

"And yeah, so that day we found out that Sir Tor wore boxers with little cartoon depictions of Arachne on them. I'm surprised he didn't challenge one of us to a duel; he was probably too shocked to think straight."

"That's so crazy," Steve said, smiling.

"Yeah..." Alan said. "Yeah."

"Hey Steve, what's up?" Nalley asked, tilting her head a little bit. "You've looked kind of out of it this whole time."

"Oh, uh," Steve said, shaking her head. "It's really nothin'."

"Hey, don't be a Fed," Nalley said, smiling. "You can talk to us about it. You've talked about your Zap stuff with both of us."

"Yeah, but," Steve said, making an unsure gesture.

"It's really okay," Alan said, also smiling. "I know I'm your boss and all, but this isn't really your *real* career anyway. I want you to feel like I'm more of a friend by the end of it than a boss."

"Uh, it's just about something I heard from Paru, and some other stuff."

"Yeah?" Nalley asked.

"Um, Alan, you used to have a Chiaroscuro, right?" Steve looked up into Alan's eyes as she asked. She saw a definite flicker of fear pass behind them, but when he responded, his tone was casual.

"Yeah, for a year or so before I sold it," he said. Nalley's expression grew unsure.

"What model was it?" Steve asked.

Alan paused for a moment before responding. "It was a Lumia," he said. "The model that Nalley based her last name on when she changed it."
"Oh," Steve said, nodding a bit. "She changed her last name."
"Yes. Isn't that right, sweetie?"
"Yes," Nalley replied, her expression unhappy.
"What's the matter?" Steve asked.
"Her parents really didn't want her to do it," Alan replied, smiling.
"What was your car's name?" Steve asked. "Paru said it was—"
"O'Malley," Alan replied a bit too fast. "Funny coincidence, huh? It wasn't—"
"No," Nalley replied, her expression dark.
Alan faltered and let his voice drop off.
"What?" Steve asked.
"I don't like this," Nalley said, her voice quavering. "I don't like this any more."
"Sweetie, please—" Alan pleaded.
"It's all I've got, Alan," Nalley said, "don't make me put it away."
Steve was silent, letting her gaze flash from Alan to Nalley. Alan's face expressed a mix of sympathy, concern, and fear.
A tear rolled down Nalley's cheek. "I didn't change my name," she said. "Alan didn't sell me!"
Steve's jaw dropped.
Nalley burst into tears and pushed away from the table, sobbing loudly. She ran from the restaurant, drawing stares from the nearby patrons. Alan looked back and forth between Steve and his fleeing girlfriend for a moment, then gave Steve an apologetic look and bolted after Nalley.
Steve was left alone with the empty trays on the table to make sense of what had just been said. She scratched her head, took a deep breath, and slowly stacked the trays, putting all of the trash on top of one of them. She walked with the tray to the trash, emptied it, placed the tray on top of the can, and exited the restaurant.

When Steve left the Kaiser Roll™, she was surprised to find that Alan was standing just outside, facing the street. He was just outside of the flood of a street lamp, standing mostly in shadow. His arms were at his side, but his shell was in one hand. It cast a soft bluish glow against his jeans, the only spot of color on him

Steve approached cautiously. "Alan...?" she said, half-expecting him to explode at her.

"Mm?" Alan said, turning a little bit.

"You okay?"

"Oh? Uh, yeah," Alan said. He sighed and ran a hand back through his hair, leaving it in a blond tousle not unlike what he wore for concerts. "Nalley wants to be alone for a bit."

"I, uh, I didn't mean—"

"I know you didn't mean," Alan said. "This is sort of my fault."

"What do you mean?"

"She's so honest, Nalley is," Alan said with a wan smile, turning toward Steve. "Trying to force a lie on her for safety's sake was..."

"Could ... you tell me what she meant?"

Alan rubbed his nose, and was quiet for a few moments. He sighed. "Thereby ... hangs a tale."

Steve chewed her lip and shifted her weight from foot to foot.

"Let's go to your apartment," Alan said. "I'll tell you the whole thing. I think that Nalley'd probably prefer I did."

"Uh, okay," Steve replied.

The two walked toward the rail station in silence.

"Steve," Alan said, carefully stepping into the apartment, "this may be the messiest apartment in New Washingtonian history."

"I like to think that by creating a protective layer of debris," Steve replied, clambering over a pile of laundry, "I'm keeping the floor from getting fucked up."

"Not like you've got too much room in here," Alan said. He soon gave up on walking and crawled over the mountains of clothing and possessions, trying to avoid destroying anything. "How much does this place cost?"

"Four fifty," Steve said. "Not a bad price for the location, but yeah it's basically a matchbox."

"Right. Um, so where should I sit?"

"On the futon is fine," Steve said, nodding and leaning back on a pile of laundry.

"Where's that?"

"You're on it."

Alan looked down at the surface he'd ended up on, and realized that it was actually a futon on a frame. Steve's homeshell was taking up about half of it, and a dropcloth on which gun parts were strewn was covering up another quarter.

"How in the hell do you sleep here, Steve?" Alan asked.

"I move the dropcloth," Steve replied, "and curl up. I don't take up that much room. Anyway, a lot of the time I just sleep on Master's couch. His second wife is a pretty good cook, and she feeds me if I crash out there."

"Is there even a kitchenette in this apartment?"

"Um, there's a bathroom there," she pointed at a small door that barely had room to open. "With a sink. And I've got some minifridges under the futon frame, and a multiheater on that pile there that I use to heat frozen dinners. Anyway, weren't you going to tell me Nalley's story?"

"So I was," Alan said, leaning back against the wall. "Okay, let me give you the history behind it."

Steve settled into her laundry.

"In May of 2225," Alan said, "I graduated from NWU with a degree in business, as you know. My parents were really happy about that. They're both really good with money, so I got a really nice graduation present: a Chiaroscuro Lumia '25. A sleek new car, a method of transportation, and status symbol all in one. I named the car Nalley.

"As the year progressed, things got difficult for me. I was still working at the Securemarket™, which I had been for a while, but I wasn't making then what I make now and anyway I was *terrible* about spending. I hadn't picked up any money-saving skills, so I was paying all of my bills with my Securemarket™ wages and not really able to save much. I was also trying to beef up my martial certs, get myself up to B-Rank pistol and CCDM. Those courses took up time and cost money, and I was eating takeout a lot. Things got kind of bad.

"So anyway, in the summer of '26, I decided that things were just getting too bad, so I made the decision that I was going to have to sell my car. I wasn't happy about it at all, but I thought it was the only option and I prepared myself to do it. And that's where the story really begins..."

19

I expected to sell my car that day. I had talked to a few potential buyers about the sale, and had actually found somebody who was willing to offer up a fair sum for the vehicle. I was not really feeling so hot about having to go through with it, nor to have to sit through an eight-hour work shift first. I liked the car; I felt like I'd really formed a good connection with her. The whole situation had put me in a pretty unhappy mood, so imagine how I felt when suddenly, first thing in the morning, somebody started banging on my door.

It was really loud, too. I was worried it was going to wake up Roger, who I was rooming with then. Still in my boxers, I rushed to the door and threw it open, ready to bitch out whoever was standing there. I stopped in my tracks, though, when I saw who was there.

It was a really hot girl. Who was totally naked. And crying. When you're a college-age guy, it's hard to stay angry with a hot naked crying girl standing at your door.

"Please don't send me away," the girl blurted. "Please don't send me away." She was shaking all over, her long black hair disheveled and plastered to her face. She didn't seem hurt, but she was clearly scared and confused.

"Iyesu," I said. "Come in, please, let's get you inside."

I ushered her in the door and closed it quickly, admittedly somewhat concerned about what any onlookers might think. She moved inside a bit awkwardly, as though dizzy or off-balance. I guided her to the couch and sat her down, then quickly rushed to get one of my t-shirts. I rushed into my room and picked up the biggest t-shirt I could find and started to rush back, then thought better of it and got a shirt for myself. Once I was wearing it, I headed back to the living room and handed the strange girl the larger shirt.

After a bit of fumbling, she got the shirt on. "Thank you," she murmured.

"Sure," I replied.

"Look I'm sorry, I'm so sorry," the girl murmured, looking like she was going to go to pieces again. "I will pay you back, I promise I'll pay you back no matter how long it takes."

"Whoa whoa whoa," I said hastily. "You don't need to pay me back. I'm just ... I don't even know what I'm doing. Do you want some coffee?"

"Um, sure," she said.

I got up to get her some. "Cream and sugar?"

"Okay," she said.

"Uh, ok." I poured her a mug of coffee, added a conservative amount of cream and sugar, and returned with it. "Here you go. Why don't you tell me what happened to you?"

"You wouldn't believe it," she said, then took a sip of coffee. "This is very bitter."

"Yes, well, it's coffee," I replied. "Do you want more cream and sugar?"

"No, I like it," she replied.

"How do you know I wouldn't believe it?" I asked. "I'm a New Washingtonian; I see weird shit on my morning commute."

"Yeah, but you've got names for it," she said. "There's magic and technology and stuff. I—I dunno."

"Why don't you tell me your name?" I asked.

That was the first time she really fixed those big brown eyes on me, and my heart just skipped a beat. I think that something inside me knew deep down that she would be able to ask me anything and I'd do it. My heart skipped another beat when she told me that her name was Nalley.

I looked at her oddly, then laughed. "Nalley," I said. "Hah, that's funny. That's the name of my car."

"I know," she murmured.

I laughed briefly, but then the laugh trailed off and my smile faded. I got a very ominous feeling and rushed to the door, throwing it open and looking outside. My parking space was empty.

I shut the door, whirled and was about to shout, but the girl looked so miserable. I also realized I didn't want to wake Roger, so I tried to stifle my sudden panic. "Where's my car?"

"I'm sorry, I'm sorry," she murmured. "I'll pay you back, I promise I will pay you back."

"What is your name," I asked in a strained tone, moving toward her, "and what did you do with my car."

"I'm so sorry," she said, her voice growing thick. "I just ... had to, I couldn't—"

"*Please*," I said, my voice very strained at this point. I leaned toward her, placing my hands on the coffee table. "Please. Tell me who you are and what has happened to my car. I really need the money that car is going to give me when it sells, because it is a very nice car that is worth a lot of money."

"Very nice car..." the girl echoed, her mouth twitching a little.

"However, I am *very poor*," I continued, "and I need to pay rent and eat, and if I cannot sell that car I don't get to do those things. So please. Miss. Tell me your name and what you know about my car. I promise I will be reasonable about this, but I need to know."

She looked at me again with those deep brown eyes and my heart jumped, which really didn't help my anxiety. "I'm Nalley, Alan," she said to me. "Please don't sell me."

I stood, I covered my mouth with both hands, and took slow, measured breaths. After a few moments, I removed my hands and said quietly, "Miss," I said, "this is really not ... not a funny joke. It's really not."

"It's not a joke, Alan," the girl said. "I'm not joking."

I opened my eyes and looked at her. Her eyes were brimming with tears; they caught mine and devoured me. If she was lying, she was very good.

"You're ... claiming to be my car," I said.

She ducked her head in a nod.

"How am I supposed to believe you?" I asked.

She held my gaze with hers. "The night that Mary broke up with you," she said, "you drove halfway home, then pulled into an open parking garage."

I stared at her.

"You pulled into a corner space and cried until morning."

I kept staring.

"I felt so bad for you," she murmured and looked down. I swear I felt a tearing sensation when she pulled her eyes away from me. "I wanted to hold you closer somehow."

Naturally I waxed eloquent. "Uh," I said.

"I can say more," she said. "Once I got towed because—"

"No," I cut in. "No, that's okay."

She bit her lip and looked up at me, rocking back and forth a little bit.

"Um, okay," I said. "Assuming for just a moment that you are telling the truth, which I still am having some trouble believing ... are ... all cars like this? Sentient beings that can turn into people?"

The girl looked puzzled. "I don't ... think so," she said.

"Are you ... human now?"

"I think so," she said, nodding.

"Did you do that on purpose?"

"Yes."

"Why?" I asked. "Why did you do that?"

"Because I c-couldn't stand the thought of n-not being yours," she stammered. A tear rolled down her cheek.

"Why ... couldn't you?" I asked.

She looked up at me once again. Her eyes were earnest and innocent. "Because," she said, "I love you."

We stared at each other. After a moment of floating helplessly in her gaze, I was able to pull away. I stumbled backward and fell heavily into a chair.

"This is all extremely implausible," I said.

"I know," she said. "I'm sorry."

"And ... there's no car any more," I said.

"Just me," she replied.

"So I'm fucked," I said.

"I'm so sorry," she said, crying again. "I just couldn't, I couldn't—"

"No, no," I said, unable to stand watching her in this state. "No, it's okay. Please don't think about it right now. Have your coffee."

"I'll work," she said. "I'll be your slave, you can take all of my money—"

"No, please," I said, leaning forward in my seat. "I really don't want a slave, I just—"

"—I'll do anything, *anything*, just please don't send me away."

"No," I said, moving across the space between us and taking her by the shoulders. "I won't send you away. I don't want a slave, but I won't send you away if you don't want to go."

I looked at her tear-stained face and her trusting eyes and sighed. "I will talk to my roommate. We'll see about finding you a job, and you can be our third roommate. At first you'll have to lean on us. I don't know how that'll work, but we'll think of something. But I'm ... not going to send you away. You can stay in my life. I promise."

Steve leaned forward on her pile of laundry, rapt.

"At the time," Alan said, "I seriously believed that I would regret putting so much trust in this girl and her crazy story. The fact that I never did is still one of those things that gives me hope for this godawful world."

"Wow," Steve replied. "She was in love with you from the get-go?"

"Yeah," Alan said. "And honestly, I thought she was attractive and wonderful from the moment I met her. But I was her protector at first, and she really felt like she belonged to me. It wouldn't have been right to date somebody who thought of herself as a possession. It wasn't until December that I admitted that I really wanted to be with her."

"What did Roger think of the whole thing?"

Alan laughed. "He thought the story was actually pretty awesome," he said. "He believed it from the start, and was happy to help shoulder the financial burden of Nalley's presence while she found a job. Funnily enough, we put her to unskilled work at first. Food service, custodial stuff ... even construction, once we found out that she was strong for her size. But she didn't like any of it; the work was too stupid."

Steve grinned. "I know the feeling."

"It wasn't until a month after she'd appeared ... when she was talking to me about one time when I was being bad about keeping up with proper maintenance, and she was talking about how her battery unit was aching because the motor unit hadn't been properly lubricated in months, and talking about how this connection and that connection were loose and if they'd kept up she was just going to stop running ... and it hit me. I asked her how much she really remembered about the way a car was put together, and she basically said she knew everything. She used to have a computer dedicated to keeping her up-to-date, after all."

Steve laughed. "I bet that'd come in handy."

"Yeah," Alan said. "We took her to a few places and managed to bypass the experience requirements and rush-certified her. Turned out that she already had the expertise of a mid-level Chiaroscuro mechanic, a job that carried a hefty enough salary to bring us back into the black."

Steve shook her head. "Wow..." she said, then looked up at Alan. "So ... what *is* Nalley?"

"She's a human girl," Alan said. "She's my girlfriend; a talented vehicle mechanic and bassist."

"But ... is she a technomantic construct?" Steve asked. "Or, like, a car morph? Or—"

"She is a *human girl*," Alan said with finality. "Who used to be a car."

Steve frowned a little bit, but didn't ask any more questions.

"Honestly, Steve, that is all that matters," Alan said, shaking his head. "It's all that Nalley wants to be. She wants to remember her history and be what she is now."

"I guess I'm just sort of curious about how it happened."

"I know. I was too," Alan said. "But it's funny, you know? This is New Washington. It's a city where legends and epics take place. There is more unexplainable stuff in this city than anywhere else in the world, and we're just scrambling to come up with scientific terms for it all. Infinite and Emergent Potential. The Law of Naming. The 26 recognized schools of magic, monster thaumotypes, and registration cards."

Steve nodded slowly. "Okay," she said. "Okay."

"You see what I'm saying?" Alan said. "We'll never catch up with all of the things we can't explain, but some people are determined to try. People who'd love to strap Nalley down and cut her apart, just to *make sure* that none of her organs were made of HD-Plastic. But I don't care. Nalley was a car once, but now she's a girl, and I love that girl."

Steve smiled. "You guys are totally adorable," she said.

Alan laughed. "Yeah, don't tell anybody." He took a deep breath and let it out. "So there you go. Nalley's big secret."

"Aw," Steve said. "It ain't so big. She's a wonderful girl."

"She is."

"Think it's okay to go home yet?" Steve asked.

"Yeah, I think so," Alan replied, shifting his weight and starting to maneuver his way toward the apartment's front door. "I'll see you tomorrow, yeah?"

"Same Securemarket™ time, same Securemarket™ channel," Steve said.

Alan finally made it to the door, opened it and looked back. "*Oyasumi*, Steve."

"*Oyasumi*, Alan. Be well."

"You too."

20

Zap trudged through the aisle, his gait slow and tired. He stopped for a moment to contemplate a shelf of disposable flatware. He spent a few minutes staring at the variety of paper plates and bowls with sleepy eyes, then put out his hand and leaned against the shelf. His eyelids slowly drooped and his head lolled slightly. His arm suddenly went slack, and he stumbled against the shelf clumsily, jolted awake. He scrambled to regain his footing hurriedly, then tried unsuccessfully to stifle a huge yawn. He resumed his slow trudge.

As Zap gradually approached the end of the aisle, To'mas walked around the corner. The half-elf halted in his tracks when he saw Zap.

"You look like a blue mutant in a sauna, dude," To'mas said, smirking at Zap.

"Precertification finals," Zap murmured.

"Bit early for them, isn't it?"

"Yeah, well see," Zap explained, "if I don't earn my precert before the retreat, I won't be allowed to use any decent magic in the simulations or exercises. You can only use weapons and magic you're certified for."

"Ahh," To'mas said, nodding.

"So I've got it all scheduled," Zap said, "so that I can get my precert in time to be able to include it in the shellwork for the retreat. And if I stick with the schedule, I can actually get four full hours of sleep a night, six if I work really hard."

"Iyesu. I hate deadlines," To'mas said, his face a mask of distaste. "You've got my sympathy, bro."

"What's going on with you, To'mas?" Zap said. "I haven't been keeping up."

An idyllic smile crept onto To'mas's face. "I have been having a *lot* of fun lately."

"Oh yeah?"

"Yes," he replied. "Remember that couple I met at the Sixth Gear concert?"

"Ahh," Zap said, echoing To'mas's earlier gesture of commiseration.

"They've decided to keep me," To'mas said. "We've been having a great time."

"Congratulations," Zap said, yawning.

"What about you?" To'mas asked. "You have a girlfriend now, don't you?"

"Yeah," Zap replied. "Her name's Pazi. She's at Ethertech too, working on an Apprentice degree in Arcane Invocation."

"A summoner?" To'mas said, grinning. "Sexy."

"I'm not really sure what you mean, but sure. Also, another thing about her—"

"You ladies plan on working anytime soon?" Steve asked from the end of the aisle.

"Can I just nap instead?" Zap asked.

"Sure, why not," Steve said. "I'll just give Paru a call and let her know that you'll be napping, and is she okay with that."

"Right, to work!" Zap said, striding from the aisle.

Zap walked across the front of the store, checking the diagnostic panel on the self-checkout machines as he passed by. He turned his head for a moment, glancing out the front window of the store. He turned back and continued his walk, then did a double-take back out the window as it registered whom he had seen.

Sir Lewis Birchmore stood just outside the store, looking in and craning his neck to try to see down the aisles. Zap's hand flew to his workshell and he tapped it, murmuring into the microphone of his store earpiece.

"Steve," he murmured, "stay in the back. Your asshole Romeo is here."

"*Son of a bitch,*" Steve's voice growled in Zap's ear.

Sir Birchmore tapped on the front polyglass window of the store.

"Do I get to go to the turret?" To'mas asked excitedly.

"Yeah, go ahead," Alan's voice said. "*Zap, please get Sir Ironsphincter to go away.*"

"Me?!" Zap said indignantly. Sir Birchmore looked irritated and knocked on the glass. He gestured to the door, indicating that Zap should meet him there.

"*Just go do it, Zap.*"

Zap very slowly and reluctantly moved toward the entrance of the store. Sir Birchmore walked over to the doorway and stood there. The door opened as the Knight passed in front of it like an arena portcullis opening on an opponent that Zap was quite ill-prepared to face.

"May I speak to Miss Steve?" Sir Birchmore asked, polite but ice-cold.

"You're really not supposed to be here, Sir Knight," Zap said slowly.

"I am not to *enter* the store," Sir Birchmore said, "thanks to the research of the toadies that your company retains. The research that you hide behind, as none of you are intelligent nor brave enough to speak for yourselves."

"You're also not supposed to like camp out in *front* of the store," Zap said.

"I have to be here for at least fifteen minutes to present any precedent for enforcement," Sir Birchmore responded. "Moreover, I do not come here to fight or argue. I come under only the friendliest of pretenses today."

"Is that right," Zap said.

"It is," Sir Birchmore replied. "I am concerned for Miss Steve; she has not contacted me in some time, and I am worried for her safety."

"Tell him I'm dead," Steve said. "Tell him I got eaten by a mimic."

"Steve is fine," Zap said, "except that she's sick today."

"Ah," Sir Birchmore said. "Perhaps I should return tomorrow?"

"Tell him I got run over!" Steve said urgently. "Say a roc shat on me!"

"Shut up!" Zap growled under his voice.

"I beg your pardon?" Sir Birchmore asked.

"Uh, no," Zap said to the knight. "She's ... got that thing going around. That lasts a few days."

"I see," Sir Birchmore said. "Perhaps that is why she missed our follow-up date."

"*Fuck*," Steve muttered. "*Fuckety fuck.*"

"Hey Zap," To'mas cut in eagerly. "*Lure him into the store.*"

"Will you two please be quiet," Alan said. "As if Zap weren't having enough trouble up there."

"Uh," Zap said. "It's possible."

"Hmm," Sir Birchmore said. "She has not been answering my messages pursuant to rescheduling."

"Oh, well, see..." Zap said, the gears in his head turning rapidly. "Steve just ... converted. To orthodox Etherism. So she can't date outside of the religion."

"*Don't tell him that!*" Steve said. "*He's Etherist! He was evangelizing at me on the lunch date from hell!*"

"Ah," Sir Birchmore said, pleased. "I see that she has heeded me. It should not be a problem, as it is I who bore witness to her."

"*Tell him a date killed my dad,*" Steve said, "*So I can't date any more.*"

"Um, I'm sorry," Zap said. "See, she converted to *really* orthodox Etherism, so she doesn't date at all."

"That doesn't ... make much sense," Sir Birchmore said, squinting his eyes suspiciously.

"*Tell him you just got a call from your manager,*" Steve said urgently, "*And I completely just exploded for no reason. Blood and guts all over the place, very tragic.*"

Zap stared at Sir Birchmore for several seconds, then cleared his throat.

"Steve doesn't like you," Zap said. There was a stunned pause from the knight, so Zap continued. "She thinks you're a creepy old man, and she wants nothing to do with you."

"*OH MY GOD!*" Steve shouted. "*OH MY FUCKING GOD I AM GOING TO KILL YOU ZAP.*"

"*Steve, ow!*" Alan said. "*I'm muting you now. Stay in the back room.*"

"What?" Sir Birchmore asked.

"I mean, do you not get this?" Zap asked, shaking his head and giving the knight an incredulous look. He found that the more he talked, the easier it was. "You pretty much ignore everything everyone else does and act like you're the most important person in the universe. That might be attractive to stupid people, but Steve's not stupid, and she thinks that basically you are an arrogant cock."

Sir Birchmore looked very angry for a moment, and Zap wondered for a moment whether he should turn tail and run. The angry expression dissolved, however, into one of shock and disbelief. "Really?" Sir Birchmore said.

"Really," Zap said, nodding. "We pretty much all think that."

Sir Birchmore's eyes flickered back and forth, his face a mask of disturbed contemplation. "Why, then," he asked, "didn't she say anything about it?"

"She was afraid that you'd throw a hissy fit if she denied you," Zap said. "That's probably why most people are so nice to you. You're honestly not a very nice man."

Sir Birchmore looked for a moment as though he were about to retort in anger, but decided to stop just short of shouting and consider Zap's words. There was a tense silence. Sir Birchmore dropped his hand and looked critically at Zap. Zap, to his credit, stood his ground and returned the knight's gaze.

"I will consider your words, Mr. Zap," Birchmore said after a pause. "Your honesty is refreshing. In the meantime, good day to you."

Sir Lewis Birchmore turned, then, and walked away from the store.

Zap turned away from the store entrance, smirked, put his hands on his hips, and nodded triumphantly at the nearest security camera.

"Holy shit," Alan said.

"Zap," Steve said quietly, "*I owe you a burrito and several sexual favors.*"

"Now," Zap said, "is the time that I do the happy dance."

He did. And it was seriously dorky.

21

Alan chewed on the end of his stylus absently, his eyes methodically scanning the surface of his tabletshell. He was near the front of the store, standing next to a wall of frozen dinners. A customer passed by, but Alan didn't look up; he was too engrossed in the message on the shell's surface.

After a few minutes, Alan seemed to come to his senses. He nodded once, sniffled, and walked to the front of the store. He tapped the shell and said, "Can I get everybody out here?"

One by one, the employees filtered to the front. Steve showed up first, her curls bobbing as she sauntered up to Alan. She folded her arms and waited. Zap trundled in, his pitch-black hair severely tousled and dark circles under his eyes. To'mas arrived shortly thereafter, trailing nearly-visible afterglow. Loren arrived, nondescript as ever, and was eventually followed by Matt, who could have been there the whole time—Alan had not seen him arrive.

"Uh, hi kids," Alan said, running his hand through his hair. "As you're all aware, we've got the retreat coming up in less than a month now. All of you are due to be there, and I hope you've all started on the administrative work that it requires. I don't want to be short on anybody's talents because they forgot to register their certs properly."

The employees nodded sparsely. Alan continued.

"Well, I'm sure most of you are also aware that this season's retreat has been particularly hellish for us, since a bunch of branches that were going to do the retreat next season are actually doing it this one. This means a lot of staff will be shifting around. Now. This is making a mess of *my* life all of a sudden, but there's one point that you all actually have to deal with: we're gonna gain a new temporary employee."

The employees exchanged looks of surprise and curiosity.

"Uh, technically he's already supposed to be here," Alan said just as somebody came in the front door.

It was a short young man, appearing to be in his late teens or early twenties, and definitely no taller than 160 centimeters, taller than Steve but not by much. He had unusually pale skin for a New Washingtonian, and his bright green hair made him stand out even more. So did his face, which was round and delicately beautiful. Perhaps most unusual, though, was the pair of insect-like antennae protruding from the front of his head.

Upon close scrutiny, a pair of insect-like wings could be seen emerging from the bottom of the neon yellow coat he wore.

"Looks like I'm just in time!" the bizarre-looking stranger said, approaching the group with a winning smile. "I'm Click, the transfer employee."

"Right," Alan said, "over here, please. Click, I'm Alan Morganstern, the afternoon shift manager. I believe you've already met our store manager Paru Dupree."

"Absolutely," Click said, shaking Alan's hand. "I'm looking forward to working with her."

Click swept a pair of caution-orange eyes over the crowd. "Hello, all," he said cheerfully. "I'm Click, and I'll be working with you for the next few weeks. I'm going to be on your team during the retreat, so I hope we all get along. And in case you're wondering, I am a faerie, so I hope that's not going to be a problem for anybody. I promise I do my work and don't prank *too* much."

"Right," Alan said. "Click, that's Steve Anderson, this shift's B-Rank employee. She's effectively the assistant manager, though not officially. When in doubt, do what she says."

"With that face, I would anyway," Click responded, smiling brightly. Steve blushed a little, but smiled and shook Click's hand.

"Down the line, our other employees are Zap Bradshaw, To'mas Bonvent, Matthew Del Fye, and Loren Waites."

Click shook hands with the other employees. All seemed at least marginally affected by the young man's infectiously cheerful attitude, and most were smiling after the introductions were done.

"Well, I think that we can learn to integrate Click into our happy little afternoon shift family," Alan said.

"I'm sure we'll be fine," Click said, confident. "We all work at the Securemarket™, after all." It sounded a bit strange, but it actually seemed to bolster the employees' confidence, and all looked cheerful.

"Okay, everybody, let's get back to work," Alan said. "Click, come with me so we can get all this stupid shellwork done."

Zap and Steve walked down the aisle together, half-heartedly scouting for customers.

"New guy," Zap said inquisitively.

"Yeah," Steve replied. "That was one hell of a surprise."

"What do you think of him?"

"I'm not trying to be offensive," Steve said, "but I haven't met a whole lot of faeries who were totally trustworthy. If this guy is, more power to him, but I'm going to reserve my judgment for now."

"I think he's nice," Zap said.

"He *is* nice," Steve said. "And he's got a smile that could melt faces like a Shadow Priest in PvP. But in some ways isn't that actually more suspicious?"

"I guess, maybe."

"No, don't get me wrong," Steve put her hands up in a defensive gesture. "I'm not saying one way or the other. He could have a Guardian's heart, for all I know. I just ain't decided."

"I wonder what his Glamour is."

"Yeah, we're gonna want to know that," Steve said, nodding. "And his certs."

Zap paused for a moment, then knit his brow. "Alan said something about stores that weren't going to go to the retreat this month actually doing so."

"Yeah," Steve said. "I'm not really privy to that kind of information, but my understanding is that some stores couldn't do this season, so they switched things around and stores that would normally be off our cycle will actually be going."

"Uh," Zap said. "Did you hear anything about the 11th Street location?"

"No," Steve said curiously. "Why?"

Click, having shed his coat and donned a Securemarket™ apron, appeared very suddenly from around the corner. "Hey guys," he said, smiling, "I'm ready for work! What's the customer load like for you?"

"Generally pretty light earlier in the day," Zap said once he'd recovered from the surprise of Click's sudden appearance, "and a bit heavier later on, toward dinnertime. When people start getting out of their shifts, that's when they really start showing up."

"Hey Click," Steve said, "we were just wondering about your certs."

"I'm a red sash in Wu-Shu style Shaolin," Click said, "which I use basic Glamour weaving to augment."

"What's your special Glamour magic?" Steve asked.

"It's kind of complicated," Click said, cocking his head. His antennae waved. "Do you know what a Granfalloon Technique is?"

"No," Steve and Zap said simultaneously.

"Then I'll explain later this week," Click said. "Once things are settled a bit. Have you got anything for me to do right now?"

"Familiarize yourself with the section locations," Steve said. "Customers get lost easy."

Click nodded and strode down the aisle, his wings fluttering slightly. Once he was out of sight, Steve turned to Zap and said, "I just realized something."

"What's that?" Zap asked.

"With you and Click, we've got two onomatopoeias working here."

"Frankly, I'm surprised you don't count Matt."

"MATT!" Matt shouted, appearing from out of nowhere and startling the other two employees. They glared at him and he smiled back.

"Hi, Matt," Zap said.

"You should buy some ice cream before you go home," Matt told Zap. "Your girl just hit her period."

Zap and Steve both stared at Matt, stricken. Steve opened and closed her mouth a few times, then turned and strode away.

"I wish you wouldn't do that," Zap said flatly to Matt.

Matt shrugged. "Just helpin'."

Zap slumped and nodded. "What flavor?" he asked.

"Azuki bean."

22

Zap stood at the end of the aisle, watching as Loren ran an automop methodically over the floor. Loren's passes of the mop were slow and carefully measured, passing over each section of the floor twice, punctuated by a single step between. The monotonous rhythm of the cleaning kept Zap mesmerized briefly, and once he was able to look away he surveyed the other employee.

Loren was possibly as ordinary as a New Washingtonian could ever be, particularly considering that he was in his late teens, generally an experimental age. He had short hair of a dark brown color, brown eyes, and a tan skin tone. He wore utilitarian clothes, just dressy enough to be professional, and had no tattoos or jewelry.

Zap suddenly had a thought. He stepped forward down the aisle and stood not too far behind Loren. "Hey, Loren," he said.

"Yeah?" Loren asked, not looking up from his work.

"What're your certs?"

"Business casual," Loren said, using a slang term for the standard businessman's certification set: a C-Rank Pistol certification and a C-Rank CCDM certification.

"Aren't you still in secondary?"

"Yeah, early program," Loren said, "about to finish. But once I was old enough, I picked up my certs during summer courses."

"Huh," Zap said. "What do you like to do?"

"I'm pretty busy," Loren said. "But when I'm not working or at school, I just do regular stuff. You know, watch the ether and stuff."

"Huh," Zap said thoughtfully. "Hang on." He turned and jogged from the aisle.

Loren sighed and continued the work that the interaction had not actually interrupted, alternating two swipes of the mop and a step. After several more rows, Zap returned, the transfer employee named Click in tow.

"Loren," Zap said, "you've met Click, right?"

"Yes," Loren said.

"Yeah, we met when I came in," Click said, a bit puzzled.

"Well, uh," Zap said, "did you shake hands?"

"Yes," Loren said.

"We did," Click said.

"Well," Zap said, "you should do it again. Just real quick."

Loren actually stopped his work, staring at Zap. He and Click exchanged a look, then shook hands. They looked back at Zap and saw a disappointed look on his face.

"Okay," Zap said with a sigh. "Never mind. As you were." He then turned and walked away.

"I wonder what that was about," Loren said.

"I don't know," Click said, then smiled at Loren. "Hey, are you as boring as you look?"

Loren paused for a moment before replying. "Yes."

"So it turns out that the matter/antimatter theory is crap," Zap said as he approached Steve. "What are you doing?"

"I'm staring down this douchebag," Steve replied, not turning to look at Zap. Following her gaze, Zap saw that Steve's eyes were fixed on the front window of the store, where a shadowy figure in a long, dark coat was standing. The figure was wearing a broad-brimmed hat, hiding most of his features from view. A long, wide sword was strapped to his back. He looked like the dictionary definition of imposing.

"Uh, why are you staring him down?" Zap asked, a little unnerved.

"It just cheeses me off," Steve growled. "Give an ether troll a big sword and a trenchcoat, and all of a sudden he thinks he's Alec Fucking Gainsborough."

"Are you sure it's a good idea to provoke him like this?"

"Provoke him my ass," Steve said. "This guy has been standing in front of the store for a half an hour. On my first three passes

I just ignored him, but he kept lurking right there. He needs to understand that he is not impressing anybody."
"What if he decides to come in here and start shit?"
"I'm kind of hoping he does," Steve said. "To'mas saw him and is already doing a little jig near the turret booth."
"I think you need more engaging hobbies, Steve," said Zap.
"No," Steve replied, "I need a more engaging *job*."
"Don't let Alan hear you say that," Zap warned.
"I won't," Steve said. "Anyway, what was that you said about anti-matter?"
"Nothing important," Zap replied.
"You wanna stare at this jackass with me?"
"No, that's okay," he said. "I think that's a one-girl job."
"Your mom's a one-job girl," Steve said.
Zap gave her a Look. "What does that even *mean?*"
"Hey, if you're not going to stare at this guy with me, isn't there something you should be doing? Like stocking things or dating customers?"
Zap rolled his eyes and walked away.

23

It was 17:30 on a Friday, deep in the heart of the week's densest dinnertime rush. The employees were all busy; Zap, Alan, and Click were at the front of the store, assisting customers with their purchases. Steve and To'mas were trolling the aisles, performing a combination of roving help and loss-prevention. Loren moved to restock items that were growing scarce on the shelves, and Matt acted, as he usually did, as a 'floater', performing whatever tasks he saw fit (or was directly ordered) to do.

Business had picked up at the Securemarket™ with the rapid onset of spring. The nicer weather had drawn more people out of their buildings and off of the Rail, and many of them decided on a daily basis to spend their time perusing the Securemarket™'s wide selection. There were easily a few dozen customers in the Securemarket™

this Friday, but the store's newly-expanded roster was able to keep up without much trouble.

At the front of the store, the employees bustled back and forth, busy but unhurried. At one point, Zap and Alan found themselves in the same area. Alan noted that Zap was back to looking half-dead, monotonously helping a customer with her bags. Alan finished assisting the customer he'd had, who was having trouble getting the checkout machine to recognize a bag of tamarind, then turned to Zap.

"How soon are the precert finals?"

"Less than a week," Zap droned. "I've been getting most of my sleep on the Rail for the past few days."

"Well, we need you in working shape," Alan said, "so be careful. The retreat's in two weeks, and it's gonna be at least as hard on you as this is."

"I know, I know," Zap said.

"Excuse me," a little old man standing near Click called to Alan, "could I have some help carrying these bags?"

"Click, would you?" Alan asked.

"Sure!" Click chirped, and moved to help the old man.

"Ah," the old man murmured, "could someone else do it?"

Click's smile turned stale and he held up his hands helplessly. He moved back to surveying the customers.

"Yes, sir," Alan said coldly, and nodded to Zap.

Zap trudged over to the man, took the bags, and carried them out of the store. Alan went back to looking over the customers, seeing that most of the transactions were going through smoothly.

Zap reentered the store, his tired face looking sour. "Old racist bastard," he muttered. "I don't know why he thought I'd appreciate him going on about how mean and childish faeries are when I work with one."

"Maybe he thought you'd commiserate," Alan replied.

"Maybe," Zap agreed. "Hey, Alan, have you heard the rumor that Paru is planning on putting a food counter in the store?"

"Well, I've heard Paru's thoughts on it," Alan said. "Word is that I have a position of authority in the store."

"What were they? Her thoughts, I mean?"

"I'm really not at liberty to say," Alan said, "but you know what *I* think?"

"What?"

"The restaurants near here are going nuts," Alan said. "The arts development in the area is drawing more people who're interested in getting ready-made food, I think. Also, we've got that office park that's changing hands across the street, which means a lot of people who want a healthy and inexpensive lunch."

"Uh-huh," Zap said.

"What's more," Alan continued, his eyes on the customers scanning in their purchases. "Our regular staff for this shift is bigger than it's been in a couple of years. If we get a deli counter, we get more customers, we make use of that extra manpower."

"So you think it's likely to happen?"

"I think it's *a good idea*," Alan corrected. "I really can't say what is or isn't likely."

"Huh," Zap said. "Will we be able to apply our employee discounts to the counter?"

"Unless corporate decides to change policy specifically for our store, yes."

"Then I think it's a good idea too," Zap said, smiling.

24

"Hey Alan, catch!"

Alan turned to see an object tumbling through the air toward him rapidly. He jerked backward, his hands flying up quickly to catch what he now saw was a pistol. The pistol hit his hands and bounced off, and Alan hurriedly caught it before it fell to the ground. A quick look revealed that it was a store-registered Dragon's Fire Forcebolt. Alan looked up and saw Zap standing in front of him, his body held in a confident stance.

Zap's eyes had dark circles under them, and a close look revealed that he was wavering slightly on his feet, but he wore a wide, triumphant smile. Zap wore a shoulder-holster rather than the hip holster he had previously worn, specifically modified to hold a wand instead of a gun. Nestled in the holster was Zap's wand, borne plainly and ready to draw. Zap drew himself up and looked pleased at Alan, waiting for words of praise.

"Zap," Alan said a little acidly, "we don't throw guns in my store."

"Aw, c'mon," Zap said, deflating. "I took the battery out!"

"We still don't throw guns in my store."

"Well I'm sorry, okay?" Zap said, then pointed at his shoulder holster. "Look!"

"You made your precert," Alan said glibly, putting the pistol in the pocket of his apron. "Did you get the shellwork processed for it?"

"Yes!" Zap said, irritated. "I wouldn't bear a weapon in the store without following procedure! Come on, I'm not *that* irresponsible!"

"You don't usually throw guns around, either."

Zap threw his hands in the air with a noise of frustration and walked away. Once he reached the end of the aisles, he turned the corner. He encountered Steve, who was running inventory, near the front of the aisle and stopped in front of her.

"Hey, Steve!" Zap said, proudly displaying his shoulder holster and openly displayed wand. "Check it out!"

Steve looked at the wand for a moment, then looked at Zap's face. "Did you do the shellwork on that?"

Zap stared at her for a few seconds, then shook his head and walked past her, down the aisle.

"What?" Steve said, confused. She turned to address Zap's back as he walked away. "What? Well, did you?"

Ten minutes later, Zap was inspecting the meat in the butcher aisle when Click walked by.

"Hey, Zap!" the faerie said enthusiastically, flashing a brilliant smile. "Say! Looks like somebody got his precert!"

"Yeah," Zap replied, smiling, then hurriedly added, "and *yes*, I did all the shellwork on it."

"Huh?" Click said. "I wasn't gonna ask you that. Are you psyched about the retreat?"

"Y'know, I kind of am," Zap said. "I think I might need to take a rest day between now and then, though."

"Probably a good idea; you look cold outta MP."
"I am," Zap said. "Literally. I don't think I've ever cast so many spells in a single week."
"You'll be casting more!" Click chirped.
"I know," Zap said, laughing. "I know. I'll be ready. Say, Click."
"Yeah?"
"You never did explain your Glamour magic."
"Oh," Click said. "Right! Anyway, so I can weave basic Glamour, like most faeries."
"But there was your specialized Glamour."
Click nodded. "Right; Granfalloon Magic."
"What is that?"
"Well, um," Click said. "What's your favorite music, Zap?"
"I like ambient music best," Zap said.
"Okay," Click said, tilting his head one way, then the other. "Where do you live?"
"Not too far from here," Zap said, giving Click an inquisitive look.
"What's your favorite color?"
"Green."
"There!" Click shouted, startling Zap. "Green!"
"What?!" Zap said.
"Green! Your favorite color is green!" Click's eyes lit up. "*My* favorite color is green! We both like green!"
Zap suddenly found himself enthusiastic, even overjoyed at the commiseration. "Whoa, seriously?" Zap asked, breaking into a wide grin. "That's fantastic, wow! That's so great!" He now felt incredibly close to Click, seeing the faerie as a good friend, a buddy, a partner. He likes green! How could things be better?
"Wait, though!" Click said, holding up a finger. "What *kind* of green?"
"Forest green," Zap said, surprised by the question.
Click eyed him coldly. "*I* like *neon* green."
Zap's heart skipped a beat. It was a betrayal, a horrible joke. How could this be? He thought there was something special between them, but how could he continue to live with the knowledge that Click liked *neon* green and not forest green? He backed away from the faerie slowly, his eyes narrowing.

And then the feeling passed with a mild wave of nausea. Zap couldn't believe that he had put such weight on color preference moments ago. "What—what was that?" he asked.

"Sorry," Click said, smiling. "I figured that showing you would be easier than trying to explain it."

"But you still have to explain it," Zap said.

"A Granfalloon is a group of people who choose or claim to have a shared identity or purpose, but whose mutual association is ultimately meaningless. Bottlecap collectors, fans of a musical artist, even New Washingtonians," Click explained. "All meaningless associations, when you get right down to it, but people take pride in them and use them to come together."

"I'm not sure I agree with that opinion, but I see what you're saying," Zap said.

"My power is to strengthen those false bonds and widen the divide between people who are in different Granfalloons," Click said. "I'm not necessarily that good at it yet, but at least with some things I can make a really, totally worthless connection and make it mean something."

"That's a kind of scary magic, Click," Zap said, shuddering a bit.

"Yeah, that's why I try to be real careful about using it," Click said, then clapped Zap on the back. "Don't worry, I'm not gonna do it to ya again."

"Thanks, I appreciate that," Zap said. "Are you planning on making a career of it?"

"Maybe at some point," Click said. "What do you think it'd be good for?"

"Motivational speaker?" Zap said. "Camp counselor."

Click laughed. "Sports mascot," he replied.

The two walked down the aisle together, talking and laughing as they went.

"Hey, Zap!" Alan shouted to Zap from across the aisle. Zap turned to face his supervisor. He saw that Alan's apron was off, and he was wearing a Plide jacket over his shirt and tie. Nalley was standing next to him in her grease-stained overalls, and towering over both of them was Michelle-Bear, dressed in a hoodie and jeans.

"Yeah?" Zap said. "Hey Nalley, Michelle-Bear."

"Hi Zap," Michelle-Bear said, smiling. Nalley smiled too, and nodded to Zap.

"We're going to head down to the range with Steve," Alan said. "You're precertified now; you wanna come?"

"Thanks, but no," Zap said. "I'm seriously practiced out. I need a day off."

"Aw, c'mon Zap," Michelle-Bear chided, pouting. "You don't have to work yourself hard; you should come! I'm not gonna shoot too much neither."

"Yeah, I thought you were a melee fighter, Michelle-Bear," Zap said to her. "That big hammer."

"Yeah," Michelle-Bear said happily. "I'm goin' for moral support, and because I'm not gonna see our boy for two weeks!"

Zap laughed. "No, sorry. I think I'm gonna go home and take a really long nap. Thank you for the offer. I'll make it up to you later, Michelle-Bear."

Michelle-Bear grinned and winked at Zap. "Will we tell Pazi?"

Zap blushed at that, and Michelle-Bear laughed. Alan and Nalley joined in. "Okay, I'll let you get away with it this time," Michelle-Bear teased, an impish smile on her face. "But I'll hold you to that whole 'making it up to me' thing. In a platonic way."

"Thanks," Zap said, managing a sheepish grin. "See you guys later."

He waved to the three as they passed by him, looking for Steve. As Zap walked in the opposite direction, Click poked his head out from around the corner, eyed Michelle-Bear's retreating form, and let out a low whistle.

"I know," Zap agreed.

"That woman could break me in half," Click said, awed, "and I think I might like it."

Zap raised his eyebrows and cast an 'after you' gesture down the aisle.

"No..." Click said. "Thanks, but I don't have the guts right now."

"Your loss," Zap said with a smirk, and resumed his travel toward the back room.

"Yeah..." Click said.

In the queue at the local shooting range, a line of Securemarket™ employees waited to register for use of the lanes. At the back end of the small group, Alan and Loren, who had decided on a whim to tag along, were having a discussion about the store. Michelle-Bear stood in the center, with Steve and Nalley nearest to the front of the line.

The line had come to a halt as a customer's shellwork near the front had some trouble processing. Nalley took the opportunity to turn back and speak to Steve. "Hey," she began. "You know, you haven't given me an update about the boy."

"What boy?" Steve asked, fidgeting.

"Zap, goofball," Michelle-Bear said from the opposite direction, leaning down a bit so she could speak quietly. "I wanna hear too."

"Nothing's up with him," Steve replied, shrugging.

"Are you getting along?" Nalley said.

"Yeah, we're getting along fine."

"Are you actually spending any time out of work together?" Nalley asked.

"A little," Steve said. "Look, it's really not ... a thing to talk about. Anymore."

"No?" Michelle-Bear asked. "So you don't have feelings for him any more; you're totally over him?"

Steve fell silent and folded her arms.

"Aw, sweetie," Nalley said, smiling at Steve. "Don't bottle stuff up. It's not good for you."

"It's irrelevant, though," Steve protested. "He's got a girl and he's monogamous and from what I hear, she seems really nice."

"Pazi is very nice," Nalley agreed, "but that doesn't mean you don't feel anything. Are you sure you don't want to talk about it?"

"Not at the *shooting range*," Steve said, hunching her shoulders.

"Line's moving again!" Michelle-Bear cut in.

"Are you gonna be okay at the retreat, though?" Nalley asked before moving forward.

"I'm sure I'll be fine," Steve said. "I mean, it's not like Pazi's going to be *there*."

Nalley and Michelle-Bear stared at Steve for several seconds. Steve's face grew uncomfortable. "...what?" she asked. After another pause, "What!"

"How could none of you tell me this?" Steve blurted, placing her hands on her head. The four were in the queue for the lanes themselves, now, waiting for adjacent spaces to open up for the full group.

"We thought you knew," Nalley said uncomfortably.

"No, I *didn't*."

"Pazi works at the 11th Street Securemarket™," Alan said. "Her store wasn't originally going to seed this retreat, but the sudden changes made it so that they did. I didn't realize you weren't checking up on the ethsite."

"Fuck ... fuck," Steve said.

"I really thought you'd know," Michelle-Bear said. "She was in the *news*, yanno?"

"She was?" Steve asked.

"Yeah," Loren replied. "She was the one who summoned a fire spirit to help fight off that plant mage who did all that damage. It was a headline."

"That was *Pazi*?" Steve asked.

"Yes," Alan said.

"Oh, fucking *guardian*," Steve said. "She's not just pretty and nice, she's a nice, pretty *hero*."

"I'm sorry, Steve," Nalley said. "Are you sure you should be handling a gun right now?"

"I think," Steve said in a strained tone, "that we're all a lot less safe if I *don't* get to shoot things right now."

No one objected.

25

"Okay!" Alan shouted over the skyport din. "Is everybody here?"

The New Washington First Precinct Skyport was bustling with activity. People of all races bustled about, walking and running, toting baggage, shouting to each other. This particular concourse, however, bustled with a unified purpose—every one of the hundred-odd passengers-to-be was an employee of the mighty Securemarket™, each one waiting to board a jet headed to the season's retreat. Shift supervisors directed frantic shouts, each one trying to determine whether all of his or her employees were present.

"Let's get a roll call!" Alan shouted, walking backward so he could address his employees. "Stephen Anderson!"

"Pong!" Steve shouted, reshouldering her backpack and moving as quickly as her short legs would carry her.

"Zap Bradshaw!" Alan called.

"Pong!" Zap barked, pulling a floating piece of luggage behind him.

"To'mas Bonv—"

"Pong!" To'mas shouted, a small shoulder bag slung across his body.

"Let me finish your name, please!" Alan shouted. "To'mas Bonvent."

"Pong," To'mas replied, rolling his eyes.

"Click o'th'Granfalloon!" Alan called.

"Pong!" Click replied, wearing a colorful messenger-bag across his shoulder.

"Matt Del Fye!"

"Pong," Matt said with just enough volume to be heard. He didn't have any luggage on him at all.

"Loren Waites!"

"Pong!" Loren called. He was carrying a durable shell-case in his free hand and wearing an oddly old-looking coat.

"Okay, I think that's everybody," Alan said. "Is there *anybody* here who hasn't checked their luggage?"

There was no reply.

"We're good to go!" Alan said. "Who's the best shift?!"
"Archmage Tea-Time!" the employees all shouted.
"Fuck yes!" Alan shouted. "Follow me!'

The afternoon shift employees were soon standing in front of Paru Dupree's form, which was even more imposing than usual due to her red military-style Securemarket™ Officer's outfit. Her jacket had several pins on it indicating her rank and accomplishments, and she wore a beret with the Securemarket™ logo on it. An Okage Arms M33-RK135 7.22 mm Automatic Rifle was slung across her shoulder, but it was not nearly as impressive as her dark eyes, which swept the crowd critically.

"Shift managers, report." She spoke in an unstrained tone of voice, somehow audible over the airport din.

"Emma Rammek," a hardy-looking woman with blue-streaked brown hair called from one side of the crowd. "Early morning shift. All employees present!"

"Alan Morganstern," Alan called. "Afternoon shift. All employees present!"

"Raye Courts-the-Shadows, late-night shift," a hollow voice called from the end of the group. Its owner was swathed completely in clothing, including a pair of goggles and a brimmed hat. His skin was a dark gray. "All employees present."

"A Shadow mutant," Zap murmured under his breath.

"Good," Paru said. "That's everyone."

"What about the morning and evening shifts?" Steve murmured to Zap.

"Don't you ever read the ethsite?" Zap whispered. "How d'you think they staff the store while we're gone?"

"No talking," Paru said in a chilling voice, silencing the employees. "This is a pretty green group. How many of you have been on a Securemarket™ retreat before?"

A smattering of hands went up. Of the afternoon shift, Alan, To'mas, and Matt raised their hands.

Paru nodded. "Not many of you. Well, I am expecting you to surprise everyone by how well you do. You are all hand-picked in collaboration between me and your shift manager. I know who you are, and I know that each and every one of you is capable of making it through this retreat. Now, this isn't a militia—many of you will have a very hard time getting through this. I cried almost all the way through my first retreat, but I made it through. And when I faced my first hostile situation in my store, I was ready for it. Thanks to this."

She walked in a line in front of the gathered employees. "This retreat will make all of you stronger. It will improve your ability to work together, it will improve your self-confidence, and it will improve your prowess both as a service worker and a fighter. Obey your superiors, stay sharp, and believe in yourselves. That is all I ask of you. Understood?"

There was murmured assent from the crowd.

"Understood?!" Paru barked.

"Yes ma'am!" the crowd shouted.

"Good!" she said, and then smiled a bit wickedly. "So, how many of you have never flown before?"

Most of the new employees raised their hands.

"Well, won't this be fun," Paru said with a small laugh.

Steve was already seated by a window when Zap walked down the aisle, looking at his seat assignment on his shell. He walked to Steve's row and stopped, looking at the seat next to her, then at Steve herself.

"Hey," he said.

"Hey," she said, and then studiously looked out the window.

Zap frowned, but shoved his bag under the seat in front of him. He took his seat next to Steve.

"Your first flight too, isn't it?" Zap asked.

"Yeah," Steve said, not looking at him.

"Little nerve-wracking," Zap said, smiling as he fumbled with his safety belt. "I've looked out of some pretty tall buildings, but it'll be different to actually zoom around."

"Mm," Steve replied.

"Uh," Zap said, looking at her. "Is something wrong?"

"No," Steve said.

"Is this about Pazi?" Zap asked.

Steve was silent.

"Look, I didn't know either," Zap said. "Her shift wasn't supposed to seed the retreat; it—"

"Zap!" Steve said. "Whatever! It doesn't matter. I don't care."

Zap gave her an incredulous look. "Honestly, Steve, I don't think—"

"I *don't. Care.*"

Zap sighed, took out his pocketshell, and booted up a game of Tetronimo.

Click, seated by the window, watched as Loren sat down next to him, then Matt sat next to the aisle. He leaned forward and looked across the aisle at Zap and Steve.

"Say, Steve looks kind of pissed," he noted.

"She just found out two days ago that Zap's girlfriend is going to be at the retreat," Loren said.

"Zap has a girlfriend, huh?" Click noted. "I always figured those two for a couple."

"No," Loren said. "They're not."

"But Steve's interested in Zap?"

"I suppose she must be," Loren replied, his tone dry.

Click canted his head a bit, his face calculating for a moment, but soon To'mas appeared and took the seat next to Zap and Steve, obscuring them from view. Click leaned back in his seat, shifting a bit to let his wings drape to his sides. "Huh," he said. "...that's interesting."

In the first-class section, Alan took his seat next to Paru, who had already settled in. Her rifle was in the holster just below the window, her carry-on baggage stowed. Alan nodded to her, and she returned the gesture. He dropped his bag and kicked it under the seat in front of him, finding the space more than adequate. He placed his pistol in the between-seat holster and then sat down.

"You realize," Paru said, "that this year they're probably going to ask you to start carrying a higher-rank weapon. You could be carrying a rifle, with your certification."

Alan sighed. "Yes, well, it was nice playing it down while it lasted. I'm really not so into the idea of toting a big hunk of plastic around the store all day, every day."

"You'll get used to it," Paru said. She did not take her eyes off of Alan, and he fidgeted under her scrutiny. "You look nervous," she finally said.

"Uh," Alan said, scratching his head. "We've got some drama going on."

Paru nodded. "I assume it's something to do with Zap and Steve," she said.

Alan nodded, chewing on his upper lip.

"It happens," Paru said. "I'm confident that you'll be able to keep things in line, and that your employees have been taught to appropriately prioritize."

"Thanks," Alan replied a bit acidly.

"Let it go, Alan," Paru said. "This is nothing. This is life. We're not the military, we're a store. These things *will* happen because we don't run a barracks."

"I know," Alan said. "I know."

Paru reached up and patted Alan on the shoulder.

Once all of the employees had boarded and sat down, a few flight attendants walked down the aisle, positioning themselves throughout the plane. The pilot's voice echoed through the resonating plates running the length of the jet.

"*Securemarket™ employees, welcome to the flight to Employee Retreat number sixty-seven. My name is Malcolm Hawthorne, and I'll be your pilot for the day. We'll be departing from the Precinct One Skyport shortly, and will be landing at the Orleans Inlet Installation approximately 3 hours later with an expected arrival time of 11:00. It's a beautiful day out there, so this should be a very smooth flight. Please look to your flight attendants for details about jet safety.*"

The flight attendants pulled out a few props and gestured with them as the pilot spoke.

"*You'll find a placard in the pocket of the seat in front of you that will reiterate these safety details. Please ensure that your safety belt is securely fastened as the flight attendants are demonstrating for you; our clasps use* triggerstone for the most effective securing method. If any of you cannot operate these clasps for any reason, please notify our flight attendants immediately. I would like to remind you all that this is a secure flight; please leave your weapons holstered and any operable enchantments or shields off for the remainder of the flight."

The flight attendants showed the seatbelt operation, then expansively mimicked turning off a bulletshield.

"Please remain in your seats with your safety belt fastened as long as the seat-belt sign is lit. Once the light is off, you may walk about the cabin if you need to use the restroom, but otherwise we ask that you remain in your seat. We will be serving breakfast during the flight. We will now taxi into position on the runway and will be leaving shortly."

In first class, Alan closed his eyes. "I never really get used to this part..."

"Really?" Paru replied. "I love watching the takeoff."

In second-class, Click pressed his face to the window. "This is going to be so cool," he said.

"Sure," Loren said, settling back in his chair and closing his eyes.

"You are incredibly boring," Click said. "Hey Matt, will this plane explode and crash?"

"No," Matt replied.

"You guys are *both* boring," Click said, keeping his attention fixed on the ground.

Across the aisle, Steve looked out the window and started to sweat. "Uh," she stammered. Her voice quavered. "I, um."

"You okay?" Zap asked her.

"I dunno."

"*Flight attendants, prepare for takeoff,*" the pilot's voice echoed through the cabin.

The plane's engines roared and it began to speed forward, pressing the employees back against their seats. After a few long seconds, it lifted off the ground.

In first class, Alan kept his eyes closed, taking deep breaths. Paru kept her eyes fixed on the outside, watching with uncharacteristic wonder as the plane lifted off.

"Guaaaaaaaardian," Click intoned, staring at the ground. "This makes me wish my wings worked for real..."

Loren snored in response.

Steve turned away from the window as the plane lifted off, and she stared straight ahead, her breathing shallow.

Zap looked at her with a concerned expression. After a moment, he moved his hand to the side and took hers. She gripped his hand hard and continued to stare straight forward, but her breathing calmed a little bit and her eyes grew a little less wide.

The great plastic bird took to the sky, slowly leaving the Legendary City.

26

The single runway on the Orleans Inlet Installation was not attached to a skyport terminal, nor was it even close to any nearby buildings. It was merely a swath of gray pavement cut through the grassy surface of the island. The only indication of its purpose was a nearby observation tower. To the left of the runway, a network of squat buildings clustered on the ground. On the right side was thick forest, a sign of modern advancement for an artificial island like the Orleans Installation.

The jet carrying the Securemarket™ employees descended toward the runway with practiced ease, orienting itself to fit on the narrow space. It landed smoothly and roared to a gradual halt only about a hundred meters from the end of the pavement.

Once it had landed, a group of five people emerged from the nearest building. Leading the group was a middle-aged Corporate Knight in a finely-pressed suit, prominently wearing a weapon-belt that carried a bulletshield and a fine longsword, attached to which was a holstered heavy pistol. As all Corporate Knights did, he wore a rose, the color of which was bright crimson with streaks of white.

Behind the CK was an older man in a deep black business suit. His tie was a bright red and had the Securemarket™ logo on its knot. His white hair was thinning, but had a swept-back look to it, as though the man had just been in a stiff wind. The old man kept both hands in his pockets and walked with a slight hunch, but his strides were long and he kept pace with the knight without trouble. His craggy face was fixed in a hawkish expression, his sharp eyes sweeping up to examine the jet. On either side of the old man walked a man and a woman with eerily similar features, both quite fit and dressed in the military-style Securemarket™ Officer's uniform. Each carried an assault rifle and kept their eyes roving, an alert honor guard.

Slightly to the left and near the rear of the small group was a handsome bespectacled man in his early thirties. He was wearing a white lab coat over a plain set of red clothing. He was outfitted as a standard corporate medic, right down to the bulky diagnostic shell holstered on the opposite hip as a sleek ionic taser.

The group walked toward the plane as its door opened and the store managers and shift supervisors began to disembark. By the time the small group of people had reached the edge of the landing strip, the high-level employees had lined up before them.

The Corporate Knight stopped in front of the line of employees, drew his sword and pistol, and held them in a Knight's salute. The employees bowed. The Knight sheathed his weapons and shouted, "At ease!"

The employees fell into a loose at-ease stance. The Knight stepped to his side and turned to face the older man. The old man walked closer, swept his eyes over the gathered crowd, and addressed them in a surprisingly clear, loud voice.

"It's good to see you here," he said. "I look forward to meeting the new members of our community, and to seeing again those who feel brave enough to come here twice. I won't keep you longer, though. Sir Erdrick?"

"Store managers, you may call your employees and sort them by shift," the Corporate Knight said.

The store manager at the end of the line tapped an earpiece and spoke a few words into it. Shortly thereafter, his employees began filing out of the jet, taking places behind their shift supervisors. One by one, the managers called their employees out.

Eventually, Paru saw the last of the employees in the group before hers exit the jet. She tapped what appeared to be a stud earring and spoke in her clear, authoritative voice: "Neimuth and 15th."

A few moments later, Paru's employees emerged from the jet and began to take their places behind their respective shift supervisors, who had turned to face the jet. In front of Alan, Steve took her place first as the highest-ranking employee; she was shaking a little bit and her face was pale. Zap, who had followed very close behind Steve, was the next to line up. To'mas was next, followed by Matt, Loren and Click.

The rest of the employees lined up without much incident, though many appeared shaken by the experience of the plane trip.

The Knight folded his hands behind his back and surveyed the crowd for a few seconds before he spoke up.

"Welcome," he said, "to Securemarket™ Employee Retreat number 67. For many of you, this retreat will be your first. Some of you have been here many times. Whatever the case, much will be expected of you here, and this retreat will not be easy by any means.

"You are not part of a Corporate Militia. In terms of military training and combat, this will not be as arduous as a soldier's training retreat would be. More is expected of you, however, than merely the ability to defend your customers. You also must *serve* them, and in this regard your training will be *more* difficult than a soldier's—you will be expected to show an ability not only to fight and to operate under duress, but also to be an effective customer service representative through it all.

"My name is Orin Erdrick," the Knight said. "You will refer to me as Sir Erdrick. I am a senior CK of the Securemarket™ Corporation, and I will be your chief commanding officer for the duration of this retreat. If I give you an order, you will obey it *promptly* and *cheerfully*. I am not cruel or strict, but I do not appreciate back-talk or laziness. If you internalize this advisement, you and I will get along fine. Before I give you your assignments, I will turn your attention to the Securemarket™ CEO, Mr. Thorvald Volnocht."

The old man stepped forward. "Hello, everyone," he said. "I am glad to see all of you here. It takes a unique person to be a Securemarket™ employee; it takes dedication and attention and effort. All of you were chosen by my store managers, and store managers were chosen in a joint effort by my top knights and myself. I believe that every one of you is capable of bearing the Securemarket™ logo and making me proud by doing so. I look forward to Sir Erdrick's reports of your excellent performances."

His brief speech finished, he turned away and Sir Erdrick stepped up again.

"All right, here's where we go now," he said. "Your schedule, room assignments and a map of the facility were uploaded to your company-issued workshell while you were on the plane. Each of you will be staying in a room with one other employee, probably from your store but likely not from your shift. Your shell will unlock your door. You have three hours to get settled in your room, get to the mess hall and have lunch. At 14:30 you are to meet your store manager in the room assignment specified on your schedule. That is all; please follow your store manager into the facility, and you are then released."

The store managers led their employees inside one by one.

Steve trudged down the dormitory hallway, dragging the rolling luggage she'd checked behind her. Like all of the other employees wandering toward their rooms, she had her workshell in her free hand and was following its instructions to get to her room. After walking for a while, she stopped and looked up at a door and the number printed on its face. She pressed a button on the side of her shell and the doorknob made a *click* noise. Steve holstered her shell, turned the doorknob and shouldered her way into the room.

The dorm room was of a modest size and sparsely furnished; it had two bunked beds, a pair of desks with a large-screen desktop shell on each one, and a compact refrigerator. A fairly large window with a polaroid control panel was at the back of the room.

There was already a girl in the room. She appeared to be in her late teens, had shoulder-length black hair and violet eyes, and was sitting on the lower of the two beds. She was wearing a white collared blouse with a sleeveless sweater over it and a knee-length skirt. She smiled when she saw Steve come in.

"Hi!" she said. "I'm Violet Crenshaw."

"Good to meet you," Steve said, pushing the handle of her luggage down. "I'm Stephen Anderson. Everybody calls me Steve."

"Okay, good," Violet responded, sounding amused. "I was sorta wondering if they'd put me with a boy."

"Yeah, I don't blame you," Steve said. "My parents are funny people."

"Well, feel free to settle in. Do you mind if I take the bottom bunk?"

"Go ahead," Steve said.

"You don't look so hot," Violet said.

"That was my first flight," Steve said, throwing herself into one of the room's office chairs.

"Mine too," Violet said, nodding. "So it's our first retreat for both of us, then."

"Yeah," Steve said. "Hey, this chair is really comfy."

"Really?" Violet said, then stood up, moved to the other chair and sat in it. "Hey, you're right."

Steve sighed and leaned back in the chair.

"What store and shift are you?" Violet asked.

"15th and Neimuth, afternoon shift."

"I'm 11th street early-morning shift," Violet said.

Steve turned her head to look at Violet. "Do you know Pazi Elwynn?" she asked.

"You heard about her from the news, huh?" Violet said. "Not really. I've met her once or twice, but she works afternoon shift, like you."

"Mmm," Steve said. "What else do you do, that early morning shift works for you?"

"I'm an apprentice bartender," Violet said with a smile. "At the Gogobera."

Steve paused, then looked over at Violet. "Whoa, seriously?" she asked.

"Mmm-hmm," Violet replied, nodding proudly. "It was one hell of a competition to get the apprenticeship, but I've got it. I work through the night and then grab some food and go to my morning shift. I sleep through your shift."

"Wow," Steve said. "Impressive."

"What else do you do, Steve?"

"I'm apprenticed to Messianic the Gunsmith."

"Ooh, cool," Violet said. "I thought your piece looked pretty."

"Thanks. It's named Polaris, and it's one of Master's favorite pieces in recent memory. Sometime I'll tell you how I got it; it's a good story."

"I'd like that," Violet said. "But in the meantime, we have an important issue to address."

"We do?"

"Yes," Violet said with a smile. "First: if my charm bracelet is around the doorknob, it means that I am fucking a boy in here. You can feel free to come in, but only if you're quiet. Or if you participate."

Steve stared.

27

The "Archmage Tea-Time" afternoon shift employees managed to find each other fairly quickly in the mess hall, congregating together at a table. Steve was the last to arrive, approaching as the other employees were all at the table.

"Hey Steve," Alan greeted her as she set her tray down and took her seat.

"Hi guys."

"So," Zap asked, "who's *your* roommate?"

Steve looked at Zap and said, "She's from the 11th street store."

Zap froze.

Steve gave him a small smirk. "Her name's Violet." Zap relaxed. Steve then turned to To'mas and gave him a pointed look. "And from what I can tell, she's basically a female version of To'mas."

"Ooh," To'mas said, grinning. "You should introduce us."

"I'm sure you don't need my help," Steve quipped. "Anyway, you look stupid happy as it is."

Alan rolled his eyes. "To'mas already has his sights on his roommate."

"He really thinks he's straight," To'mas said. "It's *adorable*."

Steve laughed. "Who's everybody else rooming with?"

"I'm with an older gentleman by the name of Arden," Zap said, sounding pleased by the fact. "He's a veteran of the 8th street war. I'm looking forward to hearing his stories."

"I'm rooming with a ghost," Click said. He seemed unsure of whether the idea delighted or unsettled him. "Named Hollow-Eyes."

"A ghost?" Steve asked, raising her eyebrows.

"An honest-to-goodness ghost," Click confirmed.

"I'm rooming with a fellow named Marlon," Loren said. "He seems okay."

"Matt?" Steve asked.

"Yeah?" Matt responded, looking up from his food.

"Who're you rooming with, man?"

"Creepy Don Stiles," Matt said. "He works at the Malachi Park store. He's an unconvicted rapist."

Everybody stared.

"Did ... he tell you that, Matt?" Alan stammered.

"Nope," Matt said, prodding at his food with his chopsticks.

"Are you planning on just ignoring it?" Steve asked him.

Matt looked up, annoyed. "Don't be fucking stupid," he said. "This asshole's not going to make it through the employee concert."

The table breathed a collective sigh of relief.

Steve looked over at Alan. "Do you have a roommate, Alan?"

"Nope, supervisors get their own room in a suite," he said. "I'm in a suite with the other two shift supervisors. Should be interesting living with a shadow mutant and a quarter-dragon. This'll be a learning experience."

"No kidding," Zap said.

"So, okay," Alan said, smiling. "You'll hear about most of this from Paru in an hour, but I'd like to give you the synopsis of these retreats that you're *not* going to hear."

The employees all sat at attention.

"This is a hard retreat," Alan said. "But just as we work hard, we play pretty hard too. If you take some time to review your schedule and map, you'll see that there's a facility bar where you can blow your account creds and hard-earned actual creds, if you have them to spare. Don't go too crazy. There's also an arcade and a nicer restaurant than the mess hall if you feel like spending money. There's an employee mixer tonight and on Friday there's a concert, and there'll probably be some smaller suite parties in between. Again, don't go nuts. You need to be in fighting shape."

He smirked. "That said, this company was founded by a traditional warrior. He believes in working yourself ragged then drinking yourself stupid. If you can keep up to that schedule, fine. Just try not to go overboard or start too much drama."

The employees all looked pleased by that, particularly To'mas and Click.

"That said," Alan said, standing and lifting his tray. "I need to go get ready for the next event. Enjoy your meals." He walked away with the tray.

"Soo ... Matt," Steve said after a pause. "You want any help setting up your creepy roommate?"

Matt smiled. "I knew you'd ask."

28

"Hello, 15th and Neimuth employees," Paru said to the assembled group. There were fifteen students in the room, a small clump in the center of a large gymnasium-like area. The three shift supervisors stood at the front of the group. "Welcome to Kekkai orientation."

There were a few murmurs from the group.

"Would the shift supervisors please step forward?" Paru asked. The shift supervisors stepped forward and turned to face the other employees. Alan was chewing his lip, looking somewhat nervous.

"This island uses top-of-the-line Kekkai technology to ensure the most realistic and safe combat situations possible. This room is currently affected by a Kekkai enchantment which I will now demonstrate by shooting your supervisors in the head."

There were loud murmurs as Paru unholstered a pistol from her hip, and the group shifted their feet. She held up a hand and they quieted a bit.

"Kekkai is the Japanese word for barrier, and it is Japanese scientists who first developed the technomagical devices that allowed for a standalone Kekkai for dueling. Originally Kekkai were only designed to reduce property damage during high-power duels and pitched battles, but it was soon discovered that the same technology could be used to protect combatants from their own actions under a very specific set of rules. What I am about to do is completely safe."

With that, she raised her gun, pointed it at Emma Rammek's head and pulled the trigger. The other side of the quarter-dragon's head erupted in a mess of blood, skull and brains. She fell heavily onto her side, what was left of her head bouncing on the gymnasium floor. Her eyes were blank.

There was a moment of silence, and then a half-elf girl among the employees screamed.

"Quiet!" Paru barked and the girl fell silent, her eyes wide. "I'm disappointed, May-May. You need to take my word. Kekkai, reset this scenario."

With a wet noise, the blood, brains and shards of bone eerily slid back to the dead-eyed supervisor, reattaching to her head. The quarter-dragon woman blinked twice and winced in memory of the pain, dragging herself back to her feet.

"You will see some horrible things happen to your coworkers during this retreat," Paru said. "This is part of your training. You are New Washingtonians and Securemarket™ employees. You need to be able to work through horror. But rest assured: you are all safe here."

She hefted her pistol again without warning and raised it to Alan's head. He had only enough time to flinch before Paru fired. Zap closed his eyes in a cringe and Steve's eyes widened a bit as the left side of Alan's head exploded, covering Raye Courts-the-Shadows (who held up an arm defensively) in gore.

The employees stared at Alan's corpse lying on the ground for a few moments, and then were interrupted as Paru shot Raye Courts-the-Shadows.

Paru turned to the employees, all of whom were visibly shaken. One employee on the edge of the group kneeled to the floor and vomited.

"I hate this orientation," To'mas murmured behind Zap.

"Kekkai," Paru said, "please reset this scenario."

The employees watched as the supervisors' heads reconstructed themselves and the two slowly got to their feet. The employee who was on his knees remained there, but his vomit had vanished.

"This will not be the last upsetting thing you'll see here," Paru said. "And don't expect that you will be exempt from *doing* them as well. If a threat needs to be neutralized in your store, sometimes that will mean lethal force. I expect all of you to be able to use it if you have to do. I do not enjoy shooting my subordinates any more than you will enjoy shooting each other. But I expect you to do your best. Is that understood?"

"Yes ma'am," the group replied.

"All right," she said. "We're done here for now. You've already been through seminar orientation and opening statements, so you're released at this point. I encourage you to go to the mixer tonight, but don't stay up too late. Exercises begin at 7 a.m. tomorrow. Mages will especially need to get a decent amount of sleep, as the first combat magic exercise will commence immediately after the morning routine. Supervisors, please come with me. Everyone else is dismissed."

The crowd, staying more or less in a clump, moved toward the exit.

"She didn't even blink," Zap said in a hollow voice. "She just shot him in the head."

"Paru's hardcore," To'mas said. "Wait'll you see her in the combat exercises; she's like a machine."

Zap shuddered.

"Chilling, no?" an iron-haired man said, approaching the group. "Difference is that back in basic, they did it to *us* instead of our officers. It was like an execution line. Pow!"

Zap smiled a little and gestured to the man. "Everybody, this is Arden Prewett, a veteran of the 8th Street War and an early-morning shift employee."

Various one-syllable greetings were exchanged. Arden shook the nearest hands.

"May I be so presumptuous to ask," Steve said, "which side you were on, Mr. Prewett?"

"The losing one," Arden said, and guffawed. "Just my luck. Why d'you ask, young lady?"

"Did you work with Lieutenant General Dukakis?" she asked.

"Why yes I did; he was my commanding officer. I was in his unit when the surrender happened."

"My Master is a good friend of the Lieutenant General," Steve said with a smile. "Grover Messianic."

"Messianic, that old bastard?" Arden asked, guffawing again. "What's a pretty girl like you doing apprentice for a drunken ol' sot like him?"

"'Cause I'm the only one who can hold Scrumpy like he does," Steve said, grinning.

"Well we're going to get along fine, Miss..."

"Steve. Steve Anderson."

"Miss Steve. We'll both have to have a glass of cider in your Master's name at the mixer tonight."

"Sounds like a plan, Mr. Prewett," Steve said.

"Hey everybody," To'mas said. Standing next to him was a cleancut looking young man with sculpted good looks and an innocent appearance. He was the employee who had thrown up at the Kekkai display. "This is my roommate, Michael."

"Pleased to meet you," Steve said, a wry smile hanging on her face. "Do you have any idea what you're getting into, Mike?"

"What?" Michael said.

"Don't worry about it, she's just ribbing you," To'mas said.

"Yeah, don't worry about it," Steve said. "Anyway, I really need a smoke. You coming, Zap?"

"No, I, um, have to go meet somebody," Zap said carefully.

"Oh," Steve said.

"I'll go, if you don't mind," Arden said. "I could use a smoke, and I'd love to talk to you about what being apprenticed to old Messianic is like."

"Sure," Steve said, perking up. "I'll see the rest of you guys later."

As the two started walking away from the group, Steve continued speaking to Arden. "First of all, I should tell you about how I ended up with this pistol. Its name is Polaris..."

29

By the time that Alan walked through the door, the employee mixer was already in full swing. Calm, ambient electronic music echoed through the space, controlled by a deejay sitting in a booth at the far end of the room. There were several long tables set up in the center of the room with light fare and small white ceramic plates. At one side of the room was a bar that served beer, cider, and wine, but at the moment no hard liquor.

Alan shoved his hands in his pockets and entered the room, murmuring to himself, "I always suck at these events."

He scanned the room for his employees. He immediately spotted Zap, who was talking to an older employee. He held a glass of beer in one hand, and the other was wrapped around an attractive young woman with short blonde hair who cradled a glass of red wine as she watched Zap speak.

"Pazi," Alan murmured, and resumed his casual survey of the room.

To'mas was leaning on his roommate's shoulder as he spoke to someone else; the look on the roommate's face was pleasant but unnerved. Loren stood near the two, looking as unremarkable as he ever did.

Matt was standing alone near the food tables, looking intently at something or someone, but Alan couldn't quite make out what the focus of his employee's attention was.

Focusing for a moment on a clump of well-dressed and elegantly poised people, Alan realized that he had located the schmooze circle of the store managers. He approached, curious, and soon caught sight of Paru. She was holding a glass of white wine and a small plate of vegetables in the same hand, gesticulating with the other. She exuded professional, subtle charm. As he neared the group, Alan became uncomfortable and veered away, choosing instead to approach the food table.

He grabbed a plate and looked over the trays of food, humming to himself. After reviewing his choices, Alan began carefully filling the plate's space with vegetables and hors d'oeuvres, arranging them like tangrams to ensure that he could get as much on the tiny plate as possible; he hadn't eaten anything else for dinner.

As he was partway through this process, he was interrupted by a honey-sweet female voice addressing him from his left. "Mr. Morganstern?"

Alan looked at the voice's source and saw a young woman dressed in what Alan found unsettlingly similar to a private secondary school uniform. The girl had black hair and striking violet eyes that Alan suspected were surgically dyed, or perhaps she was wearing contacts.

The girl gave Alan smile dripping with seductive innocence. "You're Mr. Morganstern, right?"

"Alan's fine," Alan said with a smile. "You must be Violet."

The girl's eyes widened. "You know who I am?"

"Steve mentioned her new roommate," Alan said.

"She must have described me very accurately," Violet said. Alan imagined for a moment that he could see her clenching whatever muscle she used to exude pheromones. "Or did you just really want to meet me?"

Alan laughed. "She described you very accurately," he said. "More accurately than you could know. Speaking of people who really want to meet you, though..."

Alan pointed, and Violet curiously let her gaze follow Alan's direction.

"See that pretty white-haired boy over there?" Alan said. "His name is To'mas, and he's in my shift. He mentioned wanting to meet you. What's more, I bet he'd love your help on a project of his."

"A project?" Violet asked.

"The project he's standing next to," Alan said with a smirk.

Violet knit her brow for a moment, then her eyes widened and she let out a small, high-pitched noise. She looked up to Alan gratefully. "You are a very helpful supervisor," she said, the little-girl tone in her voice gone.

"I do what I can," Alan replied.

"Y'wanna get coffee later, though?" Violet said. "I hear you're in a rock band."

"You hear right," Alan replied, dipping a baby carrot in the dollop of dressing that was slowly losing coherency on his plate. "Just lay off the act, ok? I'm a one-girl guy and I don't feel like playing faerie tennis."

Violet winked. "If that To'mas boy over there lets me in on his project, you're off the hook. I *guess*. But you can't blame me for trying."

Alan had shoved the carrot into his mouth, and replied between chews. "I guesh not," he said, chipmunk-cheeked. "I'm pretty hot shtuff."

Violet giggled and returned her sights to To'mas, beelining for him. Alan stared at her ass as she walked, caught by the hypnotic sway of her hips.

"That girl's dangerous," he murmured. He blinked and looked around again. "I wonder where Click and Steve are."

For the first time since Steve had seen it, Click's face was grave and concerned. He reached forward with a handkerchief, which Steve took gratefully.

"Thanks," Steve said, taking the cloth and dabbing her tear-stained face with it. "Sorry."

"It's ok, really," Click said.

"I'm such a mess," Steve said. "I see them together once and I go to pieces."

"The way you tell it, he really led you on," Click said, dropping to his haunches in front of Steve, who was sitting with her back against the wall.

Steve reached into her pocket and retrieved her cigarettes. "It's not like that, really," she said. "It all happened so fast. I didn't warn him, and I didn't give him any room to explain."

"He should have been forthcoming with it from the get-go," he said as Steve stuck the cigarette between her lips and lit it with a conjured flame. "He could have said something when they started going out."

"Why?" Steve said. "He didn't know it was relevant. He didn't know I liked him, and he's never liked me, so ... y'know. He didn't mean to hurt me."

"Of course he didn't," Click said. "Zap's a nice guy. He just maybe doesn't see as much as he should."

"Maybe not," Steve said. She took a long drag from the cigarette, then drew in her shuddering breath further before letting out a plume of smoke.

"He'd want you to move on," Click said. "He's probably hoping you will. He's got a girl and he's happy with her, and he doesn't want to see you hurt. I'm sure that when he sees you hurt by his actions, it hurts him too."

"Well yeah," Steve said, gesticulating with both hands, "but what am I supposed to *do* about it?"

"Start looking," Click said, giving her a smile. "There're a lot of cute boys here, most of 'em local to you. Maybe one of them would be a good boyfriend!"

"I'm really not attracted to many boys," Steve said. "I'm not sure I can just ... look. I don't usually do that. Anyway, I'm not cute enough to just pick boys."

"Of course you are!" Click said. "You're gorgeous. You just look around and give it a try. If you're at all attracted to somebody here, go for it! If you want I can help you. I'll be your wingman," he said, and fluttered his wings with a grin.

"I can't believe you just made that joke," Steve said, glaring.

"Yeah, well," Click said. "Nice to be on this side of it for once."

Steve sighed. "I don't know, I just don't. Isn't an employee retreat a kind of bad place to chase guys?"

Click laughed. "Why don't you go check out some of the other things happening at that mixer?" he asked. "A lot of people are gonna go to rooms that weren't their assigned ones tonight."

Steve laughed in spite of herself.

"Whaddya say?" Click said.

"We'll see," Steve said. "I dunno. We'll see."

"Well, at least dry your face and come get some booze," Click said. "Don't you like cider? They've got Purple Pine Brewery cider."

"Purple Pine?" Steve made a face. "More like turpentine. But I guess I could stand to have my throat stripped."

She put out her cigarette on the ground and pushed herself to her feet. "Okay, let's go back in. Thanks for talking to me, Click."

"It's no problem," Click said with a smile. "I just want what's best for you."

Steve wiped her nose and walked inside. Behind her, Click's smile took on a somewhat triumphant cast.

"Thanks for walking me back to my room," Pazi said, smiling warmly at Zap. "It's nice to have company, and I was kinda worried I might get lost."

Zap laughed. "With the tracking technology here?" he said. "That'd take talent."

"Well, I'm talented," Pazi replied, laughing too. "So. Give me a kiss and let me go inside. I need eight hours or my invocations won't be as good."

"Okay," Zap said, then leaned in. He and Pazi kissed, eyes closed. After a few moments they broke apart, and Pazi made a happy noise, then turned and slipped into her room. With a little wave, she shut the door.

Zap stuck his hands in his pockets, smiled and sighed. He turned on his heel and walked back down the hallway. When he was nearly at the stairwell, he unholstered his small workshell and tapped it, glancing at the Local Positioning System map that appeared on its surface.

He followed the path on the screen back toward the event bar, flickering his gaze up and down, ensuring both that he was on the right track and that he didn't bump into anything.

In five minutes, Zap heard the noise of the mixer as he approached the event bar. The murmur was less than it had been when Zap had left with Pazi; the event was dying down despite the relatively early hour. It wasn't yet midnight, but the threat of the early wake-up had already driven most of the attendees to bed.

As Zap re-entered, he saw that he recognized a few of the stragglers. His aging roommate Arden was engaged in an animated conversation with Steve at the bar. Nearby, Alan and Paru were chatting in a subdued tone.

Zap walked over to the pair at the bar. Steve noticed him first and waved, obviously a little tipsy. "Ping, Zap!"

Arden turned to look at Zap and smiled. "Ah, my wayward roommate. What's the haps?"

"Nil," Zap said. "You two look like you've had a few."

"A few too few, perhaps," Arden said wistfully.

"Just filling our few-el tanks," Steve added.

"I guess we're suf-few-sed with it," Arden shot back, grinning at Steve.

"It's a blood few-ed," Steve replied.

"That one was a stretch," Zap said, folding his arms.

"Ehh, whatever," Steve said. "I don't need more lip from boys."

"Huh?" Zap asked.

"Miss Steve was most unfairly treated," Arden said. "She was speaking to a gentleman who caught her eye. He seemed amiable until he heard that she liked rock music, whereupon he became very rude."

Zap frowned. "That's ... petty."

"Friggin' stupid," Steve said. "Whatever. It's few-tile."

"Have you had any water?" Zap asked Steve. "You'll be hung over in the morning if you don't get water."

"I had some water," Steve said. "Earlier."

"Were you two planning on staying much later?" Zap asked, turning to Arden.

"No, we'll both be needing some sleep," Arden replied.

"Sleep is for the weekdays!" Steve declared.

"It *is* a weekday," Zap replied.

Steve grunted.

"C'mon, let's all go," Zap said. "You're in B Block, right Steve?"

"Yeah, okay," Steve replied, getting to her feet and stretching. "I get it. We're all being responsible."

"Don't you want to do well at tomorrow's exercises?"

"It's not like I'm trying for management," Steve said. "But yeah, it'd be nice to have the cert. Let's go to bed."

The group had wandered back to the B Block dorms and dropped Steve off at her room, where Violet was already asleep.

Zap and Arden returned to their room.

"That is a mighty fine woman," Arden said to Zap as the two of them began preparing for bed.

"Who?"

"Stephen," Arden said. "She doesn't realize what a catch she is, and once she does every man will be after her."

"I like Steve," Zap said. "She's a good friend."

"She's got a lot going for her," Arden continued. "She's attractive, intelligent and talented. She just needs a little more confidence and she'll be unstoppable."

"She's a little abrasive sometimes," Zap pointed out.

"She's just being defensive," Arden said, waving the opinion away. "It's just a defensive reflex and that'll go away when she comes into her own."

"If you say so."

"Were my roving days not over..." Arden trailed off, shaking his head. He turned to Zap. "Can you honestly tell me that you've never considered what it'd be like having Steve as a lass?"

Zap paused, then looked over at Arden. "...I've got a girlfriend, Arden."

"Ehh," Arden said, waving again.

The next few minutes passed in silence as the two got ready for bed. Shortly, both were in nightclothes. Arden took his place in the bottom bunk, gently checking the latch on the assault rifle he had placed in a wall mount near his bed. Zap settled into place in the top bunk, closing his eyes.

The room was silent for a few minutes before Zap spoke.

"...yeah," he said. "I have thought about it."

30

The Tuesday sun crested fiercely, bathing the Orleans Installation in bright, powerful daylight as the Securemarket™ Trainees began streaming from their dormitories.

They gathered on a large field of well-mowed grass, marked as a standard athletic field. The store managers were already lined up at the front of the field, and at their center was Sir Orin Erdrick. Rather than a Knight's Suit, he was dressed in a warm-up suit with a representation of his rose stitched on the front. The store managers were dressed in similarly athletic clothing, though all were wearing their weapons.

The 15th and Neimuth employees clumped near the front of the field, murmuring to each other. Most were dressed in light athletic clothing to match the warm weather, except for the Shadow Mutant manager of the late-night shift, who was dressed in full-body clothing and seemed to be very uncomfortable.

Once most of the employees had arrived, Sir Erdrick raised his voice loudly enough to address the entire group of employees. "Welcome to morning exercises!" he shouted. "You'll be getting very familiar with this process, as you will begin all of your retreat weekdays this way! It is not fun to rise this early, but it is good for you! Spread out, please, and set your weapons and shell on the ground near you."

The employees moved to comply, giving themselves ample room and setting their weapons and insulated shells on the dewy ground. Those who had weapons containing real metal or unguarded electronics set their weapons down a bit more gingerly than others. Some had had the foresight to bring a bag or small tarp, which they set their weapons upon.

"We will begin with a series of stretches and exercises that we will do together every day," Sir Erdrick said. "Once we're done here, you'll move on to cycle exercises. Those of you who've already reviewed your schedule will already know what I'm talking about, but let me reiterate. Everybody here will be doing the same morning exercises, but at different times and in randomly-assigned groups. Your shell will let you know where you're to go after here. These exercises will keep you moving, limber and energetic. Now, follow me!"

Two hours later, the employees had all been released from their exercises and were wandering the halls, heading to their next destination. Steve and Zap, who had been assigned the same group, staggered through the hallway. Steve's face was flushed and she was somewhat short of breath, but Zap had fared much worse: his face was pale and he could barely speak for catching his breath.

"They don't make ya exercise at Ethertech, huh," Steve asked.

Zap tried to gasp a response, but failed. Steve patted his back.

"This'll be tough," Steve said to the winded wizardry student, "but it'll whip you into shape. Hope you've got enough energy to cast spells later."

"Me too," Zap managed.

Alan jogged up to the pair. "Hey," he said with a smile. Alan's face was flushed with activity, but he barely seemed to be out of breath. He was wearing an NWU tracksuit and had a shotgun strapped to his back.

"Hey Alan," Steve said back. "You're looking pretty good."

"Yeah," Alan said. "They work me way harder than that at Mei Kara Do practice. And they're going to work the both of you way harder than that later on. Get used to it."

"Great," Zap gasped.

"Say," Steve said, knitting her brow, "when'd you start carrying a shotgun?"

"It's covered under my rifle cert," Alan said disapprovingly, shifting the shotgun's strap. "And the higher-ups want me carrying something big and intimidating at the store. So I'm training with it from now on. Yay."

"Huh," Steve said. "Well, you'll get used to it."

"I find it inelegant," Alan said. "Anyway, where're you kids headed?"

"The range," Steve said. "I've got Marksmanship training next."

"Customer," Zap gasped, then, "Service."

Alan nodded. "I'm headed to the range too," he said. "So I'll be going with you, Steve. Think you can make it, Zap?"

"Yeah," he said. "I'll be fine. Just not used to ... exercise."

"I can't imagine not getting regular exercise," Alan said. "It just feels nice, you know?"

"It's an easy habit to drop," admitted Steve. "I don't get much exercise these days."

"Well, maybe this'll be just the thing to kick the two of you back into the habit!" Alan said, grinning.

"Maybe," Zap said, sounding dubious.

"C'mon," Steve said. "We should get to the range. I'm sure Asthma McWheezypants will make it to the seminar room one building over just fine."

"Your compassion," Zap said, "is inspiring."

"Good luck, Zap," Alan said. "I'm sure you'll be fine."

Zap leaned against the wall, watching Steve and Alan walk away for a few minutes before setting on his own way.

That evening, an exhausted and sleepy Zap Bradshaw stumbled into his room, nearly running into his roommate, who was kneeling on the floor in prayer.

"Oh—sorry," Zap stammered, tiptoeing around Arden. Arden gave a brief nod and continued with his prayer.

> *"Yea, though the snow fall around me*
> *and I am beset by beasts and monsters*
> *I know that You have given them to me*
> *as adversity that shall help me to grow*
> *and better serve You."*

Zap quietly gathered his pajamas and slipped around Arden again, heading to the bathroom. He arrived and retrieved his toiletries, beginning his bedtime preparations. As he did so, he listened to Arden's Etherist prayer.

> *"May you fortify my spirit*
> *that I may strengthen my body*
> *and raise my gun and sword*
> *and speak words of power*

to defend that which I stake as mine
and come to the aid of those I love."

Zap washed his face without hurrying, letting the hot water gather in his hands and splashing it over his face. He then turned, his eyes still closed, and pressed his face into the hand towel there. He very slowly drew the towel down his face, letting his eyes open as they were uncovered. He took a deep breath in, then let it out and hung the towel over its rack. He retrieved his toothbrush and toothpaste.

"I praise you for the strength of spirit you lend me.
I praise you for your holy gift of magic.
I praise you for adversity.
May you watch over me as I watch over mine
and may you challenge me and keep me
until the day I return to you.
Amen."

Zap was still brushing his teeth as Arden finished his prayer and raised to his feet. As Zap finished, he could hear Arden getting into bed. He rinsed his mouth quickly and said, "Sorry about that, Arden."

"No problem, Zap," Arden said from bed. "You religious?"

"A little," Zap said. "My family is Jewish. I'm a little lax, I guess, but I try to observe Passover in its entirety at least."

"We all have our own relationship with God," Arden said.

Steve arrived in her room to find Violet sitting on her bed in a full lotus position, her eyes closed and her hands perched on each knee. Steve halted, then closed the door to her room very slowly and carefully.

"Don't worry about making noise," Violet said, not opening her eyes. "I can sit zazen on the Rail when I have to."

"Oh," Steve said. "Okay."

Steve proceeded in getting ready for bed, still endeavoring to be as quiet as she could be. She finished her evening toilette and changed into the t-shirt and boxers she typically wore to bed. When she emerged from the bathroom, she saw that Violet's eyes were now open and she wore a small smile, though she was still sitting in the lotus.

"Hey," she said to Steve.

"Hey, sorry about that."

"It's fine," Violet replied. "I forgot to warn you about this. I try to sit zazen any day that I work hard."

"You're Buddhist?" Steve asked.

"Zen Buddhist, yes," Violet said. "Are you religious, Steve?"

"No," Steve replied. "Not really. My folks sort of brought me up Catholic, but they weren't very good Catholics and I'm a worse one. I don't really buy a whole lot of the dogma; I just believe in God."

"Makes sense," Violet said.

"Meditation always seemed neat, though," Steve said as she climbed up to her bunk. "Introspection over worship. I'd think that God is more interested in helping us figure ourselves out than in worshiping him."

"Perhaps you should meditate with me," Violet replied from the lower bunk. "It's very good for you, no matter what your religion is."

Steve paused. "Seriously?"

"Absolutely," Violet replied.

"I don't really know how to do it, though," Steve said.

"Nobody is perfect at it," Violet said, "but it becomes easier with practice. It's very simple. You want to try right now?"

"Sure!" Steve said.

"How much room do you have under the ceiling there?"

"A fair bit," Steve said. "I can't stand up, but I can sit up straight."

"Good," Violet replied. "Sit in a position with your spine straight, but that's comfortable to you. Crossing your legs is good..."

31

The next few days were a cavalcade of difficult training for the employees. The mornings began with grueling exercises and proceeded into seminars and exercises focusing on the certification and specialties of each employee.

All trainees went through weapon and magic practice, with more emphasis on their preferred method of combat. Zap spent a chunk of each day practicing spell use, while To'mas and Steve spent more time at the shooting range, improving their aim and reaction time. Alan and Click went through martial arts practice and evaluation in addition to the basic defense training all employees were subjected to.

All of the training had, however, been largely 'hands-off' for the employees. Seminars, target practice and exercises had been the standard fare, leaving the employees tired but seeming more like a rigorous summer camp than the 'boot camp'-style regimen that many had expected.

But tensions rose as Friday approached, for Friday brought with it the first round of Kekkai exercises. Shift would be pitted against shift to test and strengthen teamwork between employees in a combat situation. Rather than immobile targets, employees would be targeting employees of the same company, real live people who would fight back. While the test was considered safe, those who did not fight hard enough would suffer very real pain and a convincing simulation of death.

With this in mind the employees watched their schedules move inexorably forward, the number of scheduled events between the present and the Kekkai exercises shrinking. Some observed it with nervous anticipation, some with anxious dread, but almost all were so caught up in thinking about it that they scarcely thought about the concert scheduled later that night.

But no amount of anxiety or anticipation could hold the date back. Friday morning arrived, and the groups of employees gathered and went to the all-purpose Kekkai room in shifts.

The Archmage Tea-Time shift was scheduled to undergo their Kekkai exercise at noon. At Alan's behest, they all gathered in a conference room that he had reserved. The employees arrived more or less on time, sitting in a circle around the conference table and leveling serious gazes at one another. Alan cleared his throat once the last arrival, Matt, had taken his seat.

"The first thing I'd like to get out there," Alan said, "is that this is not the end-all experience of this retreat, okay? Nobody's getting fired because of this exercise.

"We're a good shift," he continued. "We have diverse talents and abilities and we all respond quickly to dangerous situations. We can do this. Remember that you're *safe* out there, so don't hesitate to do what you have to do. Fight bravely and well and we'll look good, no matter whether we win or lose. Okay?"

The employees nodded and murmured their assent.

"Okay," Alan said. "I'm gonna go report to the room and run things through. You all get your stuff ready. Check your weapons and spell reserves and whatever, and meet me in fifteen minutes."

Alan left the room. The employees fidgeted for a few moments before Steve spoke.

"Anybody know who we're up against?"

To'mas nodded. "Rose Street early-morning shift," he said. "I was flirting with a girl from that shift and asked about her schedule. They're scheduled when we are, so they're our opponents."

"Okay," Steve said.

To'mas tilted his head. "Speaking of flirting, Steve, I saw you talking to a guy at the bar last night," he said, smiling a little bit.

"To'mas, are you sure this is the time to start talking about flirtation?" Loren asked. "We should be focusing."

"You call it focusing, I call it dwelling," To'mas replied. "This helps keep my nerves down. Though if it makes Steve uncomfortable…"

"It's fine," Steve said, waving a hand. "It didn't work out."

"Why not?" To'mas asked. "Click said that you and he had caught him checking you out."

"We had," said Click, somewhat defensive. "I didn't know he was a jerk."

"We had," agreed Steve, nodding. "He got all huffy at me about not liking pigskin, of all things. He was *really* into sports."

"Huh," To'mas said. "Weird."

Zap frowned.

"Anyway," Steve said. "We're about to do this thing, huh."

"Sure are," To'mas said. "It never really gets easy."

"Any idea how it's gonna go, Matt?" Zap asked.

"Nice try, little guy," Matt replied.

"Has anybody here actually been in a deadly fight?" Steve asked.

The table went silent for a moment.

To'mas nodded, keeping his eyes on the table. "Yeah," he said. "A confrontation between a pair of yuzies on a nasty part of the Rail. They started shooting at each other and weren't really caring who they shot at. A couple of bystanders got shot, one died. I stood up and shot one of the yuzies, and he was wearing a shield but the shot knocked him down. Another passenger put a gun to his head and killed him. The other yuzie surrendered to the other passengers on the train and was arrested."

There was quiet again.

"Who's seen a killing?"

Just about everyone nodded their head, murmuring "once" or "a few times" or "possibly."

"Then we're not gonna see anything we haven't seen before," Steve said. "Except it's not real this time. Go all out. Follow Alan's orders, and if he gets fragged then follow mine. We can do this."

Everyone nodded.

The employees stood on opposite sides of the multi-purpose room, each one in a line with their supervisor in front of them. The room was filled with simple geometric obstacles; several simple blocks large enough for two people to hide behind lay scattered across the room. There were also a few tower-like structures with a ladder on the side.

A simple battlefield, and two simply-dressed teams—save for the brightly-colored Securemarket™ aprons they all wore. The Archmage Tea-Time employees wore green, the other team orange.

A voice echoed through the room, resonating from the surfaces of the objects and from the walls themselves.

"Employees, welcome to your first Kekkai training. This training will be a simple combat, one side versus the other. Fight hard and well, please, and do not hold back. The Kekkai will keep you safe. If you are disabled, tap the floor twice to drop out of the battle. If you lose consciousness or are killed you will be pulled out of the Kekkai automatically. I will be watching and will pull you out if you are disabled, conscious, and unable to tap the floor."

The employees shifted uncomfortably, images of their teammates having their arms blown off rising unbidden in their minds.

"Please remember that just like your real employee aprons, the aprons you're wearing now are an armor-weave. If you're otherwise unarmored, try to take your hits on the apron. Good luck. Please do not cross the line in front of you until my mark."

The employees tensed, gripping their weapons. Alan turned to look at his employees, surveying them. All looked back at him, tense and ready.

"Ready..." said the voice.

Alan turned back, looking at the obstacles in front of him. He looked at his employees and made a few quick gestures, indicating to them where he expected them to advance. He turned back and held up a closed fist.

"Mark!"

Alan opened his fist and his employees broke into a run.

32

The employees rushed to their positions, each one choosing an obstacle to hide behind. To'mas, barely impeded by his two pistols and the rifle strapped to his back, began clambering up the ladder to the nearest tower while Steve covered his ascent, her eyes darting back and forth.

The employees had not advanced far when a blur of blue light streaked around the corner of one of the obstacles. Something flashed, and Loren shouted as something pinned him against the barrier. Alan shouted and brought his shotgun to bear, but the humanoid figure was gone in another streak of blue before he could draw a bead.

"Zap!" Alan shouted into his intercom as Loren slumped to the ground with a large wound in his chest.

"Elven haste spell, sword enchantments, projectile shield," Zap responded. "A fighter-mage."

"Gonna tap out, boss," Loren murmured, struggling to speak through the pain of his wound.

"Do it, Loren. Click!" Alan said. The faerie nodded and moved to Alan. "Zap, I want you to counter that haste effect. Click and I will engage; cover us!"

As Loren tapped the floor twice and turned an iron-gray color, the employees moved forward, edging around their barriers with caution. They halted in their path as a hail of machine pistol fire peppered the area. Finding themselves without cover, Alan and Click threw themselves to the ground to avoid the bullets. A male human was taking partial cover behind one of the barriers, laying suppression fire over the area. Without warning, his head snapped back as a round from To'mas's rifle struck his bulletshield, throwing the employee to the ground.

"Incoming magic!" Zap called.

"Fall back!" Alan said, stumbling to his feet.

"To'mas, get down!" Zap shouted.

To'mas ducked behind the tower's short barrier just in time to avoid a magic missile that hissed through the air where his head had just been. As the employees scrambled for cover, a plume of fire washed over the area. The employees found themselves standing where they had been moments ago, where Loren's still, iron-colored form still lay slumped against the back of the barrier.

"So," Alan panted, drawing something from his weapon belt, "if my detection's on-par, that's a wizard, a fighter-mage, and..."

"A Node Caller," Zap replied. "Of fire."

"Of fire, really?" Steve asked sarcastically.

"Flashbang," Alan said, pressing a button on the object in his hand, "and we go."

The employees braced themselves as Alan tossed the small grenade around the corner. A deafening noise rocked the battlefield and the employees all turned and ran around their barriers. Sure enough, several of their opponents were reeling, stopped mid-charge by the flashbang. Alan and Click beelined for them.

Click's hands glowed with dream-fire as he hammered blows upon the nearest opponent, the human with the machine pistol. The man was thrown to the ground after only a few strikes and his body turned stone-gray.

Alan's shotgun barked as he fired at a young woman, striking her in the arm with a slug. She dove for cover and managed to make it behind a barrier without a serious wound. From partial cover, Steve fired several times at a young man holding a wand, but a pentagram glowed at his feet and the bullets dissolved in the air in front of him.

The employees on both sides exchanged fire as they ran for cover frantically. To'mas clambered halfway down the ladder and jumped to the ground, running toward the battle and dodging between obstacles.

Zap and the other wizard squared off, each standing in a circle of protection. They began battering each others' defenses; Zap would flick his wand and send a burning projectile at his opponent's shield, but the other wizard would unweave it before it could reach him. The other wizard would attempt to break Zap's protection spell, but Zap rewrote it faster than his opponent could break it down. The two fought their own battle, forming a deadly space between them that the other employees avoided.

As To'mas reached the battlefield, a man with a truly unfortunate mustache emerged from cover and fired a few potshots. One struck To'mas's bulletshield, staggering him. Steve turned and returned fire with Polaris, firing several shots. The mustached man dropped to the ground and To'mas regained his balance, rubbing his chest. He ran to Steve with a smile, but the look dropped from his face as the woman that Alan had earlier wounded stepped out from a nearby obstacle and bathed both of them in magical fire.

Alan winced as To'mas and Steve screamed in pain over the intercom. "Tap out! Tap out!" he shouted, and heard the shouts silence as the employees hurriedly surrendered. "Damn it!" he said, then ducked low and snuck around his obstacle, moving around the side of the battlefield. He muttered to himself. "Where the fuck is Matt?!"

"Okay, finally got something," Matt's voice came in over the intercom. "Click, head left and run. You won't get hit and the Caller's too busy gloating. You'll need to break her neck or she'll immolate you."

"Good to hear from you, Matt," Alan said with some relief.

"Please be quiet, I'm about to be shot. Zap, your opponent plays by the books. If you know the Three-Martini Lunch duel set, throw it at him. He won't know what to do. Now, if you'll excuse me, there's a Sparrow morph with a pair of .38s—"

There were gunshots from the far end of the battlefield and Alan winced. He quickly changed course to intercept the unaccounted-for opponent.

Zap's opponent looked increasingly concerned as Zap followed Matt's instructions, unleashing a set of disorienting and usually rather impractical spells known outside the classrooms as the "Three Martini Lunch". Once the maneuver was over, Zap's opponent was thoroughly off-guard. With a flourish, Zap brandished his wand and unraveled the enemy mage's protection spell. One more flourish wrapped his opponent in a binding cantrip, and Zap's helpless opponent collapsed to the ground and turned gray. At the same time, Zap heard a hail of gunfire from the end of the battlefield where the team had started, Alan's shotgun blasts punctuated with return fire from a smaller gun. The last shot Zap heard was a shotgun blast.

Good for us, Zap allowed himself to think. Naturally, things then took a turn.

The next moment, Zap saw Click running full-tilt out from behind his cover. He had just enough time to scream "Zap, help!" before a meteoric streak intercepted him. Click's body whirled and hit the ground. The half-elf woman above him was dressed in traditional mythril armor and carried a pair of ornately-runed short swords, both of which glowed with an ominous blue light. One was held at Click's throat.

"Tap out," said the woman, her voice deadly calm. Click obeyed and turned the same iron-gray as the other defeated employees. The woman looked up at Zap, and then broke into a run toward him.

Zap brought up his wand-arm, unweaving the charms the woman had been wearing with as much haste as he could manage. By the time she was halfway to him, her haste charm was gone. By the time she was ten paces away, her shield charm was unraveled. By the time she was within striking range, Zap had almost undone the enchantment on her swords.

Unfortunately, she cut the charm and Zap's forearm short. The young wizard watched as his hand, still clutching his wand, clattered to the floor. He brought his gaze back up to the half-elf's eyes, and she looked at him and said, "Tap out."

"She's all yours, Alan," Zap said, then tapped the wall twice with his remaining hand.

Alan emerged from cover, his shotgun trained on the half-elf. She fixed an intense gaze on him.

"Raimi And The Soft Winds Blow," Alan said. "That makes sense."

"Hi, Alan," Raimi said. "We're out of employees. Want to dance?"

Alan grunted and sighted Raimi with the shotgun. She dove for cover as he fired and ran through the obstacles. Alan backed into the open space, but when Raimi emerged, she was too fast for him. He fired and the slug went over her shoulder, bouncing off of the obstacle behind her. She brought one sword upward and sliced neatly through Alan's shotgun. Alan stumbled over the prone, plastic-hard body of one of the downed employees and sprawled against the floor, on his side.

Raimi pointed one of her swords at Alan's throat. "Tap out," she told him.

Alan looked at her impassively for a moment and raised one hand. "You ought not to do that," he said.

As fast as he could, Alan sat up and lashed out with his hand. He grasped the cross-guard of Raimi's sword and yanked backward, causing the half-elf to stumble forward. She brought her other arm toward Alan and ran him through as she fell, her sword passing through his stomach and emerging from his back.

The two were now face-to-face, Alan's pain-wracked expression next to Raimi's confused one.

"Why in the hell did you do that?" Raimi asked.

Alan's only response was to raise his free hand, in which he clutched a holdout pistol. Raimi found that with no limbs free, she was only able to watch as Alan brought the gun to her face and fired.

Five minutes later, the employees were all alive again. They stood in lines facing each other, one of the red-clad Securemarket™ officers between them. The officer spoke.

"I'm impressed with all of you," he said. "I haven't seen a harder fight yet today. I know that this was an emotional experience for all of you, but please remember that it was a training exercise. We are all on the same side here. Let's shake hands and rest up for tonight's concert. You're all going to want to have fun."

Alan and Raimi walked up to each other, each smiling with admiration.

"Well done, Alan," Raimi said, shaking Alan's hand. "You've really gotten some guts."

"And you're even more deadly than I remember you," Alan said, smiling back.

The lines continued, each employee shaking hands with the others.

"I'm sorry," the Node Caller woman said to Steve and To'mas. "I don't actually like burning people."

"It's fair," To'mas said. Steve still seemed a bit too shaken by the experience to reply. "We would have done the same if we ... y'know, had control over the element of fire."

"You're very good," Zap said to the wizard he'd disabled.

"Thank you," the other wizard said politely. "Would you teach me that set of techniques you used at the end? I was never taught that."

"They don't teach it in classes," Zap said, grinning. "But sure."

Once the handshakes had taken place, the groups moved toward the exit. Alan and Raimi were chatting with each other as the groups moved into the hallway, discussing the time that they had spent since they saw each other last. After a time, they turned back to the group.

"We're headed to the pub," Alan said. "Any of you who want to come can. Otherwise we'll see you at the concert."

The two walked off, leaving the groups to discuss the matter themselves.

"Think you guys will go?"

"Yeah, I could use a drink," To'mas said in a casual tone; he didn't seem shaken at all.

"I think I'd better take a rest, maybe," Steve said, looking a bit pale.

"I think I might too," Zap said.

"Mm," Click agreed, nodding.

Suddenly, the young man from the Rose Street store who was wearing the machine pistol he'd been carrying during the exercise walked up to the group. To Steve, specifically.

"Uh, hi, miss..." he began.

"Steve," Steve said, her discomfort forgotten in her surprise at being approached.

"Miss Steve," the man said. He held out one hand. "I'm Mike."

"Good to meet you," Steve said, shaking his hand.

"Listen, that's a really beautiful piece you have," Mike said. "Who'd you commission it from?"

"Actually, my Master made it," Steve said. "I'm an apprentice gunsmith."

Mike brightened. "Oh!" he said. "That's really interesting! If I bought you a drink, would you be willing to tell me ... I dunno, about what that's like?"

"Sure!" Steve replied, apparently forgetting her trauma. "Let's go to the pub."

The two walked off, launching into an animated conversation. The remaining employees watched them for a moment.

"Y'know, I think I actually want a drink, maybe," Click said.

"Yeah, me too," Zap said.

To'mas stared at them.

33

The bar was sparsely occupied when the ex-combatants entered it. The rank-and-file employees had lagged behind their supervisors, who already sat talking at the bar. The installation's pub was in a different area of the facility from the event bar where the employee mixer had been held, and was open more often. The pub had about it a much homier atmosphere than the event bar, complete with couches, faux-wood tables, and a fireplace at the far end of the pub.

"Oh, this place is nice," Zap said as he entered.

"You haven't made it here at all?" To'mas asked.

"Nope," Zap said. "I've been too tired."

"Pity," To'mas said.

Steve and her new friend peeled away from the group. The two hadn't stopped chatting about guns even upon arrival at the pub, and continued doing so on their trip to the table.

"Let's take a table near them," Zap suggested to the remaining employees: To'mas, Click, and two of the Rose street employees. One was Masha, the sparrow morph who had shot Matt, and the other was Dru, Zap's wizard opponent.

The employees all moved to one of the tables and sat down heavily.

"Oh 'yesu..." Zap said, sagging in his chair. "It just hit me how much that fight drained me."

"Just now?" Masha said. "I haven't been able to stop my hands shaking since I was revived." She held up one of her trembling, feathered hands.

"Anybody here not drink beer?" Dru asked, looking around.

To'mas smiled a little. "Not typically, but I can make an exception if it's good."

"A pitcher of Equator, then," Dru replied, then pushed his way to his feet. "I'll go get it."

Zap noted that Click seemed to be distracted. "How're the two new buddies doing?"

"Pretty well, looks like," Click said with a smile, breaking out of his reverie.

"Good!" Zap said. "Steve could use some positive attention."

"Yeah," Click agreed.

"And that's how I ended up with it," Steve said, patting her holster fondly.

"That's great," Mike said, laughing. "Your Master sounds like a real card."

"He's a piece of work," she replied with a grin. "I love working for him, and I think he's going to really help me become a good gunsmith. I think that my final project for him might be to modify Polaris. I've got some great design ideas."

"Well, I'm impressed," Mike said. "I love seeing different gun designs and working with them, but I can't quite imagine machining them myself."

"It's a trade," Steve replied, shrugging but smiling. She turned to look at her coworkers for a moment. "Iyesu, are they on their second pitcher?"

"Looks like it," Mike agreed. "I'm a little surprised everybody's getting on so well after shooting each other up."

"Maybe it makes them feel better about the violence to be friendly afterward," Steve said. "So, what do you think of the retreat so far?"

"It's been challenging," Mike said, "but in a really good way. I'm hoping that I can keep some of the habits they're instilling in us now."

"Wish I had the time," Steve said. "I'm feeling good too, with all the focus and exercise and everything, but apprenticeship and this job keep me pretty busy. And I like to have a little time to myself, you know?"

"And with people you like," Mike replied. "I know."

"If I keep anything from this, maybe it'll be meditation. My roommate has been teaching me meditation, which is very cool," Steve said with a smile.

"Oh, are you spiritual?"

"Not really," Steve said, shrugging. "I was brought up Catholic, but not really very devoutly. My family missed church a lot."

"Oh," Mike said.

"What?" Steve said.

"Well, I'm uh," he said, scratching the back of his head. "I'm Etherist."

"...yeah?" Steve said, a creeping apprehension working its way into her voice.

"I don't know, I guess it's no big deal," Mike said. "It just means that we couldn't date."

"It does?" Steve asked in a small voice.

"Yeah, I don't think I could date somebody outside of the faith."

There was an awkward silence.

"Listen, I gotta go," Mike said, standing. "Have a good one, okay?"

"Sure," Steve said, her face bleak.

Mike strode away from the table hurriedly, driven by an odd sense of urgency. He had made it to the hallway and was several paces away from the pub when he heard the voice of the young magician, Zap, behind him.

"Hey, hold still for a second. You've got a big ole bug on you."

Mike froze. "What is it?"

"I dunno, but it's big and gross. I'll get it."

Mike stood stock-still and felt something flickering just behind his back.

"Okay," Zap said. "I got it, you can move now."

Mike turned around and smiled at Zap. "Thanks, man," he said, then looked around. "Where'd the bug go?"

"Oh, it flew away," Zap said, adjusting his wand holster. "What happened back there?"

"Oh," Mike said. "I guess I was sort of hoping to have a chance with Steve, but something bad came up."

"I think I overheard a little," Zap said. "You must feel pretty strongly about your religion."

Mike paused and his eyes went wide. "I—no! No I don't!" he said, his face turning pale. "I'm really not that religious! What the hell did I just do?!"

"Oh, geez," Zap said.

"Oh, I'm such a jerk!" Mike said. "I don't know what was wrong with me! Why did I say that?"

"I'm sure it was just nerves," Zap said, smiling a little. "But you'd better go apologize to Steve. I think she was interested in you too, and if so that would have hurt her feelings pretty bad."

"Did she stay at the table?" Mike asked.

"No, it looked like she was heading out when I got up. She's staying in B Block. If you hurry, you can still catch her."

"Thanks so much for shaking me out of this, Zap," Mike said, shaking Zap's hand emphatically. "I've gotta go make things right." He broke into a jog down an adjacent hallway, beelining for dormitory block B.

"Yeah," Zap said quietly as he watched Mike go. His face slowly settled into a stony mask of anger as the young man got further away. "So do I."

Leaning against the wall of one of the facility's hallways, Zap saw Steve come around the corner and approach him. She had a bounce in her step and looked cheerful.

"Hey there," Zap said, smiling. "You look happy."

"I have a date to the concert tonight!" she said, more cheerful than Zap had ever seen her. "Mike came back and was really nice to me."

"That's great!" Zap said. "You think he's interested?"

"He said so!" Steve said, grinning. "I'm really looking forward to it. Have any idea of who the band's gonna be?"

"No," Zap said. "You should ask To'mas, he's pretty good about info hacking."

"Good call," Steve replied. Her look became suddenly inquisitive. "What are you doing waiting in this hall, anyway?"

"Nothing important," Zap said. "Say, were you gonna help nab that Creepy Dan guy tonight?"

"Oh yeah, Creepy Don!" Steve said and her eyes widened. "Thanks for reminding me; I gotta call Matt!"

Zap watched Steve's retreating form as she hurried away. After she had disappeared from sight, Zap drew his wand and began tracing a charm in the air.

Click exited his room cheerfully, humming the tune to *Comeback*. He had showered and changed into the clothes he intended to wear to the concert: a colorful ensemble that he thought made him look like a shiny butterfly. To enhance the look, Click had stuck a pair of micro-LEDs onto the ends of his antennae.

Click strode from the dorm area quickly, and then turned down a connecting hallway. He was somewhat surprised to find it empty, but continued his trip. Once he was a few paces into the hallway, Click thought he detected someone behind him. He halted in his tracks and did an about-face.

There was nothing behind him, of course, but the entrance to the hallway. Click couldn't shake the unsettled feeling that he was being followed, but turned back and continued his journey, more cautious than before.

Once he was halfway through the hallway, everything went pitch black.

Click spun and caught a faint glance of a ghostly figure slipping out of his line of sight. Moments later an icy, burning pain clamped around his neck. He tried to scream, but the freezing sensation was overwhelming. Click dropped to his knees as numbing, spidery threads snaked their way through his system.

Cold iron! Click thought to himself, panic rising in his gorge.

"You should be very ashamed of yourself," a distorted voice said in his ear. "Manipulating a fine young lady into feeling like she has no chance with anybody."

"I..." Click gasped. "didn't..."

"Don't take me for a fool," the voice hissed. "Do you think I didn't give you the benefit of the doubt? Do you think I didn't make absolutely sure it was you?"

Click whispered, "I..."

"Do you have any idea how you've hurt her? Did you want to destroy her confidence utterly before you moved in?"

"I—I didn't..." Click said, sobbing from the pain. "I didn't think..."

"I didn't think you did," the voice said. "Well, take a good look at yourself. If you give a damn about Steve, you'll realize what you've been doing to her."

"Who..." Click mumbled.

"I think you can figure that out," the voice said. "I'm going to end our little chat with a demand. If you want to win Steve, you will do so like an honorable man. Don't tell anyone about this encounter or I will tell her what you've done, and God help you then. Can we agree to this?"

Click nodded dumbly and gasped with relief as the icy pain disappeared, the cold iron pulling away from his neck. Click placed his hand on the wall and leaned forward, breathing hard.

"Remember," the voice said, "they've got sayings about pissing off faeries, but there are far more of them about pissing off wizards."

The darkness vanished with a sucking noise and Click found himself alone in the hallway. He gingerly touched the back of his neck, wincing at the burn there. He shook his head slowly and placed both hands over his face.

34

Pazi answered the door only a few seconds after Zap knocked. Her face seemed to bear a mix of relief and suppressed annoyance.

"There you are," she said, sighing. "You're pretty late."

"Yeah, I'm sorry," Zap said. He moved through the doorway and into Pazi's room, and she closed the door behind him. "There was something unexpected that I had to take care of."

"I guess I was just hoping to spend a little time with you before the concert," Pazi said, disappointed.

"Well, I am still staying with you tonight, right?" Zap asked.

"Yeah," Pazi said. "I just guess ... I know things have been busy, but I feel like you could have found *some* time to spend with me, you know?"

Zap's face fell a little bit and he nodded. "Yeah," he said. "You're right."

"Oh sweetie," Pazi said, moving to Zap and touching his face. "Please don't feel guilty. I just want a little bit of attention."

"You deserve it," Zap said, putting his arms around Pazi's waist. "I've been too easily distracted and haven't given you the time you deserve. I want to make it up to you."

"I'd like that," Pazi said, tilting her head to kiss Zap's jawline.

Zap put a hand on Pazi's shoulder and stepped back, looking at his girlfriend. She was wearing a flattering corset emblazoned with spirit sigils and a long blue skirt. Judging by what Zap could see between the laces on her corset, she wore nothing underneath it.

"Wow," he said.

"Do you like it?" Pazi said with an impish smile.

"It's hot," Zap said.

"I felt like representing," Pazi said. "The corset is actually a ritual corset. It was my mother's. I'm gonna wear her headband too, but I haven't put it on yet because it's sort of hard to avoid accidentally gouging stuff on the horn."

"Okay," Zap said. "Just be careful hugging me once it's on, okay?"

Pazi giggled. "Okay," she said.

"Are you going to summon a companion to bring?"

"Well, I have you," Pazi said, "but yes, I was going to bring a spirit. Any requests?"

"That little mouse-fish is pretty cute." Zap said with a grin.

To'mas and Violet sat together on Violet's bed, watching Steve preen herself with the grace of a one-legged puppy.

"This is pretty much the cutest thing ever," Violet murmured to To'mas.

"It really is," To'mas replied *sotto voce*. "I've never seen her so cheerful."

"It's really great," Violet said. She watched Steve's ineffective toilette for a few more moments before standing. "But I can't watch anymore. Steve, sweetie, *please* let me help you."

Steve gave a nervous laugh. "I think I'm a lost cause," she said.

"Don't be stupid," Violet said. "You're very pretty, no matter how much you try to hide it. Millions of women would kill to have your hair, you know."

"Mmm," Steve said. "It's a pain in the ass."

"Convenience and beauty have never gone hand in hand, Steve," Violet said, guiding Steve to the bathroom. "To'mas, babes, I'll be back out soon."

"Don't fall in," To'mas encouraged.

A few minutes later, Violet marched Steve back into the room. Steve's face now had sparse makeup applied to it, emphasizing her hazel eyes and freckles. Steve's auburn curls shone and hung in ringlets that framed her face prettily, held in place with a barrette.

"To'mas?" Violet asked.

"It's good," he said. "Very 'girl next door'."

"That's what I was going for," Violet said. "Glam wouldn't look good on her. Now we need to dress you." Violet pulled open the closet and surveyed Steve's clothes.

"You really dress for utility, don't you," Violet said. Steve shrugged.

Violet pawed through the clothes and made noises to herself. After some deliberation, she picked a pair of Steve's jeans, and then found a shirt of her own. She presented the completed outfit to Steve.

Steve balked, glancing over at To'mas. Violet made an irritated noise and marched Steve back to the bathroom. Several minutes later, the two emerged. Steve was now wearing a tightly fitted babydoll tee that said "Ultralove Ninja" on it and a pair of jeans.

"This shirt is tight," Steve said, hesitant.

"So?" Violet said. "It makes your boobs look good. You never show them off."

"I'll look fat," Steve objected.

"You're not fat," To'mas said, rolling his eyes.

"You look great," Violet said, then turned Steve around. "Go get 'em, tiger." She slapped Steve's ass, and the latter scooted to the door.

"Thanks," Steve said, smiling. She slipped out of the room.

Violet returned to the bed, where To'mas was waiting for her.

"You ready?" To'mas said.

"Your roommate is doomed," Violet said. "Our powers combined, we are dead sexy."

"To the hunt!" To'mas cried.

"To the hunt!" Violet echoed, grinning widely.

35

Pazi reached up and adjusted the horn jutting from the center of the headband she now wore. She took one last moment to check the stylized makeup she had applied, and then turned to Zap. "There," she said. "All done."

From his position on her bed, Zap smiled at her. "Awesome."

"How do I look?" Pazi said, smiling and turning in a circle.

"Like something burned the back of your neck," Click's roommate said. As best as Click could tell, his empty eye sockets were registering concern.

"Don't worry about it, Eyes," Click murmured. "It was an accident."

"It's like somebody heated up a gauntlet and grabbed you from behind," Hollow-Eyes said, floating behind Click to get a better look at the injury.

"I would seriously prefer not to talk about it," Click said, popping the collar of his shirt up to hide the burn. "Who are you going to the concert with?"

"Sir Margaret Ajeya," Marlon said with a smirk. "But that was an easy one; everybody knows about her. Ask me another one."

"Um," Loren said, "what Shadowflame has the highest contract success ratio?"

"Trick question," Marlon replied, smearing some styling cream over his hands. "There are several Shadowflames that have perfect contract success rates. The one who completed the *most* contracts successfully? Well, that'd be Alec Gainsborough himself."

"Can you count the founder of the organization as a Shadowflame?" Loren asked.

"The Hall of Records does," Marlon said as he worked the greasy cream into his hair. "Ask me another one."

"Hmm," Loren said. "Who's the Shadowflame with the highest number of *failed* contracts before being decommissioned?"

"Alan Morganstern," Paru's voice came from outside of the suite.

"Hang on!" Alan said, fumbling with the buttons on his shirt.

"You, sir, are a lousy date," Paru teased. "I should go ask Raye Courts-the-Shadows to accompany me to the concert."

"He's not *going*," Alan said as he checked himself in the mirror. He saw a bit of shaving gel nestled in his ear and grabbed a towel to clean it off.

"A minor detail," Paru replied. "Say, has that drama between your employees cleared up at all?"

"Don't I wish," Steve replied, laughing.

"How much longer, then?" Mike asked her.

"Oh, geez, I probably won't be considered a Journeyman for at least two more years," Steve replied. "I'll start being able to carry weapons I've modified under Master's supervision in under a year, though."

"Are you planning to modify Polaris?"

"Once I'm certain that I won't damage it," Steve said.

"What will you call the modified pistol?"

"Team sexy," Violet said with an expansive gesture.

To'mas shook his head. "Too plain. How about Inevitable Seduction?"

"Clunky," Violet said.

"Oh," To'mas said. "Before we get down to business, I promised that I would help a coworker of mine with something."

"Hm?" Violet asked.

"My coworker Matt has a plan for tonight, and he's calling in a few of us to help him pull it off."

"Oh," Violet said. "I think I know what this is. You guys are going to do a sting op on Creepy Don Stiles, right?"

"You bet your ass we are," Matt said.

"Whad'ju say?" the gaunt, beady-eyed man next to him asked.

"Just answering a question," Matt said. "Don't worry about it."

"Ain't nobody there." Creepy Don said. "You're weird, man."

"You have no idea," Matt said. "You ready to go?"

36

As the employees filtered outside to the daily exercise field, many were surprised to see it completely transformed. The grassy expanse now ended with a large stage that had been set up throughout the day. The stage itself was obscured with a black barrier, but massive resonance plates stood on either side of the stage, assuring the employees that they were in for, at the very least, an immersive experience.

At the side of the field, a sturdy-looking portable bar had been set up. A large awning shielded it from the setting sun and any potential inclement weather. The bar seemed fairly utilitarian, but most employees assumed it would be well-stocked, given the attitude that the company seemed to take concerning the retreat so far. Further back and to the side, a tented pavilion stood, sporting a full bar with stools, multiple grills, tables, and a multitude of chairs for those who preferred to take a less active part in the concert.

Steve and Mike arrived on the field and looked around, impressed.

"I'll say one thing for CEO Volnocht," Mike said. "The guy really knows how to let you play as hard as you work."

"It's the old-school warrior mentality," Steve said, recalling Alan's words on the subject. The two of them watched the gathering crowd for a few moments, and then began their trek to the bar.

Zap and Pazi stood in the pavilion, also watching the crowd. Near Pazi's shoulder, a small orange-and-white fish with the furry face of a mouse floated serenely in the air. The mouse-fish glowed faintly and surveyed the surroundings with great interest.

"This is what's nice about a gathering of just a few hundred people," Zap said. "They can really go all-out on treating you right."

"It's nice," Pazi agreed.

A young woman with dark skin and bright, flowy clothing approached the couple. When she drew near, her face lit up and she ran the rest of the distance.

"Oh em gee Pazi you brought Koizumi!"

"Hi Layla," Pazi said with a smile, then shouted "Horn!" in warning as the dark-skinned woman threw her arms about Pazi in a hug.

Layla drew back and surveyed Pazi. "Oh, look at you, girl," she said. "All done up like a Summoner. And look at your little friend!" She reached over to the mouse-fish and tickled it. It made a peculiar cooing noise and nuzzled against Layla's hand.

"You look really great too," Pazi said, then gestured to Zap. "Layla, this is my boyfriend Zap."

"Oh *really*," Layla said, turning to Zap and smirking. "You're the boyfriend, huh? I was beginning to wonder if you were actually here or if Pazi was making you up."

"I've been sort of busy," Zap admitted sheepishly.

"Well, I'll overlook it this time," Layla said, smiling. She reached up to where the fishmouse was floating and scritched him. "Because I'm so very forgiving, aren't I Koizumi? I'm a very forgiving girl, oh yes! Oh, who's a cute little fish mousie!" The spirit cooed, pushing against Layla's hand.

"Don't get him too hyper," Pazi said with a smile. "He'll start draining me before the concert even starts."

"Well, all right," Layla said. "And I've gotta go make my rounds. But I expect to see more of you two later."

"Sure thing," Zap said.

Layla began walking away from the two, and hadn't gone four paces before she spotted someone she knew, threw her arms into the air and ran toward her new target.

"She's so enthusiastic," Pazi said, laughing.

"She's a quarter earth-mutant, isn't she?" Zap asked.

Pazi's face registered surprise. "She is, yes," she confirmed. "You've got a really good eye, Zap."

"I do, don't I?" Zap said idly. "You wanna get some food?"

"Sure," Pazi said.

A minute later, Matt Del Fye and Don Stiles emerged from the facility. Don turned his beady black eyes toward Matt.

He began, "Do you know who—"

"Why don't you go get a drink and try to find a girl to hit on, you creepy fucker?"

Don paused, startled by the unexpected hostility. "Uh," he said. "Okay."

Thus snubbed, "Creepy" Don Stiles walked away, approaching the last bar at which he'd ever have the opportunity to buy a drink.

Meanwhile, Alan and Paru sat at the bar in the pavilion, facing toward the crowd. They watched as Zap and Pazi chatted with each other.

"They're cute," Paru said.

"I guess," Alan said.

Paru raised an eyebrow and gave Alan an inquisitive look, but did not question further. She spun on her stool, faced the bar, and placed her forearms on the bartop. "Lorenzo, my dear barkeep," she said.

"Miss Dupree?" the bartender asked.

Paru gestured to Alan as he too spun to face the bar. "My employee and I," she said, "will each have a Wyrmscale."

"A Wyrmscale?" Alan asked. The bartender whistled a low tone and went to work.

"Do you know what a Wyrmscale is, Alan?" Paru asked.

"It's one of about five drinks that both contain Dragon's Breath liquor and are non-fatal to humans."

"Right you are," Paru said. "I heard about your shift's Kekkai exercise today."

"Oh?" Alan said.

"I heard that you beat Raimi And The Soft Winds Blow in single combat," Paru continued.

"Well, that's not exactly—"

"I heard it from Raimi," Paru said. She clapped Alan on the shoulder. As always, Alan was caught off-guard by his manager's iron grip. "While she may embellish, Raimi does not lie."

Alan shrugged.

"Alan, when I first hired you I never figured you for a fighter," Paru said as the bartender worked. "When you went to uni for business, I never thought you'd achieve anything further than Business Casual combat certification. When you gained your rifle certification, I thought it was a business decision and would never be anything more."

"It was," Alan said.

Paru looked at him intently. "But you took those skills and you put your heart behind them in combat. You've gained fire, Alan, and I appreciate that. That is why you are going to have a Wyrmscale with me, and you are going to speak a dragon rune."

Alan looked more than a bit unsettled at the prospect.

Just as cheering erupted from the stage area of the pavilion, the bartender set three small shots on the bartop, all three giving off faint plumes of smoke.

Paru canted her head and gave the bartender a pointed look. "I only ordered two shots, Lorenzo."

"Be that as it may," a deep voice said, "you're not the only one who heard of this morning's magnificent battle."

Both Paru and Alan whirled to see the square-shouldered figure of Sir Orin Erdrick standing nearby. "Allow me to drink with you," he rumbled.

Alan and Paru made room for the Knight.

At the grassy open area of the pavilion, the crowd roared as Thorvald Volnocht walked onstage. He reached the center of the stage and saluted the crowd, who cheered their approval.

"My cherished employees," Thorvald said, his voice washing over the crowd, augmented by the stage's resonance plates. "On this our sixty-seventh employee retreat, we have arranged a very special group of performers for today's concert. You have trained and fought hard. You have made me proud. And it is for that reason that I am delighted to present to you..."

The magical screen flickered off, revealing a stunningly beautiful woman standing in front of a full band.

"*Ellis Manteaux!*" Thorvald shouted. The audience of hundreds cheered as though they were thousands, their surprise overtaken by their enthusiasm.

Thorvald made way for the megastar, who approached the front of the stage slowly. The employees there would later relate to their friends that the celebrity was even more beautiful in person than on the ether. She was curvy but svelte and moved to emphasize her assets. Her hair was long and lustrous, blonde with colorful streaks. She wore a silver-themed outfit, completed with a flat-topped cap.

She reached the stage and held up one hand. The crowd silenced at her command.

"You know," Manteaux murmured, her honey-like voice carrying from the resonance plates and washing over the crowd, "I've been shopping at the Securemarket™ since I was a little girl, and these days I couldn't imagine going anywhere else."

The crowd screamed. Ellis gave them a wide grin and counted off her first song. "One! Two! Three! Four!"

"Wow," Pazi said.

"Holy shit," Zap said, blinking. "That's really Ellis Manteaux. To'mas is going to spooge himself."

Not too far away, his eyes riveted to the stage, To'mas said to Violet, "I think I just came."

"You'd better save some for later," Violet scolded.

"What?" To'mas's roommate said.

"*L'Chaim*," Sir Erdrick said.

"*L'Chaim!*" Alan and Paru echoed.

The three tossed back their shots. All closed their eyes.

Nearby, Koizumi sniffed the air and made an inquisitive chirp. Pazi looked around. "Koizumi smells Dragon Magic," she said.

Zap blinked and looked briefly distant. He turned his head to the bar and pointed. "There."

"That's..."

"Wyrmscale!" Zap said, excited. "They've just had Wyrmscale! Brace yourself!"

Sir Erdrick's eyes flew open, suffused with white light. He uttered the word "*Thaum*" in a powerful, otherworldly voice. A hot wind whipped through the area.

Paru's light-filled eyes opened, she spoke "*Agon*" and all eyes nearby drew toward her.

Finally Alan, who seemed to be wracked with pain and fighting to stay upright, literally rose into the air briefly as his eyes flew open and light poured from them. He said "*Talor*" and every object nearby almost seemed to perk up, waiting for his command.

Emma Rammek, the quarter-dragon early-morning supervisor of 15th and Neimuth, who had been sitting near Zap and Pazi, raised her eyebrows. "Never would have pegged Alan as the type to say *that* one," she said.

Alan collapsed against the bartop, coughing up smoke. Paru smiled proudly and Sir Erdrick patted him on the back.

"Holy shit," Alan coughed and slowly straightened. "I ... I feel amazing."

"Let's get this man another drink," Sir Erdrick said.

Matthew watched the crowd from his vantage point, standing on the roof of the facility. He tapped his wrist and looked at the glowing numbers that appeared on his arm. When he looked up, his face was deadly serious. "It's time," he said.

"Good," the cat-eared girl crouched behind him said. "I'm tired of waiting."

Matt turned to face her. "Are you scared?"

"Yes," she said.

"You will be safe," Matt replied.

"I trust you," the girl replied.

"Let's go," Matt said.

Far below, in the throng of people, Steve and Mike watched Ellis Manteaux move and sing.

"This isn't even my style of music," Steve yelled, "but I'm fucking spellbound. She's amazing."

"She is," Mike agreed at the top of his lungs, still barely audible. "It's like I've got no conception of time while I watch her."

"No conception of—oh shit!" Steve yelled. "I've gotta go!"

"Hurry back, okay?" Mike yelled.

"Okay!"

At the other edge of the crowd, Violet tapped To'mas on the shoulder.

"Wha?" he said.

"You need to go prep for your sting operation," she reminded him.

"Oh!" To'mas said. "Thank you! Please keep Michael company for me."

He took his arm from around his roommate's shoulder, whose face couldn't seem to decide whether it should look relieved or disappointed. Violet immediately took To'mas's place, cuddling close to the confused young man.

Matt and the girl walked to the pavilion's outdoor bar. Matt surveyed the area and nodded. "Mya?" he said.

"Mya?" the girl replied.

"When that man by the taps spills his drink, he will leave. Take his place. The rest will fall into place."

The cat-eared girl nodded.

In a secluded, wooded area about a five-minute walk from the pavilion, To'mas surveyed the area. A small, glimmering magical light made the otherwise pitch-black area clear to To'mas, and he nodded.

"Just as he said," To'mas murmured, then looked under the branch of a tree. "And there's the bag."

To'mas unzipped the duffel bag and began to retrieve equipment from it.

Back at the pavilion, Stephen Anderson jogged to the edge of the covered seating area, where she could see Sir Erdrick, Paru, and Alan talking and laughing. "I'm early," she said. Her eyes swept the area and stopped suddenly as she saw that she was only five paces from Zap and Pazi, both of whom stared right back at her.

"Oh ... um, hey," Steve stammered. "Guys."

"Hey," Zap said. Pazi fidgeted.

"How's it going?" Steve asked.

"Pretty good," Zap said.

There was an awkward silence.

Not far away, "Creepy" Don Stiles approached the bar near the stage, his sunken eyes sweeping over the crowd. He shouldered past a beer-soaked man who was walking away and found his own section of the bar. He leaned on it.

His eyes suddenly caught a beautiful Pol's Cat girl in her mid-twenties standing at the bar, watching the singer onstage. Don moved in, his blood pumping in his throat, adrenaline surging. His fingertips began to burn. She was perfect.

She turned as his thigh brushed against her at the bar, excited laughter dying in her throat. Her slitted yellow eyes were reserved, but she looked straight at him and did not shy away. He wanted to push the girl down and ravage her, humiliate her and violate her in front of everyone. Ruin her beautiful face and defile her perfect body. Pull her tail, twist her ears. Reduce that cool superiority to a shame she'd never look up from. He wanted to, but he knew he could not.

Not yet.

"Hey," he said.

"Hey," she replied.

"This is a really good concert," he drawled.

"It sure is," the girl said. "I love Ellis Manteaux."

"Can I buy you a drink?" Don asked.

"Sure," the girl said. "I'd like that."

"Two rum and cokes," Don said to the bartender, who moved to comply.

"What's your name?" Don asked.

"Mya," the girl said.

"I'm Don," Don said.

"It's nice to meet you, Don," Mya said. The bartender set the two drinks down in front of them.

Mya took a sip of her drink and Don did the same. Don watched her throat move as she drank. He followed the outline of her breasts under her shirt. He looked back up at her eyes. She set the drink down.

"So," the girl said. "You're from..."

"The Malachi Park store," Don said. "Late night shift."

"I see," Mya said.

Ellis Manteaux finished the song she had been playing and the audience roared in response. Mya turned to look at the stage. Don passed a hand over the drink he had bought her, and a tablet fell from his hand into the liquid.

No one saw.

Mya turned back, smiling a little bit. The smile turned stale when her eyes moved to Don, but he did not notice or care.

Drink, Don demanded silently. *Drink it.*

"She's really good," Mya said.

"Yes," Don agreed. *Smug bitch.* He reached out and picked up his own drink, taking a long sip.

Do this, he tried to command her mentally. *Do what I'm doing.*

After a few moments of ugly silence, Mya picked up her drink with a shaking hand and took a pull from it. She stared at Don as she did so, her cat-eyes ice cold.

Don watched her drink, his mouth opening in anticipation. Mya set the drink down and blinked at him once.

"Are you having a good time?" Don asked her.

"Mm," she replied.

"Good," Don said. "Good."

Moments passed.

"I feel strange," Mya said.

"Maybe you've had too much to drink," Don said.

"I haven't even finished the one," she said. "I feel sleepy."

"You're tired," Don said. "I'll take you to your room." He advanced toward her.

She could not help but take a step back. "You don't know where my room is," Mya said.

"It'll be fine," Don said. He reached forward and took her around the waist as she lost her balance. "I'll take care of you."

"Ai'shaa protect me," Mya said and went slack in Don's arms. He heaved her arm over his shoulder.

"She's had too much to drink," he said to no one in particular.

Nearby, Steve's shell vibrated. She gasped and picked it up, then read the message she had received.

Now.

Steve rushed over to Sir Erdrick and Paru, who were discussing the next drink that they would goad Alan, who was swaying in his seat, to consume.

She urgently tapped the Corporate Knight's shoulder. He started and whirled, his hand on his sword hilt.

"Sir Erdrick," Steve said. "I—I need to report a crime in progress."

A few minutes later, Don Stiles dragged Mya Ai'o into the wooded area near the pavilion. He grunted with the effort and from the anticipation of the pleasure that awaited him. He soon found an area that suited him, confirmed that it was too far from the pavilion for him to be noticed, and dumped Mya's prone form on the ground.

"Oh yeah," he said. "You bitch. You think you're better than me, but you're not so uppity now."

He crouched and ran his hands greedily over Mya's form, pausing at her slender throat. "Now you're not fighting it. Now you want me. You want it, don't you. Well, I'm going to give it to you."

His hands fumbled with the button of her jeans and undid them. Don's hands shook with anticipation, and the sound of his heartbeat drowned out the sounds of the concert and crowd. He breathed heavily as he grasped the waistband of her jeans with one hand and began to jerk them down. His other desperate hand worked at his own pants.

"You're not so superior now," he panted. "You think you're so big—so special—but now you can't stop me. Now you want it, you whore. Now you want it."

"Light," a deep, imposing voice said, and the clearing was flooded with bright white luminescence.

Don Stiles froze where he was. One hand still gripped his quarry's jeans and panties, holding them halfway down her lightly furred legs. The other was buried within the front zipper of his pants, moments away from pulling his unmentionables into view.

Don's wide eyes fixated on the man who had summoned the magical light: the massive form of Sir Orin Erdrick, senior CK of Securemarket™ Incorporated stood before him and did not look happy. Behind him was a short girl with curly auburn hair whose face was a picture of rage and whose hand repeatedly opened and closed over the grip of a sleek-looking custom pistol.

Several moments passed where no one said anything.

"Well?" Sir Erdrick said. "Mr. Stiles, *is* this what it looks like?"

"No," Don said.

"What, then," Sir Erdrick said through a clenched jaw, "is it?"

"It's consensual," Don said.

"The lady is unconscious," Sir Erdrick said.

"She wasn't when I brought her in," Don said, his mind racing. He realized the position he was still in and let go of the kitty-girl's pants. After a few moments, he extracted his hand from his pants as well.

"The young lady behind me," Sir Erdrick indicated the curly-haired girl, "seems to have footage of you carrying the lady unconscious from the bar."

"And I," a half-elf who had not previously been on the scene said, appearing on Sir Erdrick's other side, "have night-vision footage of you dragging her into this clearing, obviously unconscious."

Sir Erdrick fixed Don with a look and waited for an explanation.

"It's fake," Don said.

Erdrick sighed. "Don Stiles," he said in a long-suffering tone, "there is one reason, and only one reason, that I do not put a bullet in your disgusting loins right now."

Don shrank visibly, placing his hands over his groin.

The CK continued. "That reason is that there are people here whose evening pleasure might be significantly dampened by witnessing a loin-shooting. These people have just done a very good thing and I want them to enjoy the rest of their night."

Don relaxed a little.

"You are, therefore, lucky," Sir Erdrick said. "You will spend the night in the brig. Your reproductive organs will not be shot, but will be removed surgically under anesthetic. Isn't that nice?"

Don gaped. "You can't do that!" he said. "I want a lawyer!"

"Somebody needs to read up on installation law," Sir Erdrick replied. "Come with me, Mr. Stiles, or I will hurt you. I will be carrying the girl, but do not assume that I need my hands free to kill you."

The knight walked to the would-be rapist, who shied away but clambered to his feet. Sir Erdrick kneeled, pulled up and fastened Mya's jeans, then lifted her. As he stood, he saw Matt standing at the edge of the lit clearing.

"...you're Matthew Del Fye, aren't you," he said.

Matt nodded.

"You orchestrated this sting, didn't you," the knight said.

Matt nodded.

"You son of a bitch!" Don said.

"You reap what you sow, Don," Matt said. "Annie Neuhart sends her regards. And her testimony, long-suppressed due to your threats." He flashed his shell.

Don blanched.

"Enough," Sir Erdrick said. "Start walking, Stiles."

In a moment, the clearing was dark again. Back at the pavilion, the crowd cheered.

"So ... I'm going to go see my favorite star now, okay?" To'mas said.

"You'd better," Matt said. "Sir Erdrick gave up a good loin-shooting for you."

"It's a shame that Mya had to end the evening unconscious," Steve said.

"Actually," Matt said, "she's going to meet somebody important this way. It's all for the best."

"Ok," Steve said. "Going back to my date now."

"All right," Matt said. "Oh, and guys?"

"Yeah?" Steve said.

"Yeah?" To'mas, slightly further away, said.

"Thank you."

Back at the concert, Ellis Manteaux had whipped the crowd into a frenzy. She strutted back and forth, fixing them all with a playful smile.

"You all seem so happy!" she said.

The audience cheered.

"But you haven't always been happy, right?" she asked, tracing a tear down her face. "Everybody has sad times. And angry times."

Music started up behind Ellis, and she walked to the time of the beat, grinning at the audience. She held up one finger. "I know that *once* you were sad..."

She held up another finger. "And you've had angry times *two*..."

Realizing what was coming, the audience started to shout their approval.

"But if you're like me you know you'll be..." Ellis said.

She gestured to the band, then sang, "*A whole lot better once you get to three...*"

The band struck up a high-energy beat and got an enthusiastic response from the crowd. Ellis sang, letting her powerful voice fill the pavilion.

> *Johnny met Ellie at the club*
> *and Johnny decided he was in love*
> *but Ellie didn't share his point of view*
>
> *After time Ellie changed her mind*

About being the Johnny-loving kind
but sadly Johnny had changed his too

The first try
they just couldn't get
The second try
no it's not right yet

We can't seem to find our luck
Isn't it time to give it up?

Ellis beckoned to the audience, who shouted in unison, "NO!" Ellis enthusiastically belted out the chorus.

What's here, what's there, what's in-between
Brown, red and green upon the trees
What is, what was and what's to be
All understand the Rule of Threes

The flower, honey and the mead
The gale, the still air and the breeze
The oak, the sapling and the seed
All understand the Rule of Threes

"How did it go?" Mike shouted to Steve as Ellis continued the song, much of the crowd singing along with her.
"What?" Steve shouted.
"How did it go?!"
"Well!"
"I'm glad!"
"What?"
In another part of the crowd, To'mas and Violet draped over To'mas's roommate Michael Duncan, whose uncertainty seemed to have been soundly trounced by the sensation of being touched by pretty people.
"Michael," To'mas said into his roommate's ear.
"Yeah?" Michael said.

"Violet is coming home with us," he said.
"Oh," Michael said.
"That sound okay?"
"Uh..." Michael said, hesitant. Violet made a happy noise, running her hand down Michael's chest.
"Yeah," Michael said, "that sounds fine."
At the covered area of the pavilion, Alan reeled. "Shouldn't ... I be getting sick at this point?"
Paru laughed, a bit inebriated herself. She slapped Alan hard on the back. "Study harder, Alan!" she said, grinning. "The Dragon's Breath you had raises your body's natural defenses; you won't be getting sick tonight. Come on, let's go dance."
"O-okay," Alan said, moving off of his stool cautiously.
Zap saw Alan pass by unsteadily and laughed. "Oh man, Paru's got Alan blitzed. She looks so steady compared to him."
"Hey Zap..." Pazi said.
"Yeah?" Zap said, turning toward Pazi.
"Kiss me," Pazi said and shifted the horn upward on her head. "I promise not to stab you."
Zap smiled at Pazi, then took her into his arms and kissed her.
On the lawn in front of the stage, Steve and Mike swayed to the thrumming beat. Mike moved his head down and gently nuzzled Steve's cheek. Steve nuzzled back. Mike kissed Steve's cheek, and she turned her head. They shared a kiss in the middle of the crowd while Ellis Manteaux sung only meters away.

> *What's here, what's there, what's in-between*
> *Brown, red and green upon the trees*
> *What is, what was and what's to be*
> *All understand the Rule of Threes*

> *The flower, honey and the mead*
> *The gale, the still air and the breeze*
> *The oak, the sapling and the seed*
> *All understand the Rule of Threes*

37

The concert had come to a close around 3:00 when Manteaux played the encore, her mega-popular cover of "Million Miles from Home". She left the stage to a chorus of excited cheers and a colorful light show.

By the time 4:00 had rolled around, most of the concertgoers had left the pavilion. Many went to their own rooms; some found themselves with different destinations. A few stragglers stayed behind for a while, but were soon ushered inside by the staff members, who were eager to clean and strike the pavilion area.

The strike was a concerted and very quick operation. The staff had moved all of the equipment and removed most of the stage by 5:00, and many of the crew left the scene then.

At 5:25, a few crew members were scattered about the remains of the pavilion, checking for leftover trash and finding little (the employee concertgoers had been informed that they would be made to perform any cleanup that the staff could not complete in a timely fashion). Soon, the field was nearly empty.

From the highest sturdy branch of a tree near the pavilion, Click watched the dwindling cleanup crew perform their duties. His face was somber and he observed the crew's activities dispassionately. Crouched on the branch, he sat still for several minutes more before unclenching his body and looking up at the sky.

A few seconds later, he reached to his side and pulled his shell from its holster. He tapped its surface several times, and then held its speaker to his ear.

It rang for what seemed like a very long time. Then a voice answered him, "Seelie Court, Lord Oberon's office."

"Uh, yes," Click said, then cleared his throat. "Um, this is Click o'th'Granfalloon."

"How may I help you, Click?" the voice asked.

"I'd just ... like a card, please."

"All right, please hold on." There was the sound of a keyboard's keys clicking. Click waited as patiently as he could manage, but even in his anxious state he knew it was taking too long.

"Is something the matter?" Click asked.

"Mr. Click, I can't seem to find you in our database," the voice said.

A cold fear stabbed Click. "Could you check the lesser Seelie database?" he asked.

"I'm afraid I already have," the voice said. "Beltane has occurred recently, Mr. Click. Would you like me to connect you to the New Washington Greater Court?"

"Yes, please," Click said in a small voice.

Hold music played in Click's ear.

The wyvern took the monkey for a ride in the sky
Because the monkey said that he could learn to fly
The wyvern tried to throw the monkey into the snow
The monkey turned around and said "Now listen Joe,"

"Oh, come *on*," Click murmured, fidgeting.

Straighten up and fly right
Don't you sting and don't bite
Straighten up and fly right
Calm down, baby, don't—

"New Washington Greater Faerie Court, how can I help you?"

"Hi," Click said. "This is Click o'th'Granfalloon. I'd like to request a card."

"One moment please," the voice said, and the hold music came on again.

—looked the wyvern right dead in the face
And said "Your story's lovely, but it sounds outta place."

Click sighed.

Straighten up and fly right
Don't you sting and don't bite
Straighten up and—

The line came to life. "Thank you for your card request. It will arrive shortly." The line disconnected.

Click lowered his shell and reholstered it. About twenty seconds passed, then Click heard a rushing noise and saw a tarot-sized card fluttering down through the air. He lashed out and caught it in his left hand, facing away from him.

He stared at the back of the card for a few moments, then swallowed and turned it over.

On the front of the card was an elaborate picture of a beautiful, black-haired woman drawn in heavy, colorful strokes. The woman looked at Click with an icy, smirking glare of triumph. A ribbon below her pale visage read "Mab."

Mab. Queen of the Unseelie Court.

Click let his hand fall slack and watched the card flutter to the ground.

Arc III

Rule of Threes

Tales from the Reynaldo's™

Michelle-Bear snaked her way through her tables, her eyes scanning the levels of drinks in their glasses, the state of food on plates. Due to another server calling in sick, she was handling twice as many tables as she usually did. Rather than falling into a frenzied state of panic, Michelle-Bear had gone into what she considered 'performance mode', a focused state of being where nothing at all existed except the small windows of interaction she had with her tables. To her customers, she was warm. To her coworkers, she was swift and efficient and spoke far less than usual.

Michelle-Bear had traveled the better part of the way to the kitchen when she crossed one of her tables that had not yet placed their order; sitting at the table was a family of four. She had made note of this table as potentially troublesome when they first arrived. It was not because they had been fussy; in fact, the family was particularly polite. The children, one of whom was in his tweens and the other probably around seven, were both well-mannered and friendly. The husband was a man in his early middle age with a warm, earnest demeanor. His wife was a redhead with smiling eyes, a clever sort who was prone to witticisms and seemed to enjoy joking with Michelle-Bear in what little time they interacted.

No, it was not the way the family acted. It was one small flower on the aloha shirt the husband wore. A rose.

Michelle-Bear stopped in front of the family's table and bent at the waist, leaning down so that her face was almost level with them. "Are you folks ready to order?" she asked. She flashed a winning smile at them.

"Yes, I think we are," the husband said. He looked over at the kids. "Jaz, would you start?"

"Okay, daddy," the little girl said. "I will have the fish an' chips, please," she said. "And a Go-Go Cola."

"Fish and chips," Michelle-Bear said as she tapped out the order on her workshell, "and a Go-Go Cola for the polite young lady. And you sir?"

"I'll have a Reynaldo's Burger with fries," the son said. "And a Spun Glass soda."

"How would you like that Reynaldo's Burger?" Michelle-Bear asked.

"Well done," he said. His father sighed and shook his head.

"And for you two?" Michelle-Bear asked the couple.

"I'll have the shepherd's pie," the wife said, "if it's made with fresh shepherds."

"The sirloin," the husband said. "As raw as possible."

"Of course," Michelle-Bear said, giving him a bright smile. She straightened to her full height, towering over the family for a moment, then strode to the kitchen to place their order.

Several minutes passed without incident. Somewhere, a rabbit ventured from its burrow, found a particularly succulent patch of weeds, and ate them. They were delicious.

At the front of the restaurant, a man in a business suit entered the restaurant. The hostess greeted him.

"Hello, sir, welcome to Reynaldo's. How many in your party?"

The man did not respond.

"Sir?" the hostess asked. "How many in your party?"

"Sir Kunimitsu," the man replied.

"I'm afraid I don't understand," the hostess said, nervous.

"Pardon me," the man said, pushing past the hostess.

The husband of the family who had been seated in Michelle-Bear's section saw the newcomer to the restaurant and froze. The family noted their patriarch's behavior soon, and each one turned to see where his gaze had gone. Each one averted their gaze in turn, realizing that the scene was about to take a turn.

"Sir Kunimitsu," the man who had just entered the restaurant said.

"Sir Birchmore," the husband of the family said.

There was a long pause. Those who had been seated at nearby tables hushed one by one as the gravity of the situation slowly occurred to them.

"You're ... waiting for a seat, I hope?" Kunimitsu said. His family remained hushed, not looking at the other knight.

Sir Birchmore cast a flat gaze at Sir Drake Kunimitsu.

"No," Sir Kunimitsu said. "I must assume not."

"Sir Drake Kunimitsu," Sir Birchmore began, "you are—"

"Sir Birchmore!" Sir Kunimitsu interrupted. "Please. My family and I are ... we're having dinner."

"Sir Kunimitsu," Sir Birchmore said. "I'm not certain that I can adequately describe the month that I have had."

"I don't—" Sir Kunimitsu began.

"Quiet," Sir Birchmore replied. "I am certain that you have heard the rumors about my company's contracts. Perhaps you have heard the rumors concerning my marriage as well. I have had a supermarket employee dress me down and I did not so much as kill him. I am not happy, Sir Kunimitsu, and if the only thing I can have right now is satisfaction from you in the form of your blood, I will take it happily."

Sir Kunimitsu's family tensed and avoided Sir Birchmore's gaze studiously.

"Have you no citations for me?" Sir Birchmore asked. "No defense?"

"I..." Sir Kunimitsu said. "I'm ... having dinner with my family."

"You leave my daddy alone!" the girl of the family said.

"Jaz!" Sir Kunimitsu said.

"Silence, child," Sir Birchmore said. "You have nothing for me, Sir Kunimitsu?"

His opponent was silent.

"Then we end this now," Sir Birchmore said, advancing toward his opponent.

Suddenly, something large and heavy swung in an arc in front of Sir Birchmore. The knight stopped in his tracks just as the head of a massive hammer struck the ground with a deafening CRACK, slamming into the plastic floor hard enough to leave a mark.

Sir Birchmore stepped back half a pace and found himself face to face with an angry woman who was nearly thirty centimeters taller than he. Her face was deadly calm, but her eyes bored holes into his head. She stared at him with a murderously intent gaze.

"Excuse me," Sir Birchmore said, not nearly as aggressively as he had hoped.

"Get out," the woman said.

"If you intend to interrupt this duel," Sir Birchmore told her as firmly as he could, "I would love to hear a citation."

"Urza," the woman said, "versus fuckface."

"W-what?" Sir Birchmore stammered.

"That's the duel where a young waitress collapsed the head of a cranky knight who was intent on killing a good man in front of his children because he was dissatisfied with the size of his penis. Care to see it play out?" The woman set her jaw and stared at Sir Birchmore.

Nearby, one of the woman's co-workers hissed an objection to her, but she was deaf to it. Her attention remained on Sir Birchmore.

Sir Birchmore's hand flew to the hilt of his sword. Michelle-Bear's hand tensed about the hilt of her maul. The two stared at each other for a few moments, and then Sir Birchmore's face softened slightly as a memory struck him. A scene seemed to run through his head, and his hand relaxed on the hilt of his sword.

"...you," he said. "You and he both..."

There was another tense silence. Sir Birchmore released the hilt of his sword and stood up straight, looking into Michelle-Bear's eyes.

"What is it about you and him?" he asked. "What is it that makes me question myself?"

"Just leave my restaurant," the woman said. "Please."

Sir Birchmore slowly turned away from her and started walking. Michelle-Bear did not relax until the knight had left the restaurant, at which point she slumped, letting the head of her maul hammer rest on the floor of the restaurant. She sighed.

"Michelle-Bear!" the voice of Charis, the shift host, trilled in her ear. "You confronted a knight! You could get fired for this!"

Michelle-Bear ignored her coworker and turned to Sir Kunimitsu and his family. She looked at them, cleared her throat and smiled cheerfully. She bent at the waist once again, this time leaning on the haft of her hammer.

"I..." Sir Kunimitsu said.

"Your food'll be out soon," Michelle-Bear said with a winning smile. "I'm sorry for the wait."

"Thank you," the wife said with no trace of humor. She was not referring to the food.

Michelle-Bear gave a small, lopsided smile and shrugged. "What ... else could I do?"

"I like your hammer, Miss Michelle Bears," the little girl, Jaz, said. "And your hat."

"Thank you," Michelle-Bear said. "You are an awesome little girl. I will get you folks your food shortly."

Michelle-Bear straightened, cast the trigger spell to release her hammer-locks, folded it and slung it across her back again. She then set off toward the kitchen, humming a nervous tune to herself.

38

Steve stirred as the sunlight that had filtered in through the window struck her face. She found herself initially disoriented that she seemed to have so much space on the bed. She wondered briefly if she had finally cleared the smithing components from one half of her bed, then remembered for the fifth time that she was not at her apartment in New Washington. She opened her eyes gradually, squinting to avoid being blinded, and was surprised again as she realized that she was looking not up at the ceiling of her dormitory room, but at the bottom of another bed.

Did Violet and I switch beds?

She rolled to her side as she mulled over the situation and found a boy there. She stifled a surprised gasp as her memory woke fully, reminding her of precisely what had happened the previous night.

Steve spent several moments simply looking at Mike's face as he slept.

"Oh," she said, her expression one of dazed wonder. She reached forward and touched Mike's face. "Oh wow."

Around the time that Steve was waking, To'mas's shell began playing a cheerful rendition of Ellis Manteaux's *Elemental*. One of the three people crowded on the nearby bed stirred; however, it was not To'mas. After one full chorus of the song, Violet made an irritated noise and crawled to the edge of the bed. She grabbed To'mas's shell, tapped it and held it to her ear.

"To'mas's shell," she said in a sleepy voice. "Mm? No, this is, uh. This is his sister. How can I help you."

Violet listened to the voice on the other end of the line.

"Oh, no kidding," Violet said. "B-Rank Rifle, huh? I'm sure he'll be ecstatic. I'll let him know once he wakes up. It'll probably be a while; he was very busy last night."

Pause.

"Not at all," Violet said. "You have a lovely weekend yourself."

Violet tapped the shell again, set it on the dresser, and crawled back into the bed with To'mas and his roommate.

"Ellis Manteaux," Alan said into his shell, holding a cold-pack to his head. "It was really something."

He tried to get up as he listened to the person on the other end of the line, but halfway up he went pale and sat down again.

"Oogh," he said. "You wouldn't believe how much alcohol Paru threw at me, Nalley," he said. "She made me drink a Wyrmscale. It's a shot that contains two drops of an alcohol that's generally considered lethal to most humanoids. Yeah."

He lay back carefully on his bed.

"I'm waiting for the meds to kick in so I can actually function, first. I don't really remember how the evening ended."

He listened to Nalley speak for a little bit.

"Yeah," he said. "I miss you a lot too. We're halfway there."

He put his hand to his temple and winced in pain.

"Iyesu, Nalley, please don't start singing."

A pleasant smell roused Zap.

"The mighty hunter," he murmured sleepily, "smells his coffee prey."

"Which his girlfriend already caught for him," Pazi teased. Zap opened his eyes and looked up at her. Pazi wore an ornately-decorated silk robe. A little sunburst with glowing spidery legs sat on her shoulder.

"Morning Pazi," Zap said. "Morning Solay."

"And good morning to you," Pazi said. She pulled the coffee pot from its housing. "I assume you want some of this?"

"Yes please," Zap said, slowly sitting up and blinking in the sunlight. "That would be nice."

"Last night was lovely," Pazi said. "Thank you for spending it with me."

"Likewise," Zap said with a big smile. "I had a wonderful time."

Mya's eyes fluttered open, then snapped shut quickly to hide from the glare of the full-spectrum lamps above her. She cautiously squinted, getting used to the light gradually. She did not recognize her location.

"Where…" she murmured.

"Oh," a voice said, "you're awake."

The face of a very handsome man in his early thirties appeared above Mya. He was wearing a pair of eyeglasses and a lab coat, indicating that he was probably a doctor.

"Am I in the infirmary?" Mya asked.

"Right you are," the doctor said. "I'm Dr. Scott Wallace. Feel free to call me Scott."

"What happened?" Mya asked, unsure of exactly how much she should say.

Dr. Wallace frowned. "You were drugged," he said. "The man who drugged you seemed to be intending to … force himself upon you, but was stopped by an intervening party of several employees and Sir Erdrick himself. You're a very lucky woman."

"Yes," Mya said, sighing with relief. "I am."

"Well, you take it easy for now," Dr. Wallace said, "but you should be feeling absolutely normal in a few hours."

"Thank you, Dr. Wallace," Mya said.

"Of course," Dr. Wallace said with a smile. "And please. Scott really is fine."

39

Zap leaned back in his chair and looked out of the mess hall's window, quietly admiring the view of the woods outside that it provided. He lifted a piece of buttered toast and took a bite out of it, then surveyed the room behind him. The cafeteria didn't have too many people in it; it was too early for the hard partiers to come seeking food but late enough that the early risers had already come and gone. Zap turned back to the picturesque landscape.

Several minutes later, he heard someone approach his table and turned around. Steve pulled out a chair and sat down. "Hey," she said, more cheerful than Zap could remember Steve being since she found out about Pazi.

"Hey," he said.

"It's a really nice morning," she said, looking out of the window. "We got really good timing for the concert."

"We did," he said. "Thanks for coming, anyway."

"Sure," she said. "I haven't seen that much of you. It's nice to spend some time with you."

Zap looked at her suspiciously, then studied her face. He leaned back, smiled and nodded. "I know that glow."

Steve blushed.

"I guess things went well with Mike," Zap said, smiling.

"Yeah," Steve said. "We really connected. It was good."

She paused and sniffed once.

"And 'yesu was it a relief," she said, grinning. "Do you know how long it's been since I got laid?"

Zap laughed. "Okay, good; you're not possessed," he said. "I was beginning to wonder if it was really Steve in there."

"Hey, shut up," Steve said. "How were things with Pazi?"

"Pretty good," Zap said. "Pretty good. Oh! How was the sting operation?"

"Successful," Steve replied. "Creepy Don's probably been sterilized by now, if Sir Erdrick was serious. If he's feeling benevolent, they might extradite him to New Washington to give him a 'fair' trial."

"He's in Malachi Park, though, isn't he?" Zap asked. "That's ... what, Precinct Eight?"

"I think it's Eighteen now," Steve said.

Zap shuddered. "He'll be lucky if he gets just forced sterilization and exile."

"Hi-def," Steve said. "Did you hear about the executive they caught embezzling from the municipal funds?"

"Didn't they throw him into the Labyrinth?" Zap asked.

"They did," Steve confirmed. "And gave him a pistol, just to add insult to injury."

"Barbaric, man," Zap said, shaking his head. "Remind me to cancel my Merc District vacation."

"Your Labyrinth vacation, too?" Steve joked as she got to her feet. "Hang on, I wanna get something to chew on."

Zap nodded and Steve left, curls bobbing behind her as she strode away. Zap watched her ass as she went, formless though it was in the overalls she'd worn to the cafeteria. He turned back to the window and surveyed the landscape.

"We should go to the lagoon," he said to no one, "before we have to go home."

A few minutes later, Steve returned with a food-laden tray. "Ping," she said.

"Pong," Zap replied.

"You know who I didn't see last night but expected to?" Steve asked.

"Who?"

"Click," Steve said. "I didn't see him at all."

"That *is* weird," Zap agreed, though he didn't turn away from the window.

"I wasn't surprised to see that Loren hadn't come…"

"Now that's something," Zap said, now turning to Steve, "I have been wondering about. Do you really think that any New Washingtonian could possibly be as boring as Loren is?"

"Well," Steve said. "Sure, maybe. Some people just don't want excitement."

"But Loren just has *nothing* going on. It seems weird, doesn't it?"

Steve rocked her head back and forth for a moment. "You think he's a Guardian?" she asked.

"Maybe," Zap replied. "But usually they have more colorful identities."

"A dragon?"

"No dragon could voluntarily be so low-profile."

Steve tapped her chin. "Maybe he's an ancient mage."

Zap nodded. "It's possible," he replied. "I have thought about that one."

"Maybe he's just a normal guy," Steve said with a smirk.

"I suppose that should at least be in the pile," Zap agreed.

"Oh by the way," Steve said, "Mike said that the Rose Street employees are planning a Suite Party tonight. You wanna come?"

"Possibly," Zap said. "I'd kinda like to know what else is going on. Has Violet mentioned 11th Street planning anything?"

"I haven't seen Violet since the concert, Zap."

"Oh yeah," he said absently.

"You should come," Steve said, then turned around and looked around. "Oh hey, there's Click." She indicated a table at the far corner of the mess hall.

"'zat right?" Zap asked without looking. He picked the toast up from his plate and bit into it again.

"He looks pretty down," Steve said. "I wonder if something happened to him."

Zap shrugged and continued his breakfast.

40

Zap knocked on the door to the suite. He allowed half a minute to pass in the hopes that someone inside would hear him over the din inside. They did not. Zap raised his fist and pounded on the door hard, eliciting a few startled noises just inside the suite.

The door swung open. Abruptly, Zap was confronted by the clouded but still intense eyes of a drink-addled half-elf. She had one hand where her swords would be, if she were wearing them.

"Yayzoo, tryin' knock th' door off?!" she demanded in a voice loud enough that it echoed down the hallway and back up.

"Evening, Miss And the Soft Winds Blow," Zap said politely.

"Whooo...?" Raimi asked, squinting her eyes and tilting her head. She studied his face for a few minutes and Zap watched recognition slowly dawn in her eyes.

"Ohh," she said. "Yer that whizzer boy. Sap."

"Zap," Zap agreed. "May I come in?"

"Yah, sure," Raimi agreed, grinning widely and stumbling inside. "But only if y' stop using my last name 'n conv'rsation."

Zap stepped inside the suite. It was a very spacious suite, obviously the store manager's, but even then it was occupied from wall-to-wall. Securemarket™ employees from every shift and most of the stores packed the suite, talking, laughing and drinking.

Raimi groped at a nearby side table and picked up her drink, a dark-colored fizzy concoction in the kind of cheap red tumbler commonly associated with University parties. She gestured to Zap and indicated that he should follow her, then slipped out of sight in the press of bodies.

Zap cursed and attempted to follow, shouldering his way through the crowd as fast as he could while trying to keep his eyes on Raimi's mousy brown braid. He passed between the clumps of partiers and avoided drink-bearing hands as best as he could. He had almost caught up to his guide when a hand clapped him on the shoulder roughly, halting his progress.

Zap whirled, a wandless defense spell forming in his mind before he saw who had grabbed him: it was To'mas's roommate. The young man looked wild-eyed and nervous.

"You're To'mas's coworker, right?" the roommate said.

"Uh-huh," Zap confirmed. "Michael, right?"

"Right," Michael said, then looked around as though searching for armed pursuers. "Are ... Violet and To'mas here?"

"I dunno," Zap said. "I just got here."

Michael grabbed Zap's shoulders. "I don't know what to do," he said. "I—I can't control myself around them."

"Yeah, that happens to people," Zap said, glancing in the direction Raimi had gone. Naturally, she was completely obscured by the crowd, so he turned back to Michael.

"I did things with them last night," Michael said, stricken. "*Both* of them."

"Okay," Zap said.

Michael stared at Zap, who responded with an unimpressed look.

"*Both* of them!"

"Uh-huh," Zap said.

"They ... that isn't right; they can't *do* that!"

"Okay," Zap replied. "They didn't force you or anything, right?"

"Well no," Michael said, seeming a bit surprised. "But—"

"Did you say 'no'?"

"No," Michael said, slowly realizing that he was losing ground. "But—"

"Did they even *pressure* you?" Zap asked.

"...kind of?" Michael said uncertainly.

Zap put his hand on Michael's shoulder.

"Michael, my man," Zap said. "I'd love to feel sorry for you, but even *I* see you as prey."

"What?" Michael whimpered.

Zap clapped his shoulder once more and walked back into the crowd, leaving Michael confused and helpless behind him.

Zap wandered through the press of bodies, trying to pick out the lithe form of Raimi And The Soft Winds Blow. Even the concert had not seemed this crowded, and Zap found himself having to fight the urge to throw elbows at the nearby partiers.

After a few minutes of fruitless searching, Zap sighed and tapped the nearest partygoer, who turned to him. He was a morph of equine stock, a bipedal, muscular horse-man of average height and with grey fur.

"*Sumimasen ga*," Zap said. He found it difficult to raise his voice over the crowd's talking, having nearly blown it out at the concert last night. "Have you seen Raimi And The Soft Winds Blow?"

"Whose winds?" the horse morph said.

"Raimi And The Soft Winds Blow," Zap said loudly. "The Rosebud supervisor!"

"Oh," the morph replied. "I don't know anybody from Rosebud. I'm from Malachi Park."

"Oh," Zap said, then looked curious. "Did you work with Creepy Don Stiles?"

"Yeah," the horse-man said. "I heard he got arrested for attempted rape."

Zap nodded. "He did," he said.

"Good fuckin' riddance," the horse said.

"Hi-Def," Zap agreed. "Hey, where can I get a drink?"

The horse morph pointed in a direction Zap had not been headed in. "Just go until you see somebody towering over everybody else. That's the store manager, Basil, and he's manning the booze table."

"Thanks!" Zap replied, and then resumed his journey through the party.

Once Zap was about halfway there, he saw a man with curly brown hair rising above the rest of the crowd. Zap continued on his path, beelining for the man. He was eventually able to push his way past the press of bodies, which had gotten denser as Zap approached the table. Once he was nearly to the table, he realized that he had found his quarry; Raimi was involved in animated conversation with the large man.

Raimi soon caught sight of Zap. "*There* you are!" she said. "Why din't you follow me?"

Zap laughed. "You moved too fast."

"Bullshit," Raimi said. "Anyway. Sap, this is Basil McCabe, the store manager of Rose Street."

Basil grinned down at Zap. Zap noted that Basil appeared to be both the largest and the most outwardly jovial human that he had ever seen.

"Sap!" Basil said, extending a huge paw. "Pleased ta meet ya!"

Zap shook Basil's hand and found it to be far less crushing than he had expected.

"Hear you an' yer team put up one helluva fight against me Buds."

"We did our best," Zap conceded with a smile.

"Fantastic," Basil said. "Time was, 15th street wasn't nothin' but dull sugarknives: fragile an' useless. Since Paru took over, things is changed."

"Paru's very motivational," Zap said.

"Paru's *scary*, man," Basil warned. "I'm not sure if you've ever seen her in a fight, but I hate getting pitted against her. Woman's scary accurate with an assault rifle and cool as an ice mutant on Shiva Street."

"I'll keep that in mind."

"So, you want something, my man?" Basil spread his hands to indicate the bounty in front of him, which was quite impressive. While not a full bar, Basil had all of the basics and quite a few more eclectic choices. Zap's magical awareness noted a familiar tingle behind the table and realized that Basil was keeping a bottle of Aura and probably several other rare liquors back there.

"Uh," Zap said. "I'll have a Grabet and Go."

"Pong," Basil said, his hands moving to the Grabet whiskey and a nearby bottle of Go-Go Cola.

"Hey Sap," Raimi said to Zap.

"Zap," Zap corrected glibly.

"Whatever," Raimi said. "So what's up wi' me seeing you with two diff'rent girls alla time? I talked to Alan one time an' he said you were only seein' one girl."

"I'm only seeing one girl," Zap said. "Pazi Elwynn, from After Elevens."

"Oh," Raimi said. "So yer jus' friends with, uh ... Scott."

"Steve," Zap corrected. "And yeah."

"Right, Steve," Raimi said, nodding. "I was kind of confused."

"No problem," Zap said. "It's easy to confuse."

"Grabet and Go," Basil said, holding out the ice-cold drink. "Or stay, whatever."

Zap took the drink, ignoring the overused pun. "Thanks!"

"No problem!" Basil said. "Hey, listen, I heard that a few employees from your shift ran into Creepy Don Stiles raping a girl."

"Not quite," Zap said. "They got there before it started, thankfully."

"That's good," Basil said, then turned to Raimi. "Who'd you say the girl was?"

"Mya Ai'o," Raimi replied. "A Pol's Cat from Rising Elevens."

"That's Violet's shift, ain't it?" Basil asked. "D'you know Violet Crenshaw, Sap?"

"Zap," Zap said. "And yeah. Violet's Steve's roommate."

"Oh, Violet's a trip," Basil guffawed. "I like to hang out with those kids. Violet an' Tea an' Dead Kate Smiles an' the Aphid Kid."

"Hey, isn't that your friend Steve over there?" Raimi said, pointing.

Zap turned. Next to a press of chatting partygoers, Steve stood against the wall, pinned there by her new friend Mike, who was kissing her passionately. Steve seemed to be enjoying the attention a great deal; her eyes were closed and her fingers twined with Mike's.

Something thrashed in Zap's gut and he looked down at his drink, then up at Basil.

"Hey, uh," he asked. "Where's the bathroom?"

"That way," Basil said. "But good luck getting to it. Find your way back; I'd love to chat with you more, my man."

"Maybe," Zap said, and pushed into the crowd.

41

To'mas and Zap sat on the roof of the dormitory building, their backs pressed against the smooth industrial plastic of the building's Communications Multitower. The crisp, clean ocean air swept by in a gentle breeze, gently tugging on the tops of distant foliage. The moon, nearly full, cast a bright light onto the island, nearly overcoming the floodlights surrounding the facility.

The boys were still wearing their party clothes, and To'mas had brought one of the red plastic tumblers with him, filled to the brim with an unhealthy-looking University-strength drink. After a minute or two of watching the moon, Zap sighed and reached into his shirt pocket, pulling a pack of rose cigarettes from it.

"Thanks for taking me up here," Zap said, flipping open the pack and withdrawing a cigarette.

"No problem," To'mas said. "You looked pretty unhappy when I ran into you. I was going to refresh my roommate's conditioning, but a guy's got to have priorities."

"Well, I appreciate it," Zap said as he stuck the cigarette in his mouth. He traced a pattern in front of it with his finger. "*Zenthi amaerys feu.*" A pentacle glowed in midair, and Zap moved the tip of the cigarette into the pentacle and drew in a breath.

"What was going on?" To'mas asked.

Zap pulled away from the cigarette and finished inhaling. The pentacle faded from the air. A thin wisp of smoke hung in front of Zap, and he dispersed it by exhaling. "Nothing," he finally said, turning to look at To'mas.

To'mas looked back for a few moments, then settled back against the wall and looked at the moon. "Lemme tell you a story, Zap," he said.

Zap looked at him quizzically. To'mas took a drink from the cup and winced slightly at the strength.

"Once," To'mas began, "there were a man and a woman who loved each other very much. And they were both magic users, right? They were invokers, to be exact."

"Okay," Zap said.

"Now it bears mentioning that each one had something they really loved. The guy had this seriously sweet gaming shell that he used to play all of the latest games. It had OMF capability, it could do holos, he was on an upgrade program. It was just a really awesome machine. And it just so happened that Eternal Light Productions was about to put out this really guardian new component that'd run your shit twice as good as whatever rig you mighta had before, but it was *really* expensive; we're talking crash-your-bank-server expensive. Almost as pricey as the shell itself."

Zap nodded.

"Now the woman had this effin' beautiful motorcycle. It was really awesome, very fast, very sleek. It would turn heads. It was quiet and well-designed and was ready for all of the upgrades. In fact, there was this one generator upgrade that the woman had been considering saving up for, but it was such a huge deal that it cost almost as much as the motorcycle."

Zap knitted his brow, the cigarette hanging from the edge of his mouth.

"So Yule comes along. The guy thinks, 'I care for my beloved so much, there is nothing I wouldn't give up for her. I want to get her something that will really show her how much I care.' So he goes to the upgrade shop to get her bike spec'd for the upgrade. The guy there looks at it and says, 'It's gonna cost you 5,000 creds.' Naturally the guy is stricken; he can't afford that kind of thing. But he really wants to get this generator upgrade for his beloved. He sits and thinks about how happy her face will be toolin' around on that thing."

To'mas took another drink. "So you know what he does?" he resumed the story. "He goes and sells the upgrades from his shell. He sells the holo unit, he sells the OMF compatibility card, he sells the realism hardware. He gets enough money to buy this generator upgrade for his girl and he buys it. They're like 'no refunds, dood,' but he doesn't care. He's so happy to have gotten this thing for his beloved. He takes the upgrade home and prepares it for Yule."

"I think I see where this is going," Zap said.

"Shuddup for a second," To'mas said. "If you're going to let me get this far, you've got to let me tell the end. So Yule happens, and he and his beloved exchange gifts. And she opens the present and looks not happy, but dismayed. Her love is stricken; he can't understand. He says, 'I thought you would love this gift! It's what you wanted more than anything else!'"

Mimicking the couple, To'mas spoke passionately to the sky. "And she turns to him and says, 'My love, of course! I truly wanted this more than anything else. But I sold my bike in order to get you the latest mod for your gaming shell.' And he looks at her and says, 'Oh ... I can no longer use that mod, having sold all of the upgrades that would make it work.'"

To'mas picked up his cup and drank from it, finishing the beverage.

"So?" Zap said.

"So what?" To'mas asked.

"What happened?"

"Oh, I dunno," To'mas replied. "Presumably they eventually got enough money to buy their shit back, and they learned not to sell possessions to get gifts for each other or something."

Zap shook his head. "And ... why were they invocation mages, anyway? What'd that have to do with anything?"

To'mas shrugged. "It's the title of the story. *Gift of the Mages*."

Zap stared, the ash on his cigarette growing long. "Why did you tell me that story?" he asked, incredulous. "I mean, what did that do for me just now?"

To'mas smiled slightly at him. "It passed the time."

42

Zap cracked his knuckles and leaned forward. He let his fingers dance over the keyboard, opening his e-mail client and composing a new message. He chewed his lip for a moment, then began.

> Dear Mom,
>
> The second week of the retreat is flying by. They're keeping us busier than a mind flayer at a MENSA meeting, and

it's making the time go fast. I guess a two-week retreat isn't that long, is it?

Anyway, we've gotten back into exercises and training, so I've had very little time to hang out with the new friends I've made. Luckily, the Rail is there for us and I've already gotten over a dozen new ethadds on my contact list.

"Weren't you going to get some food before the impro magic seminar?" Arden's voice came from the bathroom. "You were really enthusiastic about this one. Wouldn't want you to faint or something."

"I've got 45 minutes," Zap replied. "I can eat fast."

He resumed typing.

I can't type for long; I've taken it upon myself to pick up a few seminars that I thought would be good for me. Makes me even busier, though.

Everybody's mind is on the Store vs. Store combat exercises near the end of the retreat, and the subsequent retreat party. The exercise seems like a more intense version of our fight with the Rosebuds, which is a bit scary. If the party's anything like the concert was, though, it should be a lot of fun.

Anyway, I

"Do you know if Miss Steve is planning on attending the firearms modification seminar?" Arden called again.

"I think so," Zap replied.

His train of thought derailed, Zap stared blankly at the shell's monitor for nearly a full minute. He cautiously raised his hands to the keyboard and began typing again.

Anyway, I have been doing well and it hasn't been too hard on me. The exercises nearly kill me every day, but I'm dying a little less each time. This is a good incentive to start really exercising once I get back.

I hope things are working out for you at the Atelier. Let me know if you have any interesting new components come in.

Love,

Your Son Zap

Zap hammered one the shortcut keys that sent the message into the ether, then whirled in his chair and stood.

"Right," he said. "Food."

"Oh, you're finally getting going," Arden said.

"Yes, yes," Zap said. "I wonder if I'll get to cite my use of the Three Martini Lunch combo from Friday's exercise."

"Not sure what you're talking about," Arden said, "but I could go for a three martini something."

"Want to meet up at the pub after your seminar?" Zap asked.

"Sure," Arden said. "Sounds like a plan. Save a martini for me."

"I'll make sure they don't run out of olives," Zap said as he slipped through the door.

"I guess that I relied on my band members as friends a little more than I realized," Alan said. He tore a chunk off of his bread bowl.

"You're missing them?" Steve asked, a chopstick-held bundle of noodles halfway to her mouth.

"Yeah," Alan said. He ripped smaller pieces off of the larger chunk, placing them one by one in his soup. "It's like I got here, and I went to parties, and I suddenly got all shy. That's not really like me."

"I agree," Steve said. She took a large bite of sesame noodles.

"I think that's probably why Paru took me to the concert as her date. She knew I needed a direction. Shouldn't I be doing that on my own, though? I'm a shift supervisor."

Steve mumbled something through the mouthful of food.

"Exactly," Alan replied. "It's a learning experience like everything else here. Oh, hey Zap."

"Hey Alan, Steve," Zap said, approaching with a tray full of food. Zap took the seat next to Steve, who scooted over a little bit to accommodate him. Zap set his tray down and took his seat.

Alan continued. "So I think it's something I'll learn from. How's everything going for you? Picking anything up?"

"Hell yeah," Steve said with a nod. "I always figured that I could do with a little more time on the range, but I didn't realize how much it would help. My marksmanship scores have shot up, and my quick draw's faster than ever."

"How about you, Zap?" Alan asked. He took his spoon and dredged through his french onion soup to find the now soup-soaked bread. He soon extracted a piece, catching a thread of cheese as he lifted it.

"Well, I have to admit that being in AP wizardry, the magic practice here isn't much more than practice," Zap said as he laid out his place on the table. "Even the improv magic seminar only taught me a little. What I'm really doing is getting in shape. Exercises don't tire me out *quite* as much."

"You could have fooled us," Steve teased. She gave Zap an impish grin. "You still look like you've just crawled through the Northern Wastes every morning."

"Not all of us are of hardy peasant stock," Zap said a bit sourly.

"Now now, girls," Alan said, his mouth full. "You're both pretty."

There was a minute of silence as everyone ate, which was interrupted when Loren, carrying a tray with only a single plate of food and a glass of water, arrived.

"Hey Loren, how's—are you eating plain pasta?" Steve said.

"It's not plain," Loren replied, sitting at the table. "It's got butter on it."

"That's the loneliest tray ever," Steve said mournfully.

"Anybody else try the french onion soup?" Alan said. "It's awesome."

"Yeah, I got a bowl," Zap said. "It's good?"

"Plus one delicious," Alan replied.

"HD," Zap said, pulling his cup of soup to him. He began blowing on it to let it cool.

"Steve," Loren asked, "how is your new boyfriend?"

"We're doing great," Steve replied. "It's been ages since I got l—since. Uh."

"Since you had a boyfriend," Zap filled in.

"Since I had a boyfriend," Steve agreed.

"Congratulations," Loren said with a smile. "You deserve somebody good."

"Why thanks, man," Steve said, surprised at Loren's vote of confidence. "I think so too."

"Where does Mike live again?" Alan asked.

"About a block north of Rose street. It's only ten minutes on the Rail," Steve replied.

"Iyesu!" Zap exclaimed.

Everyone turned to look, surprised by the outburst.

"This soup really *is* awesome!" Zap said.

"See?" Alan said.

Steve and Alan stayed at the table for fifteen minutes after they had finished their food, but when Loren finished his plate of spaghetti the three decided to part ways. This left Zap alone at the table, poking at the last of the food he had taken and debating whether he was hungry enough to eat it.

After a few minutes of deliberation, Zap forgot about what he was trying to decide and set about playing with his food instead. The remaining mashed potatoes on his plate became a canvas on which he began drawing. Humming to himself, Zap practiced runes in the surface of the mashed potatoes.

Zap was soon so absorbed in the action on his plate that he failed to notice Click's approach until the faerie set his tray on the table with a loud *clack!*

The young wizard started violently, looking up into Click's eyes. Click, who had dark circles under his eyes and looked very frayed around the edges, stared back at him. The two remained in this tableau until Click finally spoke.

"Zap," he said. "I'm Unseelie."

"Hur dur," Zap said, drawing from a richly empathic part of his soul.

"I didn't *know* it, is the thing," Click said, sitting down at the table. "The fae ... we do our own thing, really, and introspection isn't really much of a thing we tend to do. I hadn't seen my card in months until Friday night. I *used* to be Seelie, Zap."

Click's wild-eyed desperation sent a twinge of sympathy through Zap, who sighed. "Who was your card?"

"Mab," Click said.

Zap winced. "Oogh," he said. "Not even Kallisti?"

"I half-expected her," Click said, "but not Mab. I can't have come this far."

"Well, Click," Zap replied. "You were in the middle of a plan that entailed destroying a girl's self-esteem so you could get with her. That's pretty ... that's pretty scummy, man."

Click put his head on the table.

"Well," Zap said, somewhat uncomfortable, "only thing to do is start checking yourself, right?"

"Right," Click said, his voice heavy. He picked up his head and looked at Zap.

"So..."

"I'm going to try to avoid using Granfalloon magic at all," Click said.

"And," Zap prompted.

"And I'll take a more direct hand with anyone I feel like trying to influence."

"And Steve?" Zap asked.

"Steve..." Click thought about it for a moment. "I mean, if she breaks up with this guy, I can try pursuing her like a normal person? I guess? And if not, I'd better leave her alone."

"Ok," Zap said. "Good words. If you can actually *do* it, you should be okay to switch back by Yule."

"Big if," Click said.

"It's in your hands," Zap said. "But whatever the case, you've got to stop moping. That won't help anybody. Get some sleep, think on it, fly right."

"Why did you have to say that," Click said.

"Say what?"

"Never mind," Click said.

"Look," Zap said. "There's another suite party tonight. I'm not going, but you should. Just loosen up a little bit, just ... not *too* much."

"Okay," Click replied.

"Anyway, work on that. I'll see you later, Click."

"All right," Click said, still looking pathetic. "See you later."

Zap stood and picked up his tray. Once several paces away, he shook his head. "I threaten a guy once and all of a sudden I'm his fucking psychiatrist."

43

Layla McPhee heard the lock to her room's door unlatch as she approached it, responding to the downloaded key on her workshell. She turned the knob and pushed the door open, expecting an empty room. She was therefore surprised to see her roommate Pazi sprawled on one of the beds.

Pazi turned her head to look at Layla, but didn't move the rest of her body. A familiar of hers, Inryu, was draped across her chest and she petted him idly. Inryu resembled nothing so much as a little dragon-dog, with a serpentine but furry body and an adorable canine face. A contrast to her familiar, Pazi's face was currently less than adorable.

"Hey, girl," Layla said. "What're you doing here? I thought you were going to go hang out with your boy."

"He's busy, apparently," Pazi said. "Doesn't have enough time to just hang out."

"Oh," Layla replied, her face falling into a sympathetic expression. "Pazi, that sucks."

"I guess I could have given him more warning," Pazi said quietly. "I didn't really ask him about it until yesterday."

"It's a retreat," Layla said. "He should have been able to make at least a little time."

"Whatever," Pazi replied petulantly. "He likes Steve better than me anyway."

"Don't say that, now," Layla shot back. "There's no need for you to get like this. If he's not giving you the time you need, go get your needs met somewhere else."

"I don't want to do that," Pazi said. "I like Zap."

"Like him however much you want, but don't give him the benefit of no doubt he didn't earn. You should tell him he needs to shape up or you're gone."

Pazi was silent, petting Inryu with her eyes averted.

"Pazi, I want you to tell that boy that if he doesn't take you somewhere tomorrow, you are through with him and his disregard. Can you do that?"

"I guess," Pazi said.

"You guess, or you will?"

"I will."

"And so they calculated the absolute maximum load amount that the animal could carry, and made some reasonable assumptions about how much it could conceivably throw and how far," Marlon said. "Having that knowledge, it was really only a matter of setting a time limit and making the calculations."

"But it's not about how much it *could* throw," Steve said. "It's about how much it *would*."

"Well, I think that we can safely assume that if given the ability, the groundhog would prefer to move as much lumber as possible."

"Who are you again?" Steve asked.

"That's my roommate, Marlon," Loren said.

"Ohh," Zap said. "You're the guy who memorized the Hall of Records' ethsite."

"That's me!" Marlon replied proudly.

Zap and Steve exchanged a look.

"Anyway," Zap said to Steve. "Where're you headed now?"

"I'm headed to the range," Marlon said. "I'm not really so enthusiastic about fighting; I think that stock memorization is really where I shine."

"That's great, Marlon," Zap said. "But—"

"I mean, enough of my coworkers are fighters," Marlon continued. "With Raye Courts-the-Shadows as my shift supervisor, what we really need more of are regular employees. Anyway I got basic rifle certification and usually use a shotgun."

"Ok, Marlon," Zap said.

"That's why I took it upon myself to keep track of all of my store's inventory—"

"I'm also headed to the range, Zap," Steve said loudly, talking over Marlon, who looked irritated but fell silent.

"Okay," Zap said. "I guess I'm free, then. I'll walk partway there."

"I'm going to the range too," Loren said, "but it's cool, don't ask or anything."

The four employees walked out of the classroom and into the hallway, where employees who had been released from seminars and exercises were wandering. One who had been standing nearby approached the group.

"Oh, Pazi," Zap said. "Hi!"

"Zap, I need to t—" Pazi began, her expression stormy. Her sun-spider paced her shoulder, clearly agitated.

"I'm free all of a sudden," Zap said with a bright smile. "You wanna hang out for a while?"

Completely thrown, Pazi's eyes went wide and she stammered a bit. The sun-spider grew completely still, its legs vanishing into its orblike body.

"Yeah, no?" Zap asked. "Are you busy?"

"Um, no," Pazi said.

"Then let's hang out! Do you want to take a walk to the lagoon? Maybe we could go swimming."

"I ... that sounds nice," Pazi said a bit weakly.

"Great!" Zap said. "I'll see you guys later, ok?"

"Yeah," Steve said, already walking away.

"Ok, see you, Zap," Loren said.

"That's a Sunburst familiar," Marlon said matter-of-factly. "I hear that they are very versatile and can handle a lot of energy for being a low-level familiar. Have you ever tried feeding it extra energy?"

"Yes," Pazi said. She still seemed a bit dazed. "Actually, a few weeks ago at my store—"

"I hear that it's capable of some very powerful fire magic in a pinch," Marlon said. "Though it's not very efficient, in the long run. So I've read, I mean. If you—"

"Marlon, we're going to be late," Steve said loudly, talking over Marlon again. Marlon stopped talking, looking sour. Zap nudged Pazi, put an arm around her and guided her away from the others. After realizing that his quarry had escaped, Marlon turned and followed Steve and Loren as they walked down the hallway.

"You know, guy, it's really great that you know all this drek," Steve said to Marlon as they walked, "but it makes you a serious pain in the ass, ok?"

44

Raimi And The Soft Winds Blow stood in the center of the practice room floor, her eyes closed. Her mail armor had been replaced with an HD-Plastic sports jacket, not unlike a pigskin player's padding. The weapons she wore on each hip were not her short swords, but a pair of sheathed sticks, weighted to simulate the heft of her blades but padded to prevent injury.

Standing in a ring around Raimi were six people, each one bearing similar armor. Three carried padded weapons, one held a rifle-like device and two carried nothing at all. All stared at the half-elf with determined eyes.

A voice from above called, "Begin!"

Raimi's eyes flew open and her lips began to move, murmuring arcane words under her breath. Three of her six opponents dashed forward, their padded blades held aloft. The warrior with the rifle aimed at Raimi and fired, launching a soft ball toward her at high speed.

The half-elf's haste spell finished first. Her arm blurred to her side and drew a stick with impossible speed, cutting the projectile from the air. Her lips began to move again, preparing the next spell even as she drew the other stick.

The three melee fighters reached Raimi and attacked. She parried madly, knocking their weapons aside with practiced ease and preternatural agility. Before she was able to return their attacks, however, a trio of magic missiles arrived, hissing through the air toward the combatants. Raimi leapt into a backward somersault. The missiles veered to follow her, but couldn't turn fast enough; they barely missed Raimi's close-range opponents and struck the far wall.

Raimi hissed a flurry of arcane words, finishing the interrupted spell. A bubble of magic snapped up around her, then faded from view. The close-range fighters were upon her in a moment, but Raimi was ready; a forceful swipe with one stick disarmed the opponent in front of her and she dove through the gap she had created, neatly tumbling under a lateral swipe with a forward roll.

As soon as Raimi gained her footing she pointed both sticks at the rifleman, who had been unsuccessfully trying to draw a bead on her. She barked a few words and energy ran down the length of the sticks. A pair of missiles fired from the sticks, tracing an arc toward the rifleman. He tried in vain to dive away, but was struck by the missile and tumbled to the ground.

"Number four," the omniscient voice said. The rifleman punched the ground in frustration and picked himself up, nearly unharmed from the sparring missile's impact.

Raimi's bubble shattered abruptly, and she turned her head to see that the mage who had not yet acted had just completed a dispel cantrip. The bubble had taken the spell's effect, however, and Raimi retained her magical speed; she streaked toward the effect-mage with her weapons raised. She was forced to dive to the side, however, when another flurry of magical projectiles struck the ground she had been running toward.

Raimi growled to herself and ran again, tracing the edge of the room. The melee fighters tried to intercept her, but were not quick enough. The projectile mage's breath was forced out of him as one of Raimi's padded sticks struck him hard in the stomach.

"Number six," the voice said. "Careful now, Raimi."

"Shut up!" Raimi shouted, lunging toward the unprepared melee fighters. Her sticks blurred in dangerous arcs as they struck her opponent's weapons away. A blow from one stick struck one of the fighters in the chest as the other collided with another fighter's head. Raimi whirled and struck down the third fighter with both sticks.

"Numbers one, two and three," the voice said.

Raimi leveled a gaze at the support mage, who blanched and raised both hands.

"And that's match," the voice said.

Raimi looked up. "No editorializing when I'm practicing," she said firmly. "Ever."

"'yesu, sorry," Click said, clambering down from his perch on one of the support beams.

"You should know better," Raimi said.

"'Thanks for calling my sparring match, Click,'" Click said in a high-pitched voice, then switched to a lower tone. "'Oh, sure, Raimi, no problem. Glad to help you.'"

Raimi rolled her eyes. "I should know better than to scold a faerie, I guess," she said.

"Yes," Click said. "Yes you should."

"Dismissed," Raimi called out to the training assistants, who scurried to comply. She turned back to Click. "Now what did you want to talk to me about?"

"Uh," Click said. "Some time ago, you said that if I needed a frank, unbiased opinion about something you'd be the person to go to. Remember?"

"Yes I do," Raimi said. "That relationship was a total failure, by the way."

"And I'm sorry about that," Click said, holding his hands up. "I might not be the best judge of character on earth. That's why I'm coming to you."

"I'd tell you some of the things he did, but it would be unladylike to mention them."

Click was silent for a moment. "Now I'm interested," he said.

"Ask me your question, churl," Raimi replied. Her tone was curt, but a small smile graced her angular face.

Click sighed. "Mike Lewis," he said.

"An employee of mine," Raimi said. "And Miss Steve's new boyfriend."

"What do you think of him?" Click asked.

"He's a good employee," Raimi replied with a shrug. "Doesn't get in the way, does his job. He seems all right."

"What about his personality, though?" Click asked. "Does he seem like the sort of person who's ... I don't know, easily influenced? Weak-willed?"

"I wouldn't really know," Raimi said. "He doesn't really run in my friendwheels."

Click chewed on his lip. "Ok," he said. "I'm going to give you a hypothetical situation that didn't happen, it's just hypothetical. So you can't hold anything I say against me, because it didn't actually happen."

"Because it's hypothetical," Raimi said dryly.

"Exactly," Click said. "It's hypothetical. So let's say there was this guy. This guy who there isn't, really."

"Because he's hypothetical," Raimi added.

"Yes," Click said. "He's hypothetical. So. This guy who doesn't exist has a magical ability that affects emotions and opinions. Like projective empathy."

"Or Granfalloon Magic," Raimi suggested.

Click looked pained. "Hypothetically, yes, he could be somebody who had the exceedingly rare ability of Granfalloon Magic, that is possible, since this is, you know..."

"A hypothetical situation," Raimi said.

"Yes, exactly," Click said. "It's hypothetical. So this guy, who doesn't exist, and for the purposes of this story let's say he's a faerie with Granfalloon magic, *hypothetically speaking*. So this guy is maybe doing some kind of unethical things with Granfalloon magic that he will seriously regret and be sorry about later."

Raimi raised an eyebrow.

"Hypothetically speaking!" Click said, holding up a finger. "And anyway he regrets it a *whole lot* later, so let's just not talk about that any more. So he ends up using it on ... another guy. Another hypothetical guy."

"Let's call him Mike," Raimi said, canting her head a little bit.

Click looked pained again. "Sure," he said. "Totally hypothetical, so let's just call him Mike because really his name could be anything. So this guy, this Granfalloon guy uses his Granfalloon magic on this so-called hypothetical 'Mike' guy."

"Mm-hmm?" Raimi said.

"And, uh," Click said. "It's ... really really easy. Really unexpectedly easy."

Raimi's expression grew more serious.

"Pretty much like taking candy from a baby. So our hypothetical guy, whose name is really seriously not Click, knows from experience that stronger-willed people are much harder to influence with this kind of magic. They have to be worked up to it, or it has to be about unimportant things. And this 'Mike' guy gets really easily affected by something and acts very out of character with very little pushing."

"Meaning that..." Raimi prompted, obviously recognizing Click's point.

"Meaning that Mike is—hypothetically speaking—extremely weak-willed," Click said. "And let's say hypothetically that Mike starts dating somebody that our guy really likes a lot."

"Click," Raimi said, holding up a hand. "I don't think that I can talk about this."

"But—" Click said, his eyes pleading. "It's hypothetical!"

Raimi gave Click a look that hushed him immediately. The two stared at each other for ten seconds.

Raimi finally leaned in very slowly and murmured, "Watch him closely. Be ready to help her when the inevitable occurs. And do not think about revenge for even a moment."

Raimi then turned and strode away, leaving Click and his ruminations alone in the dojo.

45

Steve woke abruptly to the sound of someone pounding on her door. She sat bolt upright, alert but not yet fully awake. Below her, Violet made noises of intense dissatisfaction.

"Steve!" someone's voice came from outside. "Are you in there?"

More pounding on the door.

"I'm up!" Steve shouted. "I'm up!"

"Shaddap!" Violet murmured.

"You slept through exercises!" The voice, which Steve now recognized as Zap's, had a definite sense of urgency in its tone. "Our store-wide match is in less than an hour!"

Steve sat silently for a moment as her sleep-addled brain slowly processed the information. Her eyes went very wide as she realized what day it was. "Oh, shit!" she said. "It's Friday!"

"Yes!" Zap shouted. "Get your ass out of there! Paru's going to flay you if you're late for briefing!"

"I'm coming!" Steve threw herself out of bed, tumbling as she hit the floor. She rushed through her morning routine, skipping her shower under the rationale that she'd be getting dirty soon anyway.

Several minutes later, Steve stumbled into the hallway, where Zap was waiting. "Speedy," he admitted. "C'mon."

The two hurried down the hallway, talking as they went.

"Why the hell did you sleep in today, of all days?" Zap asked, clearly a little irritated at having to rescue his coworker.

"Violet and I were up late talking," Steve said. "We were catching up on gossip and shit."

"Gossip?" Zap asked, a bit incredulous. "You?"

"I like knowing what's going on," Steve replied acidly. "Sue me."

"Anything out there about me?" Zap asked with a small smile.

Steve was silent for a moment. "We can talk about it later," she said.

"Whoa, what?" Zap asked, his eyebrows raised and eyes wide.

"Don't worry about it," Steve said. "We've got bigger things to focus on."

"You—" Zap spluttered. "You can't just *do* that! It's going to gnaw at me until you tell me! What're people saying about me?"

Steve chewed her lip. "People think you're neglecting Pazi," she said.

Zap started, and then shook his head. "I'm not ... no, I'm not neglecting her," he said. "We're all really busy."

"But we're all trapped in the same facility," Steve said. "And it's not like we don't have free time. I think you hang out with me more than you hang out with her. And much as that's cool for our friendship and all, that doesn't exactly make you boyfriend of the year, you know?"

Zap lapsed into a fretful silence.

"Look, you really need to not think about that now," Steve said. "We've got a match. You know who we're fighting?"

"Malachi Park," Zap said.

"That should be interesting," Steve said, clearly apprehensive.

"I know," Zap said. "Nasty neighborhood, tough employees. Lotta intrinsics."

"At least they're down Creepy Don," Steve said.

"More's the pity," Zap said.

"Yeah, you've got a point," Steve replied. "I'd love to cap that motherfucker in a company-sanctioned environment. If I could get to him before anybody else."

The two power-walked out of the dormitories, close now to the briefing room.

"Do *you* think I'm a bad boyfriend?" Zap asked.

Steve looked away. "Maybe you just haven't..."

"Haven't what?"

"Never mind," Steve said. "Yeah, you could be better."

Zap frowned.

"Aight, here we are," Steve said. She looked over at Zap. "You ready?"

"No," he replied.

"Me neither," she said. "Let's go."

In the control room of the installation's Kekkai battlefield, several employees of the Securemarket™ were getting ready for the upcoming match.

"Good morning, kids," Sir Erdrick said to the inhabitants of the control room, closing the door behind him as he entered. He was wearing his standard kit; a business suit with his sword and pistol sheathed at his side. He was also carrying a large travel mug.

"Good morning, Sir Erdrick," Mya chirped.

"That's a little too cheerful for ten o'clock, Miss Ai'o," the knight said.

"So sorry," Mya said with a smile. "Won't happen again."

"Bullshit," Sir Erdrick growled. "But you're cute so I'll let you live."

"Sir Erdrick, Miss Ai'o is still technically under my care," interrupted Dr. Wallace, the bespectacled young on-site physician. He was looking out of the window of the observation booth, watching the parties gather below. "I would appreciate it if you toned down your flirtatious banter."

"Scott," Sir Erdrick said, raising his eyebrows, "if I want your opinion, I will carve it into your brain myself."

"Have some coffee before you talk any more, Sir Cranky of Pants," Mya suggested.

Sir Erdrick sighed heavily and took a sip from his coffee.

"Kekkai or no, I still hate all this," Dr. Wallace murmured.

"It's good for them," Sir Erdrick said, walking up to the large window and peering out of it. "Hard, but good. Every New Washingtonian should have to go through this sort of thing."

He turned to one of the two Kekkai technicians, who sat near a console shell at one end of the room. The other was at the back of the room, his eye darting between several screens.

"How's the generator holding up?" Sir Erdrick asked the technician.

"It's running fine," the technician said. "Won't be due for a service until after today's exercises."

"Good," the knight replied. He turned back to the observation window. "This should be very interesting."

"Why's that?" asked Dr. Wallace.

"Malachi Park's employees have, on average, the best weapon certification at this retreat. They've grown up in a tough neighborhood and felt threatened most of their lives."

"And you're looking forward to watching them mop the floor with 15th Street?" Dr. Wallace asked.

Erdrick laughed. "No," he said. "I'm looking forward to seeing how Paru handles a challenge."

Paru surveyed her employees carefully. "All right," she said. "You've been assigned your groups: Alpha, Beta, Gamma and Delta."

The employees, all gathered in their respective groups, shifted their feet; they were all a bit nervous. Alpha group, comprised of some of the more direct combatants in 15th street, stood directly in front of Paru: Alan, Arden, Click, and Loren's roommate Marlon.

Beta was just to the side, another group of short-range fighters: Emma Rammek, the quarter-dragon supervisor, To'mas's roommate Michael, May-May Dunaway, and her roommate Prue Smith (the latter two stood very close to each other for reassurance).

On the other side of Alpha was Gamma Team, the longer-range gunners: To'mas, Steve, and Loren (who had been placed in Gamma mostly because his skill with a pistol was far better than his skill as a ground combatant).

Delta Team, the specialists, stood in the rear. The swathed form of Raye Courts-the-Shadows, the floating apparition everybody called "Hollow-Eyes", Matt, and Zap.

"As you're all aware, you're facing a lot of firepower," Paru said. "Malachi Park has a high level of weapon proficiency, and they'll be ready for yours. We'll be using our magic in ways they won't expect, and that should give us an edge. That doesn't mean you can falter on the offensive, because a lull in our attack will let them know that something else is coming. Fight as though Delta Team doesn't exist. I expect you to give everything you have and more."

Paru shouldered her rifle and swept her gaze over her employees. "We will succeed," she said. "But only if you use everything you have and kill without mercy. Do you understand?"

The employees murmured their assent.

"I'm sorry, do you understand?" Paru asked again.

"Yes sir!" the employees shouted.

46

"Shall I give the opening announcement, Sir Erdrick?" one of the Kekkai technicians asked.

"I'll do it," Sir Erdrick said, walking to the resonator mic and picking it up.

The knight pressed the button on the side of the mic. "Employees, welcome to the final exercise of the retreat. This will be a combat simulation of the largest magnitude that you have faced here, and probably the largest one you've experienced at all, except for you militia veterans."

Sir Erdrick released the button, cleared his throat and took another sip of coffee.

He pressed the button again. "This Kekkai exercise operates under the same rules that the previous one did. Tap a surface twice to be pulled out; we'll pull you out if you get disabled, unconscious, or dead. Wait for the signal then fight like hell, kiddies."

Sir Erdrick set the mic back down on the Kekkai console.

"That's ... not the official spiel, sir," the technician said.

"It isn't, is it?" Sir Erdrick said. "How's the generator?"

"It's fine," the technician replied.

"Great. Let's set it on fire, ey?" Sir Erdrick walked to the observation window.

The technician, clearly a bit annoyed, picked up the resonator mic and pressed the button on its side. "Ready," he said, paused, then, "mark!"

Below, the two teams leapt into action.

Paru weaved between the objects in front of her, her assault rifle held at the ready as she ran. Behind her, two of her teams followed. The sound of their shoes and boots was a rapid, erratic staccato as they pushed themselves to keep up with their manager. Paru kept herself very aware of the noise, most notably when she heard it in front of her as well as behind.

"Heads up," Paru said. "Enemy approaching."

Paru slowed her pace near the end of an obstacle, only to come face-to-face with a shotgun-toting human wearing a bandanna.

Reacting instinctively and spurred by a surge of adrenaline, Paru snapped the butt of her rifle upward with jaw-breaking force. She was instantly rewarded with a sharp cracking noise as the young man's head snapped backward, the shotgun falling from his hands.

"Find cover," Paru said calmly into the intercom. She backed up rapidly, training her rifle on the space where the man had emerged. She saw brief movement and fired a short burst at the obstacle, halting any further approach. She reached to her belt and pulled a grenade from it. The young man in front of her, writhing in pain, slapped the ground twice and turned iron-gray.

Paru pulled the pin on her grenade and murmured, "Sir Erdrick, we who are about to die salute you."

The sound of gunfire echoed not far away, and then a sharp explosion rocked the battlefield.

To'mas, crouching atop one of the flat obstacles, pressed his lips together. He turned back and watched as Steve clambered out of a sticky pool of shadow.

"Hurry," he said. "They've engaged." Steve nodded and dragged herself out of the shadow a bit faster. "You ready, Loren?"

"I feel useless," Loren said bitterly.

"Chin up, man," To'mas said. "Today, you're a specialist."

Loren looked across the sparse collection of flat-topped obstacles, each one no less than three meters from the next. "Is Zap's jump charm actually going to last long enough for us to get to the action?"

"I think a more important question," Steve said, yanking her foot from the shadow, "is whether we will be noticed and shot as we jump from surface to surface."

"I have the answer to both of your questions!" To'mas said cheerfully. "And here it is: shut the fuck up!"

Steve glared.

"Let's go," To'mas said.

Alan fired his shotgun at the small group of combatants and cursed as he watched the slug deflect against a bulletshield with a spark.

"We need some slow ballistics here," he said, ducking as the area where he had been standing was peppered with gunfire.

"May-May!" Prue's voice shouted from nearby.

"Prue!" Alan shouted. "Need slow ballistic support!"

"They got May-May!" Prue shouted, turning toward Alan. Marlon leaned around his obstacle and fired a useless spray of buckshot at the cluster of employees.

"PRUE!" Alan shouted, startling the half-elf. "She'll be fine! We need you!"

Prue stumbled to Alan's side, drawing her hand-crossbow. She prepared to turn the corner, but flinched as a volley of gunfire sliced the air in front of her.

"We've got a blockade," Alan said into the intercom, then heard a clinking noise. It was a moment before he realized that a grenade had been thrown. "Fire in the hole!" he shouted, and everyone dove for cover.

"Five employees already down," the Kekkai technician said.

"Spread?" Sir Erdrick asked.

"Three Malachi, two 15th," the technician replied.

"Good start, Paru," Erdrick said. "But you're going to regret trying to set up snipers."

From his position on one of the obstacles, To'mas signaled to Steve and Loren, each of whom had taken their own positions atop the structures. The three employees brought their weapons to bear and fired.

To'mas saw the employee whom he had shot stumble heavily, protected by armor but stunned by the impact of the high-caliber bullet. Seizing the opportunity, Click darted forward and pummeled the man insensible.

"Good," To'mas said, chambering the next round.

He adjusted his aim and fired on another exposed employee, an air mutant. Unprotected by armor and too slow to react with magic, the employee dropped to the ground and turned gray.

"Good," To'mas said again, chambering the next round mechanically and looking for the next target.

A snarling noise startled To'mas, and he lowered his gun and looked to the side. The sight of a hulking creature clambering onto the surface of his obstacle greeted him.

"Oh, shit," he murmured.

"Werewolf!" To'mas's voice came over the intercom. "We've got a werewolf up here!"

"Hollow-Eyes," Paru said into the mic.

The ghost ceased his activity, which had been delivering harmless but distracting blows to a group of enemy employees. His voice crackled over the intercom band. "Yeah?"

"Go help," she said.

"But werewolf claws—"

"That's an order!" Paru barked. "Steve, there's your distraction."

"Workin' on it!" Steve said. "To'mas is down, and it's going after Loren."

"Take care of it," Paru said grimly. She shouldered her rifle and led another charge forward.

Steve turned her eyes away from the werewolf, who had suddenly been accosted by the swift ethereal form of Hollow-Eyes. With shaky hands, she released the magazine currently loaded in Polaris and grasped another one, which had a piece of silver tape marking its base. She slammed the clip home and looked up in time to see the werewolf tear the ghost into two pieces, its spirit-attuned claws rending the immaterial being. Luckily, the Kekkai's effect took hold and froze Hollow-Eyes's torn spirit in place.

The werewolf was about to fall upon Loren when Steve sighted it with her pistol and fired.

It barely flinched. "Chambered round!" Loren shouted, scrambling away from the beast.

"Oh yeah," Steve said and fired again. The werewolf roared in pain as the silver bullet hit it. Steve continued to fire, forcing the werewolf to drop to the ground from blinding pain and confusion. Steve stopped firing and surveyed the beast. The werewolf raised one claw and slammed the top of the obstacle with it twice, then turned the dead gray of a defeated Kekkai combatant.

"Woo!" Steve shouted. She said into the intercom, "Paru, I got 'im!"

She paused.

"Paru?"

"Impressive," Sir Erdrick said. "15th Street did its homework. Or Paru did, at least."

"Speaking of which, sir," the Kekkai technician said. "Dupree is down."

"Is that right?" Sir Erdrick said, surprised. "Spread?"

"Only seven 15th Street employees left," the technician said, "and twelve Malachi Park employees."

"That means Paru's frontline is nearly annihilated," Sir Erdrick said, frowning. "It's unlike her to calculate so poorly."

"It's really ugly down there," Dr. Wallace said with distaste, but seemed unable to tear his eyes from it.

"Say..." said Mya. "where's that prodigy wizard boy? Zap?"

"How's the Kekkai holding up?" Sir Erdrick asked.

"Would you please stop asking me that?" the technician replied, annoyed. "Obviously I'm monitoring it! If something goes wrong, I'll tell you!"

There was a silence as Sir Erdrick stared at the technician.

The technician sighed. "It's fine, sir," he said. "Nominal condition."

"Come to think of it," Mya said, "Where's that shadow mutant supervisor?"

At long last, the arcane words ceased to issue from Zap's mouth. Breathing deeply, he slowly walked to the center of his pattern labyrinth. Once there, he slowly lowered himself to the ground and sat cross-legged.

"Are you ready?" a voice whispered.

"Almost," Zap murmured in an entranced voice.

"Well, hurry it up," the other voice replied. "We're only 45 seconds from Matt's mark."

"Hush now," Zap whispered.

Zap took a deep breath and let himself become a conduit for the energy for which he had drawn the labyrinth. He turned his inner-eye toward the multi-planar facets of the dream-lines he had drawn, admiring the non-Euclidean angles of the impossible shape. He watched the energy flow, like thick, black blood, down the rivulets he had carved in reality. He breathed in as he felt the pleasure-pain of the energy channeling through him.

He was darkness. He could dip the world in ink. The brush named Zap...

"Zap," the honey-voice of Dark-Being slid through Zap's senses. "Almost everyone is out. Steve and Loren are down. Alan is holding back nine people by himself."

"You are beautiful," Zap said, hearing his voice echo through several spheres of existence.

The voice was silent for a moment, caught in the echoes of Zap's empowered words.

Zap opened his eyes, which were pitch black in their entirety. "I am ready," he said. "I will fill the Kekkai with you."

In the observation booth, the previously silent Kekkai technician suddenly spoke up. "A spike in Eldritch signatures, sir."

Sir Erdrick hurried to him. "What's the analysis?"

"Shadow magic," the technician said. "But classic W-Encoding. Class B."

"Class B..." Sir Erdrick murmured, and turned to the observation window. "No one in that room should be capable of a ritual as pow—"

The window suddenly went pitch black, obscuring everything past it. Dr. Wallace and Mya recoiled abruptly.

"The generator!" Sir Erdrick shouted, whirling.

"Fine!" the technician said. "It's—it's running nominally! All of the monitoring is coming through!"

"That shadow magic just released," the other technician said. "This is an elemental field."

Sir Erdrick leaned back, his mouth forming an 'o'. He slowly nodded. "Well played, Dupree. Well-played."

"Ping! Somebody come in!"

"I'm hearing you, but I can't see—ack!"
"Arbus? What just happened? The—urg!"
...
"You guys?"

"Four ... three," the technician said. There was a pause of ten seconds. "Two."

Sir Erdrick chuckled deeply. "Bradshaw," he said. "Zap Bradshaw casts a heavy shadow elemental field and augments it with Raye Courts-the-Shadows's intrinsic stores, allowing the mutant to pick off their remaining opponents while they're helpless. Fucking brilliant, Paru. Mind, in a real situation it'd probably kill Raye when the field dropped..."

"I can't believe Bradshaw was capable of such a wide-ranged and heavy elemental field," Dr. Wallace said, looking at the glass as though hoping to see through the veil of darkness.

"One," the Kekkai technician said.

"Yes," Sir Erdrick murmured. "And I can't help but wonder how Paru knew about that. Bradshaw's record doesn't really show anything like the magic we just saw; she'd have had to see him pull off some really impressive field-based magic, like an isolation ward or a pocket realm."

"And that's everyone," the technician said. "15th Street win."

"All right, let's have a reset," Sir Erdrick said. "I'm going down there." He turned to walk away, then paused. "How's the generator?"

The employee glanced at the screen, then stared at Sir Erdrick.

"All right, fine," Sir Erdrick said. He turned and exited the room.

47

In the great multipurpose hall of the Orleans Installation Facility, the walls echoed with the loud murmur of scores of employees spending the last of their time together at the retreat. They milled about in clumps, gossiping and sharing stories of the day. On a raised stage at the end of the hall, Securemarket™ CEO Thorvald Volnocht approached the podium with slow steps.

He looked over the crowd, then spoke. The microphone point on the podium caught his voice and routed it to the walls' resonators.

"Securemarket™ employees." Volnocht's voice sounded clearly throughout the room. The employees hushed and turned to look at the stage.

"When I was fighting in the Aramis-Sawtooth War," he began, "I made some acquaintances behind the sandbags. Don't think I would have done what I've done if not for those soldiers. When you're getting shot at most hours out of every day, and it's just these people watching out for you, you start to forget about ideology and religion and all of that. It's just you and them and the guys on the other side, and you just need to get done what you came there to do. The men and women fighting with you are the closest thing you'll have to friends, even if you wouldn't give 'em a word outside of the sandbags."

Volnocht cleared his throat.

"We had a lull in the action," he continued. "And we started talking about kids. Some of us had 'em already, some of us was going to. Some of us, like me, had no intention, but we got talking anyway because that's what'd been brought up. The topic was how hard we were going to train our kids to fight and why. Back then, the arms culture hadn't settled in quite so much, and many folk didn't wear weapons on the streets at all. Well, being soldiers most of us agreed that we would train any kids we had in how to fight properly. Then the question came up of why.

"Most common answer was 'Because it's dangerous.' The post-Snowfall world doesn't suffer weaklings, and nobody wants to see his kids die early. Just about everybody was bound and determined to make sure that any successors would be well able to defend themselves. Another interesting answer was just 'So they'll be strong.' Kinda macho thing that I don't really hold so well to, much as you might not think it of me. The answer I thought was just the best came from Private 'Big Bird' Daniels—who we all called 'Big Bird' for reasons I'm not going to discuss here. He just looked at us and he said, 'Because this is what I know, and I'll be damned if I can't pass *something* on to my kids.'

"That struck me right deep. It's a big world and there are a lot of us sentients on it. All of the great philosophers have discussed this business of significance and finding your place in the world, but when you get right down to it everybody wants to leave something behind.

"Well, kids, I'm good at two things: fighting and making customers feel cared for. I was a grocery clerk, then a store manager, then a soldier, then a store manager again. Now that I run the Securemarket™, I've finally got the chance to pass on everything I learned from all of those jobs.

"I am happy to say that at the end of this, the sixty-seventh Securemarket™ retreat, I am pleased and relieved to see the progress and dedication that I have seen out of all of you. You have all done me proud. Now stuff your faces with my food and guzzle my booze, y'ungrateful dogs. You've earned it."

Volnocht grinned as the employees roared.

48

Zap sidled into the middle seat of the row and kicked his carry-on luggage under the seat in front of him. He settled back and looked at Click, who appeared to be asleep and leaning against the window of the plane.

"I told you to drink more water," Zap said.

Click groaned.

"I just told you, is all I'm saying."

Across the aisle, To'mas and his roommate, Michael, buckled their safety belts.

"So there are two of them?" Michael asked hesitantly.

"Yes, T'y and Teak," To'mas said with a smile. "I'm sure they'll be really excited to meet you."

"I have no idea what I'm going to tell my mom about all this," Michael said.

"I recommend telling her that you've just met a lot of really interesting people."

A few seats back, Steve and Mike leaned against each other. They had taken the window and center seats, and the aisle seat remained open. Steve nuzzled against Mike's shoulder, and he smiled down at her.

"Do you want to come have dinner with my folks sometime soon?" Mike asked.

"Isn't it kinda early for that?" Steve asked, but smiled back.

"My folks are important to me," Mike said. "And I'm sure they'd like you."

"Well, ok," Steve said, laughing a little. "I'm not really that great with parents, so far as I know."

"You'll be fine."

The remainder of the employees took their seats without much fuss, chatting to each other as they went. The pilot's voice came over the plane's resonator plates.

"*Securemarket™ Employees, welcome to the return flight for Employee Retreat number sixty-seven. My name is Malcolm Hawthorne, and I'd like to welcome you back and hope that you had a good time at the retreat. We will be departing from the Orleans Installation runway in just a few minutes and will be landing at the Precinct One Skyport approximately three hours later, at 12:30. We anticipate clear weather the whole way. The flight attendants are going to help me out with this safety spiel again, so those of you who actually paid attention the first time can go ahead and tune out now.*"

The pilot continued talking as numerous conversations restarted.

In first class, Alan smirked at Raimi And The Soft Winds Blow, who seemed to be having the same morning that Click was.

"Do you have any idea what you did last night?" Alan asked.

"Vaguely," Raimi croaked. "I remember ... chocolate."

"Very good!" Alan said with a grin. "You wrestled Emma Rammek in the chocolate fountain."

"Did I win?"

"Basil and Paru hauled both of you out before a winner could be determined," Alan said.

"I would've won," Raimi grumbled.

"I don't know," Paru called from across the aisle. "Emma just about had you on the ropes."

Raimi was silent for a few seconds, then muttered, "I would've won."

"*Flight attendants, prepare for takeoff,*" Malcolm said over the resonators. "*Those of you who had too much fun last night might want to locate your barf bags.*"

A few minutes later, the great silver bird took to the sky, returning to New Washington.

49

Steve sprang up the stairs of the Rail entrance with rapid-fire steps. She grinned at how much easier the physical feat seemed post-retreat; she had first noticed the difference the previous evening at the range, where her scores were markedly higher than they had been two weeks before.

She hurried down Neimuth Avenue at a brisk pace, weaving her way through the slower-moving crowd. She was not quite halfway to her store's street corner when a raspy voice broke her commuter's reverie.

"Wait now, dearie."

Steve didn't stop walking, but glanced to the side and saw an old woman with dark skin, kinky black hair, and a simple gray hoodie that was a size too big. The woman was tucked into the corner of an alley entrance. She was looking directly at Steve. Steve hurriedly averted her gaze and quickened her pace.

"I have answers for you, nut-brown rose!" the woman called as Steve passed by her. "You need answers now, old Aggie knows. You come back now, or you'll be back later."

Steve didn't stop walking until she had reached the store's entrance.

Steve shoved the door of the store open with her shoulder, walked a few paces inside and stopped in her tracks. Her eyes went wide.

Someone clapped her on the shoulder and she jumped in surprise. She turned her head to see the offender and was met with Alan's grinning face.

"Don't look so surprised, Miss Anderson!" he said cheerfully. "I've been hearing you guys toss this rumor around for weeks."

"Yahbut..." Steve protested, turning her head back to the object that had startled her. "I didn't expect for it to happen while we were away!"

Standing like a gleaming altar on the left side of the store (from the entrance) was a polished, beautiful deli counter, displaying rows of meats, cheeses, breads and various different salads. The polyglass glare of the counter was obscured for a moment as Paru emerged from the corner.

"Ah, hello Steve," she said with a smile. "Do you like it?"

"Uh," Steve said. "Well, it looks really great! But do we really have the staff to..."

"We'll have a quick meeting about that once the rest of the shift gets here," Paru said with a nod. "In the meantime, you'd better start going through your B-Rank duties. Coming back from the retreat doesn't excuse you from working."

A few minutes later, Steve's shift takeover duties were complete and the rest of the afternoon shift employees had arrived, each one taking a few minutes to ogle the new deli section. Click was absent, naturally, not being an employee of the 15th and Neimuth store in the first place. Paru called them all to the back room, and they gathered while the morning shift watched the store.

"Well," Paru addressed the employees. "Welcome back, everyone. You all did an excellent job at the retreat, and I look forward to seeing you use the skills you learned there in the store."

She gestured at the door to the rest of the store. "You may have noticed that we now have a deli counter. I put in the application for one months ago, but it's only recently been approved. I think it'll be an excellent way to drum up business, given the number of restaurants in the area."

"I realize that some of you may be a bit concerned about our ability to cover the deli counter, particularly since we'll be running it at dinnertime. In response, Alan and I have interviewed a number of applicants and I am pleased to introduce you to the two newest members of our shift team."

She walked to a door to the small room that served as a multipurpose office and shell station and knocked on its door. "All right, you two can come out now."

The door opened. The first person behind it ducked her head and sidled under the doorframe to get through. The other person, being nearly half a meter shorter, simply strode through. Paru gestured to the two new employees.

"I think most of you know Click," Paru said. The faerie flashed the gathered employees a winning grin and bowed a little bit. He was already wearing his employee apron over flamboyantly-dyed clothing.

"And our other new employee might also be familiar to some of you, I understand. To those for whom she is not, may I introduce Michelle-Bear Urza."

"Hi guys," Michelle-Bear said, her smile a little bit sheepish. She was wearing her white bear-ear hat, a powder-blue hoodie (which was emblazoned with a cartoon version of her own bear-hatted head) and a pair of cargoes, but no employee apron.

"Michelle-Bear?" Steve said, astonished. "I thought you worked at Reynaldo's!"

"Uh, I'll explain later," Michelle-Bear said, scratching the back of her neck. "Management and I had a disagreement about some customer service of mine."

"Needless to say," Paru said, "we didn't consider it a valid disagreement on the management's side. We believe that Michelle-Bear's customer service habits will suit the Securemarket™ very well."

Michelle-Bear smiled.

"Unfortunately," Paru added, "we had no employee aprons that were a good fit for Michelle-Bear, so we have requested a special one from Corporate. Now, I expect everyone to participate in the acclimation of our new employees to the 15th and Neimuth working environment. However, As our only B-Rank employee, Steve will be overseeing Click and Michelle-Bear's training."

Both of the new employees smiled, though Steve noted that Click's seemed a bit wooden.

"Okay," Steve said. "I'll do my best."

"You'll do well, I'm sure," Paru said. "Now everyone to work, please. I would like to release the morning shift."

50

Steve looked at the array of ingredients sitting in front of her, then turned her head to look at the pictorial sandwich-making instructions on her shell. She looked back at the ingredients and sighed.

"I'm going to be honest with you guys," she said, "and tell you that the last time I made a sandwich there was an apartment fire. I pretty much live off of instant food and restaurant fare."

Michelle-Bear's arpeggio laugh preceded her ample hips, which she used to push Steve away from the counter. "Scootch," she said. "I've worked food service, and not just as a waitress."

"*Makaseta*," Steve said, gesturing to the food. "I'll be over here. Supervising."

"Me too," Click said.

Michelle-Bear flexed her Saf-T-Mem-gloved hands and surveyed the ingredients. "I'm assuming we have to do this by the book."

"Yeah," Steve said. "Substitutions are okay, but no experiments the customers don't ask for."

Michelle-Bear began to assemble the sandwich, her eyes flicking back and forth between the instructions and the ingredients. "This reminds me of when I used to work at SubFleet. That was a pretty shitty job. Not in my worst five, but definitely up there."

"You've worked a lot of jobs, Michelle-Bear?" Click asked.

"I went through a lot of them early on," she replied. "The Reynaldo's job is the longest one I've held to date."

"Why the turnover, if you don't mind me asking?" Click asked.

"Excuse me," a curly-haired man said, peeking over the counter. "Can I get a sandwich?"

Steve pointed at the sign on the counter:

Securemarket Deli™ Coming Soon!

"Not yet," she said. "We expect to be serving by the end of the week, sir."

"You shouldn't be working behind the counter if you're not serving," the customer replied.

"Thank you for the observation, sir," Click replied, smiling cheerfully.

The would-be customer grumbled and moved on.

"The reason I lost a lot of jobs early on," Michelle-Bear said, "is because I hadn't realized that my size would affect my career too."

"What do you mean?" Steve asked.

"In school, I got teased and beat up because I was big," Michelle-Bear said. "Eventually I formed a clique and got decent at fighting back, so I got left alone. That doesn't work so well in the job market. People still didn't like my size, so they antagonized me and I got fired a lot for no reason. There!"

Michelle-Bear slid her knife into the middle of the sandwich and closed it around the blade. The three surveyed the sandwich.

"Looks fine to me," Steve said. Click nodded.

"Okay, awesome," Michelle-Bear said.

"What did you do?" Click asked. "About the jobs, I mean?"

Michelle-Bear sighed. "I got ingratiating. Subby," she said, and shrugged. "I'm a skilled suckup now. I'm friendly anyhow, but that's not good enough for people who can't handle a woman who's a head taller than they are."

"That sucks," Steve said.

"Yeah, well," Michelle-Bear said and shrugged.

"So, Click, I think I've got to watch you make a sandwich," Steve said, "but unless it's a total disaster I think I'm comfortable with saying that you guys are fine to run the counter. You'll have other shift employees assigned to help you out, two during dinner hours."

"Sounds good," Click said.

"Maybe," Steve said. "We'll see how it pans out in practice."

"This sandwich is too dry!" To'mas shouted, throwing both of his arms over the counter from the other side. "I demand more hoisin sauce! Where's your supervisor! I'll have your job! My marriage is falling apart and service personnel are the only available targets for my impotent frustration!"

Michelle-Bear laughed. "I'm so sorry, sir," she said. "Would you care to insult me for a solid half hour with baseless attacks on my behavior?"

"Aw, how cute," Click said. "I think she thinks he's exaggerating."

"Oh no," Michelle-Bear replied, rolling her eyes. "No, no I don't."

"I'm going to make racist comments and expect you to commiserate now! Half-orcs all belong in jail! Mutants are dangerous freaks! Having sex with a morph is like bestiality!" To'mas droned.

"Okay, To'mas, shut up now," Steve said.

"How dare you speak to me that way!" To'mas said. "I'm going to have you killed! I know people! I—" he cut off abruptly as a cherry tomato bounced off his face.

Zap was nearly to the end of the aisle in his inventory when a customer, a dark-skinned man with laugh lines and a long coat, walked around the corner.

"Excuse me," the man said.

"Yes?" Zap replied.

"Could you help me find a few things in the frozen foods aisles?"

"Sure," Zap said, tucking his workshell back into its holster. "What do you need help finding?"

"Happy Cow Burgers," the man said. "I'm having a barbecue."

"Right this way," Zap said, walking ahead of the man. The man followed.

"Have you heard about Better Living?"

Zap laughed a little and glanced back. "I live in this precinct, so…"

The man laughed and shook his head. "No, I mean recent news."

"There's news? I just got back into town," Zap said. The two turned into one of the freezer aisles, where ambient light from the temperature-isolation fields bathed both of them.

"Just last week," the man said, "Better Living launched an offensive against Lorenz Municipality and claimed all the way up to Peterson Street, which they've been fighting over for ages."

"Yeah, wasn't that block part of a UZ at one point?" Zap asked.

The man nodded. "It was," he said, "but Lorenz has had it for years now. But Better Living just took it and it looks like Lorenz doesn't have the resources to take it back."

"I'll have to congratulate Sir Drake," Zap mused. He halted in his tracks, gestured to the shelf and smiled to the customer. "There you are, sir," he said. "Happy Cow farms. You should try their Reddi-Fry skillets; they're new."

"But you know what I think?" the man continued, seeming oblivious to his destination. "I think that Better Living needs to stop treating Lorenz like its only enemy. Mayfield Limited would benefit greatly from the destabilization of this precinct's municipal corporation."

"That's an interesting observation," Zap said.

"Oh yes," the man said. "Most of our defense funds are in the Lorenz detail, which is now in the form of an occupying force. What happens if something hits at home?"

"Mmm," Zap mmmed. He took his workshell out of his holster and did his best impression of a man who really needed to get back to work.

"I'll tell you: chaos. Mayhem. You'll see, my friend. I am stockpiling weapons and rations, and—"

"Is—is there anything else you needed, sir?" Zap asked.

"No," the man replied, looking a bit put off.

"That's fantastic," Zap said cheerfully. "Please feel free to find me if there's anything else you need."

Zap walked away. The man sighed, a bit annoyed, and opened the fridge case. After taking several boxes of burgers, he walked to the front of the aisle. Matt was standing near the auto-checkout machines, studiously not using the automop in his hands.

"Don't nobody want to hear the truth, is the problem," the customer said to Matt.

"Don't get me started, man," Matt replied. "Anyway, can't you see I'm mopping the floor?"

51

"Eighty-five!" Michelle-Bear shouted.

"Do you do substitutions?" an iron-haired woman said, holding up her handshell. It displayed the number '85' in a large font.

"At this hour?" Michelle-Bear said piteously. "...sure, what'll it be?"

"Eighty-six!" Click shouted.

"I want the chipotle mayonnaise on my cheesesteak," the woman said.

"I'm eighty-six," a blue-haired woman in her forties said.

"Excuse me, *I'm* eighty-six," the bald, cuckolded customer from Chapter 1 said.

"Okay," Michelle-Bear replied to the woman with gray hair. "That's fine. What kind of cheese?"

"I beg your pardon!" the blue-haired woman said. "Are you trying to cut in line?!"

"May I see your shells, please?" Click asked.

"Provolone," said the iron-haired woman.

"Okay!" Michelle-Bear said.

"No, I'm not!" the bald man said. "I am number eighty-six."

"If you'll show me your shells, please—" Click tried to interject.

"Eighty-three!" Zap said, appearing between Michelle-Bear and Click. He held a wrapped sandwich over his head triumphantly.

"I'm eighty-three," a man said, and tried to shoulder his way through the crowd.

"I am eighty-six!" the blue-haired woman shouted at the bald man.

"I'm sorry, folks, but I'm going to eighty-six both of you if you don't show me your shells," Click hissed through a plastic smile.

The two, startled, stopped arguing. They pulled out their shells and opened the Securemarket™ Applet.

"Oh," the blue-haired woman said. "I'm eighty-*nine*."

"Can I please see your applet real quick?" Zap asked as the customer reached for the sandwich. The customer nodded and fumbled at his belt, then showed its surface to Zap.

"Okay, sir," Click asked. "How can I help you?"

"Do you do substitutions?" the bald man asked.

"At this hour?" Click sighed. "Sure. What'll it be?"

"Iyesu," Steve said, surveying the crowd at the deli counter.

"Well, it's clearly popular," Alan said.

"I'm not sure I'm going to be able to handle that shit," Steve said. "I definitely heard the word 'substitutions' at least four times as I *casually walked by*. If somebody asks me to do a substitution I'm pretty sure that there will be a fire."

"It's not nice to joke about hurting customers," Alan chided.

"That's not what I meant," Steve said. "I'm talking about what happens when I try to take liberties with a recipe."

Alan made a noise of uncomfortable understanding.

"Eighty-nine!" shouted Zap, holding up a sandwich.

"It's about time," said the blue-haired woman.

"Ninety!" Michelle-Bear followed, also holding a sandwich.

"How much longer is shift?" Click asked, folding the sandwich on the counter over his knife.

"Two and a half hours," Zap said.

"Shoot me," Michelle-Bear murmured as she handed the sandwich off to a customer.

"Good bid," Click replied, "but nobody behind this counter has a gun."

Michelle-Bear sighed. "Ninety-two!" she shouted.

"Do you do substitutions?"

"At—sure," Michelle-Bear said. "What'll it be?"

"How are Click and Zap?" Steve asked. She peeked around the corner at the Deli Counter, where the subjects of her inquiry stood as if in a daze.

"They're a little shell-shocked," Michelle-Bear replied, still looking as bushy-tailed as ever. "I don't think either of them expected it to be this busy."

"Damn good thing we had an experienced waitress working the counter," Steve said.

"Oh, it's nothing," Michelle-Bear said. "Anyway, I'm going to take the boys out for a drink to help them get over their trauma. Want to come?"

"How long'll you be there?" Steve asked. "I'm gonna go to the range first."

"You going every day now?"

"Yeah!" Steve said with a grin. "My aim improved so much on the retreat, I wanna keep in the habit."

"Good for you," Michelle-Bear said. "Call me when you're done!"

"If Nalley wants to come, can she?"

"No," Michelle-Bear said with a sunny smile. "I fucking hate that bitch."

"Aight, I'll ask her if she wants to come."

"I think I'm going to go make myself a sandwich," Michelle-Bear said. "I'm hungry."

"Bring me back some olives," Steve said. She dug in her pocket and retrieved a credit chit. She glanced at its color and tossed it to Michelle-Bear.

"Will do. See you tonight!"

"Maybe," Steve corrected.

"See you tonight!" Michelle-Bear said, then turned and bounded toward the counter.

"Mark!" Steve shouted.

In unison, Nalley and Steve raised their pistols and fired five measured shots. They lowered their pistols and surveyed their handiwork; a small smile crept onto Steve's face.

Nalley raised her eyebrows. "Steve, that's ... you're getting really good."

"I know," Steve said happily. "Gotta say, things are really looking up for me."

"Yeah, about that!" Nalley said as she ejected the magazine from her pistol. "I need to hear more about this boyfriend of yours!"

"Well, he's into guns," Steve said as she released her own magazine. "And he's very sweet. I'm going to have dinner with his parents this week."

The women picked up a handful of bullets and began to refill their magazines.

"Are you nervous?" Nalley asked. "I was very nervous about meeting Alan's parents for the first time. Uh, as a person."

"Yeah, kinda," Steve said. "But Mike's an adult, you know? It's not like it matters that much if his parents approve or don't approve. I'll try to make a good impression, but I'm not gonna let it stress me out."

"Okay," Nalley said with a nod.

The two slid the magazines home, turned toward the refreshed targets and chambered the first round. They took a ready stance, their pistols pointed toward the ground in front of them.

"On my mark... —oh!" Steve began, shouting as she remembered something.

Nalley twitched. "Don't do that!" she admonished.

"I trust you to not kirk out on me," Steve said. "Listen, do you want to go out for a drink after this?"

"Sure!" Nalley replied.

"Michelle-Bear took Zap and Click out. They've had a stressful day."

"Oh, okay." Nalley furrowed her brow. "Wait, didn't Zap have a date with Pazi tonight?"

The girls exchanged troubled looks.

"Did he?" Steve asked.

"I think so," Nalley said. "I thought he said something like that."

"Huh."

"Do—do you think we should call and remind him?"

Steve set her jaw. "Far as I have come, *I* am not going to call Zap to remind him that he should be lubing up his girlfriend with a dinner date."

Nalley blushed furiously and stared at the floor.

"But maybe," Steve said, sighing, "you should give him a call, yes."

"Okay," Nalley said, flicking the safety of her pistol on and setting it down. She reached for her shell.

Outside of the 15th Street Watering Hole, all was quiet.

A young man burst from the bar's doorway and ran down the street full-tilt.

A homeless man watched him run by, smoking a cigarette.

52

Steve skipped up the steps from the Rail station, her backpack slung over one shoulder. She hurried down the street while humming a tune, a slight nervous edge to her gait.

"Thursday Thursday Thursday," she sung tunelessly.

Steve was preoccupied enough as she moved that she failed to notice the homeless woman sitting by the side of the road.

"Just a moment, dearie," the woman called.

Steve froze, caught off-guard.

"You've got something you're looking forward to tonight, haven't you?" the woman said. "Old Aggie knows."

Steve turned toward the old homeless woman, instantly angry. "I don't need this, you crazy old bitch," she said, her jaw tight.

"But you're nervous," the old woman replied. "Is that because this is your first time doing this sort of thing? Or perhaps you know something, deep down..."

"Shut up," Steve said, advancing on the old woman. "Shut *up*. If I see you again I'm going to call the cops on you."

"Yer a strong-willed, capable woman," the old woman said, her dark eyes fixed firmly on Steve. "You deserve somebody who's the same. Think you've found him?"

Steve and Aggie glared at each other for a few moments.

"G'wan ta work now," Aggie said.

Steve wheeled and strode away as fast as she could go.

"Pull!" To'mas shouted.

Zap hurled the jar high into the air, then threw another upward. He then broke into a run toward the other side of the loading dock.

To'mas reached for his hip, drew his pistol and fired. The first jar burst into pieces with a sharp report. To'mas fired again, then a third time. The first shot went wide, but the second found its mark; soon Zap was being pelted with the falling bits of both jars.

"Nice!" Steve said, her hands in her pockets.

"Hope I take to the rifle like that," To'mas said. "So far my training's a little bit rocky."

"You're not doing the cram track for your cert, are you?" Zap asked from the lower area of the dock.

"No," To'mas said. "So I've got time. My practice registration has gone through, and I'm going to go to the range tonight. Does anybody want to come with?"

"Can't," Steve said with a smile. "I'm going to meet Mike's parents tonight."

Both To'mas and Zap failed to look happy for Steve.

"I'm going to go see a certified Path Seer," Zap said. "It's actually a requirement for school."

"Why?" Steve said, stepping up to the edge of the dock's lip.

"I think that it's one of those precautions to make sure they're not producing evil wizards and stuff," Zap replied. As he spoke, Zap went to the empty jar pile and took a jar from it.

"Does it ever actually detect any?" Steve said. "Oh, I want to do three jars."

Zap blinked. "Three?" he asked.

"Have you seen me shoot lately?" Steve asked.

"Ok, three," Zap said. "And yes, actually; there was a big to-do a few years ago when all of the Path Seers said that they'd found the reincarnation of Baba Yaga and that she'd doom us all if she got certified. Unfortunately, her parents were pretty influential, and they got pretty upset when they refused to certify her."

"That's messy," Steve said.

"No kidding, lawsuits all over the place," Zap said. He walked toward the red X on the floor of the dock, which was now surrounded by plastic shards. "I'm a little nervous about it. I don't want to be declared unfit for certification just because of something one of my past lives apparently might have done. If there *are* past lives."

"I went to a Path Seer once," Steve said. "My parents took me."

"Yeah?" Zap said as he shifted the jars in his hands, preparing to throw one.

"Yeah," Steve replied. "They actually got a trace on my soul, they said. Not sure I believe it."

"Who were you?"

"Some woman," she said. "I don't remember her name. *Pull!*"

Zap hurled each jar into the air, one after the other. Steve drew her pistol neatly and shattered them all with three precise, measured shots.

53

Steve sat as stock-still as she could manage, trying to match Mike's family. She couldn't help but picture herself as a smear of red ink on a black-and-white photograph: distracting and unwelcome. She cleared her throat and smiled, trying not to think about how poorly she forced smiles.

"This is a really lovely condo, Mrs. Lewis," Steve said cheerfully.

Mrs. Lewis stared at Steve, then said what Steve thought was, "Thank you, Miss Anderson," but also closely resembled "shut up" in tone and intent.

"Michael tells us that you're a gunsmith, Stephen?" Mike's father said with a tone of apology in his voice.

"An apprentice," Steve said.

"Ah," Mike's father said. "To, ah, which company?"

"Er, to an artisan gunsmith, actually," Steve said. "Grover Messianic."

"I've never heard of a *Grover Messianic*," Mrs. Lewis sneered.

Steve bristled, but said nothing.

"We ensure that Michael buys only from major companies," Mrs. Lewis continued. "It ensures a quality weapon."

"This pasta is very good, Mrs. Lewis," Steve lied through clenched teeth.

"Yes," Mrs. Lewis agreed. "So. Stephen. You have a peculiar name, don't you?"

"Stephen?" Steve said, a little surprised. "Er—no, it's a very old name."

"Traditionally a male one," Mrs. Lewis replied.

"It's been gender-neutral for several generations," Steve said. "Just like Peter and Etienne. And Mason."

"Mmm," Mrs. Lewis said. "We're a very traditional family."

"But ... you're Etherists," Steve said, confused. She stole a glance at Mike, who was staring intently at his pasta.

"What of it, young lady?" Mrs. Lewis said acidly. "Etherism has its roots in many ancient monotheistic religions. We believe in following their traditions without their limp-wristed attitude. What religion are *you*?"

"My family is American Catholic..." Steve began.

"Miss Stephen," Mike's father cut in. "It's our understanding that you and Michael met at the Securemarket™ Retreat."

"Yes, we did."

"And how did your store do at the Kekkai exercises?" Mrs. Lewis asked.

"We won both of them," Steve said, deciding not to mention that one had been against Mike's store.

Mrs. Lewis raised her eyebrows. "With you on the team, even?"

Steve's ears rang as she felt blood rush to her face. Pushing her rage down, she swallowed and replied, "I understand your surprise, but they actually forgot to apply a handicap to offset my high skill."

Mrs. Lewis stared at Steve.

Steve stormed away from the condominium as fast as her little legs would carry her. As she expected, Mike interrupted her departure by calling from its entrance. "Steve, wait!"

Steve whirled. Her face expressed a mixture of indignation and hope as she shouted at Mike. She did not lower her voice even as he halted about two meters away from her. "Mike, I want an apology and a promise and I want them right now," she said. "I want you to apologize for not warning me about your mother, and I want a promise that I will never have to see her again!"

Mike shifted from one foot to the other. "I ... can give you an apology and a promise."

Steve waited a few seconds for his reply, then threw her hands forward. "Waiting!"

Mike scratched the back of his head. "Steve, my family is really important to me, you've got to understand."

Steve stared at Mike, then dropped her hands.

"My mother seems really harsh, I know, but—"

"She *insulted* me, Mike!" Steve shouted. "She insulted my breeding, my skill, my store, my friends, my employer..." she gesticulated wildly, trailing off.

"She just doesn't want me to settle for somebody who doesn't deserve me," Mike said. "And you rubbed her the wrong way."

"I don't care how I rubbed her," Steve said. "I care how I rub *you*. Please, Mike. An apology and a promise."

Mike looked at Steve a few moments, then averted his eyes. "I promise you will never have to see my mother again, Steve."

Steve's stomach dropped a meter at his tone.

"And I'm sorry," he continued, "because this isn't going to work out. I'm sorry."

Steve stared wide-eyed at Mike. He did not return her gaze.

"What?" Steve finally asked, incredulous.

"This isn't going to work out," Mike said. "I can't be with ... it's ... my family is very important to me. I'm sorry."

Without looking up to meet Steve's eyes, he turned and walked away.

It wasn't until he was nearly halfway to the condo entrance that Steve found her voice. "You—you aren't doing this to me!"

Mike kept walking.

"You can't be that spineless!" Steve shouted. "It's not possible! You're *twenty-two*; leave the *womb*!"

Mike ducked his head further, but did not slow his approach to the building's entrance.

Steve watched him go, tears in her eyes. When he reached the door, she screamed, "Fine! Fuck you, you son of a fuck! I hope that you find somebody who deserves you, because what an *icy bitch* she's going to be!"

Steve turned and ran full-tilt away from the hulking monolith of the condominium building.

"Can we kill him, maybe?" Zap asked. "I'm for murdering him in an alley."

"Yes!" Steve sobbed. "Yes, please do!"

"No," Nalley said firmly, "no killing. No death."

Steve went back to sobbing, crouched between Alan and Nalley while Zap paced the floor of the apartment. Nalley gently stroked Steve's back as she cried.

"You really didn't date him for very long—" Alan began gently.

"Shh!" Nalley shushed. Alan quieted, clearly out of his element.

"Maiming?" Zap asked. "Maybe we could maim him?"

"Yes!" Steve said.

"No." Nalley corrected. "No killing or maiming or hurting."

Zap let out an explosive breath and resumed pacing.

The sound of a key in the door caught everyone's attention. When it opened and Roger stepped through it, he found everyone's attention on him. His crimson-flushed eyes flickered to Steve's, which were nearly as red from weeping.

"I'll just go to my room then," Roger said. Alan nodded. Roger slipped past the group and disappeared down the hallway.

There was an awkward silence for a minute.

"I'd like to reopen the consideration for killing and/or maiming," Zap said.

"I second the motion," Steve said.

Nalley sighed.

Pazi sat on the bed of her dorm room and hugged herself fiercely. Her dog-dragon familiar snaked around her body, making concerned noises as he did so. She unclenched and reached out a hand to pet him. The creature made more noises of worry.

"Inryu," she asked the familiar, "I really thought that Zap was doing better. Why does one missed date bother me so much?"

Inryu headbutted her hand.

"If he called first, does that make it okay that he canceled?" she asked. "If so, why do I feel so bad?"

Pazi fell back onto the bed. "Is it because I know without asking that this is about Steve?"

Inryu snaked up to her face and lapped it with affection and concern.

"And because I assume that because it's probably about Steve, does that mean that I'm jealous of her?" she asked.

She sighed. "And is that because I believe that Zap is in love with her and not with me?"

She looked at her familiar, running her hand down his long, winding back.

"Should I break up with Zap, Inryu?" she asked.

There was a long pause.

"When I become a better Summoner, will I be able to Call familiars that speak English?" she asked.

"Graow," Inryu replied.

54

Steve did not bother trying to take a straight route to work. She emerged from the Rail station and began to search the street, her eyes sweeping each alleyway as she passed it. She was halfway to the store by the time that she located her quarry: a dark-skinned vagrant woman, leaning against the corner of a building.

"You!" she shouted. "You!"

"Aye?" the homeless woman who called herself Aggie replied. She saw Steve's face and cackled. "Seen the wisdom of Old Aggie's words, have yeh?"

"You knew!" Steve hissed, bearing down on the woman. "You *knew* what would happen."

"Old Aggie knows a lot of things," Aggie replied, leaning her head against the wall.

"You should have told me! You unfeeling cunt!" Steve spat.

"Watch your tongue! I *did* tell you, brat!" Aggie snapped back, her demeanor hardening. "You heard what you wanted to hear. That's always been your way, girl."

"What else are you keeping from me?" Steve asked. "Are you an Oracle?"

"I'm Aggie," the old woman said, then cackled. Her casual tone returned. "I yam what I yam and that's what I yam."

Steve threw her hands skyward and turned in a tight circle. She jabbed a finger at Aggie. "You know, I always figured that Matt was particularly obnoxious, but I now see that fortune-tellers are just *like that*."

Aggie cackled again, then broke into a wracking cough. Once recovered, she said, "Del Fye? He's a softie. Good work with that scumbag Stiles, though."

"So you're an oracle," Steve said with a nod. "Right. What the fuck am I supposed to do now? This *hurts*. It's the first chance I've had in a long time and this bastard blindsided me. I want somebody who isn't going to *do* that."

"If you're looking for a perfect partner," Aggie rasped, then put two fingers to her head. "Shoot yourself! Then ask Yesu if he'll fuck you in the ass!" Aggie burst into wheezing, painful-sounding belly laughter.

Steve stared at her, then slowly took a few steps away. Seeing that the old woman was not close to being over her own joke, she turned and walked away.

"We need to get the cops to patrol this neighborhood better," Steve muttered as she walked into the store.

"What?" Alan asked, looking up from his tabletshell. "Why?"

"Don't worry about it," Steve said. "Is Matt here? I'm going to put him on cleaning the bathrooms."

"*Matt* on the bathrooms? But they actually *need* cleaning," Alan objected.

"Restocking, then," Steve growled. "Anything unpleasant."

"Steve," Alan said, "I understand that you're going through a lot right now, but you know that Matt's gift is erratic. If he could have warned you, he would have."

"That's not it, it's—never mind!" Steve stormed away.

"Iyesu," Alan said.

Zap walked through the store's entrance. "Ping!" he said.

"Pong," Alan replied a little absently. "Hey Zap, have you been keeping current on the occupation of the contested territory?"

"A little," Zap said.

"So 'no', then," Alan said with a nod. "Seems that Better Living is devoting a lot of staff to keeping the area."

"Is Sir Drake deployed?" Zap asked.

"Not sure," Alan said. "Maybe we should ask him. How's Pazi with your cancellation?"

"Mm?" Zap said, caught off guard by the question. "I haven't called her since. She seemed okay when I made the call."

Alan gave Zap a look. "You should do something for her tonight," he warned. "You don't just cancel something and not make it up."

"Oh," Zap replied. "Okay."

Michelle-Bear arrived on the scene, her hat's ears barely clearing the doorframe. "Good morning, boys!"

"Morning, Michelle-Bear," Zap said.

"Morning, kiddo," Alan said. "Steve's having a bad day, so be nice to her, okay?"

"When am I ever not nice to anybody?" Michelle-Bear asked, confused.

"*Extra*-nice," Alan said. "Give her some Michelle-Bearapy."

"Oh!" Michelle-Bear said. "Okay!"

"Ping!" Click said as he walked in.

"Pong," Zap said.

"Pong!" Michelle-Bear replied cheerfully.

"Pong," Alan said. "Click, be nice to Steve. She's just had some rough news."

"Oh?" Click said, raising his eyebrows. "Okay, will do."

"Also, I'm afraid I have to put you on restroom-cleaning," Alan added.

"That's fine," Click said. "I just bought a new set I wanna listen to." He walked off.

There was a short pause. Michelle-Bear's expression was troubled. "Zap, could you be on LP?"

"What's up, Michelle-Bear?" Zap asked.
"I dunno," Michelle-Bear said. "Click didn't seem…"
"Didn't seem what?"
"It's probably nothing," Michelle-Bear said with a wave. "I'll go prep the deli."
She walked away.
"Ping," Matt said as he walked in the store. "Restocking, right."

Click shouldered his way out of the back door of the store and around the loading dock to the alleyway. He walked halfway into the alley and leaned against the wall. After a few moments, someone joined him.

"How's the landscape?" the other person asked.

"Steve's as cranky as can be expected," Click said. "She seems to be trying to take it out on Matt."

"Makes sense."

"Also, from what I heard of him on the phone, Zap is in the doghouse with Pazi. He skipped out on a date to be with Steve last night."

"Hm," the stranger said. "All right. Anything else?"

"Not really," Click said. "Are we still on for tomorrow?"

"If you can call for me without making wiseass comments, sure. Anyway, I'd better be going."

"Okay, see you," Click said.

The person began to walk away, but Click called, "Wait a second."

The figure stopped.

"Is this really the right thing to do?" Click asked. "This … meddling?"

The figure shrugged slowly. "Maybe, maybe not."

Click shoved his hands in his pockets.

"But on the other hand, nothing is being said that isn't already known," the person said. "We are just making those things a little harder to ignore."

Click nodded. "Okay," he said.

The figure walked off into the busy New Washington street and was lost in the crowd.

Click sighed and walked back toward the store.

"Here we are, ma'am. Aisle four," Alan said, pointing down the aisle. "Powdered, dehydrated, and reduced goods. Bonito flakes should be on the right, near the end."

"Thank you," the woman said, and then started down the aisle.

"Hey Alan," Zap said, rounding the corner from the next aisle. "Those yuzies I kicked out yesterday are back with like three more friends. They're all pretty well-armed."

"*Mattaku*," Alan cursed. "What are we now, the Merc district? Who picks a fight at a reputable Securemarket™? Who does that?"

"Did somebody say fight?" To'mas asked, his head poking out from above the aisle divider, which he had climbed on top of.

"To'mas! How many times have I told you not to go up there?"

"You never mean it," To'mas said with a smile. "So ... stun turret?"

"They're not in range," Zap said. "They headed straight to the back of the store."

"All right, let's go put the Fear of God into 'em. Click! Loren!" Alan called to the two, who were helping customers with the checkout machines. "We need you!" Click finished his business and jogged to the growing group of employees.

"Ok, kids, remember the manual," Alan said as they set out toward the back of the store. "Don't draw unless they do, but keep your weapons visible and your hands near them."

At the back of the store, a group of four young men and two women, all of whom openly bore deadly weapons, paced. The one in the front, a boy in his late teens with a military-style buzz cut, was actually holding a shotgun drawn in one hand. When he saw Zap emerge from around the corner of an aisle, a predatory grin spread across his face.

The grin faltered somewhat when three other employees emerged from behind Zap.

"Put that gun down, chall," Zap said, not slowing down. "Drawn piece say words you don't mean."

The young man's only response was to sneer, then turn away. The entire group about-faced and began walking in the opposite direction, toward the produce section.

Their way was abruptly blocked when a shopping cart rolled into the aisle's intersection, propelled by Michelle-Bear's foot. Though she smiled sweetly to the yuzies, she was ready for action: her hammer was unlocked and unfolded, held to her back by its sling.

The yuzies' faces registered disbelief that a single employee would try to block them, but for whatever reason none of them seemed willing to move past Michelle-Bear's towering form. Their only remaining choice was the aisle leading all the way back to the front of the store.

As they walked through the aisle, Zap, Alan, and Click followed them while Michelle-Bear, Loren, and To'mas circled around to block the way to other aisles at the front of the store.

A minute later, the yuzies had been herded peacefully outside, cowed by the prospect of facing a well-trained and unified employee force. They stood outside of the store jeering and cursing for a grand total of one minute before the police arrived, scattering the group.

Alan watched cheerfully as the ringleader of the group and one of his friends who had been caught were put in cuffs.

"Good job, everybody," he said, turning around. "You're all—wait a second."

"What?" Matt said.

"Matt, what the hell are you doing here?" Alan asked. "I thought you were on deli."

"No, Michelle-Bear was," Matt replied.

"There seemed like trouble," Michelle-Bear said. "I wanted to make sure everything was okay."

"Well, you helped and all," Alan said with a growing sense of horror, "but is there *anybody* helping Steve with the deli?"

As if to answer, the fire alarm went off.

55

"Ok, girl," Layla said, raising her eyebrows and giving Pazi a pointed look. "Let's practice this."

"O-Okay," Pazi stammered.

"I'll be Zap," Layla said, then changed her expression and lowered her voice. "Pazi! Hi!"

"Hi, Zap. Listen, we really have to talk," Pazi began.

Pazi was waiting for Zap at the top of the escalator. Her expression was very serious. Zap smiled and waved to her.

"Pazi! Hi!" he said.

"Hi, Zap," she replied. "Listen, we really need to talk."

"Can't we talk later?" Layla said in her Zap-voice.

"No, it has to be now," Pazi replied flatly.

"What, at the top of an escalator?" Zap said, laughing. "Can't it wait?"

"No, it has to be now," Pazi replied.

"Well, ok. What's up?" Layla asked.

"I really feel like you've been neglecting me, Zap."

"You do? I'm really sorry," Layla said.

"Sorry really isn't good enough anymore, though." Pazi said.

"Well, okay," Zap said. "What's going on?"

"I really feel like you've been neglecting me, Zap."

Zap sighed, then nodded. He ran a hand through his hair. "...I know. You're right. I haven't been paying enough attention to you or giving you the time you need from me. That's not fair, and I'm really sorry."

"Uh," Pazi said, momentarily thrown off. She shook her head and said, "Well ... sorry really isn't good enough anymore, though."

"Well, how can I make it up to you?" Layla said. "Maybe we can go to dinner sometime?"

"But it's always 'sometime', Zap, and it never happens," Pazi said to Layla firmly. "The few times we do go out are really nice, but you just don't devote the time to me that I deserve. I'm beginning to wonder if you really care at all."

"You know, you're right," Zap said. "Sorry *isn't* enough. Things need to change. I've been leading you on and I want things to change. It's not fair to you. I want to start by taking you to dinner as soon as possible. I'll clear up any evening this week for you. We could do it tonight, if you wanted."

"But I ... what?" Pazi said, completely thrown off course. "I'm just ... beginning to wonder if you care...?"

"I do care, Pazi! I care!" Layla pleaded as Zap. "I'll make it up to you someday, I promise."

"I can't do this anymore, Zap," Pazi said. "Maybe we could be friends sometime, but things as they are can't go on. I'm breaking up with you and I'm doing it now, and nothing you say is going to change my mind."

"I don't blame you for thinking that," Zap said. "And me saying it won't mean anything. If we're going to do things properly I need to make some time for you, starting now. So, dinner? Tonight?"

"I ... okay?"

"Okay, good." Zap smiled warmly and leaned in to kiss Pazi on the cheek.

56

Steve emerged from the Rail station and fished out her pack of cigarettes. She withdrew a cigarette and lit it with a small fire spell, then put away the pack. Re-shouldering her backpack, she walked on.

She had no intention of going straight to work, of course; she veered toward the alleyway where she knew Old Aggie would be ensconced. Sure enough, the ugly old vagrant crouched there, waiting for Steve.

"Hate the cunt, but keep coming back, eh?" Aggie rasped. "You're just like a man!" She expelled a grating laugh.

"Ugh," Steve said, grimacing. "Shut up."

"You said it first, dearie," Aggie said, then spotted the cigarette in Steve's hand. "Bum a fag, eh?"

Steve glared at the old woman, but dug out her packet of cigarettes and withdrew one. She offered it to Aggie delicately.

"Thank yuh, dear," Aggie said. "I can't die fast enough fer my tastes."

"So," Steve said. "Anything for me today?"

"Got a light?" Aggie asked.

Steve pointed at the cigarette and a dancing flame appeared at its tip for a few seconds. Aggie took a drag from it and grinned, displaying a set of teeth resembling a lumber pile at the end of winter.

"Well?" Steve asked.

"Nope," Aggie said.

"What?"

Aggie shrugged. "Nothing for you today."

"For this I gave you a cigarette?" Steve asked.

"No," Aggie said. "You gave me a cigarette to help me to th' grave. An' I thank y'h for that."

"...right," Steve said. She turned and began to walk away.

"If yeh want some news," Aggie called, "there's always the Ether!"

Steve gave Aggie a dismissive wave as she walked away.

Steve walked through the door with her personal shell in hand, her eyes fixed to the screen.

"Hey, look who's early!" Alan said, glancing up from his own shell only briefly.

"I had an appointment I thought would go longer," Steve replied. "What do you think of this whole Better Living occupation thing?"

"I think Better Living is putting too many of its eggs in one basket," Alan replied.

"Maybe," Steve said, "but what other threats are there? Lorenz is kind of our only rival."

"True," Alan said. "Maybe I'm just being paranoid."

Alan looked up from his tabletshell. "How're—how're you doing?"

Steve looked up. "Me?" she asked. "Oh, well..." She shrugged. "I'm doing ok," she said. "I'm not happy about what happened, but I'm moving on. It's not like I was dating him for very long, right?"

Alan nodded.

"Just another one in the pile, right?" Steve said. "I'd say that I'm probably going to end up a cat lady, but I hate cats."

"Don't think about it like that," Alan said. "You just haven't found the right person."

Steve sighed, somewhat irritated by Alan's attempt at placating her. "I—Alan, you know, I can understand why you'd say that. You've got a perfect relationship. You get along just right, you have the right amount of arguments and agreements, you love each other ... I can see why you'd be like 'you have to find the right person'."

Alan blinked.

"But for the rest of us?" Steve said. "There is no right person. It's a matter of settling for the *least* fucked up relationship you can find, because there's never gonna be a 'right' one. Look at me, man. If I'm *really really lucky*, I'll find somebody who's willing to put up with me and who doesn't piss me off too bad."

"I don't know about that..." Alan said lamely.

"Well," Steve said, "obviously I don't either. But I know I'm not going to get anywhere looking for 'the one'. Just ... 'one'. We'll work from there."

"Okay," Alan said.

Steve sighed. "Sorry," she said. "I'm sorry. I'm just frustrated." She turned and walked toward the back of the store.

"Steve," Alan said. Steve stopped and turned. "I hope you find the best person for you that there is."

Steve paused and stuck her hands in her pockets. "Thanks, Alan," she said, then turned and kept walking.

A dark figure in a wide-brimmed hat stood outside of the store. It was tall and fearsome, with a black coat and a face obscured by a mask and a large sword strapped to its back. It stood in the middle of the store's front windows, looking directly in and barely moving. It had stood there for several minutes by the time Steve walked nearby and spotted it. She had gone nearly halfway across the checkout lines by the time she realized that the figure was familiar.

"You again!" she said, pointing an accusing finger at the figure. She walked up to the bulletproof polyglass and gesticulated violently at the figure. "What do you *want!*"

They stared at each other for a while, then Steve tapped her store earpiece. "Alan, that weirdo with the wide-brimmed hat from a few months ago is back."

"Just leave it alone. If it's still there in fifteen minutes, we'll call the cops."

Steve scowled, still staring at the figure.

After about a minute, she sighed and waved the figure over to the front door of the store. The mysterious stranger obeyed, walking to the front door until it opened. Steve stood in front of the stranger.

"What do you want?" she asked.

"I seek..." the stranger whispered. "...the Eternal."

"It's been discontinued," Steve said. "Go away."

She left, leaving the figure standing by itself in front of the store.

57

"Hey!" Alan said as Zap walked into the store. "How nice of Mr. Bradshaw to *deign* to join us!"

"Please don't shout," Zap said, his voice tired.

"Only forty-five minutes late, even! On a Friday!" Alan said.

"Alan," Zap said. "Please."

Alan gritted his teeth. "Could you please call next time?"

"If I'm awake next time," Zap said, "yes."

Alan made a noise of irritation and walked away. Click, who had been standing nearby, walked up to Zap. "What's the deal, man?"

"I was up really late with Pazi," Zap said. "Really, *really* late."

"Oh!" Click said, and gave a thumbs up. "Awesome! It seems like you're really rekindling things with her!"

"Yeah," Zap said, not sounding terribly excited.

Click frowned. "You're beat, man. You want me to take your deli shift?"

"Please. I will give you sexual favors," Zap said.

"Don't make offers you don't intend to follow up on," Click warned. "But you got it; I'll cover for you." He clapped Zap on the back and walked away.

Zap made a noise of exhaustion.

Click approached the deli counter and noted that the employee currently behind it was To'mas.

"Speaking of sexual favors," Click said with a grin.

Click went through the counter's gate and joined To'mas, who had just finished making a sandwich for a customer. He handed it to the customer.

"The rush is late today," To'mas remarked.

"I'm noticing that," Click replied. "Hey To'mas, how's your couple?"

To'mas smiled. "Things are going great with them. I don't think things are going to work out long-term with us and my retreat roommate, but at the very least we'll let him go with a lot more experience. And fewer hangups."

"Keep the faith," Click said.

"Amen," To'mas replied.

"Hey guys," Loren said, entering the area behind the counter. "Looks like the rush is late."

"Yeah," To'mas said.

"Hey Loren," Click said. "Have you got a girlfriend?"

Loren blinked, caught off-guard by the question. "No," he replied.

"Have you ever?"

"Yeah," Loren said.

"Who was your last girlfriend?" Click asked.

"A girl named Sally, from school," Loren responded. "Why?"

"Don't you have any *stories*, man?" Click asked. "Any embarrassing anecdotes or wacky adventures? C'mon."

Loren stared, then shook his head. To'mas and Click looked at each other and shrugged.

Matt walked up to Zap with his shell in his hand. "Hey Zap, listen to this."

Zap looked up from his restocking task.

Matt read aloud. "'Mayfield Limited Withdraws Forces'. That's the headline. Aight. So. 'This week, municipal company Mayfield Limited withdrew its militia forces from a number of fronts, all of which were directly related to recent expansion efforts. Mayfield has repeatedly been criticized for its governing practices, which include unrestricted corporate monitoring of citizens, relaxed requirements for search warrants and police raids, and an alleged business connection to nearby drug lord Iwato Blumgardener. There are speculations that the cause of the withdrawal—'"

"Wait—" Zap said, holding up one hand. "Wait. Why are you reading this to me?"

Matt shrugged. "Thought you'd be interested."

Zap knit his brow and shook his head. He was quiet for a few moments, then said, "I really don't know what you're getting at, Matt, but I can't deal with your head games right now. If you think I should read that article, just forward it to me. Now please leave me alone."

Matt shrugged again and walked away. Zap muttered curse words under his breath.

58

"Okay," Michelle-Bear said, "so let's try another example. Somebody wants a roast beef sandwich with lettuce, mayonnaise, sprouts, horseradish, and activated fi-root on wheat bread. Go."

Steve sliced open the bread and began to make the sandwich; she spread horseradish on one side, mayo on the other, placed several slices of turkey and some shredded fi-root—

"Stop!" Michelle-Bear said. "Okay, you're going to cause a fire. Why?"

Steve stared at the sandwich.

"Because," Michelle-Bear said, "horseradish should not be activated. It'll catch fire when you put it in the activator. You need to put the horseradish on after the fi-root so that you can activate it on the sandwich."

"Oh, riiight," Steve said.

"Okay, so let's say that a customer wants the same sandwich but with fennel bread."

Steve paused, then looked up. "We ... won't serve that."

"Why?"

"Because fennel will also catch fire in the activator?"

"Yes," Michelle-Bear said.

Steve shook her head. "I wonder if making sandwiches was this dangerous before the Snowfall."

"I dunno," Michelle-Bear said with a shrug. "Probably."

"Hey Zap," Click said.

"Yeah?" Zap replied, looking up.

"You're looking better today."

"Thanks," Zap said, smiling. "I got more sleep."

"How're things with Pazi?" Click asked.

"Pretty good," Zap said.

Click frowned. "D'you want to go snag a drink after work and talk about it?"

Zap paused, then sighed and shrugged. "Yeah," he said. "I guess that'd be a good idea."

"How about Dog Street?" Click proposed. "It's in the arcade district, but the H Rail goes more or less straight there."

"That sounds fine," Zap said, then smiled. "Hey, man, I'm impressed. You're really doing a good job of turning over a new card."

Click laughed. "You have no idea," he said, "but yeah. I'm really trying. Thanks."

"Um," Zap said, "by the way, your deli shift's on. I think that Michelle-Bear's done training Steve."

"Whoop," Click said and skipped away.

Zap smiled and crossed his arms, then turned toward the front window of the store. His smile dropped from his face as he noticed a dark, mysterious figure in a wide-brimmed hat standing directly in front of the window. After a moment of staring, Zap tapped his earbud.

"Alan," he said, "that guy in the wide-brimmed hat is back."

"*I'm calling the cops,*" Alan said. "*Just ignore him.*"

Zap turned and hurried down an aisle, thoroughly unsettled.

"What's going on?" Loren asked.

Zap, who was standing near the end of an aisle, had been watching Alan give a report to the police officer who had arrived on the scene. The stranger was gone, having left before the police arrived.

"Alan's giving a police report. I'm going to give one too, in a second. There's been this creepy guy stalking the store."

"Weird," Loren said, and began to walk away.

"Yeah," Zap said. "Wide-brimmed hat, dark coat, big wide buster sword."

Loren stopped in his tracks and turned back. "Oh?"

"Yeah," Zap said. "He looked like a Shadowflame, if you ask me."

"Did you get a look at his face?" Loren asked.

"Uh, no," Zap said. "Come to think of it, I think he might have been wearing a mask."

Loren looked at Zap for a few seconds.

"You okay there, Loren?" Zap said. "I think that's the first time you've ever asked a detailed question about anything."

"Yeah," Loren said. "Just curious."

Zap, Click, and To'mas (who had caught wind of plans and insisted that he attend) approached the entrance to the Dog Street Bar. A bouncer was posted directly outside of the building: a fit-looking bovine morph, whose unusually-patterned black-and-white-furred skin made her stand out even more than her unusual clothing and piercings might have.

"Hey," Click said to the bouncer as he passed her. She gave him a quick wave.

Once inside, To'mas let out a low whistle. "I know who that is!" he murmured to the others. "She's an associate of Oddzer's!"

"Who?" Zap asked.

"Oddzer!" To'mas said, exasperated. "The *Shadowflame*."

"She sort of looks like a Shadowflame herself," Zap said.

"I'd hit it," Click said appreciatively.

"She'd hit *you*," To'mas said. "And you wouldn't get up."

The three took seats at the bar.

"Memory dump, user," Click prompted Zap. Zap looked a little apprehensive, glancing at To'mas..

"It's cool, Zap," To'mas said. "Mum's the word. Promise."

The bartender appeared from out of nowhere. "Get you gentlemen something to drink?"

"A Faerie Dust," To'mas said.

"Something Shiny and Green," Click said.

"Uh," Zap said. "What's on tap?"

"Guy, Guy Lite, Cooper, Cooper Lite, Guinness, Sing-Sing-Sing, Trout, Lyre, and Fishhead Dog IPA."

"I'll have a Sing," Zap said.

"All right," the bartender said.

Zap turned to Click. "You ordered 'something shiny and green'?"

"I ordered *a* Something Shiny and Green. Melon Liqueur, sour mix, seltzer water and a lime wedge."

"Sugar shock," Zap said, shaking his head.

"So," Click said. "Mind shedding a little light on the Pazi subject?"

Zap sighed. "Okay," he said. "It's like this..."

Two hours later, the three stumbled out of the bar. After they had gone their separate ways, Click drew his shell and tapped it several times.

He held the handpiece to his ear and waited several moments. He then grinned and said, "Hey! Have I got some really interesting news for you."

59

It was Friday.

Stephen Anderson skipped up the last few steps of the 14th Street Rail station and lit a cigarette. It was unusually cool for late summer, and a moderate breeze blew her curly hair around her face. She pushed it back with one hand and exhaled a lungful of smoke, looking into the sky and watching the cloud dissipate.

Pazi Elwynn sat on the side of her bed and watched as the door to her dorm room closed. Her tear-filled eyes swept from the door to the table near her bed, where an exquisitely-designed velvet-plastic rose lay. She shook her head and let out a long sigh. After a few moments, she smiled a little bit.

Zap Bradshaw stood in a dormitory elevator. His eyes were somewhat tired and red from crying, but his face showed an unparalleled sense of relief. He wiped his face with his sleeve and smiled.

Matthew Del Fye held a camera up to his face, looking through the viewfinder at various objects. He mimicked pushing the shutter button, making shutter noises with his mouth as he did so. He let the camera rest against his chest, held by the strap, and shook his head. "Damn, man," he said. "Damn." He retrieved his handshell and made a call.

Michelle-Bear Urza made a face at her available wardrobe. "Gotta do laundry," she murmured to herself. She waffled between her two choices: a top that her mother had bought her (whose pattern was a crime against humanity) or her expensive Dura-Kev sundress, which Michelle-Bear liked the look of but was honestly too heavy to wear to work. After a minute of deliberation, Michelle-Bear sighed and pulled the armored dress off of its hanger. "Suffering for fashion," she remarked.

Alan Morganstern sat atop the divider between aisles next to To'mas Bonvent, reading the news. His expression darkened as he read and he shook his head. "I don't like it," he murmured. "I don't like it at all."

Click o'th'Granfalloon clapped Raimi And The Soft Winds Blow on the back and nodded to her. Raimi looked back and returned the nod, then walked away, a theatre mask in one hand.

Ro Z'kerr tightened the strap to his massive sword, then readjusted his facemask. He regarded himself in the mirror briefly, and then retrieved his wide-brimmed hat from the nightstand. Today would be the day. Even if he had to kill innocents.

Curtis Mayfield leaned back in his comfortable desk chair and smiled broadly. Everything was laid out, marking the easiest and most significant gain in Mayfield Limited's history. He reached out one hand and tapped the intercom panel on his desk. "Maria," he said, "give General Fawkes the go-ahead. Today's the day."

60

Aggie was already waiting in her alley when Steve arrived on the scene. Steve held out her pack of cigarettes, and Aggie reached forward and took a cigarette from it. Steve reached out a finger and ignited Aggie's cigarette.

Aggie took a drag. "Horizon's roiling with clouds," she said. "There's a bond 'bout to break, if it hasn't already."

"Whose?" Steve said.

"Be ready for it," Aggie said, "because it was more binding than it was freeing, but someone newly-freed may stumble into others."

"Huh," Steve replied.

"Also—did you read the news?"

"Yeah," Steve said.

"I'm worried about all that," Aggie said.

"You're 'worried about all that'?" Steve asked, somewhat incredulous. "That's a weird thing for an oracle to say."

"You know," Aggie said, "I never said I was an oracle. I'm just a good listener. You could stand to pick up that skill."

"Whatever," Steve said, annoyed. "Why are you worried?"

"How many Knights have you seen walking the streets this week?" Aggie asked. "Where is our army?"

"...okay," Steve said. "Um, anything else?"

Aggie stared at Steve, took a deep drag of the cigarette, then said, "Being impulsive isn't always being wrong."

Steve nodded slowly. "D'you want a cup of coffee?" she asked.

"Fuckin' One I do," Aggie said. "And a sandwich. Get me those. And a bottle of whiskey."

"I'll be back with coffee and a sandwich," Steve said.

"Hey guys," Zap said, looking up at To'mas and Alan. He passed by and moved toward the deli counter. A few seconds later, he came back and looked up at the two. "Uh, Alan, aren't we not supposed to sit on the aisle dividers?"

"If you can't beat 'em..." Alan began, still reading the news on his shell. "Be a dear and prep the deli, okay?"

"Where's Steve?" Zap asked.

"She came in, bought a coffee and a sandwich, said she'd be right back and walked out," To'mas said.

"Ok," Zap said, then turned to walk away.

"Hey Zap," To'mas said, prompting Zap to turn back. To'mas gave Zap a questioning look and Zap nodded. To'mas nodded back, then Zap walked toward the deli.

A few minutes later, Alan put away his shell. "Okay," he said to To'mas. "Down." The two vaulted to the floor just as Steve returned. "Hey guys," she said. "How's stuff?"

"Not too bad," Alan said.

"Hey Steve," To'mas said. "You should talk to Zap."

Steve tilted her head. "Why?"

"You just should."

Steve shrugged and walked off. To'mas smiled to himself and walked down the next aisle over, leaving Alan, who was booting up his work tabletshell, alone at the front of the store.

Matt appeared without warning and with an expensive camera slung around his neck. Alan scarcely had time to look up before Matt raised the camera and took a picture. Alan blinked.

"What—what was that?" Alan asked.

"Taking photos today," Matt said.

"So it seems," Alan said.

Matt walked off.

"You'd better actually do work while you're carrying that thing around!" Alan shouted after him.

"Hey Zap," Steve said, approaching the deli counter.

"Hey," Zap said.

Steve leaned on the counter. "To'mas said I should talk to you about something. What's up?"

"Oh," Zap said. "Um. I broke up with Pazi last night."

Steve was stunned silent.

Zap shrugged. "I just ... I wanted to be in love with her, I guess, but wasn't. So I talked to her and we broke up. She took it well. I think she'll like me better when she doesn't have to think of me as a boyfriend. And vice versa."

"I'm sorry..." Steve said.

"No, it's a good thing," Zap replied. "I hope I can be her friend. I feel like I couldn't have been a good boyfriend to her, even when I was trying. There was nothing behind it."

"Yeah," Steve said. "...so, um."

A shutter noise interrupted her; Matt had arrived and taken a picture of the two of them talking over the counter.

"Uh," Steve waxed eloquent.

"Matt," Zap asked, "why do you have a camera?"

"For taking pictures," Matt replied.

"Oh really?" Zap asked.

"Yeah," Matt replied. "Really." He walked past them.

"What do you make of that?" Zap asked.

"I have no idea," Steve said.

Zap looked at Steve. "Do you..."

"What?" Steve asked.

"...mmm," Zap said. "Never mind. I'm not in a great place, I'm sure that's all it is. Today just ... feels weird."

Steve knit her brow. "Have you read the news lately?"

"No," Zap said. "Why?"

"No reason," Steve said.

Michelle-Bear approached the two, a bemused look on her face.

"Ping, Michelle-Bear," Zap said.

"Ping," Steve echoed.

"Pong, guys," Michelle-Bear said. "Do you know why Matt is carrying a camera around and taking pictures of everybody?"

"No," Zap said. "We were actually sort of wondering that too."

"Maybe he's picking up a new hobby," Steve said.

"I asked him why he took my picture, and he said, 'For the epilogue.' I was like, 'What epilogue?' and he said 'Of the story.'"

"Weird," Steve said.

"Textbook Matt, though," Zap said.

The girls both nodded and murmured in agreement.

To'mas wandered up the aisle with Alan's tabletshell in hand, taking inventory of the store. He was humming Ellis Manteaux's *Rule of Threes* along the way and taking about twice as long as he needed to.

He was interrupted by Matt, who stuck a camera in his face. To'mas grinned photogenically and Matt snapped a picture.

"How does it look?" To'mas asked.

"Gar!" Matt said, giving a thumbs-up.

"Schveet," To'mas said. "What's the occasion?"

"Gotta wrap it all up," Matt replied.

"Wrap what up?" To'mas asked.

"It all," Matt replied with a shit-eating grin.

"You're a trip, man," To'mas replied, laughing.

"Hey guys," Loren said. Matt immediately whirled and took his picture.

"Uh," Loren said, "why did you just take my picture?"

Matt's expression grew perturbed. "I don't really know," he said.

"Okay," Loren said, rolling his eyes a bit.

61

Friday soon kicked into gear. The deli was swamped with hungry customers and the Friday shopping rush started early, filling the store with nearly more customers than the employees could handle. Even Matt helped nearly all of the time, fielding questions somewhat enigmatically but, for the most part, sending customers on their way.

It wasn't until around 15:40, right around the time that the deli crowd was thinning a bit, that things took a turn.

Michelle-Bear, To'mas, and Zap were busy at the deli counter, filling orders and making sandwiches with polished grace.

With no warning whatsoever, a scream pierced the air. All three employees froze in place, as did the customers they were serving.

A rough voice echoed from the front of the store. "I will see all of the employees of this store at the front!"

A pause.

"If I do not, I will begin killing your customers."

The stranger got his wish; within seconds every employee was at the front of the store and pointing a weapon at him. Some of the bystanders, too, had their weapons out and were pointing them all at the stranger; the others didn't seem to want to make themselves into targets.

Steve and Zap immediately recognized the man in the wide-brimmed hat. He was even more imposing than he had seemed when he was outside the store; the man could not have been shorter than Michelle-Bear and was probably even more muscular under his heavy coat. One of his gloved hands was holding aloft a massive sword with seemingly very little effort. The naked sword was almost as fearsome as the figure himself—it was half a meter wide, a luminous gold color, and inscribed with strange symbols along its entire length. His head was tilted back somewhat, and everyone could see that the man was wearing a dark-colored mask with tinted lenses over his eyes and a set of vertical slits where his mouth would be. The figure was also holding a terrified-looking businessman aloft by the shirt with his free hand.

"If anyone takes action against me, they will face the consequences," the figure said. "I have a simple request, and once it is fulfilled I will depart."

"To'mas...?" Alan murmured under his breath.

"All of the aura readers on this thing measure this guy as off the charts," To'mas's voice muttered in Alan's ear. "I seriously doubt the gun would even faze him."

"Okay," Alan said aloud, "state your demands, terrorist."

"I am no terrorist," the man said. "I am Ro Z'kerr, brother of Lath Z'kerr and heir to the fourth royal laboratory of Mu."

The bystanders murmured among themselves, mostly about how crazy the man had to be.

"Mu doesn't exist," Steve said derisively, keeping the stranger's head in her sights.

"The stupidity of your historians is immaterial," Z'kerr rasped. "I am Ro Z'kerr and I demand that the Eternal face me."

"We have no knowledge of an Eternal," Alan said. "We are all mortals."

Z'kerr pointed his sword straight at Alan, who raised his shotgun in response. "You lie!" he shouted. "My divinations have been exhaustive and conclusive! The Eternal is here and I demand restitution for what he has done!"

"What would that be?" Zap asked, looking down his wandpoint at Z'kerr.

"The Eternal destroyed the minds of my brother and his fellow scientists!" Z'kerr said in a hoarse roar.

"Or," Loren said, stepping out from the crowd, "this Fourth Royal Laboratory was looking into the unknowable, and staring directly into it was too much for their simple minds to withstand."

Ro Z'kerr's reaction was instant; he tossed the businessman into the crowd, knocking down several nearby onlookers. He strode across the floor in two impossible paces and grabbed Loren by the apron, hoisting him aloft as he had done with the businessman.

"You know nothing of the Royal Scientists of Mu," he hissed at Loren. "And for your insolence, you die."

He drove the blade through Loren's midsection, running it straight through and out his back. The wound sprayed blood all over Zap, who shrank away from the gore. Loren's body convulsed in Z'kerr's hand. Zap cringed away and several members of the crowd shrieked.

"You certainly are Muan, aren't you?" Loren asked from behind Z'kerr. His shirt and apron were undamaged, and he stood casually with his hands in his pockets.

Z'kerr looked back at Loren, then up at the empty space where his hand now held nothing.

"Something troubles you, so you choose to hit it with your livemetal until it goes away," Loren said, tilting his head a bit. The empty look in the eyes of their coworker unsettled the employees who caught them.

"It is because you think it will work," Loren continued, then spoke in a formal tone as though quoting. "Nor again is there anyone who loves or pursues or desires to obtain pain of itself, because it is pain, but because occasionally circumstances occur in which toil and pain can procure him some great pleasure."

Loren clasped his hands behind his back. "This is not such a circumstance."

Z'kerr slowly lowered his hand and his blade. "You," he said.

"You know, Ro, I have a name now," Loren said. "Lorem Ipsum."

Z'kerr lunged forward and lashed out in a deadly arc with his sword. It passed through empty air.

"Most of your people chose to learn a lesson from the fate of Laboratory Four," Loren asked, standing calmly on the ceiling. "Did you just not get it? Were you too busy praying to Maal to give you long life?"

Z'kerr threw his sword at Loren. It traced an unnaturally straight line up to the employee, who merely held up his hand. The sword hit its mark, but seemed for some reason to be disproportionately small; it appeared that only a small knife had pierced Loren's hand. Looking directly at the sword, it seemed to be the correct size, but so, somehow, did the hand. Many onlookers looked away, rubbing their aching temples.

Ro Z'kerr growled and beckoned to the sword, which shot out of Loren's hand and returned to him.

Loren wiped his hand on his apron unnecessarily; there was no blood. Also, he was now on the floor in front of Z'kerr, not on the ceiling. He did not seem to have actually moved or disappeared. More bystanders clutched their heads.

"I am unwilling to fight here any longer," Loren said. "I am already damaging the weaker minds among the onlookers. I was happy to be a placeholder here and I care for these people. Together we will leave this place and finish this feud once and for all. If you don't wish to begin your search anew, I strongly suggest that you leave them alone and follow me."

Z'kerr did not seem pleased, but did not make any overt physical action; it seemed that he acknowledged that Loren could escape if he so chose with little effort.

Loren turned back to the other employees—all of whom had long since lowered their weapons in shock—and smiled.

"Sorry, Alan," he said. "I don't really have the flexibility to give my two weeks."

"Uh," Alan said, "that's—that's okay."

Loren waved to everyone else. "I'm afraid that none of you are ever going to see Loren Waites again," he said. "It's been real. I'll miss you."

The employees and the crowd were all silent as Loren stripped off his apron and folded it neatly.

Finally, Steve blurted: "We'll miss you too, Loren. Um, Lorem."

Loren laughed. "Please, still Loren. If only for a little longer."

Alan tapped his nametag twice and held his hand out, palm up: the Service Worker's Salute. One by one, the other employees followed suit, tapping their badges and holding out their hands. Loren returned the salute, and then did something extraordinary: he took himself off.

Quite a few members of the crowd cried out in pain as Lorem Ipsum 'doffed' Loren, who dissolved into a mass of archaic-looking code text. Lorem, whose features seemed to elude the senses, highlighted the text with his hand and made a flicking motion, and the Loren-code vanished. Matt raised his camera and took a picture.

Lorem Ipsum took one last glance at the employees of the 15th and Neimuth Securemarket™, then turned to his opponent. Ro Z'kerr tensed and readied his weapon, but Lorem had no intention of fighting. A noise split the air like someone violently running all of their fingers across the modulation patch on a mixer, and then the two enemies were gone.

Everyone gaped. Zap stuck a finger in his ear and twisted it around. To'mas's voice sounded over the store's PA system.

"Attention shoppers. We apologize for the inconvenience. Please return to your Securemarket™ shopping experience. Remember, it's Data Deal Friday! Please check our ethsite for Data Deals valid today only!"

After a few moments, the crowd's New Washingtonian instincts took over. They murmured amongst themselves in bemusement and wonder as they dispersed outside or into the aisles. The employees all gathered at the front of the store, forming a half-circle around Loren's discarded apron. Alan leaned down and picked it up.

"This is going to be a hard one to file," he said, then started. He looked at his shell, which informed him that he had an incoming call. "Scuze me." He moved away from the group. "Hey, Paru," he said as he walked away.

"That was really something else. I think that today couldn't possibly get any weirder," Click said.

Everyone stared at him.

"What?" Click asked.

"You don't *say* that," Steve said.

"Why not?" Click said.

Alan interrupted before Steve could reply. "Paru called," he said urgently. "Mayfield's sent an occupation force into this neighborhood. We've got a war on our hands!"

62

"Customers of the 15th and Neimuth Securemarket™," Alan began. The mic near his mouth picked up his voice and amplified it over the PA system. Alan's calm, clear announcement reached every corner of the store, drowning out the confused babble of the crowd.

"Mayfield Limited has declared a state of Official Opposition against Better Living Limited, our precinct's current municipal corporation," Alan began. He had unslung the shotgun from his back and held it one hand, rested against his shoulder. The customers near him stared, alarmed. "Please remain calm and follow my instructions to ensure the safest Securemarket™ experience."

The nearby employees bustled about, moving customers out of the aisles. Steve paced the front of the store with Alan's tabletshell, issuing commands to the store's defense mechanisms. Clear HD-Plastic shutters emerged from the ground just in front of the shelves, protecting the products but leaving them on display.

"My employees are already enabling the Securemarket™'s built-in defenses, designed to convert the Securemarket™ building to a C-Class Defense Structure. Should you choose to remain in this building, you may be asked to aid in the defense of the building and our municipality. All current Securemarket™ guests are welcome here, as are any other residents of the precinct who should wish to take shelter here."

Small, clear barriers, not unlike those that covered the shelves but only slightly above waist-height, rose between the aisles, providing a bulletproof plastic 'bunker'. Sections of the aisles lowered into the ground and left gaps through which the employees could travel.

"If you cannot or will not abide by these conditions, Securemarket™ Incorporated must ask that you leave the store at this time," Alan intoned. "We strongly suggest that you proceed to the next secure location available to you, whether it be your home or the nearest Rail station."

There was relative silence for a moment. The vestiges of Alan's announcement echoed off the walls of the store. Alan closed his eyes and sighed, then spoke again.

"Some of you may be aware of Mayfield Limited's Opposition tactics," he said in a less official voice. "To those who aren't: please understand that being outside when Mayfield's forces arrive is *not safe*. If you feel unsafe taking refuge with the Rail employees and your home is not nearby, you should consider staying here. But please make your decision now."

Some of the customers left, murmuring about family members and friends.

"Okay," Alan said. "All employees and customers to the front! I need everyone who has a weapon proficiency of B or better to stand in front of checkout device five!"

Only a few minutes later, the customers had been successfully sorted. To'mas ushered those who were not physically capable of combat or had insufficient certification to the back of the store. Steve and Alan placed the employees in support positions, leaving places for themselves in the front lines. Matt walked to the control booth to man the stun turret. As the preparations were being made, Click turned quickly, his eyes alert. "Listen!" he barked.

Everyone went silent for a few moments. The sound of gunfire floated by.

"They're here," Steve said. "It's good to know we actually have some militia forces around."

"What's the strategic point?" Zap mused.

"It could be us," Alan replied. "It wouldn't be the first time that an occupational force tried to take a Securemarket™ as a base of operations."

"What happened last time?" Zap asked.

"Let's get in place!" Alan barked. "If they break through the line, we need to be ready for them before they get here!"

The employees shouted orders to the customers who had been assigned to them and they all bustled into their places. Zap stayed behind.

"So," he murmured, "what happened last time?"

"What do you think?" Alan replied in a low voice. "They took it."

Zap frowned. The moment was broken when someone screamed from outside. The sound of gunfire came from outside, very close now.

"All right!" Alan said, pushing Zap. The two of them started jogging toward their positions behind one of the folded checkout kiosks.

They were halfway there when a familiar voice cried for help outside. Alan froze.

"Help! Somebody!" the voice called from outside.

"Nalley!" Michelle-Bear shouted.

Zap turned back and faced Alan, who stood stock-still in indecision.

Alan's gaze swept over the gathered forces; people he was sworn and expected to lead as store manager. Breaking his position and going outside would be abandoning his post, yet someone he loved was outside. The battle hadn't even begun, but...

The sound of automatic fire and Nalley's shriek from outside broke Alan's reverie. He turned to run toward the door, his instincts taking control.

"Stay where you are, Morganstern!" a familiar voice—not Nalley's—crackled to life in his ear. Alan stopped.

"Your beloved is coming to you," the voice said.

There were shouts from outside and the gunfire stopped. Moments later, a dumpy-looking woman in dirty gym clothes bounded into view with superhuman agility. Tucked under the figure's arm was Nalley; in her other hand was a beautifully-crafted elven sabre. The woman ducked into the Securemarket™ as the gunfire resumed, bullets caroming off the polyglass of the store's front window. The woman set Nalley on the ground; Nalley ran at top speed to Alan and threw her arms around him.

"Aggie?" Steve asked, eyes wide.

Alan looked up from Nalley, whom he held tightly. "...that's Raimi's sword..."

"Correct," Aggie said, then reached up to her face. "...and correct." She wrapped her hand around her face. With a sucking motion, it pulled away like a mask, drawing all of the woman's 'old' features along with it. The face's features gradually simplified into those of a plain theatre mask: 'tragedy'. The woman moved the mask away; it was Raimi And The Soft Winds Blow.

"...you?" Steve said.

"Get into place, Morganstern," Raimi said. She grasped the hem of the hooded sweatshirt and pulled it off, revealing that she was already wearing her mythril armor underneath. "That's the last order I'm going to give you. You're commanding *me* now."

Alan blinked a few times, then shook his head. He locked eyes with Nalley and pointed to one of the groups. She nodded and jogged toward it.

Alan took a deep breath and squared his shoulders. He looked outside and saw that Mayfield soldiers were gathering outside. They were clad in black, complete with masks and gloves; they looked far more like a pack of assassins than militia members. Easily two dozen of Mayfield's finest positioned themselves just outside of the bottleneck of the front entrance door of the Securemarket™, which Steve had sealed just after Aggie and Nalley's entrance.

One of the soldiers began to place sonic resonators on the store's door. Alan turned to the gathered forces. "Get ready!" he shouted. "We will hold this store!"

The soldier placed the final resonator. The employees and recruited customers hunkered behind their barriers, their weapons pointed directly at the door. The soldier tapped a military shell at his side and the resonators activated.

The door shattered, Mayfield's soldiers poured through and the battle was joined.

63

The first wave of Mayfield's troops did not stand a chance. They poured through and were immediately gunned down as the entire front line of employees unloaded upon them. All fell to the ground, wounded or dead. The second wave made a slightly better show, stopping most of the bullets with riot shields. Unfortunately for them, most were still in Zap's circle of effect when he triggered the hung spell there; a towering inferno set the hapless soldiers ablaze. Matt targeted the remainder with the stun turret and they were gunned down under a combination of stun bolts and bullets. The soldiers did not seem discouraged, however; they rallied and attempted another entry.

The defenders fought back.

"*Raimi's taking over for me in the back,*" To'mas's voice sounded over the employee radios. "*Taking sniping position.*"

"Right," Alan replied. He sighted an intruder over his barrier and fired. "Focus on commanding troops or those with special armaments. Or few armaments."

Steve and Zap crouched behind the same barrier. Zap finished murmuring a spell and a bolt of lightning shot from the tip of his wand. It struck a group of three soldiers who had just come through the door, who staggered and lost control of their shields. Steve took aim and fired three times, hitting each of the soldiers in the forehead.

"Fuck," Zap said a bit shakily.

"Yeah, I'm kind of a crack shot these days," Steve replied.

"No, I mean," Zap said. "We're killing people. We're actually killing them. I mean, have you ever done that before?"

Steve set her jaw. "No," she said. "Don't think about that right now."

"Right," Zap replied, then closed his eyes and started chanting.

One of the soldiers staggered past a hail of gunfire and stun bolts and made it to one side of one of the checkout kiosks, crouching just behind it. His shoulders fell in a sigh of relief. With no warning, Michelle-Bear stepped from behind nearby cover, swung her maul in a lateral half-circle and struck the soldier in the side, crushing him against the side of the kiosk. He fell to the ground, clutching his arm and struggling to breathe. Michelle-Bear stepped back under cover as a few other soldiers turned their fire on her.

Before the soldiers could regroup and send another party in, Zap stood and shouted a few arcane words. A wall of light streaked across the entrance of the store, blocking the door-shaped hole.

"That'll give us some time," Zap panted, then dropped into a sitting position and leaned against the HDP barrier.

The defenders hurriedly worked to reload their weapons and recuperate. Michelle-Bear ran out from her cover, collecting weapons and shields from the fallen soldiers. What few were still alive and conscious received a gentle tap to the back of the head, rendering them unconscious.

"Hey," Steve said to Zap, looking up briefly from refilling a magazine with bullets.

"Yeah?" Zap said, not looking up. He was rifling through a duffel back filled with plastic sandwich bags, each one holding a small amount of material spell component. He had removed some of the bags, placing them in small piles next to one another.

"I looked up the name of the woman I'm a reincarnation of," she said.

"Who was she?" Zap asked, his attention still absorbed.

"Oakey," Steve said. "Ann Oakey."

Zap stopped what he was doing and stared at Steve. "Oakley, you mean?" he asked. "Annie Oakley?"

"Yeah!" Steve said, smiling. "You've heard of her?"

"Crack shot indeed," Zap said, shaking his head. "My dad has a video to show you when we get out of this. What the hell's that?"

Zap pointed at a strange device at Steve's feet. It looked not unlike a rotary fan with curved blades made of shiny gray plastic. It had what appeared to be a red-battery assembly in its center and had several protruding cables.

"That," Steve said proudly, "is an attachment to Polaris that *I* made. It uses a standard energy converter to change Polaris into a hybrid energy pistol."

Zap recoiled a bit. "Is it ... safe?"

Steve looked ceilingward, shrugged, and made noncommittal noises.

"What do you call it?" Zap asked.

Steve grinned. "The Spur," she said. "On account of its shape."

Zap continued to watch Steve as she returned to the task of refilling her magazines.

"You're really something else, you know that?" Zap said.

"Hmm?" Steve said, looking up at him.

"I..." Zap began. "Would you—"

"*Incoming!*" Alan shouted.

There was a deafening blast. Zap's magical shield shattered, driven inward by an intense explosive force. All of the defenders' eyes shot to the roiling cloud of smoke where the door had been. Through the smoke rolled a massive hunk of gleaming plastic, a hulking personal tank just small enough to be able to fit through the plastic hole that it had just widened.

"Oh, no," Nalley breathed. "A Juggernaut Suit."

64

"Duck and cover!" Alan shouted.

As if in response, the Juggernaut Suit opened fire on the employees and customers, who shouted in dismay and alarm. The half-size barriers shuddered as automatic rifle bullets pounded them, barely able to shield the defenders behind them.

Taking advantage of the break in defenses, Mayfield soldiers poured in behind the suit.

"Suppression fire!" Alan barked. "Hold them back! Zap, *do* something to this monster!"

"*It's 'slippery',*" Matt replied over the radio. "*Looks like they painted it with all the nicest shielding.*"

Alan subvocalized all of the German curse words that he had learned from his grandfather as he lay down suppression fire, forcing some of the soldiers to take cover behind the entrance hole. After a moment of thought, he spoke over the radio.

"Okay, everybody, focus fire on the soldiers. Anybody with HE rounds, explosives or other high-level ordinances, switch to them and target the Suit. Nalley, I want—"

"*Specs,*" Nalley interrupted. "*Got it.*"

"Please don't interrupt me, love, but yes."

"*No, I mean I have them already,*" Nalley said.

"Awesome," Alan replied. "Upload, please. Everyone else, defend the store and protect yourselves. Personal safety comes first."

The employees and customers renewed their defense of the store. Guns blazed, both to hold back the tide of soldiers that were slowly making headway into the store and to attempt to damage the nigh-invulnerable Juggernaut Suit.

"*The Juggernaut Suit is literally the finest technology available in corporate warfare,*" Nalley read. "*Outfitted with the finest magic-resistant bulletproof armor, with explosive-resistant defense mechanisms and carrying a heavy arsenal of deadly weapons, the Juggernaut is the smallest, most potent vehicle in its defense class. Its design was a compromise of the previous Dreadnought class street tank, whose—*"

"Weaknesses!" Alan shouted. "Skip to weaknesses!"

The Suit seemed to be a one-unit turning point in the battle; a single pass of its automatic rifle forced all of the defenders in range into hiding. Zap rose from behind his barrier and unleashed several strong spells, most of which glanced off the plastic hide of the tank. Zap cursed and took cover behind a break in the shelves. He was covered in sweat and panting heavily.

"You need a break," a nearby customer said. He was a nondescript man in his early twenties, dressed in drab, unassuming clothes.

"Can't," Zap panted. "I'm the only dedicated mage here."

"You have a point," the man said. "Here, take this." He handed Zap a vial that contained a thick yellow liquid and a small ginseng root.

"Oh, 'yesu, thank you," Zap said, taking the vial. He nearly dropped it as an explosion rocked the store. Some of the defenders cried out.

"It's throwing grenades at us!" Steve shouted. "Nalley!"

"*Here it is!*" Nalley said over the radio. "*The Juggernaut Suit's defensive capabilities, while formidable, are by necessity somewhat reduced from those of a larger-sized street tank. The Suit's armor is treated to be extremely resistant to magic and is—*"

The defenders threw themselves to the ground as another grenade exploded in their midst. "Medic!" Click yelled.

"You know," the customer said to Zap, "you really should ask her. Don't let yourself get interrupted."

"What?" Zap said.

"That girl you like," the customer said. "You should ask her whatever you were going to ask her."

Nearby, Alan shouted. "Can we get to the good part, please, Nalley?"

"*...is able to shrug off most gunfire under fifty caliber,*" Nalley continued, "*But its magic and energy shielding is all focused in the top armor layer, which is susceptible to concussive force. While the Juggernaut's ambient field will divert most explosions, high explosives or low-speed rams will bend its armor easily, exposing the sensitive circuitry within. The area near the cockpit is particularly susceptible.*" Nalley read.

"We don't have any explosives better than grenades," To'mas said over the radio.

"You shouldn't listen in on people's conversations," Zap said, a little flustered. "And anyway, I didn't say that I liked her."

"Well," the man said. "You should ask her anyway."

Zap knit his brow at the stranger. "What's your name?" he asked.

"Marc," the man said.

"Thanks, Marc," Zap said and held up the vial of liquid. "If we make it out of here, I owe you a burrito." He drank the contents of the vial and made a face.

"Click, how're you doing?" Alan asked over the radio.

"Been better," Click said, "*But it's nothing critical. I can still fire a stolen gun.*"

"Please do so," Alan said.

"I think we need to find something physical to throw at it to dent the armor," Nalley said. "*The manual mentions ballistas and rams, but also sledgehammers.*"

There was a pause.

"*On it,*" Michelle-Bear said over the radio, her voice a deadly monotone. "*Cover me.*"

Before anyone could react, Michelle-Bear leapt from her cover. She held one of the Mayfield riot shields in front of her and held her maul in the other hand. With a deafening battle cry she charged at the Juggernaut Suit. The suit could not turn in time, but other soldiers noted her charge and turned their fire on her. Soon Michelle-Bear was running through a fusillade of bullets. The other employees saw several bullets strike her in the arm and shoulder, but her pace was not slowed.

Alan found his voice. "Zap!" he shouted. "Buff her! NOW!"

Zap had already stood and was chanting the arcane language as fast as he could. His eyes were rolled back into his head, his wand pointed directly at Michelle-Bear. Steve rushed to stand behind him, gunning down any of the soldiers she saw take aim at the young wizard.

Michelle-Bear bore down on the Juggernaut Suit quickly, ignoring the rounds that pummeled her and keeping her head behind the shield. She was only a few meters away when Zap's spell took hold. Michelle-Bear's muscles bulged as supernatural strength coursed through her body; she roared, threw the shield aside and drew back her hammer with both hands.

The force of her impossibly strong blow not only buckled the armor plate it struck but also the joint of the suit's grenade-arm. The weapon was effectively useless from a single maul-blow.

The machine rifle, however, was still free to move.

A full round of automatic fire struck Michelle-Bear full in the body, throwing her meters away from the suit like an oversized rag doll. She hit the ground and slid, leaving a large smear of blood on the tile floor behind. She was not moving.

"NO!" Nalley screamed.

His leg injury forgotten, Click clambered over his barrier with several customers. All held the Mayfield riot shields in place to protect them, and the customers formed a wall around Michelle-Bear's body. As Click and a customer moved in place to drag the body, the Juggernaut suit turned toward them and primed its gun.

"Not on your fuckin' life!" Steve shouted, standing on one of the shelves. She hefted Polaris, which had the spur-shaped accessory mounted to its top. The Spur was spinning rapidly and the red battery glowed with activity.

Steve quickly took aim and fired. With a strange whine, a beam of light fired from Polaris and struck the Juggernaut Suit's exposed circuitry with deadly accuracy. Sparks and smoke poured from the gap as the cables inside fused together, causing numerous short circuits and burning even more of the suit's delicate electrics system. The entire suit seemed to shudder; then, with a loud groan, it stopped moving. A thumping could be heard from inside the suit as the pilot tried to force his way out of the powered cockpit, but the shell of the suit had already begun to fuse together as white-hot internal fires melted the armor plating.

Michelle-Bear's defenders dragged her body away, trying to ignore the screams of the Juggernaut's pilot as he burned to death.

Steve turned away in disgust just in time to see Zap waver on his feet. "Zap?"

"Too much," Zap said. His eyes rolled backward and he collapsed heavily on the floor.

"Zap!" Steve shouted.

"Michelle-Bear, Michelle-Bear," Nalley cried as her friend's prone form was dragged back into cover. The unoccupied employees and customers renewed their defense of the store, firing on the soldiers who continued to press inward. Mayfield was gaining ground.

Alan rushed to Michelle-Bear, a small medical kit clutched under his arm. "How is she?"

"Armor," Click said, awed. "She was wearing an armored dress. That's the only reason that she's not torn to pieces."

"But how is *she*?" Alan asked again, kneeling down.

Click gave Alan room. "Not good," he said.

"No, no, no," Nalley cried.

Alan checked Michelle-Bear's pulse and found it, but it was faint. He pulled away her armored apron, which had been torn completely to shreds. The Dura-Kev dress underneath had saved Michelle-Bear's life, but not protected her completely; many holes had been punched in it and Michelle-Bear was bleeding heavily underneath.

"Okay," Alan said and took a deep breath. "Okay."

Steve helped a groggy Zap to his feet. She slung an arm around his waist, propping him against the shelf. She could feel his breath on her cheek. "Are you okay?" she asked.

"Muh..." Zap said. "Michelle-Bear?"

"She's ... ok," Steve said. "She's alive."

"I should have cast protect," Zap said, delirious. "Not strength."

"We might still be dealing with the Juggernaut if you hadn't cast strength," Steve said. "You made the right choice. Don't get yourself worked up; you overtaxed yourself with that spell."

"Are..." Zap said, breathing heavily. "...we going to die?"

Steve leaned her head out to look at the pitched battle. With several key employees out of action, the defenders were losing ground.

"I don't know," Steve said.

"Ok," Zap said.

"I need to grab an SMG and fight some more, ok?" Steve said. "You should rest."

"Steve, I'm sorry," Zap said, trying to slow his breathing a little.

"Why?" Steve asked.

"Because I didn't give you the chance I should have, you know?" he said. "The timing was so bad."

"Sit down, Zap," Steve said.

"It's just," Zap said. "I think I'm in love with y—"

"Stop!" Steve said. There were tears in her eyes. "Stop! Stop. You are not doing this to me now. I am not having any fucking final confessions, because that is not fair."

Zap looked at her, surprised.

"No, Zap," Steve snapped. "We are *not* going to die. And this is a *bad time* so you don't get to tell me you're in ... you're in *anything* with me. Okay?"

Zap nodded dumbly.

"When we get out of this—" Steve said adamantly. Her tearful eyes burned. "*Which we will*—I might c-consider letting you t-take me on a date."

"Okay," Zap said.

"To dinner," Steve added. "Somewhere nice, yuh-your treat. *Maybe.*" She sniffled. "So you sit right fucking there and don't die."

"Um," Zap said. "Okay."

Steve glared at him, and then snatched one of the Mayfield submachine guns from the ground. "I—I can't fucking *believe* you!" She ran to the barrier and gunned down three soldiers in quick succession.

"Hot damn," said Marc, who had been eavesdropping.

"I don't know what just happened," Zap said.

"Shit!" Click said. "What's—that means stabilize her. Stabilize her." He was fervently trying to cross-reference the medical diagnosis software on Alan's tabletshell and its manual on his own workshell.

Alan reacted swiftly, jamming a hypo of stabilizer against Michelle-Bear's neck. He then returned to his work, trying to staunch her bleeding while removing numerous high-caliber shells from her body.

"Ok—it looks like she's lost a lot of blood," Click said.

"No fucking shit!" Alan barked, then wiped his forehead. "Sorry. Sorry." He turned the valve on the tube of replacement plasma snaking from the first-aid kit.

"We're running out of the plasma too," Click said. "I think that's what that icon means. I wish we could have Nalley on this."

"Nalley's..." Alan said shakily. "Nalley's out."

Nearby, Nalley was shuddering, curled into a ball.

"Her stomach's ready to self-repair," Click said, "but the battery's almost out on the cure crystal and Zap ... Zap can't cast any more magic."

"Find a red battery!" Alan said. "Use some of your own magic! You're a fucking faerie!"

"I don't know how to jury-rig a glamour-to-mana converter, Alan!" Click replied. "Nobody here does!"

"We've got a multimag-converter in the back," Alan said, then pointed at a frightened-looking customer on the front line. "You! Go get the converter kit from the back room. It's in the closet."

The customer ran.

"Oh, oh fuck," Click said, trying to hold back tears. "Alan, we're losing her. The kit's almost out of everything we need."

"We need a doctor!" Alan said, pulling back. His hands were covered in Michelle-Bear's blood. "This—this isn't enough."

He shook his head.

"I—we can't do this," Alan said. His voice rang with a horrible finality. "She's going to die."

65

Raimi pushed the customer out with the converter kit.

"If they're that desperate..." she murmured. She listened for a moment to the sounds of battle from the front of the store.

She turned to the people whom she had been assigned to protect. They were mostly children and the elderly, with a few men and women unsuited to combat scattered among them.

"I'd like those of you who are willing to join me in a prayer," she said to them.

All of those gathered in the back of the store formed a circle and joined hands. Once they had come together, Raimi spoke.

"To the Powers that Be," Raimi said. "Whoever they might be. I have never been terribly religious, so I'm not sure exactly how to address you."

She cleared her throat.

"An ongoing thread throughout all of the dogmas that I've run into seems to be that you want us to improve. We have to face adversity and discover within ourselves the strength that will allow us to persevere, to keep on keeping on despite all. That's why you test us, why you put us through such awful shit.

"It's why you give us abusive spouses and cruel strangers, why you throw tempests and hurricanes and monsters at us. It's why you inspire us to hate each other, give us the tools to kill. It is all, apparently, to better us and to give us that mental shielding. We have to get used to the fact that sometimes bad things happen to good people, that sometimes decent people die for no reason.

"But out there in the store right now is a set of really great people. There's a young couple desperately trying to figure out how to love each other. There's a big-hearted girl, the sweetest I know, dying of two dozen bullet wounds. There is a misguided little sprite who is kind of a dumbass, but is trying very hard to be a good guy. And I like him a lot, anyway.

"These people are the heart of New Washington. They are everyday people in the most colorful and interesting way. They live and love and are so full of personality, and they just exemplify everything about our city that makes it special. I am in love with them. If they get snuffed out because of this—this ill-conceived power-grab, it will be a surer sign that all this destiny talk is a steaming pile than any of the saddest bards' songs.

"Basically, I guess that what I'm saying is ... throw us a fucking bone, ey?"

There were a few seconds of silence. Suddenly, a voice seemed to come from everywhere. "Hello?"

Raimi blinked.

"God?" she asked.

"Uh ... no," the voice said, obviously a bit weirded out. "Scott. Is that you, Raimi?"

"God!" Raimi said, her eyes wide. She practically flew to the door.

"We're seriously running low here," Click said, his voice taking on a desperate edge.

"Just keep her alive!" Alan said, pulling the pin on a grenade. "We are *not* letting her go gentle into that whatever night!"

"What?" Click said.

"The—I was quoting—forget it! Just keep her alive until death tears her from your claws!"

"That's going to be—*throw that fucking grenade!*" Click shouted.

Alan turned and hurled the grenade, scattering a group of soldiers. Click and Alan ducked as the grenade went off. The soldiers regrouped too quickly for Alan's tastes.

"That's going to be soon, Alan!" Click shouted.

"Just keep her alive!" Alan snapped, firing his shotgun into the crowd and ducking back into cover. "In the off chance that ... I don't know, a doctor materializes out of the ether—"

"*Poof*," Raimi said over the radio. "*You've got a guest.*"

Alan turned back to see two familiar forms running toward them. His eyes went wide.

"Dr. Wallace!" he said. "Mya!"

The Pol's Cat grinned and struck a pose. Dr. Wallace held a full-service medkit aloft. "Point me at the patient, Alan."

"She's right there," he said, pointing at Michelle-Bear's prone form. "Please be careful; there's no good cover near her. Why the hell are you guys here?"

"Matt asked us to meet him for lunch," Mya said as Dr. Wallace approached Michelle-Bear in a crouching scuttle.

"Are my guests here?" Matt asked over the radio.

"I owe you so big," Alan replied.

"I'd tell you to pay it forward," Matt said, *"But you already are. Tell my guests that I'm sorry, but I'm busy shooting people."*

"This is really bad," Scott said. "I'm not sure that I can save her."

"Please try," Alan said.

"I'll give it everything I have," Scott said, setting to work.

"Is it just me, or am I the only person who's killed any soldiers in the last five minutes?" To'mas asked over the radio.

"It's the blockades," Alan said. "They're setting up a perimeter inside the store."

He looked at the remaining troops. No one had been lost, but he could see several wounded fighters continuing to hold their positions. Even Zap, who looked barely conscious, was clumsily firing volleys of automatic fire at the enemy, leaning against Steve as she did the same.

Click, who was covered in blood, limped over to Alan. "This is too much, Alan," he said. "We have to surrender."

"Click," Alan said, shaking his head. "That is not an option. If Mayfield takes this precinct, we are well and truly fucked. This is the only strategic point in the area. We have to hold until forces get here."

"There *aren't* any forces, Alan!" Click said. "They're all in other precincts."

Alan set his jaw and took a deep breath, surveying the forces. This wasn't a fighting force. In a real war, people would be dying, ground would be gained and lost. People would be expendable. This wasn't war, though, and his fighters weren't soldiers. They were not his comrades in arms, they were his friends. Losing even one of them would be more than he could bear.

It was at his most shamed, on the crest of his most difficult decision, that Alan was saved from having to make it.

A pair of amplified voices shouted from outside. "For the Company!"

Sounds of chaos and battle followed. The soldiers stationed inside craned their necks to see what was going on.

The voices cried out again. "For the Precinct!"

More chaos could be heard outside of the visual range of the store. The soldiers inside registered alarm. The fighting in the store dwindled as employees, customers and soldiers alike tried to see the source of the disturbance.

"For New Washington!" the voices cried.

Then entered the Cavalry.

Five Mayfield soldiers were pushed through the door and scattered, revealing the triumphant figures of Sir Lewis Birchmore and Sir Drake Kunimitsu behind them. Both were in traditional Knights' Combat Suits, finely-pressed business attire designed for maximum ease of movement. Each had his sword and pistol in either hand, and they moved together like a well-oiled machine.

The soldiers in their way fell like leaves, cut and gunned down by soldiers of the highest skill. Behind the Knights came a small squadron of Better Living, Ltd. soldiers, covering their Knights in a tight formation.

The employees stared, dumbfounded, as the battle was swiftly won.

Less than five minutes later, the surviving Mayfield soldiers had surrendered and been led away by Better Living Military Police.

Sir Kunimitsu ran up to Alan. "Please say that I am not too late."

"I..." Alan stammered, pointing at Sir Birchmore. "He..."

Sir Birchmore drew himself up and said in a pained tone, "The possibility of losing this territory to a company as unethical as Mayfield is more important than ... than petty rivalries."

"Sir Birchmore and I have declared an all-points truce until this conflict is over," Sir Kunimitsu said. "He met with my company shortly before the attack, when we were preparing to move."

"You—anticipated this?" Alan said.

"Wasn't it obvious?" Sir Kunimitsu said, a little incredulous. "Mayfield's withdrawal of occupation forces made it plain to us. What we miscalculated was the time of the attack; had you not held this ground until our arrival, we might have lost the territory."

The Knight clapped Alan on the shoulder. "You have done very well, Alan," he said. "Very very well."

"Hello!" Dr. Wallace called out. "Crisis not over! Dying girl!"

Alan skipped to the doctor's side. "What's going on?"

"Too much organ damage for a physic alone," Scott said, shaking his head. "I can't do this without magic, and that is not my department."

"Get Zap over here!" Alan shouted.

"No!" Steve said, wrapping her arms around Zap's dazed form protectively. "He's exhausted! He'll die if he tries to cast anything more!"

Sir Kunimitsu gaped at Michelle-Bear's heavily damaged body. "That's..."

"The waitress who confronted me," Sir Birchmore said.

"You were the CK she stood up to?" Click barked. "Your antics got her fired!"

Sir Birchmore was quiet for a moment. "So I suppose it's my fault that she's here and wounded, eh?"

"More or less, yeah," Alan said, somewhat worried about what the knight's reaction might be.

Sir Birchmore reached into the pocket of his jacket and withdrew a small container that looked rather like a glasses case. "I'd been saving this for a special occasion," he said, "but I've got to make amends with the young lady. I suppose that saving a life is special enough."

He tossed the case across the room at Steve, who snatched it out of the air.

"What is this?" she asked.

"Give it to your tired friend," he said.

Puzzled, Steve opened the case. A luminous golden ball slipped out of it and floated just above the surface of the barrier.

"Beautiful," Click breathed.

"It's a shot of Aura!" Steve shouted. "Zap, drink this!"

"Fuck yeah," Zap murmured. "I could use a drink."

Steve moved her hand around the ball and tipped it into Zap's mouth. He closed his eyes. A warm glow surrounded him for a moment, then his eyes snapped open, energetic and full of alacrity. In a single fluid motion, Zap righted himself, vaulted over the barrier and ran toward Michelle-Bear. He was already chanting in the arcane language; in one of his hands was a green leaf he had withdrawn from his duffel bag. The leaf trailed a faint blue glow behind it.

Zap reached Michelle-Bear, placed the leaf on her ravaged midsection, and clapped his hands together. The words of his spell echoed through the room, bouncing off of each other and building a powerful, surging momentum. Dr. Wallace worked behind him, diverting the healing energies with his diagnostic device and using gauze to staunch Michelle-Bear's wounds.

A few minutes later, Zap stopped chanting. He fell back into a sitting position, panting heavily but lucid.

"She's stable," Dr. Wallace said softly. "Very badly damaged, but stable."

Nalley burst into a fresh bout of weeping. Alan gave Sir Birchmore an earnest look. "We owe you one," he said.

"No," Sir Birchmore said. "Only repaying a boon."

"You owe *me* one," Dr. Wallace said.

"I'll get in on that too," Zap panted.

"Yeah, me too," Matt joined in, sauntering out from the stun turret booth.

"Sure," Alan said, rolling his eyes. "I owe everybody one except Sir Birchmore. Now let's account for our customers and secure the door so I can make a report."

As the employees bustled about gathering customers and consolidating weapons, Zap struggled to his feet and leaned heavily on the nearest shelf. After a moment, he realized that Steve was hovering near him.

"How do you feel?" she asked.

"Like I'm going to sleep for twelve hours," Zap replied.

"Okay, I can wait that long," Steve said.

Zap blinked. "For what?"

"For my date," Steve said. "That you are going to take me on."

"Oh," Zap said. "Okay."

"But I am *not* going to wait twelve hours for a kiss," she said.

Zap and Steve looked at each other for a few moments. Steve closed the distance, reaching up and wrapping her arms around Zap's neck. She brought his face down to hers and their lips met softly. They shared a kiss that lasted several seconds before the sound of a shutter interrupted them.

They broke the kiss and stared at Matt. Matt lowered his camera, grinned, waved to the couple, then moved along.

Steve and Zap's eyes met again. Unhurried, they moved in for another kiss.

This time, no one interrupted them.

Epilogue

That evening, Matt opened the door to his apartment, walked inside, and shut the door behind him.

He went to his widescreen TV-shell, leaned over, and plugged his camera into it. As the welcome splash page appeared on the large screen, Matt dragged an easy chair over to the TV. He straightened and punched a few buttons on his stereo system. An epic-style remix of Ellis Manteaux's *Rule of Threes* began to play.

Matt sat down in the easy chair, picked up his shell, and smiled at the audience.

He tapped a key on the shell and an ensemble picture of the employees cleaning the war-ravaged store appeared.

"The forces of the evil Mayfield Corporation were vanquished," he began. "Our heroes had held their ground and pushed the enemy away. The 15th and Neimuth Securemarket™ made the news that evening, and was later awarded the coveted Erdrick Award for the collective bravery of the employees there. All gained an employee rank."

He tapped the shell. The picture changed to Alan, with a picture of Nalley next to it.

"Alan and Nalley married three years later. Nalley became a certified technician for several brands of vehicle, ensuring a steady income for the family. Alan eventually quit his job at the Securemarket™ and became the full-time manager for *Sixth Gear*, which attained moderate success and made the family very happy. They had a talented and intelligent son."

He tapped his shell once more. The picture of Steve and Zap talking over the deli partition appeared.

"Steve and Zap's relationship lasted three weeks. It ended with a screaming match at work that nearly lost both of them an employee rank."

He tapped his shell again. Click and Michelle-Bear appeared, looking surprised.

"Click rejoined the Seelie Court at Yule and stayed Seelie for the rest of his life. He became a motivational speaker and was successful at touring schools and businesses, but remained a good-natured rogue at heart. Michelle-Bear, who made a full recovery within a few months, eventually got a waitstaff job at the Aquarium Restaurant and eventually rose to the status of maître d'. She settled down with two boys whom she loved very much and had two kids: one with each of her partners."

He tapped his shell. A picture of a blood-drenched Dr. Wallace appeared with Mya at his side. Dr. Wallace's smile provided a bizarre counterpoint to his gory attire.

"Mya and Dr. Wallace got married. After extensive tutelage under Sir Erdrick, Mya decided to enter the Honorable Academy of Corporate Knights and was named Sir Mya Ai'o of Securemarket™."

He tapped his shell. A picture of Pazi, standing at the door of her dorm room and looking baffled, appeared.

"At Zap's urging, Pazi got a job with the Bradshaw Atelier just out of school. In a few years, she and her familiars were running a satellite lab nearly on their own. Pazi eventually quit the business to become a professor of Invocation Magic at Ethertech University. She married a member of the administration. While she took many apprentices, she never had children."

He tapped his shell with a flourish. A picture of Raimi And The Soft Winds Blow appeared, leaning against Paru with a grin on her face. Paru appeared to be tolerating the action, though only barely.

"Raimi and Paru continued to serve the Securemarket™ for years. Paru's store remained one of the most acclaimed ones in Securemarket™ history, and Paru gave birth to a single child, whom she alternately gave a very hard time and spoiled rotten. Raimi And The Soft Winds Blow never married or bore children, though she and Click had another abortive attempt at a fling. Somehow, they managed to stay friends afterward."

He tapped his shell and a boring-looking image of Loren appeared.

"Lorem Ipsum and Ro Z'kerr disappeared, never to be seen by our heroes again." Matt frowned. "Probably."

He tapped his shell once more. The picture of To'mas, smiling brightly, appeared.

"To'mas?" Matt laughed. "That's another story entirely."

Matt tapped his shell. A posed picture of Sir Kunimitsu and Sir Birchmore appeared.

"Sir Drake and Sir Lewis decided that after their landmark cooperation in the face of adversity, they should set aside their enmity and attempt to foster cooperation between their companies. To their credit, they managed to hold this peace for a full year, at the end of which they had a heated argument about how to cook steak. They had a total of forty-three minor duels over trifling matters from that point forward. Sir Kunimitsu barely came out on top with a total of twenty-four wins. The duels eventually stopped when Sir Kunimitsu had a minor heart attack. When he died, Sir Kunimitsu bequeathed his sword and pistol to Sir Birchmore. Sir Birchmore returned the favor unprompted: he supported Kunimitsu's family until his own death."

Matt smiled. "Wanting to emulate her one-time hero, Jaz Kunimitsu became a Dancer Rank Maul fighter by age 16. She will probably have a story written about her at some point."

He thought for a moment. "Did I miss anybody important? Oh yeah!"

He picked up the camera and pointed it at himself. A moving image of him appeared on the TV.

"Matt went and got a beer," he said. "Then he took a shower and played video games for four hours. It was awesome."

He set the camera down, rose from the chair and walked away, leaving the camera pointing at the wall and displaying that on the television.

Thirty seconds later, he returned with a beer.

He sat back down in the chair, drew his shell, and tapped it. The image on the television changed to one of Zap and Steve locked in a kiss.

"Steve and Zap dated two more times after that. The second time was for three months, the third for three years."

He took a pull from the beer and gave us an earnest grin.

"Evidently deciding that the third time was the charm, they got married," he continued. "Steve finished her apprenticeship with Grover Messianic and began work as his partner. When he died, she took over the business and remained an artisan gunsmith in her own right. Zap got a job at his mother's Atelier. After a decade, recognizing her son's talent, she handed him the business and retired. Soon thereafter, Zap and Steve decided to merge the businesses, forming the magical smithy 'Messiah Arms'. Despite fighting nearly all the fucking time, Steve and Zap loved each other and their only daughter until their deaths."

Matt stood up and turned to walk away, then turned back for a moment.

"You know, I trust you guys not to tell them before it happens. Ok?"

He turned to his stereo console, and then slowly faded the lights and music out at the same time. He walked away, forgetting to turn the television off. It displayed the picture of Zap and Steve's kiss until morning.

Glossary

8th Street War: The most recent major Official Opposition prior to Mayfield Limited's actions against Better Living, fought over the rights to hotly-contested longevity research.

activator: A device roughly the size of a 20th-century microwave that uses a sensory enhancement spell to emphasize the flavor of certain foods. Can cause adverse reactions in certain substances that have strong elemental affiliations.

adblitz: A heavily researched and precisely-timed advertisement campaign, designed to present striking and new advertisement schemes at the precise time that they would be best received. Adblitzes often involve performance art, flash mobs and 'googolbombs'—campaigns to influence ether search engines.

Ai'Kiall'Tchall: Colloquially known as **Pol's Cats**. A race of people with feline features but no relation to cats, the Ai'Kiall'Tchall claim to be a race created directly from humans by a deity named Ai'shaa. Their apparent 'blessings' have become curses in the modern day, however; their blood, skin and hair are all used in salves, medicines and drugs. Though many make a living from donation, many also disappear mysteriously every day.

Ai'shaa: The goddess said to have created the Ai'Kiall'Tchall. A non-jealous but secretive goddess, valuing martyrdom and service over all things. Ai'shaa is said to have been a panther once, but her creation of the Ai'Kiall'Tchall sapped her power, rendering her a housecat. While her existence is obviously contested, the inclusive nature of her religion has drawn many non-Tchall followers.

Ajeya, Sir Margaret: A Corporate Knight sworn to Andiron Industries. Arguably the greatest Knight currently living, Ajeya sports a perfect mission record, encyclopedic knowledge of **citations** and flawless grace in combat.

Arachne: A six-armed Shadowflame mercenary known for her cybernetic cable-reels and six-pistol combat style.

Aramis-Sawtooth War: One of the more noteworthy instances of Official Opposition in the past fifty years, the Aramis-Sawtooth War was a vicious conflict fought over a piece of territory discovered to be on top of a strong ice-element node.

armor-weave: A technique of creating a non-gel flexible armor, using the thaumochemical integration of durable materials into real textiles. Not the best armor available, but light and comfortable compared to stronger methods.

artisan: An honorific title affixed to the front of a vocation. By law, a crafter is only an 'artisan' after she has distinguished herself sufficiently to exceed standard means of certification.

atelier: A workshop. In New Washington, the term is usually used for magical artifice shops and stores carrying nonstandard magical items.

Aura: A magical liqueur whose origin and method of creation are a closely-kept secret, Aura is so heavily enchanted that it floats several inches over whatever surface it is placed upon. Aura is known for giving the user a magical 'high' once imbibed, and can allow someone exhausted by magic to feel completely refreshed in an instant.

automop: A simple but brilliant technomagical creation, the automop conjures water by drawing a minute amount of magical energy from its user, and combines that water with a small soap cartridge installed near its base.

bulletshield: A technomagical field generator designed to widely distribute the force of any object moving at a sufficient speed toward its user. Responsible in large part for the popularity of melee weapons and shortbows in New Washington.

card (faerie court): A tarot-style card representing one of the innumerable faerie courts. Assigning every faerie to one of these courts, and categorizing them twice a year by their glamour type, is one of the few governing practices recognized by most faeries.

CCDM: Civilian Class Defense Magic. Developed in a laboratory, CCDM is the simplest and easiest magic to learn in history. No matter what kinds of magic a New Washingtonian citizen knows, a few CCDM spells are inevitably part of his vocabulary. The 'trigger' spell, used to trip magical switches and hanging effects, is one of the most important and common spells.

certification: The system of merit measurement recognized by nearly every institution in New Washington. Most certification is earned through education or apprenticeship, though some can be achieved through self-study and testing.

chargebus: An encoded serial bus device with a specific amount of money on it, which can be spent like a gift card.

chit: A small card encoded with a set amount of **credits**. Some chits are a fixed value, but others contain coded stripes indicating their value and can be changed.

citation: A declaration of precedent before a duel between **Corporate Knights**. Previous duels are quoted to establish what terms should be used, and every CK is expected to have near-encyclopedic knowledge of important duels. The Knight with the highest number of duels memorized is likely to set the terms of the duel.

Corporate Knight (CK): Trained for six years by the Honorable Academy of Corporate Knights, CKs are the best and brightest of the modern Corporate army. Most Knights wear high-quality bulletshields and duel with a formalized sword-and-pistol style. Knights show their allegiance through the colors of the roses worn on their lapels.

credit, or **'cred':** The standard unit of New Washington currency, denoted by the ₢ symbol.

Data Deal: A standard Securemarket™ promotion offering competetive prices to customers willing to sign up for an **ether** mailing list.

datasoul: The 'heart' of a home computer; holds licenses, critical data and operating system structures. Effectively allows a New Washingtonian to turn any basic shell into their personal computer, even a public console. Datasouls are frequently very heavily encrypted through both technological and magical means.

Dragon's Breath: A liquor brewed by dragons and for dragons. Even a small quantity can be lethal to humans, but there are a few drinks that, very carefully mixed, can be tolerated. The thaumobiological effect of such drinks is usually striking.

Dura-Kev: The brand name and material respected as the most reliable and comfortable armor manufacturer in New Washington. The material itself is a flexible, clothlike armor-weave, arguably the best currently manufactured. It is rather expensive.

easy-sling: A simple, consumer-grade levitation device designed to make carrying heavy loads by hand easier.

Eternal: A being that has, by any of a wide range of means, achieved an indefinite lifespan. Most beings referred to as Eternals have a host of abilities or intrinsic attributes held in esteem by society at large.

ether: A vague term that can mean either anything related to New Washington's digital information network or anything related to magic. Attempts have been made throughout the years to adequately differentiate the two halves of the term from one another; so far, none have been successful.

ether address, or **'ethadd'**: A point of contact that can act as an e-mail address, instant message username and phone number rolled into one. Users may choose to have an ether address that only has certain features, but by federal mandate all citizens must have a government-supplied ether address that they check on a regular basis.

Etherism: A monotheistic religion created in New Washington, and one of the most popular. While marginally similar to Christianity,

Etherism frames adversity as a gift from God and emphasizes that defending loved ones, land, and possessions is a God-given duty.

ethersite, or **'ethsite'**: An umbrella term referring to a static site within New Washington's digital information network, the **ether**. An ethersite can be a streaming source for a television program, a static website, an audio serial, or even a routing site used for data management alone.

Ethertech University: The premier establishment for magical education in New Washington.

Forcebolt: A model of technomagical pistol manufactured by Dragon Flame Atelier. Fires a low-grade but high-efficiency bolt of magical force, drawing magical power directly from the user via a pair of contacts in the pistol's grip.

Gainsborough, Alec: A well-known hero from the time immediately post-**Snowfall**. Alec Gainsborough founded the **Shadowflame** Mercenary organization, originally intended as a supplemental law enforcement agency but eventually evolving into a more media-oriented company.

glamour: The inherent magical energy unique to and generated by faeries. Fae produce a high quantity of glamour at all times and use it to power their spells. Each fae has a unique brand of glamour that can be used in a personal way, and similarities in glamour seem to draw certain 'types' of fae together.

Ghost Blade: A **Shadowflame** mercenary assassin. While Ghost Blade is best known for his look—he wears a long trenchcoat and a long nodachi sword at all times—his most remarkable ability is that he can blend effortlessly into the background, whether in a crowd or alone. When Ghost Blade does not wish to be noticed, he will not be.

Gogobera: One of the most popular clubs in New Washington.

guardian: A cybernetically and thaumobiologically enhanced officer of New Washingtonian law. Guardians are fast, strong and principled, and are one of the iconic representations of New Washington's advances in technomagical innovation. Guardians are so well-respected that 'guardian' has also become a slang word meaning 'excellent'.

handshell: A small computer carried everywhere by nearly every New Washingtonian. A handshell is a personal organizer, music player, mobile phone, credit card and ID all rolled into one.

HDP: High density plastic. HDP is an umbrella term used to refer to any of a number of polymers used to make nearly everything in New Washington.

hi-def, or **HD**: Excellent, clear, understandable. Can also be used to mean "I know what you're saying."

Holiday, Johnny: A **Shadowflame** mercenary known for his unusual armaments: a pair of katana, as well as a pair of intricate machined gauntlets.

IHDP: Industrial High Density Plastic, the main subset of **HDP** used for construction.

iyesu kristo: Literally, 'Jesus Christ'. A common New Washingtonian epithet, but few who use it recognize its religious origins.

kekkai: A technomagical field designed to allow for safe and reversible combat simulation.

kit: The standard equipment carried by a **Corporate Knight**. Consists of an **armor-weave** business suit, **bulletshield**, sword, pistol, and a rose signifying the company to which the Knight is loyal.

Labyrinth: A sprawling slum to the south of New Washington. Rumored to be a zone where magic works poorly and gods walk the streets. Most New Washingtonians are deathly afraid of the Labyrinth.

livemetal: A term unknown to most New Washingtonians. Scholars who study the myths about the ancient city of **Mu** say that Muan royalty commanded a living metal. Some even posit that elven mythril may have been based on Muan metal. This is not a popular theory.

Manteaux, Ellis: One of New Washington's premier pop stars. Pretty, talented and capable of producing incredibly catchy songs, Ellis Manteaux is a household name known by every New Washingtonian. Some like her and some hate her, but all agree that few artists are capable of capturing a crowd with the same aptitude that Manteaux shows.

mimic: A cunning, highly intelligent creature capable of shapeshifting but too consumed by hunger to think of anything but devouring other creatures. Mimics can imitate nearly anything, and are considered one of New Washington's most obnoxious pests.

morph: Created by an unfortunate fad sometime post-Snowfall, morphs are the descendants of either humans given bestial form or anthropomorphized animals. They are now their own race, and are one of the most downtrodden races in the city.

Mu: An ancient city that may or may not have existed at one point.

multiheater: Effectively a combination microwave and convection oven, with special settings for prepackaged foods.

municipal company: The corporation that acts as the local government for any given precinct. Their relation to the federal government is not unlike feudal lords to a king.

mutant: The result of a human tainted by elemental radiation while in the womb. The resulting being has brightly-colored skin, natural elemental magic and weaknesses, and is doomed to lifetime prejudice. Mutants are seen as second-class citizens at best, natural menaces at worst.

New Washington: The largest city in the post-Snowfall world. New Washington is the greatest center of technomagical research in the world, but is incredibly insular due to being walled in on all sides by hostile nature. The xenophobia of its citizens does little to ameliorate this.

New Washington University: The largest educational company in the city. The University provides educational certification for nearly every major, though deep and detailed education tends to be easier to find through vocational certification.

node caller: A mage capable of summoning and controlling a particular element. A powerful and dangerous form of magic, frequently found through talent rather than study, node callers are under constant psychological scrutiny as many go mad.

Oddzer: A Shadowflame mercenary who is distinctive for being a patchwork of animal features on a human body: he sports a scaly tail, feathery wings and furry ears.

Official Opposition: Corporate war. While more organized and civilized than traditional war, official opposition between companies heralds much death and sorrow.

Orelyn-Neimuth: A powerful and influential elven mage from the early days of the Snowfall, indirectly responsible for the creation of the city of New Washington. Along with the headmaster of Ethertech University, Orelyn-Neimuth attempted and failed to form an official wizard's council.

ping: Slang term, derived from the computing jargon of the same name. A common greeting, to which 'pong' is the appropriate response.

pocketshell: A particularly small handshell.

Pol's Cat: See Ai'Kiall'Tchall.

polyglass: A form of HDP that is perfectly clear like glass, but capable of withstanding concentrated gunfire if thick enough. Clear material in New Washington is no longer associated with fragility, as polyglass has almost completely replaced its namesake.

pong: See ping.

precinct: A subsection of New Washington's Districts. Precincts were originally spheres of police coverage, but now represent the areas of influence by the city's **municipal corporations**. The borders of precincts change periodically, as corporate alliances are made and takeovers occur (see **Official Opposition**).

primary (school): Grades 1 through 7; the only required education that a New Washingtonian obtain.

Rail: The New Washington Rail System (NWRS), New Washington's mind-bogglingly comprehensive (and occasionally redundant) subway system. Having a comprehensive knowledge of the entire Rail system is nearly impossible, but knowing one's neighborhood is a very handy skill.

rank: One's level of **certification**, whether martial, magical, vocational or educational. Different types of certification use different rating systems.

red battery: A battery designed to stimulate magical production in a living being if current is run through it. Many technomagical devices use these batteries to generate power directly from the user. See **automop, Forcebolt**.

Rubeus: A talented musical artist whose hallmark is the dramatic and risky surgery that allows him to sing complete harmonies with himself.

secondary (school): Grades 8 through 12. Optional, but still completed by many New Washingtonians as having a SEC (secondary educational certificate) is a prerequisite to many other types of **certification**.

Shadowflame: A celebrity mercenary. The Shadowflames value form and function equally, completing contracts publicly and in as flashy a manner as possible.

shell: A computer of any kind.

skyport: The New Washington term for its only airport.

Snowfall: The strange disaster that occurred just as the year 2000 turned, when a gentle rain of intangible, snowlike substance fell from the sky. Magic returned to the world overnight, throwing society into chaos. Centuries later, there are still areas of the world that have yet to recover from the upset.

sugarknife: An elven invention whose technique of creation is a carefully-kept secret. The sap from an unknown tree produces 'sylvan sugar', which is then somehow spun to a literally monomolecular edge. Sugarknives are very fragile, but can cut through nearly anything if used with proper technique.

triggerstone: A partially synthetic, magically-reactive substance that becomes alternately hard and soft when a **CCDM** 'trigger' spell is cast upon it. Used in many daily household objects, since the trigger spell is known by over 90 percent of New Washingtonians over the age of 18.

uni: See **New Washington University**.

Unpoliced Zone (UZ): A gap between precincts, usually caused due to **Official Opposition** or aborted alliances. Some UZs are temporary, while others are hotly contested and remain unclaimed for years. Some are very dangerous, but others are policed by organized gangs that keep the peace themselves.

weapons culture: A term used to describe the prevalence of self-defense equipment and training that marks a New Washingtonian. One's visible armament is a noticeable message to a New Washingtonian, and carrying too many or too few means of self-protection can be a serious risk.

Wyrmscale: One of the few drinks made with the **Dragon's Breath** liquor that is considered non-lethal to humans. Causes a flood of dragonmagic in the user, allowing them to speak a single word in the draconian magic language.

yuzie: Homophonic with 'UZ', yuzie is a derogatory term for someone living in an **Unpoliced Zone**. The term has spread to mean any street punk, and is used freely and excessively by the bourgeois.

Made in the USA
Charleston, SC
28 February 2010